Netherworld

**Book One of the
Chronicles of Diana Furnaval**

By
Lisa Morton

JournalStone
San Francisco

JOURNALSTONE
YOUR LINK TO ARTISTIC TALENT

JournalStone books may be ordered through booksellers or by contacting:

JournalStone
www.journalstone.com
www.journal-store.com

The views expressed in this work are solely those of the authors and do not necessarily reflect the views of the publisher, and the publisher hereby disclaims any responsibility for them.

ISBN: 978-1-940161-08-2   (sc)
ISBN: 978-1-940161-09-9   (ebook)
ISBN: 978-1-940161-26-6   (hc)

JournalStone rev. date: January 10, 2014

Library of Congress Control Number: 2013950839

Printed in the United States of America

Cover Design: Rob Grom
Cover Photograph © Shutterstock.com

Edited by: Joel Kirkpatrick

Endorsements

Netherworld is a crazily fun romp, compulsively readable and full of wit, engaging characters, and wonderfully weird supernatural twists. Lisa Morton has created dazzling entertainment that's a great ystery, historical thriller, spy story, and horror novel all rolled into one. **– David Liss,** Bestselling author of *The Twelfth Enchantment* and *The Whiskey Rebels*

"Disturbing, chilling--and wonderful! Lisa Morton's Netherworld is a tale that grips you from beginning to end. And it's the kind of book you pick up again and again--marveling at the wonderful atmosphere created that sweeps you in--and stays and chills with you into the dark of night." - Heather Graham, New York Times-bestselling author of *Blood Red* and *The Night is Forever*

"Hold on to your hats for this one, people. Right from the first page Lisa has you and you will not be able to stop...Lisa has delivered a book that firmly cements her place as one of the best writers working today...in any genre. With *Netherworld - Book One of the Chronicles of Diana Furnaval* Lisa has created a heroine for the ages that is sure to please any reader that likes grand adventure, intrigue and outright terror." - **Peter Schwotzer**, *Literary Mayhem*

"Action, suspense and deep horror are the hallmarks of Lisa Morton's 'Netherworld'. The protagonist Lady Diana Furnaval is the most compelling female adventurer since Evy Carnahan of 'The Mummy' franchise, as she travels the world fighting an ancient evil world of monstrous beings lurking just beyond ours. Morton's cinematic style effortlessly delivers Victorian era England, Canton, Calcutta and Los Angeles, which must mask many fine hours of research; and paces the story so that the book is near impossible to set down. You may recognize a source of your own terrors as you follow Lady Diana and her companions through challenge after terror after revelation. The best fiction is part myth, part cold reality and *Netherworld* doesn't fail either of those counts – the first novel in what promises to be a series of what the Victorians would have called 'rollicking adventures'." – **Rocky Wood**, Bram Stoker Award-winning author of STEPHEN KING: A LITERARY COMPANION

Fast-paced and intriguing, *Netherworld* is the kind of book that you wind up reading into the night because you can't wait to find out what happens next. It crosses genres over mystery, intrigue, and horror. *Netherworld* is non-stop action and its plot travels the world, and Morton seamlessly changes cultures as Diana travels. I do recommend that you read this book, especially if you are attracted to 19th Century gothic works with a modern twist. Highly original, I can't say I have ever read anything quite like *Netherworld*. - **Jeani Rector, The Horror Zine**

Netherworld

The Western World

Chapter I

October 31, 1879
Hertfordshire, England

"I'm not entirely comfortable with this," said Constable Quilby, as he struggled to extract his boot from a particularly noisome patch of grave mould. Even though the low-lying, thick fog hid his feet from view, Quilby grimaced at the feel of the earth pulling at his shoe, and the wet sounds the extraction made.

Lady Diana Furnaval risked opening the lantern by her side just long enough to check the time on the pocket watch she carried in the mens' waistcoat worn beneath her riding jacket. "It's twenty minutes until midnight, Constable. We haven't much longer to wait." She put the watch away, then bent to stroke the head of a small gray tabby cat that sat at her feet, its head just breaking the surface of the mist.

"That's not what I meant," Quilby said, resettling himself into a less damp patch of grass while casting a sideways glance at her. "It's...well, your clothing, mum. I've never seen a lady dressed like— like—"

"A man, Constable, is what you're trying to say."

"Well...yes."

Quilby grumbled something else Diana couldn't make out. She glanced down at herself in the tiny shred of light coming from the lantern, and was actually rather pleased: She'd chosen suede riding pants, high boots, a cap, and even sported an ascot. With her slender figure and long auburn hair tucked loosely up under the cap, she thought she looked quite dashing. "What about George Sand?" she asked.

The constable's bushy brows screwed together for a moment before he answered, "Can't say as I know the chap."

"The *chap* was actually a she, a Frenchwoman, died a few years ago; a writer and quite famous for dressing as a man."

Quilby harrumphed. "Well, French, certainly…but mum, you're English. And a Lady, at that."

"It's simply a matter of practicality, Constable," she told him. "I assure you I shall return to my skirts and petticoats once we're done with this graveyard."

The constable seemed to accept that, if his grunt was approval.

Diana eased the lantern shade down again, and the night went black. They squatted in the damp graveyard twenty or so yards from the entrance to the church itself, Diana's bag between them. The night was cold, of course, and because of the fog the chill clung to them like a funeral shroud. The moon had not yet risen, and the only light came from the stars overhead and a few candles left burning inside the church, spilling a weak glow out into the surroundings. All Diana could make out was the bulk of the church in front of them, the darker outlines of bare branches guarding the graveyard, and a few of the larger markers. During the day it was probably quite charming place. But at night, especially a dank Hallowe'en…well, Diana put those thoughts aside. Her nerves were quite steeled, thank you, and she had no intention of letting them weaken now.

Diana was leaning against a headstone indicating that one Abner Lindley had expired in 1793. Through even her leather gloves the stone was so cold it almost burned, and she was thankful for the one small patch of warmth provided by the cat, Mina, who crouched atop her feet. She knew Mina was scanning the darkness anxiously, perhaps already sensing the gateway they sought.

Quilby cleared his throat nervously and pulled his collar closed. "Tell me again what to expect," he asked, even though they'd already discussed it at least a dozen times. Diana was slightly irritated to have to answer his query yet again, but she reminded herself to be grateful for Quilby's presence; she'd needed someone from the village to act as her guide and an assistant, and stout Quilby was the only one who'd offered his aid. His wife had initially objected (*"to be out at that hour on Hallow's Eve, Henry Quilby, and on a devil's errand with a* woman, *no less!"*), but apparently Quilby regarded closing a gateway to the world beyond as part of his constabulary duties.

The five pounds Diana had paid him hadn't hurt his decision, either.

Still, Diana was growing tired of repeating herself. She stifled a sigh, pulled at her gloves to warm her fingers, then told him (sounding for all the world like a patronizing school teacher): "At exactly midnight the gateway will open and we'll see a procession come forth from the church entrance, made up of the spirits of all those from the parish who will die during the coming year. Remember, Constable, no matter what you see during that procession you are not to move or cry out. Once it's complete, Mina will lead us to the exact location of the gateway, which I suspect is inside the church itself. At that time I will close the gateway, and then we will return to the inn where you may indulge in ale while I shall enjoy a hot buttered rum."

"I still don't understand why we need—" Quilby gestured at the cat, who ignored him, "—that animal."

Mina looked up at Quilby, her eyes flashing green even in the darkness, and she gave him one look of pure disdain before returning her attention to the church.

"Cats," Diana answered, "are the only animals which have a connection to evil even though they remain basically good. Although I know there is a gateway in this area, I don't know its exact location. Gateways to the netherworld are invisible, unless you're lucky enough to actually see something coming through it. Mina will show us the exact location of the gateway after it opens."

Quilby shivered. "I wouldn't call anything about this *lucky,* mum. Take that church, for instance: I don't fancy going in there on this night. You know who they say we'll see preaching there—Satan himself, dressed as a monk."

"Rubbish," said Diana.

"But Mary Edwards, she claims to have seen him herself, she did."

"If Mary Edwards did indeed see anything, it wasn't Satan, but some lesser demon."

"Oh, well, that's reassuring," Quilby answered with considerable sarcasm. "What if he sees *us?*"

"I shall handle him."

The constable clutched at himself tightly, then asked, "You've done this before, haven't you, mum? Closed one of these gateways, I mean?"

"Six already, Constable."

"Six? Criminy. How many of these things are there?"

"There were eighty-one to begin with; now there are only seventy-five left open."

Quilby pulled his coat tighter and stamped on the ground, trying to inject some warmth into his feet. "And you mean to seal them all, do you?"

Diana's jaw tightened as she answered, "As many as I can. Some are more difficult than others; there's one in China, for example, which will be quite arduous to travel to. There's one in the middle of a Scottish loch, which may even be under water. Some—like this one—open only one night a year. But I have made it my life's purpose to seal as many as I can, yes."

Quilby gulped, then asked, "What happened with the ones you sealed? Did you see...things?"

Diana smiled grimly. "Oh, indeed I did, Constable." As she remembered, she unconsciously ran the fingers of her right hand up her left wrist, caressing the skin beneath the coat and shirt. "The second one I closed, for example, was located in the woods near Little Chester. For many years it had been the site of various incidents, of hauntings and murders. Many of the people of Chester Green claimed to have seen the spirit of a young child with snow-white hair, or heard a child crying in the night."

"Blimey," murmured Quilby. "So what did you see, when you closed it?"

"An eight-foot tall horned demon," replied Diana.

Quilby's jaw dropped beneath his thick moustache. "A horned—oh, come now, Lady Furnaval, you surely can't expect me to believe that."

"You believe Satan appears in a monk's frock in this church at midnight every Hallowe'en, but not that I've seen a horned demon?"

Quilby could only shrug, slightly abashed.

Diana said, "Believe it or not, Constable; it makes no difference to me. But I would remind you that the horned man is not unknown in these parts...."

Quilby thought for a moment. "The old sculptures, from the pagan days...."

"Yes," Diana said, nodding, "the ancient Celts worshipped a horned entity called Cernunnos. I believe the demon I fought may have been the inspiration for the Celts' deity."

"You *fought*?" Quilby considered for a moment, then asked, "How did you...fight this thing? It sounds like it could easily tear a man apart. Oh, begging your pardon, mum—or a woman."

"Oh, it certainly tried. It had me by one wrist and three feet off the ground at one point."

Quilby's eyes widened. "Sweet mercy! So how did you...?"

Diana reached into her satchel and retrieved a large, ancient-leatherbound book; brass reinforced the corners, and the volume was so weighty that Diana had to reposition it carefully to display it to Quilby. "This is *The Book of Gateways, Conjurations and Banishments* by Dr. Martyn Fox. It reveals the approximate location of all the netherworld gateways, and contains spells for the banishment of dark things that may come forth through them. In the case of the horned man, for instance, I discovered it was vulnerable to rowan wood, and used that to drive it back. Then I closed the gateway it had been using, so it could no longer return to our world."

"Then, mum," Quilby asked nervously, eyeing the cat, "are you a witch?"

Diana burst into laughter. "No, Constable, so please don't have me burned at the stake any time soon."

"Mum, we haven't burned a witch in these parts in centuries!"

Quilby was quiet after that, and Diana opened the lantern to check the time again.

Two minutes until twelve.

She sealed the lantern, then felt Mina stir at her feet. The cat bristled, and Diana could just make out the hair along Mina's back and tail; it stood straight up, stiff with tension. The little feline's back was arched, and she made a low growling in her throat as she faced the brooding entrance to the church. Diana followed the direction of Mina's glance, and felt her own hackles rise.

The weak flicker of the candles had given way to a distinctive blue glow now emanating from the windows of the church. It grew in radiance, outlining the headstones and tree branches, spilling over onto the slimy stones of the church walls.

Quilby stirred uncomfortably beside Diana, and uttered a low moan. "Quiet!" she whispered.

And then the spirits appeared.

They floated through the closed door of the church entrance, transparent yet solid enough to make out facial features and details of clothing. The first wore the garb of a baker; he was a man of late middle age, with portly build. He hung motionless in the air as he floated forward, his passage leaving the fog beneath him motionless. He soundlessly levitated towards them, along the path that led from the church porch through the graveyard and then out through the surrounding fence to the road.

Quilby gasped when he saw the apparition, then blurted out, "Fowles, the baker!"

Lady Furnaval made no attempt to silence him this time, since his outburst had gone unnoticed by the spirits that now included a wizened old crone, an elderly man in dressing gown, and a well-dressed woman in her forties. The silent, phosphorescent spirits proceeded down the pathway, and simply faded away into the night once they passed the gate and drifted beyond the grounds of the church. Behind them, the blue glow from the church continued, painting the grounds with unearthly luminescence.

Diana had glanced down at Mina when Quilby convulsed beside her, uttering a strangled, "No!"

She looked up, and immediately saw what had caused his distress.

The latest spirit to issue from the church was a man in a constable's uniform. A man with bushy brows, a thick mustache, and a hefty midsection.

There was no question it was Quilby.

"No, it can't—that can't be me—!" He jumped to his feet and started forward, but Diana grabbed his arm to hold him back.

"You can't interrupt the procession, Quilby! Just wait—"

He was panting, but held his ground, his eyes riveted to the ghostly vision of himself not five yards away now. Diana had to admit it was startling, to see the living, wide-eyed, trembling man next to her, while his bluish, transparent spirit-self floated serenely past, almost close enough to wave a hand through.

Suddenly the spirit constable stopped. A small look of confusion seemed to cross its face, and it wavered while other wraiths moved past.

"What's it waiting for?" whispered the living Quilby.

"I believe this might be good...hold on," counseled Diana.

After a moment, the spirit Quilby turned and, moving right through the other spirits, made its way back to the church. Quilby and Diana watched it disappear through the doorway.

"What happened?" asked Quilby. "Why did I—I mean, why did it—do that?"

"According to legend," said Diana, "any spirit that leaves the procession and returns to the church means its owner will suffer a significant illness but recover that year. You're not going to die, Constable."

Quilby sagged in relief, falling nervelessly to the ground. "I won't die...I won't die...." he mumbled over and over.

But Diana's attention was away from Quilby now, and centered on the church. The last of the spirits (a grotesquely fat man in his fifties) had now passed through the graveyard, and the blue glow emanating from the windows had changed, replaced by a red color, casting the surrounding graveyard into a hellish light. There was sound, now, as well—a strong voice reciting something that might have been scripture.

At Diana's feet, Mina suddenly yowled and then darted forward. She ran to the closed church door and scratched at it, the crimson glow from beneath painting her paws red.

Diana moved to tug Quilby to his feet, but then decided she could do what had to be done alone. Quilby had served his purpose—he'd brought her to the isolated country church in the dead of night—and there was no need to expose him to what came next.

She feared it might be beyond anything Quilby could comprehend. Her mind was disciplined, her will strong, and her experience already deep for a woman who had just barely turned thirty.

Her eyes reflecting the fiery effulgence, she took her satchel and followed Mina to the door, pausing there long enough to place her ear against the old, thick wood to listen.

What she heard made even her experienced breath quicken.

The voice beyond the door was plainly not human. It was deep and had a coarseness to it no man's larynx could produce; it was more like the roar of some large, savage animal—one that could speak while making that horrible sound, that is. And the words…they were an eerie gibberish, and yet Diana sensed there was something familiar about them.

"*Live morf su reviled tub, noitatpmet otni ton su dael….*"

She ran through the words in her mind, comparing them to facts about the myriad of demons, monsters, creatures, vampires, warlocks and fallen angels she'd studied, and she finally had it:

It was *The Lord's Prayer*—backwards.

Mina began to howl and scratch frantically at the door, and Diana knew her opportunity was limited; this gateway opened at exactly 12 a.m. on Hallowe'en, but she had no idea how long it would remain open. If she hesitated, she wouldn't have another chance to seal this gateway for a year.

She had to move quickly.

She reached into her satchel and considered the items therein. She unsealed the lantern, and by its light flipped *The Book* open to a banishment spell she'd previously bookmarked. Then she rummaged through the other contents of the satchel—garlic cloves, candles, herbs—and selected a dagger with a double-edged blade and a black handle. She stashed the knife in a pocket of her outer jacket, balanced the open book in her left hand, and while holding the lantern with her right she cautiously opened the church door.

She blinked and turned away, blinded by the intense radiance; despite the hellish hue, the interior of the church was even colder than the sodden grounds outside.

Looking down, waiting for her vision to adjust, Diana saw Mina bolt in and rush straight down the center aisle, pausing at the base of the altar to look up and hiss at—

—Satan.

Diana squinted, paralyzed by the sight of him. Even forty paces away, at the opposite end of the church, he towered over her. He was the classical depiction of the Devil come to life, with reddish skin, large ivory horns sprouting from either side of his brow, pointed ears, bearded cheeks and chin, and long, clawed fingers. He wore priests' robes, and his cloven hoofs were visible beneath its black hem. Smoke and fire poured from his mouth as he continued the obscene prayer, his voice booming, multiplied as it echoed down from the rafter:

"...*eman yht eb dewollah, nevaeh ni tra ohw*...."

Diana assured herself that this couldn't be Satan; although she still had no idea if Lucifer actually existed or not, she felt certain that if he did he was far too important to risk a journey out of the netherworld merely to play a grotesque Hallowe'en joke on some small English village. No, this was merely some lesser demon, and as such he could be dealt with.

He'd have to be confronted, because he was standing in front of the gateway. Mina stood now at the foot of the dais, hissing – but not at him. Instead she was fixated on the unseen *something* directly behind him.

The fiend stopped his reading and glanced up, froze when he saw first the spitting, snarling cat below him, and then the petite woman in masculine garb holding up a lantern in one hand and a book in her other.

"You've got that backwards, I'm afraid," Diana said to the demon, as she advanced on it, "and I also don't care much for your tone."

The demon gaped at her in disbelief.

"In fact, I'm so unimpressed by your performance that I'm going to send you right back to Hell."

The demon snarled at her and she felt the heat from its flaming breath. Diana had to admit *that* was impressive, at least.

She paused halfway down the center aisle and, after placing the lantern down onto a pew, began a strange spell, reading from the book: "By the sacred names of Adonai and Elohai, by the angels Raphael, Uriel, Gabriel and Michael, I adjure thee o foul spirit to return to your realm of darkness—"

The monster roared, trying to drown out her voice, but Diana could out-shout it.

"—the white powers obey me, and will cast thee from this plane into the bottomless abyss between worlds—"

The demon flexed and ripped most of the monk's cassock away as if it were made of paper. It revealed huge, rippling muscles and stepped to the edge of the altar, apparently about to launch itself at Diana. Five-inch long, half-inch thick claws reached towards her.

She saw the motion and calmly reached into her jacket pocket, removing the dagger, which she held point-up before the demon.

"I did not come unprepared. But you did."

It saw the blade and screamed in terror. Diana pressed her advantage, momentarily forgetting the incantation to simply advance on the monster with the upheld blade. "Yes, it's iron. Something you don't much care for."

She renewed her chanting. "By the sacred names of Adonai and Elohai...."

It lunged at her.

The move wasn't entirely unexpected, though, and Diana dropped the book as she leaned back, feeling the demon's hot breath on her cheek. Its other hand shot towards her throat, and she simultaneously ducked and thrust upward with the knife. She felt it drive through the flesh of the creature's hand and she yanked it out. Shrieking and clutching its wounded palm, the demon staggered back.

Diana wiped the blade clean with a handkerchief, then returned the cloth to a pocket to retrieve the book. She found her place and continued reading. "...by the angels Raphael, Uriel, Gabriel and Michael...."

The demon continued to back away, until one hoof vanished from view, and Diana knew it had passed through the gateway. Too late it realized its mistake. Diana tossed the book aside and leapt up onto the altar, where she thrust the knife into the monster's face. It bellowed its impotent rage, and this time Diana felt pain as she was singed. She was dimly aware that something on her face was smouldering, but it would have to wait....

...because the demon had just fled back through the gateway, and now Diana had her chance to seal it forever.

She held the knife between her teeth and quickly tore off her jacket, flinging it carelessly behind her. Then she undid the cuff on her left sleeve and rolled it up, baring her tender skin between wrist and elbow. Taking the knife in her right hand, and without hesitation she drew its sharp blade across her left arm, drawing a two-inch thin line of blood. As she waited for the blood to well, she called out in a clear, steady voice:

"By my will and by my blood is this gateway sealed forever!"

She flung her bloodied arm at the gateway, showering it in crimson droplets. She heard a final roar of fury from the other side and briefly saw the outline of the fiend behind the frozen beads of her blood—

—and then the air before her was clear and silent.

Diana hesitated a moment, just to be sure. It took another few seconds for her to realize that the only light within the church now was her lantern, and the only sound was the voice of Quilby from behind her:

"Lady Furnaval, are you—did that thing—!"

She turned and saw Quilby staggering with his coat askew and capless up the center aisle towards her and she forced a smile at him. "I'm fine, Constable, thank you."

She stepped down from the altar, but her knees nearly gave. Now, with the task accomplished and the energy of her fortitude draining away, she allowed herself to drop into the nearest pew, limp and exhausted. Mina rubbed happily around her ankles, purring in triumph.

Quilby leaned over her, eyeing her with great concern. "Mum, your face...."

"What?" Diana cried out, involuntarily reaching up, feeling for serious damage.

"I'm afraid that beast's fire...well, it seems to have burned away an eyebrow."

Diana ran a hand over her forehead, and discovered that indeed, most of one eyebrow seemed to be missing. Still, it was a relatively small price to pay for victory (and was easily remedied with cosmetics).

Quilby comically bobbed his head, swinging between the altar, the rest of the church, and Diana. "When it fell backward and disappeared—"

"Through the gateway," Diana added.

"The gateway—is it...did you—?"

"It has been sealed," she told him. "No more midnight Hallowe'en processions in your parish, I'm afraid."

"This must be some blade!" he picked up the knife to better see it. "Is it blessed?"

"Iron," she told him. "Demons can't touch it. Burns them worse than fire burns us."

Then he saw her wound, and actually squeaked. "You're bleeding, mum—!"

Diana realized she'd forgotten about the cut. "Oh, yes...."

She had Quilby retrieve her satchel for her, in which she kept materials for cleaning and bandaging the wound. Quilby watched her, dismayed to see the scars that ran up her arm. He counted five— no, six....

"Lady Furnaval," he finally asked, "the scars on your arm...one for each gateway?"

"Quite. One for each gateway," she replied, then went on after a small, sad pause, "...and all for my William."

"William?" Quilby asked, then remembered. "Oh, right—your late husband. Sorry, mum."

"It was three years ago, Constable, no need to offer condolences."

Quilby shifted uncomfortably, and Diana patted his shoulder in what she hoped was a friendly manner. "I believe you're catching on to this gateway-closing business at last. Perhaps you'd care to join me in Cornwall, where they believe in a group of demonic huntsmen called Dando's Dogs, and are unaware their wild hunters are merely trespassers through a gateway that needs closing...?"

"Not me, mum!" Quilby answered, and then sneezed three times. "Besides, I think I've got a cold coming on."

She drew a calming breath and gazed about the beautiful, lantern-warmed sanctuary. Moments before, it had been a hellish place; now, even shadowed, it was inviting and serene.

Diana retrieved her jacket, then snuggled Mina down into the satchel, which she hefted up as she moved to the doorway. "Something tells me it's going to be a nasty cold, Constable Quilby...but I think you'll survive."

Chapter II

November 5, 1879
(and memories)
London

Diana was happiest when she was in London.

Even though she'd spent the five best years of her life in the country (when William was still alive and they'd lived together at the Furnaval's ancestral home of Hampstead Hall in Derby), she was really, at heart, a creature of the city. She loved its crowds, its intensity, its energy, its boisterous clattering streets, its shops.

As comfortable as she found her masculine attire, she still enjoyed the latest fashion, and always looked forward to a visit with her London tailor. William had sometimes accompanied her there, and she still heard his voice complimenting her when she tried on a lovely new morning dress in a princess-line, mentioning that its pale blue print matched her eyes. He might have teased her about how she needed to cut her auburn curls before they became the scandal of the society pages, but he'd always offer up such comments with a half-smile.

London was admittedly bittersweet now, without William, but the great metropolis still held Diana in its thrall. She was excited by the city's progress, by the growth and new industries. Even though the factories belched filth into the skies and could be savagely unsafe, those evils still felt like the future to her; she trusted, as did other believers in reform, that the poor would soon be lifted up by the powers of business and government. She was intrigued by new discoveries and inventions; she'd recently acquired a new gadget invented by a clever American, called a gramophone, that could actually replay recordings (admittedly tinny) of music inscribed on wax cylinders. She'd even traveled to London merely to see the display of electric lights outside the Gaiety Theatre on the Strand, and had been as dazzled as the thousands of onlookers. Her breast had swelled with the great promise of science.

A passionate reader of classics, she also studied Charles Darwin's *The Descent of Man* when it was first released eight years earlier, and although she found Darwin's theories about female inferiority truly appalling, she thought the rest of his work to be quite remarkable. Diana felt (with an irony she was well aware of) that man would not truly progress until he gave up his superstitions and put his faith in a world he'd studied, categorized, and created himself.

She often pondered the clash between her reliance on science and progress with her dealings in darker matters. Before meeting William, she hadn't believed in ghosts, monsters, demons, or the existence of the soul. She was raised a Protestant, but even as a child had doubted most of what she heard in church. By the time she'd reached adulthood, she'd become an atheist, although she'd confessed that fact to very few.

William had laughed when she'd told him, during a lunch he'd arranged on a boat floating down the River Avon.

She'd found his laugh musical and charming, but had asked, "Why the laughter?"

"Diana, you may be in for a few surprises," he answered. Then he kissed her, and that was a most pleasant surprise. William, she discovered, might have been a member of British aristocracy, but he was also playful and impulsive.

Several months after they were engaged to be married, he introduced her to her first ghost.

She remembered it well. William had taken her for a nighttime walk to the edge of his estate; the moon was full and so bright they required no lantern. They strolled past the hulking ruins of the old hall and the landscaped gardens, and he told her there was something very important she needed to know about him—something that might change her mind about their coming marriage.

Diana had stopped him; there, in the moonlight, she'd taken his hands in hers, and assured him nothing could change her mind. She was deeply in love with the handsome young Lord Furnaval, her William, with his easy grin and waving black hair and the jokes he whispered in her ear when they attended stodgy society functions. And she knew that love was well and equally shared.

"Still, darling, I do think you need to know of this," he'd told her. Then he'd turned and gestured behind him, as if they were just taking a nature walk and he was serving as guide. "Do you see that slight ridge, the one with the trees growing on either side of it?"

Diana could easily make out the ridge, which of course she'd seen before. It rolled up from the surrounding landscape, standing perhaps ten yards higher. Only grass grew atop it.

"That's one wall of an ancient Roman fort which once existed here," William told her. "If we were to dig into the earth, we'd find the old stones."

"Yes?" she'd asked, wondering why William was bothering with this if he had something so important to tell her.

And then she'd seen the ghost.

It had seemingly appeared from nowhere, and at first looked perfectly solid: A Roman soldier, fresh from battle in muddied mail and tattered cloak. Oh his head he wore a plumed, dented helmet. He'd materialized perhaps twenty yards away, and was walking towards them, sword in hand; yet he trudged forward with stooped shoulders and obvious fatigue. As he neared, though, Diana realized that she could see parts of the moonlit ridge directly *through* him.

There was no denying that Diana had felt a chill course up her spine, that first time.

The ghost walked towards them but stopped, glaring with some indefinable rage.

"William—" Diana cried out in alarm.

"It's fine, dear, just watch," William assured her.

She had…and after a moment the spirit turned away from them, as if bored, and walked on. After perhaps another dozen steps it vanished from sight. Diana was too stunned to move or speak.

And that was when William explained the gateways.

The Furnaval family had been the keepers of the Derby gateway for generations. They carefully watched what apparitions came through their gateway, and performed banishment spells on any especially troublesome manifestations. Others that were harmless—like the war-weary Centurion, or an old man who looked like a groundskeeper— were allowed to exist, and had even become minor local tourist attractions.

After the sighting of the ghost, William had taken Diana back to the house, and shown her the family's copy of Dr. Martyn Fox's *The Book of Gateways, Conjurations and Banishments*. Fox was a sixteenth-century magician who had lived near a gateway in Dartmoor, and somehow harnessed a demon who then revealed the location of all the gateways to Fox, along with certain useful spells on controlling what came through them. The Furnavals' copy was an original first edition of the book, bound in leather with brass hardware and with marvelously antiquated type; the page margins were crowded with numerous handwritten annotations made by various Furnavals over the centuries, noting where certain spells hadn't functioned or more precise locations for some gateways (the book gave very specific directions for finding some gateways, while others were apparently obvious to detect by the amount of activity that occurred around them; a Welsh gateway, for instance, not only attracted numerous spirits but was centered in a fairy ring).

Over the next few days they spent all their daylight hours in the library. Diana read through the book, consumed every other occult volume she found and deluged William with questions: Did he know all the other gatekeepers? (No. In fact, he wasn't even sure there *were* other gatekeepers.) Were there more gateways in Britain? (Yes, there were eleven, including locations in Little Chester, Wales, Cornwall, Scotland, Ireland, and even one on the Isle of Man.) How many times had it been necessary for him to perform banishment spells? (William answered this by giving her his own journal to read, and she read with astonishment of his two banishings: Once of a pesky will-o'-the-wisp that insisted on leading nocturnal travelers over cliff edges, and once a genuinely frightening demon that slew several local children before William trapped it and returned it to its netherworld). What was on the other side of the gateway? (William didn't know, and hoped to never find out.) Why not just close the gateway permanently?

William had smiled at that and told her he most happily would, but he didn't think it was possible.

"I don't believe in a door that can't be closed," she said. He'd smiled then, not with condescension, but with the acceptance of Diana as a valuable new partner.

If anything, William's new status as heroic gatekeeper, standing against ancient evils, only made Diana love him more. They were married, and Diana had been eager to share his duties with him. Over their five years of marriage, she'd seen things she would never have imagined or believed possible—an entire troop of marching Roman soldiers; a ring of wicked fairies, sporting sharp teeth, black wings, and tarnished gold tunics, cavorting beneath the starlight; a great black hound with glowing red eyes—and she came to accept these entities as merely part of a natural order of things, no more unusual than a horned toad or a giraffe. After all, she'd reasoned, once something supernatural was proven, then it was no longer *super*natural, was it? Of course she never discussed what she'd seen outside of the bounds of Hampstead

Hall—she'd even laughed at other accounts of mystical or occult phenomena—but she reconciled her own belief systems to encompass what she now knew of the world.

And then William was killed.

They'd received a letter one day, in a battered and dirt stained envelope, from a little known province in Eastern Europe called Transylvania. William and Diana had been in the Derby sitting room, planning an upcoming dinner party, when Howe, the Furnavals' butler, had set the letter before William. Diana had seen the way his brow creased as he attempted to decipher the cramped script, and she'd joined him, bending down over his shoulder to read.The letter was one from one János Rákóczi, who claimed to be both a descendent of Transylvanian royalty and a watcher over a particularly troubling gateway. He claimed to be literally under siege by demonic forces, and begged for help. He asked William to come to him.

Diana had immediately told William she believed it to be a trap. For one thing, this Rákóczi made no mention of how he'd found William. Although *The Book of Gateways, Conjurations and Banishments*, showed that there was indeed a gateway at the location indicated, the area was remote and unlikely to have a gatekeeper. Perhaps, reasoned Diana, the forces of darkness were tired of William's exorcisms, and they gained a better chance of removing him permanently if they could lure him to a primitive area where he'd have none of his usual protections. Diana reminded him that he had no brother and they hadn't yet produced an heir, so if anything happened, the Furnaval title would die with him.

William had agreed with her, but was nonetheless intrigued by the prospect of meeting another gatekeeper. He penned a response, telling Rákóczi he would come. As he finished the letter and sealed it into an envelope, Diana begged him not to send it. By way of answer, he rang for Howe and asked that the letter be posted immediately; when Howe had left, William had turned to Diana and vowed to exercise extreme caution; he would take weapons both natural and supernatural.

But he wouldn't take Diana.

She'd fought him vigorously on this, of course, but had finally given in when he'd suggested that this whole trip might be nothing but a ruse to lure him away from his own gateway. If she stayed behind, she could continue to guard their Derby portal.

Before he left, William made copies of all the spells he thought he might need from *The Book of Gateways, Conjurations and Banishments*, and left the original with Diana. Diana accompanied him to London, where he made his travel plans, which involved weeks via boat, rail, and carriage; and he left detailed instructions on all matters relating to running of the estate. He also made sure his will—which left the estate to Diana—was in place and that she was well acquainted with their solicitor.

On the morning he left, she stood on a London dock, ignoring the sounds of shouting sailors and laborers, of crates being loaded and groaning ship timbers, and begged him one last time to stay. He'd kissed her and told her he must, and then stepped aboard the vessel that took him from England...and her.

When she returned to Derby, it was to a house that felt as cool and dull and lifeless as a tomb.

As he'd traveled, he'd written to her daily, describing every step of his journey. She couldn't respond, but cherished those letters, filled in William's precise penmanship, and kept them all in a large leather album. In the final, hurriedly-jotted letter, William told her he arrived at his destination—a small mountain village in the heart of Transylvania— but had yet to locate Rákóczi. William had already decided to journey on to the next village should Rákóczi prove impossible to locate in this one.

The next letter she received, four days later, was from a local magistrate writing in broken English to inform her that her husband had died. He'd last been seen, apparently well, leaving the inn in the company of an unknown man; that man had since vanished. The following morning, William was found badly wounded in the nearby forest, and was taken back to the inn, where he survived only two hours before succumbing to his injuries. His belongings had been freighted back to her already; his body then temporarily interred in the local cemetery, pending further instructions from Diana.

Diana had crumpled to the floor, the letter slipping from nerveless fingers.

Howe rushed to her side. He glanced at the letter, and immediately discerned the horrifying nature of its information. Howe was a thoughtful, attentive man who knew of the gateways, and had even assisted William in performing one of the banishments. There was no person better equipped to offer Diana comfort at that time. Her own parents were both gone, her mother having died six months earlier, and Diana had no siblings.

Howe made the arrangements to have Lord William's remains returned to England for interment in the Furnaval family crypt, while Diana became obsessed with the gateway. She'd spent every night for weeks wrapped in one of William's coats, sitting on the ridge near it, somehow hoping for some clue as to his demise, or something to lash out against, but the portal hadn't so much as shivered. She'd ceased her nightly watches only when they led to her becoming ill with pneumonia. She'd missed William's interment as she'd hovered near death herself; doctors at one point had even pronounced her beyond help, but she'd been determined to recover, because if she couldn't save William she could at least avenge him.

It took weeks. Howe and the wait staff attended to her with loving care, and under their ministrations her vitality slowly returned. The doctors stood back, shaking their heads in amazement as her breathing eased, fever subsided, and strength returned. When she'd thanked one of the doctors, he'd said, "Don't thank me, my dear – will power alone saved your life."

He was right.

While she recuperated, Diana's thoughts had circled back to one thing so often that she knew it must be her life's mission from here on: She would find a way to close the gateways, and put it into effect throughout the world. She distressed Howe greatly by returning to her studies in the library *weeks*, he stressed, before she should have left her bed.

She believed it was possible, although at first she had no proof. She'd reread *The Book of Gateways, Conjurations and Banishments*, looking for any clues, but found none. She endangered her health further with all-night searches; Howe frequently found her still in the library come dawn, hollow-eyed and trembling but reading, desperate for any clues. When the pneumonia had threatened to return, she'd reluctantly agreed to take to her bed again...provided books were brought to her and the bedroom lights left burning.

When she was strong enough at last, Howe could not prevent her reaching out, to seek answers that the Furnaval library did not hold.

As distasteful as she'd found them, she'd joined occult societies, gaining access to secret papers and journals; again, she'd found nothing but chicanery and nonsense. She then befriended every antique bookseller in England, offering considerable sums of money for ancient occult tomes. The Furnaval library soon required expansion, and carpenters were brought in to build additional shelves to house new acquisitions; yet - despite containing certain useful bits of information – none of those volumes had yielded that vital data she most sought.

And then one day a special letter arrived for her from a dealer in London, one she'd never encountered. Chappell and Sons Booksellers had a rarity they thought might suit her needs. They handled a *very* exclusive clientele, and saw customers only by appointment. They were apprised of her wants by a fellow dealer, and so had taken the liberty of contacting her.

She had immediately replied by return post informing them that she'd like to see them the next day, and she'd provided the address of her London house in Eaton Place.

An hour later she'd been on the train to London, feeling almost giddy with anticipation. The following morning she'd received a note at her London address providing a time and directions to the store. The note contained nothing else, only the name of the shop embossed at the top.

When she arrived at the scheduled time and place, she at first thought she might have made some mistake; although it was a good area located just off the Strand, there was no cheery shop window filled with books, no sign with name and hours. There was only a number on an unremarkable door. However, since it matched the number she'd been given, she told her carriage to wait and rang the bell beside the door.

She was met at the door by a strikingly handsome young man, with serious, dark features. Accustomed to shopkeepers nearly more ancient than their precious merchandise, she assumed this fellow might be a clerk. However, he greeted her professionally and introduced himself as Stephen Chappell before leading her down a short hallway to a large, windowless room filled with bookshelves.

He told her they had no windows because sunlight was potentially damaging to many of the books they possessed. It took a moment for her eyes to adjust to its shadows, then she saw no visible cash register, only one small table, a fairly comfortable-looking reading chair, and a few lamps.

And books everywhere. They were lined up in double rows on the shelves, stacked on the floors, and piled on the table. Diana was used to crowded bookshops, but this one felt both unusually claustrophobic and open to immense vistas of knowledge.

Diana perused the first few shelves nearest her, and was surprised by the value of what she saw there: It was a collection of occult tomes that surpassed even her own. She ran a gloved finger over the spines of titles that she'd heard of but presumed to be non-existent; there were first editions she'd read had been destroyed immediately after printing. Her pulse thrummed as she withdrew a copy of Dr. John Dee's *Monas Hieroglyphica* and saw that it contained additional chapters on "communion with Spirites"; there, just below it, was a handwritten grimoire by the infamous eighteenth-century necromancer Thomas Moreby. When she removed a copy of *The Book of Shadows* bound in some sort of animal hide she couldn't name, the bookseller commented, "You have most refined tastes."

The attractive young Mr. Chappell, whom she assumed now to be the *and Sons* part of the Chappell business, excused himself for a moment. He disappeared behind the stacks, leaving his client to commune alone with the magnificent collection.

Diana breathed in the dust of centuries of knowledge, feeling sure that she would at last find her answer here. The thought of all the lore and wisdom contained on just a single shelf made Diana wish for several more lifetimes.

She was just replacing a rather brittle binding on its high shelf when Mr. Chappell reappeared bearing a huge book in a custom made slipcase. He set the folio down on the table, and, with gloved hands, opened the slipcase to reveal a thirteenth-century illuminated manuscript bound between sculpted copper sheets. The manuscript, by some unknown monk, was written in Old English, and so Diana could only understand parts of it; but when Mr. Chappell came to a page reading: "Spelle for Immediate and Permanente Sealing of Darke Gateways", she quietly asked him to close the book and told him she'd take it. Of course, it had cost her no small fortune, but she would gladly have foregone years of luxuries to possess it and the secrets it held.

Back in her apartment, she pored over the book, certain it was the key to her own future, but the archaic language frustrated her and she knew that any mistake in translation could prove deadly.

The following day, she took the book to a university scholar of Old English, who assisted her in making sense of the most difficult passages. She transcribed several copies of the sealing spell so that she could stow the original book away in a secure place. According to the instructions, she'd need only herself, an *athame*, or ceremonial dagger, and a cat.

She returned to Derby and began preparations. She'd been gifted with an appropriate blade during her brief associations with occultists, and Mina had been an easy acquisition (although the way the kitten had run up and rubbed against her when she'd entered the miller's house, she often felt as if Mina had acquired *her*). After she brought the cat home, she explained its real purpose to Howe and showed him the ancient manuscript. He'd learned to stop questioning her, and had instead responded only with, "Yes, mum," when she'd told him she was now certain she could close the gateways.

She strode out that very night, intent upon her mission. The new moon and cloud cover necessitated a lantern to light her way, and Howe had insisted on accompanying her. Mina (as she'd named the kitten) lived up to her promise and tore towards the gateway with such astonishing speed that Howe and Diana momentarily lost track of her. When they found her again, she was seated on the grassy rise, peering up and hissing, back arched, gray fur on end.

Although Diana couldn't see the gateway, she trusted completely in her feline accomplice's sense, and she'd quickly pulled up her sleeve. Gritting her teeth, she used the knife to slash her arm, and then hurled both blood and incantation at the gateway.

She knew she'd been successful only because Mina abruptly ceased her hissing, and playfully turned to bat at the hem of Diana's skirt, all memory of the gateway already gone.

Howe had related his dislike of the gate-closing ceremony in no uncertain terms, berating Diana all the way back to the house as he daubed at her bloody arm. "The spell won't work without it," she tried to explain.

"It's not the spell I question, mum; I just wish you'd warned me in advance."

Diana assured him she wouldn't be so forgetful in the future.

"But," Howe added, after his anger had abated, "you've done a fine thing tonight. His Lordship would have been very proud."

Diana wasn't entirely ready yet to accept that it had worked. She spent the next month keeping a careful eye on the gateway; she slept during the day and spent her evenings with Mina on the ridge. But there was absolutely no further sign of ghostly or demonic activity. Plus, the area simply felt different, free of some sort of oppressive aura, and Mina scampered after field mice or slept. Diana was satisfied, and quite certain that it was effectively sealed.

Still, a sense of victory eluded her. The Derby gateway had always been home to mild activity; surely other gateways wouldn't be so easy.

The next proved that presentiment correct.

The second one was located not far away, in an oak grove near a village called Little Chester. Although Diana arrived with the usual collection of protective implements, including *The Book of Gateways, Conjurations and Banishments,,,* she had to admit later that she'd still been overly confident.

Because she'd no sooner peeled back her sleeve when the eight-foot tall horned man stepped through and shrieked at her.

For an instant Diana had frozen in terror, staring at that monstrosity before her. It had a curling rams' horns, a fierce, saturnine face, dark skin and furred, goat-legged haunches. It howled in the night, and then turned glowing green eyes, reaching out with long, filthy fingers; a musky scent filled the air as it loomed over her. She might well have died right then and there, her paralysis guaranteeing her fate, had it not been for Mina. The fearless little cat uttered her own piercing screech and launched herself at the nightmare, ears laid back, claws extended.

That action had awakened Diana from her terror, and she swore it would be the last time she was ever caught unawares.

Mina laid a long gash into the creature's furry flank and then dashed away, leaving the horned man to howl in pain and spin about in a vain attempt to locate its tiny attacker. That confusion gave Diana the time to dive for her copy of *The Book*, flip it open to the section of banishment spells, and read the first one her eyes fell upon.

The creature whirled then, its attention riveted on her. It lowered its great head, the curved horns chipped from other battles, and studied her for a moment with clear, malevolent purpose.

And then it came at her *fast*.

She leapt aside at the last instant, and cursed the skirts that caused her to trip. She stumbled backwards and fell, coming to rest with her right hand near the satchel of herbs and charms. Before she could react, the demon ran forward, driving its head—and horns—down at her. She twisted slightly to one side, and the horns struck the ground on either side of her slender figure. In the few seconds that it took to raise its head (with its foul, spitting face over Diana's midsection), she scrabbled for the satchel. Just as the demon jerked its head back and was aiming the deathblow at Diana, she grabbed whatever she could from the satchel and flung it at him.

Later, Diana would realize she'd been lucky;. This particular type of demon could be sent running by the use of rowan wood, and Diana had inadvertently thrown several rowan twigs at it along with a handful of other herbs and barks. The demon reared back, screaming, and retreated through the gateway. Diana scrambled to her feet and sealed it. When it was done, she fell back against the trunk of an oak, her strength nearly spent.

After resting for a while, she'd managed to gather up her things, small pains alerting her to bruises she'd acquired in the fight. She hobbled back to Little Chester, ordered a brandy at the pub, and thought about everything she'd done badly.

She hadn't made those mistakes again. She'd sealed five more gateways since, and, having engaged in several more battles, discovered that true confidence came from experience and knowledge.

It was during the sealing of the fourth gateway that Diana met the medium.

This gateway was located in London, in a rather unsavory section of the East End, and turned out to be in the ground floor of an abandoned, haunted house. Diana and Mina had entered the house unnoticed (or so they thought), and although she saw a few spectral forms, nothing had impeded the closing of the gateway.

Afterwards, as they left the house, they were surprised to find a woman waiting for them on the street outside. She was perfectly ordinary looking, of middle age and unremarkable dress, except for the ornate, life-sized scarab brooch at her neck.

"You closed it," she said, regarding them with evident wonder.

That simple pronouncement startled Diana more than any ectoplasm or ichor. She gaped at the woman for a moment, then answered only, "Yes."

"I didn't know that was possible," the woman told her.

"It is. I've done it before."

"I wonder if I'll still be able to hear them," the odd woman had said.

Diana, eyeing the colorful brooch, said, "May I ask about your scarab?"

"Oh. For good luck," the woman replied.

An hour later, with dinner between them at the woman's cramped little Bethnal Green flat, Diana heard the whole story.

Her name was Isadora Feduchin. She'd lived in the house next to the haunted one for twenty years. Isadora had a penchant for gathering odd items, and her small sitting room was lined with cases cluttered with books, stones, vases, and dolls made of old corn husks. She apparently possessed some sort of natural ability to receive emanations from the residents of the netherworld, and over the years she'd mentally acquired all sorts of messages, everything from the locations of other gateways to cries of captivity to clues from dead men.

That last, of course, intrigued Diana greatly. Although initially skeptical about Isadora's claims of mediumship (London had caught the fever of spiritism some years before, and fraudulent mediums abounded, all too ready to deprive the gullible of thousands of pounds), Diana soon realized the woman did possess the talents she claimed. She had heard of Diana's battle with the horned god (it was she who had first supplied Diana with the name Cernunnos, which research into Celtic mythology soon proved to be correct), and she had no interest in setting up shop to charge for her services; she survived from a small inheritance. It turned out that closing the doorway only slightly dampened the connection, and Isadora would continue to receive her "psychic messages." She and Diana became fast friends, and whenever Diana was in London she visited Isadora, braving the East End's pubs and streets full of dangerous urchins.

Of course Diana had to admit the visits weren't entirely out of friendship. She desperately hoped that someday Isadora would provide her with a clue as to the mechanics of William's doom. Isadora had promised Diana to do what she could; unfortunately, the clues she received from the netherworld weren't a two-way communication—she had no control over what she would "hear," and at best she could only try to filter the messages for information that was wanted.

The netherworld wouldn't give up its secrets easily.

So it was on this November eve in 1879 that Diana found herself on her way to visit Isadora. She was curious to know if her friend could offer any clues about the nature of the demon she'd fought in Hertfordshire; she'd never previously heard of a lesser-being trying to pass for Satan himself. Under one arm Diana carried a large wrapped package: Isadora dearly loved the works of Anthony Trollope (who Diana personally detested), and Diana had just purchased his new three-volume novel *John Caldigate* for her friend.

It was the evening of November fifth, or, as it was more popularly known, Guy Fawkes Day. For more than two and a half centuries this day had been one of raucous merriment in England, celebrating the foiling of a plot (involving one Guy Fawkes) to blow the House of Lords to kingdom come. Diana knew that back home in Derby the surrounding hills would be alight with bonfires. Here in London, the streets were thronged with soot-covered boys capering about effigies and crying out rhymes:

"Pray to remember

> *The fifth of November,*
> *Gunpowder treason and plot,*
> *When the king and his train*
> *Had nearly been slain,*
> *Therefore it shall not be forgot."*

One little chap, dressed in rags, face smeared with charcoal, ran boldly up to Diana and extended a hand. "A penny for the Guy, Miss?"

Diana smiled, juggled the books to reach into her purse, and tossed him a coin. The boy caught it and doffed his hat to her.

"Thank you, Miss!"

He ran off to rejoin his fellows, and Diana continued on her way, amused by the ritual.

She arrived at Isadora's house, and after exchanging greetings and the gift (for which Isadora, whose budget left very little money to spare for books, was thrilled), they sat down with a plate of Bonfire Parkin cake between them. "Beastly stuff that I know will only fatten me up," laughed Isadora between mouthfuls, "but I can't resist it. At least it's only once a year."

As they exchanged tea and pleasantries, Diana noticed one new acquisition perched on a nearby table; it looked like a very old dinner roll.

"Oh, there's a lovely story behind that," Isadora said. "Do you know about soul cakes?"

Diana nodded. "Yes. They used to be quite popular at All Souls' Eve. Weren't they given to beggars in exchange for prayers on behalf of deceased loved ones?"

"Your knowledge never disappoints me—yes, quite right. In some areas, though, they were given to neighbors as well, and it was thought to be good luck to keep one for a year. Well, that one was given to a lady who not only kept it for all of her eighty years, but passed it onto her daughter. That cake's two-hundred years old."

"Please tell me you're not about to serve it."

They both laughed, and Diana felt a surge of affection for her eccentric friend. She made a mental note to search out a more unique gift for her next visit.

"Is there any news from the other side?"

Isadora shook her head. "Sorry. I've been off to Whitby looking after my sister Beatrice—she took ill with fever, and she's got no one else to care for her. But she recovered and sent me home—she's a bit of a hermit, that one—and I just returned yesterday."

"Could we try to make contact now?"

Isadora rose. "That we could. It might even help to have you right here in the room—sometimes the spirits have specific messages for those with me."

Unlike the fake mediums, Isadora didn't turn out lights, seat guests around a table, or close her eyes and pretend to enter a trance. There were no spirit cabinets, or musical instruments levitated with strings by hidden assistants. She and Diana seated themselves on the sofa, and Isadora merely gazed intently at her friend. After a few moments, Diana saw her eyes take on a glassy look, even as her brow furrowed slightly. "Oh," she murmured at one point, but Diana knew better than to interrupt and waited silently.

After perhaps ten minutes Isadora's attention came back to Diana, and her eyes widened. She jumped to her feet, and paced a few steps before Diana addressed her: "Isadora, what happened?"

The medium stopped pacing, took a deep breath, then looked down at her. "At least you're already sitting down. You'll need to be, for what I have to tell you."

Diana didn't respond. Isadora sat next to her, and took both of Diana's hands in her own. Torchlight flared outside the window, and Diana heard the raucous cries of the boys out in the street celebrating as they lit their effigies on fire:

"A pound of cheese to choke him,
A bottle of beer to wash it down,
A jolly good fire to roast him—"

Irritated by the merrymakers, Diana spoke to her more sharply than was necessary:

"Tell me, Isadora!"

"Diana," Isadora said, biting a lip between words, "I was told that your husband isn't dead."

Diana stared at her friend for a moment, then barked a harsh laugh. "That isn't possible. His body rests at this very moment within the Furnaval family crypt in Derby."

"Didn't you tell me that William was killed in some village in Eastern Europe?" asked Isadora.

"Yes. In a province called Transylvania."

"And the body was shipped back to you?"

Diana felt a chill steal over her. "Yes...."

"Did you ever actually see the body?"

Her chill became a shiver. "I...no, I...I'm sure our man Howe did."

"How sure, my dear?"

Diana was the one pacing now, as possibilities raced through her mind. Surely it couldn't be...? She'd received a letter from a legitimate magistrate, telling her about William's death—why would this magistrate lie? *Unless...was it possible they'd mistaken someone else's body for William?* Or was the letter a fake, written by someone merely pretending to be a magistrate? *And if William wasn't really dead, merely vanished, then where was he?* Still in Transylvania somewhere? No, it'd been three years, he would have found some way to contact her. Amnesiac in some hospital, perhaps? *Not likely.* No, there was only one place William could have disappeared to:

The Netherworld beyond the Transylvanian gateway.

"Diana," Isadora said, drawing her friend's attention back from her troubled thoughts, "there's something else...."

Diana stopped pacing. "What?"

"William kept a journal, did he not?"

"Yes," Diana answered, "in all the time I knew him he never missed a day. And yet when I received his belongings back from the inn where he'd stayed, his final journal wasn't among them. I wrote the inn several times, asking them to check the room again, but they swore it was nowhere to be found."

"It *is* somewhere to be found. In fact, it's *here* in London."

Diana was suddenly bending over her friend with great urgency. "Where is it, Isadora? Do you know?"

"It wasn't a complete message, dear. All I got was that it's in a chapel in London. I'm sorry it wasn't more specific."

Diana pondered the strange information. "A chapel in London...how many chapels do you suppose there are here?"

Isadora shook her head. "I don't know. Dozens. Maybe even hundreds?"

"Then I'll have to search every one of them," Diana answered. She considered briefly, then turned back to Isadora. "How could William's journal have wound up in a chapel?"

"I'm sorry, Diana, I don't know the answer. The...emanations, or impressions I get are rarely even as complete as that."

Diana said, "We should be able to rule out most by simply using common sense." After a few seconds, she added, "Unfortunately, by applying common sense I'd rule out *all* of them. It is a bit baffling."

"Maybe," suggested Isadora, "the journal was found by a travelling priest."

"Perhaps," admitted Diana.

Isadora added, "There's another possibility we should consider."

Diana stared at her, raising her eyebrows (including the one just now growing back).

"Something could be toying with you, my dear. This could all be a lie, some great scavenger hunt to send you running to all the chapels in London instead of closing more gateways."

Diana considered that, then answered, "That's certainly possible. But if there's any chance William is alive somewhere—even the tiniest, slightest chance—you know I'll pursue it. And locating his journal would be my best way to learn what happened to him."

After that they sat for a while, and finally the revelry outside began to die down; the bonfires sank to a few sputtering embers, and the boys drifted back to their homes, to await next year's Guy Fawkes holiday.

It was after midnight when Isadora offered, "Why don't you just spend the night here? It's getting awfully late, and I'm not sure I like the idea of you walking the East End streets alone at this hour."

Diana had to smirk at her friend. "Dory, I was battling a demon who fancied himself to be Satan less than a week ago, I think I can handle the streets of East End."

At Isadora's look, she relented. "—but your offer is really quite kind, and I'd be happy to accept."

Isadora made sure Diana was comfortable in her guest bedroom, and then excused herself for her own bed. Once alone, Diana didn't immediately undress, but rather stoked the fire in the small hearth, pulled an overstuffed chair nearer to the warmth, and seated herself, resting her chin on one hand.

As far as investigating William's death, it wasn't a particularly difficult matter, although the process would be far from pleasant: She'd have to pay a visit to the Furnaval family crypt and open her husband's coffin.

As to the matter of locating the mysterious chapel...she forced herself to analyze that dilemma carefully. What sort of chapel would have journals? Was there some other meaning for the word *chapel*? A chapel that didn't belong in a church? One that housed—

—*books*.

Of course!

It was 1 a.m. when she dashed out of her bedroom and down the short hall to Isadora's closed door, onto which she frantically pounded. "Dory—"

Seconds later her friend appeared in her nightdress, looking blearily concerned. "What's wrong?"

"I know where William's journal is. It's not a church chapel, it's a bookstore specializing in occult texts called Chappell and Son".

Isadora wearily nodded. "Oh, that's wonderful, dear. Now go back to bed."

"But, Dory—!"

"Diana," her friend chided her, "you can't very well visit a bookshop in the middle of the night, can you? Now go back to bed."

Isadora shut her door, and Diana returned to her room...but she didn't fall asleep until nearly dawn, and then she only dreamed of her William.

Chapter III

November 6, 1879
London

Diana awoke after only a few hours of troubled sleep; in her dreams, William called to her from the end of a long, dark tunnel, but—although she ran towards him in desperation—she was never able to reach him. And unseen things lurked along the sides of the tunnel, things with strangely shaped eyes—some in sets of three or four—that glowed at her as she passed. When she'd awakened she felt more fatigued than she had when she'd fallen asleep.

She left Isadora's and returned to her own house, where Mina greeted her with loud meows of displeasure at being left alone for the night. Diana's parlormaid assured her the cat had been fed, and Mina seemed to calm down once Diana gifted her with a few moments of lap time and some loving strokes. By 10 a.m. she'd arranged a noon meeting with Chappell and Son.

The two hours 'til noon were among the slowest of Diana's life. She paced anxiously, petted Mina, paced some more, drank one small cup of tea, and paced still more. By the time 11:30 arrived, she had literally worn a slight circular groove into the Persian carpet adorning her drawing room floor. She called for her carriage and departed.

At precisely noon she was met at the unmarked door by the elegant younger Chappell, who actually offered her a smile this time. Before they'd even reached the bookshop, she had asked if they ever acquired journals.

"Yes," Chappell answered, "provided they contain significant enough content or provenance to be of interest to our clientele."

They entered the cloistered shop, and Diana immediately turned to face him. "I'm looking for a journal by my late husband, Lord William Furnaval."

"Ahhh," the bookseller responded, then added, "I'm very sorry, Lady Furnaval, but I know our stock quite well and I'm certain we have no such volume."

Diana was instantly crushed. She'd been so sure: it'd felt so right. Perhaps Isadora's suggestion that they'd been misdirected was accurate. Or maybe she would simply have to search every church chapel in London—

"Where did you say your husband died, Lady Furnaval?" asked Chappell, interrupting her thoughts.

"Oh, in Eastern Europe. A place called Transylvania."

"Did his reasons for being there have anything to do with some sort of gateway?"

Diana's heart skipped a beat. "Yes, they did."

"Ahh. Then I apologize. If you'll follow me..." Picking up a lamp, he walked back through the stacks, and Diana followed. They passed row upon row of tall cases, and Diana couldn't help but wonder how it was possible–the shop gave no impression of such size from the street. Finally the bookseller turned right down an aisle and stopped before a section that held a curious collection of folios and unmarked volumes. Diana barely had time to wonder how he could possibly remember what each of these untitled books were when he pulled one out and passed it to her. "This hasn't his full name. Would this be the journal?"

Diana's fingers trembled as she received the book: she recognized it instantly. It was considerably more battered than when she had last seen it, but otherwise all of William's journals were identical, bound in Morocco leather with gilt edges and a ribbon marker. His initials— W.F.—were embossed on the front board. "Yes, this is his," she could only whisper.

Chappell leaned over her with a polite nod and flipped the book open. "As you can see, we received this volume absent a number of pages from the beginning." Indeed, Diana saw that at least twenty pages had been torn out; several others were filthy beyond readability. The book looked as if it had lost a boxing match with a hurricane. Fortunately the remains, perhaps fifty or so pages, were intact and legible, although the last few were blank.

"How did you get this?" Diana asked, trying to keep the quaver from her voice.

"We have agents working for us throughout the major European cities. Our man in Belgrade, I think it was, encountered this in an antique shop, and upon scanning its contents he thought it might be of interest to us." Chappell suddenly caught himself and looked at her very seriously. "Lady Furnaval, I should forewarn you: This won't be a pleasant read for you. Your husband was involved in an extraordinarily dangerous undertaking surrounded by any number of occult forces—"

"I'm well acquainted with my husband's activities, Mr. Chappell," she snapped, but immediately regretted the remark. "Thank you for your concern, but if you knew some of what I've seen—"

"Oh," he responded, unoffended, "I understand. You've undoubtedly dealt with some rather...*alarming* beings coming through the gateways."

She gaped at him in open-mouthed astonishment for a beat, then caught herself. "You know of the gateways?"

"We wouldn't be great bookmen if we didn't at least attempt to acquaint ourselves with the contents of our stock, Lady Furnaval," Chappell answered.

"How much of your stock *do* you know?" she asked, beginning to view the bookseller with interest that went beyond his engaging appearance.

The bookseller gestured with the lamp, and began strolling back toward the front room. "Of course I haven't read *every* book in here, but I'm familiar with most major aspects of occult and paranormal philosophy and history. The gateways are certainly very significant."

Diana surprised herself by what she said next: "Stephen, I'd very much like to talk to you further about your knowledge."

He stopped and turned back to smile at her; his smile wasn't dazzling, like a sunny meadow, but rather it promised mystery - a moonlit stroll across a moor. "I'd enjoy that as well, Lady Furnaval."

"Are you available for dinner any evening?"

Chappell answered, "Would this Sunday evening be acceptable?"

Diana nodded. "Eight p.m.?"

They agreed to dine at the Pall Mall Restaurant. Stephen led her back to the front room where she purchased the journal, which Chappell sold to her at a considerable discount ("I wish I could just give it to you, but we did expend a fair sum getting it ourselves").

As she returned to her apartment—desperate to tear open the wrapped package containing William's journal—she found herself both anticipating her dinner engagement and being vaguely ashamed of herself.

What am I doing? I should be at home disinterring William's corpse, not imagining dining out with this handsome stranger.

Still, it had been so very long since she'd enjoyed the company of any man other than Howe or Quilby, and she quite looked forward to the appointment.

Before tea time, she was settled into her private railway car bound for Derby, with Mina curled up on the seat beside her. She was normally disdainful of hiring a private car—she didn't feel herself to be so far above the other passengers—but today she needed the solitude to study the journal. The weather was appropriately gloomy, and she was grateful for the warmth of Mina's small form in her lap.

Then she opened William's journal, and after moving past the pages that were no longer intelligible, she found the first clean page and, trembling, allowed herself to imagine William's voice speaking to her as she read.

Chapter IV

From the final journal of Lord William Furnaval:

- had the last English-keeping innkeeper translate my papers into Romanian, because it's been some time now since I've encountered anyone who speaks Eng. My fellow passengers on the current coach seem to be a mix of Romanian and Hungarian. We had a German on the coach, with whom I could converse a little, but he left us at the last village.

The coach is now climbing up a steep mt. road, with a sheer drop only yards to the left of us. The condition of the road does little to reassure, but our driver seems unconcerned and the horses very strong and steady; the great beasts are indeed most impressive equine specimens, far removed from our more genteel Eng. steeds. The l.s. is a mix of wild forest and craggy rock, splintered here and there with brooks which shatter into mist as they cascade over some cliff's edge or other. (Oh dear, I fear this bumpy ride is doing little for my pensmanship!)

6:40 p.m.

We've arrived at a stop which can't even truthfully be called a village, since it consists of little more than a single inn. We supped on a very decent meal of a rich and flavorful meat stew and a local red wine, and I've been provided with a serviceable, if not exactly luxurious, room. I'm writing this now by the light of the small fire, which is calming and cheerful after the strenuous ride here. I confess I sometimes wish I had D's nerves when it comes to confronting these difficult positions! She would not only have not minded the rough road and vertigo-inducing downward views, she would probably have exulted in them. Dear Diana…I miss her more than she can know, and I do regret not being able to have her accompany me on this tr. How often I wish our lives were those of normal folk, whose greatest concern is what to have for breakfast or remembering to pay the glazier who fixed the broken window. (Good god—did I remember to pay the glazier? Oh well, no great matter—if I did not, D. can certainly handle <u>him</u>.)

I know D. would be curious to know of the books on the small shelf here in my room. Of course they are in the native tongue and so incoherent to me, but I can make out enough to know that one is, of course, a Bible (the crucifix embossed on the cover makes it rather easy to recognize), and one seems to be some sort of history. I see a large portion of this book is dedicated to an ancient hero who seems to be greatly worshipped in these parts. The Eng.-speaking landlord of a previous inn told me his name was Vlad Dracul, meaning "Son of the Dragon", and that he was a 15th-century prince of extr. bravery and cruelty. The l.l. took particular delight in regaling me with the unsavory story of how this "Dracula" (who is apparently the source of many local legends) had 30,000 of his own people impaled, and then ordered that his nobles join him in a feast at tables set in the very heart of this nightmarish tableau. Whilst dining, this barbarian noticed that one of his noblemen was vainly attempting to cover his nose against the foul stench of rotting bodies and bodily emissions, and he ordered this gentleman impaled <u>above</u> the rest of the corpses in order that he no longer be forced to endure the odious smells.

It should reveal much of the savage nature of this land that these people hold this monster in such great esteem.

Enough; I shall think of him no more. Tomorrow afternoon we are due to arrive at my final destination, a village known as Urveri. From there I will meet with this János Rákóczi, assist him with this unknown dire matter of his, and then hopefully be bound home to Eng. & D. within the wk.

April 30, 1876

Imagine my surprise when I awoke at sunrise this a.m., dressed, gathered my things, and stepped out of the security of my little room only to discover that the entire inn had been redecorated during the night!

It took me a few minutes to remember why: Tomorrow is the delightful celebration of May Day in Eng., but here in the more ancient and primeval areas of Eur. tonight is Walpurgisnacht. I remember this odious date as a night of peculiar events in Goethe's <u>Faust</u>, and I gather it is still a time of superstitious danger in these parts. In the main room of the inn I found branches of some sort fastened above all doors, while the local women sat at tables fashioning torches from an herb I could identify (by its scent) as rosemary. Outside some of the men were placing crosses above the doors of the stable.

Most interesting to me, though, were the strings of whole garlic bulbs strung around all windows. Before leaving for this tr, D. and I used our library to study the folklore of the area. We've come to believe (or at least I have—I think my darling wife may still be somewhat skeptical, as is her nature) that there's some kind of factual basis behind nearly all folklore. I believe that the Russ. witch "Baba Yaga", the Egyptian sphinx, and the N. Amer. Indian thunderbird may all represent creatures that have traversed gateways from the netherworld. Our research on this area of Eur. revealed belief in the vampire—creatures returned from the grave after death to feed upon the blood of the living. Romania's neighbor Hungary experienced a veritable frenzy of vampire belief in the 17th century, not unlike the witch-hunting madness that possessed other parts of Eur., and in these outlying areas, away from the more sophisticated cities, Walpurgisnacht represents a potential orgy of vampires, witches and other evil entities.

And given the prox. of this area to a gateway, these people may be wiser than we city folk in employing these protections.

After a breakfast of a tough local bread, thick butter and a strangely-scented herb tea, we piled into our coach again and continued our journey. This time the going was easier, as our rt. took us through forests so thick I wondered if sunshine ever shone within them, and past occasional crag faces where we glimpsed abandoned mines. Apparently the whole of this country was highly prized by the Romans for its mineral resources, which included gold, copper and salt; but many of the mines have been abandoned, either because they were worked out or were too difficult to reach.

We arrived at the village of Urveri at about four in the p.m. The sun was still high in the sky, but I suppose because of the particular day, the villagers were already bolting doors, leaving only a few of the men outside, with clusters of the homemade rosemary torches. The village consists only of an inn, a general store, a church, a few homes, and several abandoned businesses which I gather once served the area's mines. I inquired after Mr. R.; I displayed the note the innkeeper had written for me, and the original letter I'd received from this R., but no one in the village was able to identify such an individual. I posted a letter to D., then retired to the inn.

As I write this, I'm seated in a cozy corner of the inn's main room. The sun has set outside, and I'm trying to gather my wits as to how to deal with this problem of my non-existent host. The only possible explanation must be that I've somehow arrived at the wrong village; is it possible there are two villages named Urveri? If only someone here spoke Eng., I could query them further; alas, they can barely pronounce my name, and I confess I've gained no Romanian whatsoever. I'm apparently stuck here until the next coach passes through, at which point I shall board it, ride on to the next stop, and make my inq. there.

It's full night now, and a very strange scene greets my eyes beyond the windows of the inn: The local men roam about with their lit torches of rosemary, waving them about overhead in quite a mad fashion. I seem to recall hearing of some practices conducted in Scotland on Hallowe'en (at the exact opposite end of the calendar from Walpurgisnacht, or April 30), in which torches were waved overhead to frighten off witches, so my guess is these Rom. are indulging in something similar. The inn smells (pleasantly, in my opinion) of garlic, from the ubiquitous strings of bulbs. The women sit near me, looking morose, reading from their bibles, and glancing up nervously from time to time.

Later—I must have dosed off, and have just now been awakened by the sound of a carriage pulling up outside. According to my watch it's just past 11, which seems rather late for a coach, doesn't it? The villagers seem anxious about this new arrival as well. The driver is stepping down from the coach, and approaching the door. He's knocked; the women are conferring among themselves, apparently deciding whether to open the door or not. The men who were outside with the torches must have wandered off, for the night is dark as pitch and quiet.

The women seem to concur, and the door is opened. A caped and behatted man stands in the doorway, his face invisible but his build powerful—wait, I hear my name! Could this be my contact, the mysterious J. R.?

May 1, 1876

I'm very weak and may not have long to live, but I must get down as much of this as can. D. must know. I will pay one of the innkeepers to be sure this journal reaches her.

Diana, dear one, if you are reading this, then you know by now that I have been declared dead. You also know, of course, that you were right, as always—the letter inviting me to come here was a trap. The most obvious of deceits, and yet I believed it. I've likely paid for that belief with my life…if not indeed with my soul.

As I mentioned in my last entry, it was shortly after eleven when a weird visitor arrived at the inn: A tall, strongly-built man whose face was invisible in the shadows of his large hat and high-collared cloak. He uttered my name, in a deep croaking voice that caused more than one of the women near me to cross herself. I rose and advanced towards him, uttering the name, "János Rákóczi?"

He heard me, swiveled in my direction, and executed a deep, very old-fashioned bow. He swept off his hat, and a collective gasp sounded behind me: He was indeed a very unsettling-looking individual, with whitish-grey skin, a few wisps of black hair crossing a protruberant skull, deepset eyes and hollow cheeks, and a wide, almost lipless mouth. His smile was not a pleasant thing to behold; but he spoke Eng., and my relief at hearing my own tongue was enough to cause me to disregard some of my trepidations.

"Lord F—," he said, gesturing towards the carriage with his hat, "if you don't mind. We need to be at the gateway by midnight. It's nearby, but we haven't much time."

I told him I'd join him momentarily, and retreated to my room, wherein I sought my coat, hat, gloves, and the pages of <u>The Book</u> I'd copied out. Before I left the room, I also took one of the loops of garlic bulbs from above my window and secreted it in my leather traveling bag, which I slung over my shoulder under my coat. I returned shortly to the main room, and then left it to join R. outside at the carriage. Even his horses were strange—they were gigantic and jet black, with eyes that rolled whitely in their sockets. The carriage looked quite ancient but sound enough, and yet I was still reluctant to enter it, with so many questions unanswered.

"Mr. R., why exactly have you summoned me?" I queried.

R. merely gestured with some annoyance at the open carriage door. "Please, my Lord, all will be explained, but time is of the essence."

"I'm sorry, sir, but I'm not going anywhere until some of my questions are answered," I told him.

For a moment, his countenance seemed to change, resembling more some great enraged beast than a fellow human being, and I confess I stepped back in some alarm as he loomed over me. Then he seemed to catch himself, and reached forward as if for the carriage door.

"We have less than an hour to reach the gateway," he said, "and seal it."

It was the one thing he could have said that would have persuaded me to enter that carriage just then.

"The g.w. can be sealed? How?"

"It can only be done on this night, Walpurgisnacht. Now, if you please, Lord Will.—your questions will be answered when we arrive at our destination."

Fool that I am, I entered that carriage.

It was not done without some last hesitation, at least, but the idea of closing a g.w. overwhelmed my better judgment. R. closed the carriage door behind me and assumed the position of driver. I glanced back once at the inn, and caught the village women all staring out at me with absolute horror in their faces. One even frantically ran up to the carriage, gesturing and madly spewing words in her own language, but a glare from R. sent her scurrying back to the safety of the inn.

The carriage took off with such sudden force that I was thrown back against the seats, which I was dismayed to find smelled of mildew and age. I wondered how on earth R. dared drive the horses so fast in the dead of night, on a forest road that was undoubtedly treacherous on even the brightest of days; yet our tr. transpired without incident, and it was perhaps 10 min. later when we bumped to a halt.

After a few seconds R. appeared at the side of the carriage and opened the door, gesturing me out. I stepped down, rounded the carriage, and gaped at what was before me:

We had stopped before the entrance to a large and very old cemetery.

I turned to stare at R., who was removing a lantern from the carriage and approaching the cem. "The g.w. is within, Lord F—" he said, gesturing towards the graveyard.

I don't mind relating that I very nearly demanded just then that we return to the inn. The notion of a g.w. situated in a graveyard was simply too monstrous. Although g.w. were invisible (at least to the human eye), they always precipitated strange, sometimes deadly, events: Hauntings, monster sightings, cases of madness and murder...and unholy desecrations. Certainly a cemetery could be mistakenly started near a g.w.—but the swiftly mounting numbers of occult phenomena would cause any sane people to soon cease burials in the area and relocate.

This was a very large cemetery.

My host obviously saw my trepidation. He stood at the perimeter of the necropolis and said, "Lord F—"

"Are you saying your g.w. is within this cemetery?" I queried.

He nodded. "It is."

I asked, "And to seal this g.w. requires both of us?"

He nodded and answered, in that strange croaking voice, "Tonight is Walpurgisnacht, a night of great power. I have discovered an incantation which will allow us to seal the gate forever, provided it is performed on this one night and by two gatekeepers."

"How did you find this 'incantation'?" I asked. I myself had incurred some expense searching for such a solution; I would certainly have sealed my own g.w., had it been possible.

Rákóczi answered: "A 14th-century necromancer's spellbook held the incantation for the closing of the g.w."

What a fool I was to follow him into that graveyard.

I can barely describe the utter desolation and bone-chilling dread of that place. The markers were largely rotting wood crosses, a few still adorned with withered bouquets or wreaths; what few stone monuments were present were large and baroque carvings, of bony reapers or grieving angels. The most macabre showed a skeletal musician playing a flute made from a human thighbone. There was no fog at this high elev., but there was a strong, freezing wind blowing that made me shiver beneath my heavy outer coat, and somewhere off in the distance thunder rumbled.

R. led the way, and it seemed that we walked for kilometers, although of course that couldn't possibly have been the case. This cem. seemed long forgotten, and more than once I tripped over ground that had frozen, thawed, and cracked many times, creating numerous obstacles for the unwary visitor. Roots from dead trees still poked up through the earth in places, clutching at my ankles as we walked by.

Finally R. came to a halt, and after holding the lantern high and peering about briefly, he murmured. "We are here."

I looked around and saw nothing that would indicate this area of the cemetery was any different from the rest of it. "Where—"

Before I'd finished speaking, R. held the lantern out to me and with his other hand pointed into the murk before us. "There, Lord F—" he suggested.

I took the offered lantern and stepped forward a few paces, looking carefully but seeing nothing…at first. I was about to turn and query him further when some small movement caught the corner of my eye, just off to my left, and I swung the lantern there to look.

The ground was moving. It pulsed upwards once, twice, just a small area.

Something underneath was trying to come up.

I confess I lost the power of movement. I just stared, stupidly, as the ground finally broke, and five tattered fingers with long, claw-like nails pushed through. The hand scrabbled about for an instance, as if testing—

—and then the earth around it exploded outward and the vampire rose into view.

Its head, torso and arms came first, and then it pushed itself into a standing position, dirt and splintered bits of coffin wood falling from its grave clothes. The clothing was that of a peasant's best, a homespun suit in the local style. It was, of course, filthy now, and much of the outer coat hung in tatters. But as bad as the thing's hands and clothing were, it was the face that was the worst.

It had evidently been long dead, to judge by the sunken, skull-like features. It was nearly hairless, nothing remained of the nose but a stub of cartilage and an open hole beneath, and the eyes were red fires glowing from within sunken pits. The lips were cracked and peeling, and pulled back to reveal two long fangs where the canines should have been. Even from twenty paces away I was nearly overcome by the thing's foul stench, which was somehow reminiscent of decaying fruit.

The only thing that saved me then was the vampire's movement—it was slow and jerky, as if its joints no longer quite properly worked. It was staggering towards me, its crimson eyes fixed on my neck, but it was so slow I could have easily outrun it.

Had there not been another one behind me.

For just as I turned to flee, I beheld a second monster forty feet off in that direction. This one was female, bloated, shambling, but with a bloodlust that had fixed on me.

I started off in another direction—just in time to see a wooden cross topple over as the earth disgorged another vampire.

I was turning in every direction, hopelessly, and seeing the fiends everywhere now. There were at least a dozen, of varying ages and stages of decomposition, but all stumbling towards me with insatiable and demonic appetite.

And R. was nowhere to be seen.

The first vampire had nearly reached me when I broke my paralysis and frantically scrabbled for the leather satchel under my coat. I found the garlic necklace and fairly flung it at the nearest of the fiends. It hissed and stopped its advance, then staggered back.

The garlic worked. So much for the villagers' superstitions being ridiculous.

I started spinning, holding the garlic out towards the monsters. They had formed a ring around me now, but were evidently repulsed by the herb to the point where they dared approach no closer. I was just beginning to formulate a plan for escape when something hit me from behind. Before I could react, my arms had been pulled back from behind me, and the garlic had fallen to the ground.

"Very clever, Lord F—," croaked R., and I realized it was he who held me, "but not clever enough."

The first sank its fangs into my neck as R. held me immobilized.

I was instantly overwhelmed by pain and the horrible odor of the thing. I struggled in vain against his grip, but the man—if such he were—seemed impossibly strong.

Another of the things fell to its knees before me, ripped my trouser leg open and bit into my ankle.

Behind me, R. pulled my right arm away, and I felt the icy fingers of more vampires gripping my wrist. That sensation was followed by greater agony, as they tore into the pulsing veins there.

That's the last thing I remember.

When I came to, it was a.m., and I lay on hay in the back of a villager's bouncing cart. The pain was gone, but I was too weak to move. I lost consciousness again for a while, and woke up in the inn just before I started to write this.

The sun is setting outside the window now, and I fear it sets permanently for me. I've no idea why I'm still alive, and even should I survive my current condition, I'm sure that monster Rákóczi—for now I'm certain he must represent some particularly loathesome species of the netherworld—has something else planned for me. The res. of Urveri are a sturdy, courageous people, but they can't possibly hope to stand against R. and his vampire horde, should he choose to invade here.

Diana, my love, if you read this…you must understand what has really happened here. Something has changed in that unknown world beyond the g.w. Those in charge there—for something has masterminded this—are no longer merely content with using the g.w. to perpetrate minor horrors. They lured me here, where they knew I would be vulnerable, for a very particular reason. I wish I could tell you what that reason was, but I fear I shall go to my deathbed without discovering it.

You must exercise extreme caution from now on, D. You will now become the heir of the F— legacy, and the new g-keeper. It could well be, dear, that you are the last surviving g-keeper anywhere on earth. Should that be the case, the same creatures that have ingeniously plotted my demise here will undoubtedly be after your life, as well.

Promise me, D., that under no circumstances will you come to this region. They may try to lure you here; perhaps I have been left alive to further such an evil scheme, and they will try to convince you that I'm alive and awaiting you to rescue me. Do not believe it, even if they offer proof. My concern extends beyond my considerable love; you may be all that stands between our world and theirs.

Night has now fallen, and I've just become aware of some great commotion downstairs. I hear shouting, cries of alarm and of pain. A woman just shrieked; I can't imagine that horrid sound coming from anything not facing its own demise. Footsteps are coming up the stairs now. Towards my room. Oh God, the smell

Chapter V

November 6, 1879
Derby

There was nothing after that, save for a few brown spots which might have been blood.

William's blood.

The train whistle shrieked and Diana jumped, then set the journal down and stared out the window at the passing landscape, her mind reeling. William, her William, murdered by revenants, as part of some fiendish plot to attack those who guarded the gateways. What had Rákóczi really been? Another vampire? Or something worse, some sort of netherworld captain sent to oversee the vampire attack on her husband?

But was William truly dead? Isadora had received a message from the Netherworld saying he wasn't. Had he somehow survived the vampire attack? It didn't seem likely, given the journal's horrific ending. Had Isadora been lied to in the psychic message?

Diana went over her conversation with Isadora, thinking about what exactly the medium had told her. She'd said only that William was not dead. Then she asked Diana about his remains, shipped over from Eastern Europe....

Oh dear God. William's remains had been shipped over in a *sealed* casket. William had last been attacked by vampires.

Diana mentally urged the locomotive on to greater speed.

It was dark as the hansom cab pulled up the lane towards the front of Hampstead Hall. Howe was somewhat shocked to see her, but not as shocked as when she revealed her purpose in returning so soon.

At first the stolid butler was aghast; disinter his Lordship's corpse? And even if it were true…there'd been no vampiric attacks near the grounds. But Howe had had enough experience dealing with the supernatural that he listened when Diana explained her reasons, and finally agreed to assist her.

Diana had been anxious to proceed immediately to the family crypt, but Howe had convinced her to at least do some research into the vampire folklore before proceeding. After all, she knew little about dealing with these denizens of darkness, and there were no instructions provided for dispatching vampires in *The Book of Gateways, Conjurations and Banishments*; fortunately, though, the Furnavals had their extensive library of occult and historic references, and she had no difficulty winding through her earlier clutter to locate what she sought: Augustin Calmet's *The Phantom World*, the English translation with several handwritten letters from the author on vampires included. She was also glad that Howe had convinced her to wait, since Calmet strongly indicated that vampires should only be exposed during the day, when they were essentially powerless. She also discovered that there were ways to render a vampire unable to leave its coffin, and some—such as placing a holy wafer in the mouth—were quite simple.

Although Howe had retired, Diana was unable to sleep that night; she paced the library, pulling still more reference books and re-reading William's journal. She discovered that Rákóczi was a famous name in Transylvanian history—George I Rákóczi was a seventeenth-century ruler who had presided over Transylvania's golden era—and Diana castigated herself for not doing more investigation into the supposed gatekeeper's letter before letting William ride off to his doom. It was obvious that whomever—or whatever—had written the letter had simply chosen a name from the province's history. How easily deceived she and William had been.

Shortly after dawn Howe appeared, dressed in his hunting clothes. He'd just come from the kitchen, where he himself had selected a cord of ash wood and carved a lethally-pointed, heavy stake from it; he'd also gathered a sexton's spade, crowbars, garlic, and lantern (since the crypt interior was dark).

A few moments later, Howe and Diana (with Mina trotting by her side) were off for the crypt. Hampstead Hall included its own small chapel and graveyard, located a short distance from the main house, with an extravagant family mausoleum that had housed all the deceased Furnavals for the last three centuries. The sun had barely risen above the surrounding trees as they passed the ruins of the old hall and reached the crypt; the day was hazy and cold, and Diana shivered as she waited for Howe to thumb through his huge key ring. He finally found the key to the crypt door, unlocked it, and entered first so he could light the way for Diana.

Half-a-dozen steps downward led to a large stone chamber with ledges around all the walls, on which were stacked caskets. A stone pedestal in the room's center still held a sarcophagus, which Diana knew contained William's casket; his casket would be moved out to one of the ledges when the next Furnaval passed on and was placed within the sarcophagus—Diana herself, in other words.

Howe jumped slightly as the crypt door swung closed behind them, sealing them in the dank, stone chamber. The only light came from his lantern, and fell upon the dusty, cobwebbed surface of the huge, heavy sarcophagus. As Howe moved the lantern along the length of the stone lid, Diana took her place on the opposite side, Mina rubbing around her ankles. That the cat was calm gave no comfort to either of them.

Howe finally set the lantern aside and looked at Diana. "Are you ready, Lady Furnaval?"

She took a deep breath. "As I'll ever be, Howe. Let's get this done with."

Howe picked up the crowbars and handed one to her, then placed his own beneath the lip of one side of the sarcophagus lid. Diana joined him, and together they levered the weighty stone top far enough ajar that they were able to lift the edges and set the covering aside. Howe raised the lantern, and they peered down into the sarcophagus, where William's ornate coffin lay, its polished wood only slightly dusted with age.

Diana started to reach for it, but Howe cautioned her: "It's been nailed shut. We'll need the crowbars."

Diana nodded, and picked up her crowbar again. She took a moment to gird herself; she wasn't sure which she feared more—finding him or *not* finding him. And if she found him, she'd be witness to either his withered corpse, long and truly dead, or something far worse.

"A moment, Howe."

Howe thoughtfully gave her the time she needed—and then she leaned over the edge of the sarcophagus and placed her crowbar's tip under the coffin's lid. Howe did likewise, and they started straining against the lid's bonds.

This lid was harder to move than the sarcophagus lid, and Diana was breaking into a mild sweat, despite the clammy chill of the crypt, before it came free, nails squealing out from the wood with banshee-like cries. They moved the crowbars down to the other end of the lid, and that portion worked free with less effort. Finally Howe set his crowbar down and reached in. With a few seconds of tugging, he finally freed the lid completely. He looked up at Diana, who nodded, and then he pulled the lid from the sarcophagus and set it aside.

Diana cried out involuntarily when she saw what was in the coffin.

Whatever ghastly thing she'd expected—a bloated monster, a bloodstained revenant—it hadn't been this horror: A corpse, showing the effects of three years' decay, and with twisted hands upraised at chest level.

He had evidently been buried alive, and fought in vain to escape.

Diana turned away in horror, and struggled to keep from retching. "Oh my William...no...William, no...!"

Diana barely heard Howe as he exclaimed, "There's something in the mouth...."

It took several seconds for those words to work through her tortured brain, and suddenly she whirled. "Howe, don't—!"

Too late. Howe had removed a white, disc-shaped object from the corpse's mouth and was holding it up to the lantern's rays. "It's a holy Eucharist—"

Mina suddenly hissed and began backing away to a corner. At the same moment the corpse's withered hand shot upward and grasped Howe's throat in a lethal stranglehold.

Howe uttered one choked gasp of surprise, then he was struggling vainly to free the dead fingers. The corpse was rising to a sitting position now, baring fangs as long as Diana's little finger. Its eyes popped open, and revealed a hellish red glow, fixed on Howe.

Diana instinctively leaped forward, raising her crowbar. She brought it down on the vampire's arm, and was satisfied to hear the rotting bones snap, severing the arm just above the wrist.

The severed hand continued to strangle Howe.

Diana overcame her revulsion and grabbed the thing with both hands, but realized she would be unable to free Howe from the deathgrip before the vampire would be on her. She upended the bag of supplies they had brought, grabbed for a string of garlic bulbs, and held them up before the vampire, struggling to rise. It snarled and hissed, then fell back into the coffin, twisting its head aside to avoid the garlic scent.

Diana threw the garlic chain onto the writhing monster, then grabbed Howe's stake in her left hand and the spade in the right. She hesitated, trying to recall exactly what the books had said about this process: The stake needed to be driven cleanly through the heart with one blow of the spade. It would have been difficult for a strong man under the best of circumstances. But Howe was grappling with the severed hand clawing the life from him, and she knew if she didn't act quickly Howe would surely die here, in this nightmarish crypt.

"I'm sorry, William," she whispered, then placed the stake's pointed tip above where she hoped the fiend's heart was. The vampire's twisting made this nigh impossible, and she fought to hold the stake steady.

With a deep breath, she raised the spade high overhead, and brought it down with all her might upon the stake.

The beast's response was instantaneous and astonishing. The vampire screeched, a deafening and unnatural sound that was amplified in the stone crypt until it was literally painful. Thick, noxious vapors geysered up out of the thing's convulsing chest, and Diana staggered back, crying out. Howe gulped in air as the severed hand released its deathgrip on his throat and tumbled lifeless to the floor.

When she could catch a breath again, Diana turned to Howe. "Are you all right?"

Howe was pale and still sucking in air, but he nodded as he fingered his throat, already purpling with bruises

Diana swallowed back her fear and stepped forward to look down at the thing she had slain. The corpse, now dusted with the fetid essence Diana had released from it, lay unmoving. Diana studied it...and gasped before reaching into the coffin.

Howe saw the motion, and choked out, "What is it, Lady—?"

She touched the head of the ruined corpse, which still bore the hair of its former life. A thick head of light brown hair, now matted with debris.

William's hair had been black.

"It's not him, Howe. This is not William."

Howe looked down, saw the hair, and then looked up sharply at her. "Lady Furnaval, this is my mistake. I should have unsealed the coffin when it first arrived—"

Diana cut him off. "That doesn't matter now. What does matter is that this isn't William. My William may still be alive somewhere!"

Howe looked at her, not daring to tell her there was surely very little chance of that.

There was still some work left, though. Diana had just enough strength to raise the spade overhead and sever the vampire's head from its body with one blow; then she shoved one of the garlic bulbs into the putrid mouth, and finally the horrific thing was done.

As Diana turned to leave the crypt, Howe called up to her, "Lady Furnaval...what should we do with this?"

She turned to see he was gesturing to the coffin and the newly-dead-again thing within it. "We'll burn it tonight in secret, Howe. It would be a dishonor to the Furnaval name to leave it resting in our family crypt. But just right now...I'd desperately like to clean myself up, if you don't mind."

She didn't see Howe's nod, but she did hear Mina's winsome meow, and leaned down to stroke the feline's back before she left the crypt.

"Yes, Mina, I'm glad that's done, too."

Howe caught her when, halfway back to the house, her knees gave way and she crumpled to the ground, both strength and senses gone.

Chapter VI

November 9, 1879
London

Diana returned to her London house in time to see Isadora before her meeting with Stephen Chappell. She was anxious to hear if her friend had received any further spirit communications, but Isadora told her the netherworld had been strangely quiet for the last few days.

It had taken Diana a full day to recover from the horror in the crypt. Howe told the rest of the staff she'd taken suddenly ill, and had given a bonus to a young groundskeeper to help in the burning of the coffin while Diana had recuperated. She'd spent the first twelve hours in a feverish state, shivering and nauseous. As the shock passed, she'd pondered William's situation. She believed the warning in his journal had been apt, and that the nameless vampire in William's coffin had undoubtedly been sent as a deadly trap. She also thought it unlikely that William was still alive somewhere in Transylvania; in fact, she thought it unlikely that he were alive anywhere on the planet. At least not the planet on *this* side of the Netherworld.

Her biggest question right now was: Who/what had relayed the messages to Isadora? Most of the communications Isadora received from the netherworld were from specific spirits attempting to reach loved ones on this side. In fact, Isadora's messages had given Diana her best conception of what the netherworld must be: She thought of it as the place where mankind's fears were made real and dwelled;

terrible entities always seeking to gain entrance to our world. She wasn't sure why they didn't cross over more often via the gateways.

What she did learn was that these nightmares had been coming through the gateways in far greater numbers for the last hundred years. And actually, for a thousand years, supernatural events with documented origins near to gateways were surprisingly few and far between; despite a few particularly gruesome fairy tales, there was little evidence that human deaths had occurred near any gateways—until roughly ten or fifteen decades ago. She and William both had known this, and they discussed it at length, but had never come up with an answer for the unnerving phenomenon.

And, there had been no deliberate attempts made on the lives of the Furnaval gatekeepers of past generations. No, something was changing in the unknown place beyond the gateways. The netherworld was somehow shifting.

Diana was troubled by the notion that Stephen Chappell might have more answers than he'd so far let on.

And even if he didn't…well, he was still terribly pleasant to look at.

She arrived at the elegant Pall Mall just prior to eight p.m., and was pleased to find that Stephen was punctual; he joined her at five minutes before the hour. He had reserved a private dining room for them, a gesture that Diana found very appealing. After they were seated, with a fine claret ordered up and on the way, Diana took a few moments to study her dining companion.

Tonight Stephen Chappell looked quite different, although their dining room was only slightly brighter than the dimly-lit confines of his bookshop. For one thing, Diana had never noticed his eyes before, and she was quite startled by their depth and hue—they were a clear and pale blue, like a cloudless sky reflected in ice. He had a face that was very nearly ageless—he could have been any age between twenty-eight or fifty—and had long, delicate fingers. There was something vaguely familiar about his face, but Diana couldn't place what that was, and so ended up deciding that he reminded her of a figure in a painting by an old master, Raphael or Michelangelo.

"So," he began their conversation, "tell me more about the gateways."

Diana smiled at him, saying, "Funny, Mr. Chappell, I was going to ask you the same thing."

"It's Stephen, please."

Diana nodded. "Stephen, then. And please call me Diana."

"Very well, Diana," he replied, "I think your experiences with the gateways will be rather more personal than mine have been."

"How so?"

"Very simply: Your knowledge of the gateways has been obtained from a rather close vantage-point."

"Ahhh, Stephen. I see. Yes, it's true, I've confronted a number of gateways and have hopefully sealed them, and yet I still feel as if I'm not entirely sure what they are. I was hoping you might have some insight into their history."

He peered at her strangely for a moment, and then admitted, "I do know…a little."

The wine arrived just then, and Diana was forced to wait while Stephen examined the bottle, allowed the waiter to uncork it and pour his glass, sampled it, and nodded his approval. The first of the eight courses (an excellent turtle soup) was brought, and then they were alone. They shared a brief toast, and then a moment of silence before Stephen continued: "Let's begin with something simple: Do you understand why there are eighty-one gateways, Diana?"

She looked up from her spoonful of soup and blinked in surprise; she'd never stopped to consider the number itself, and confessed as much to him now.

"Oh, the number itself is very important. Nine is a number of power in magical workings: The Egyptians believed in ninefold cosmic levels. The Greeks honoured nine Muses. The Christians know of nine orders of angelic choirs in nine circles of heaven, and likewise there are nine orders of devils within the nine rings of Hell. There are numerous mathematical games centering on the number nine: For example, take any two-digit number, add the two digits together, then subtract their total from the original number, and the result will always be a multiple of nine."

Diana sipped her excellent bordeaux, then followed his thought, "So, there are eighty-one gateways because eighty-one equals nine times nine."

Stephen nodded, pleased. "A number of extraordinary magical power."

Diana considered, then offered, "Then by closing the gateways I must be causing some serious interference to that power."

Stephen's clear eyes seemed to cloud over for an instant. "Indeed you are. You've upset some serious balance, and there are those on the other side who aren't very happy about that. Hence the trap you recently managed to avoid."

Diana felt a raw chill pass through her. "How do you know about that?"

"I didn't, actually. An educated guess."

She didn't believe him.

The way he was looking at her, for one thing; under other circumstances, his long, unblinking study of her would have been flattering, but now she felt it to be slightly disturbing, and she had to fight an urge to turn away. "Stephen, how much do you know?"

His gaze remained riveted on her as he answered, "I know you've become the focal point now in a very old war."

"A war?" Diana asked. "Between whom?"

"On one side, the netherworld."

"And who is on the opposing side?"

Stephen actually chuckled slightly before answering, "You, mainly."

Diana didn't join him in laughter. "So I'm fighting a war alone?"

His amusement completely vanished, and she thought she'd never seen another human being look so serious. "You're not alone. Have you become so skilled at recognizing the forces of darkness that you can no longer see those of good?"

"Would that be you, Stephen?" she asked.

He leaned back in his chair, setting his glass down. "I'd like to think we're on the same side, yes. I am...*constrained* from fighting as you do, but I offer assistance whenever I can."

There was a long silent moment between them, and Diana suddenly wanted very much to touch him. She tried to put that thought from her mind by asking, "Tell me what you know about the netherworld."

"Do you believe in life after death?" he asked.

"Yes and no," she answered. "If you mean do I believe in those nine circles of Hell and those nine heavenly choirs, the answer is no. If you're asking if I think some netherworld spirits were once human, the answer is yes, though I can't explain it."

"You're close," he said. "The netherworld was originally a place inhabited by what we would think of as monsters. You've met one of the oldest of their kind, I believe—a horned man...."

"Cernunnos," Diana offered.

"Yes. There used to be separation between our world and theirs, but then the gateways were discovered, and some of the netherfolk found they had a taste for human life. Spirits came here and those who saw them either fled in terror, worshipped them as gods, or were slain by them. Any human being slain by one of the netherfolk will find his own spirit trapped in the netherworld; likewise, any human who should cross through a gateway and die in the netherworld will remain there."

Diana was dumbfounded; for some reason, it had never occurred to her that travel through the gateways could go both ways. *William is over there....*

As if reading her mind, Stephen told her, "Only the most foolhardy of humans would ever dare to cross through a gateway into the netherworld. It almost certainly means death, followed by an eternity of roaming that dark plane as a bodiless, tormented spirit."

Oh dear god, if William were to die over there....

"Diana!" Stephen barked, drawing her attention back to him, "as I told you earlier, you're not alone in your fight against the dark forces—but were you ever to be so stupid as to venture through a gateway into the netherworld, your allies would desert you."

Diana answered, "My husband is my best ally. And he may be in the Netherworld."

"Your husband is dead," he said softly.

Diana gaped in astonishment for a moment, then could only whisper, "How could you know that?"

Stephen leaned forward now, and boldly took one of her hands in his. His palm was warm and comforting, his fingers strong as they wrapped around hers. "You must trust me. William's gone. You can never get him back, and you can never enter the netherworld."

"But my friend Isadora...." she began.

"Your friend is being misled by the same forces that sent the vampire against you."

"How do you know all that?!"

He ignored her question to go on: "Think, Diana: They probably meant for you to face the vampire earlier, but when that didn't happen they defrauded your medium friend with that fake message. You read William's journal, you know that he couldn't have survived that attack in the inn."

She did know it.

And yet she *didn't want to know it*. A part of her—a large part—still believed that Isadora hadn't been lied to, that her heroic William had somehow survived, and was alive there even now.

"Diana, you're doing the right thing in closing the gateways, but you will be tempted and tested and tricked and attacked in the times to come. You will need to find reserves of strength and willpower within you that you don't even know exist yet. And you need to start by acknowledging to yourself right now that William is dead."

Diana nodded—yet at the same time pulled her hand from his.

The rest of the dinner passed largely in silence. Diana found herself regarding the elegant silver-striped wallpaper, the oil paintings of placid crowds and lovely flowers, the perfect manners and suits of the wait staff, the excellent beef...anything but her companion. At the end of the evening, Diana feared she was being rather rude in telling Stephen that she'd take her own carriage home. She was intrigued by him, even attracted to him...but she also feared him. He knew things about her that no one else knew. She believed that he was good—she dismissed instantly the possibility that he was some sort of creature of the netherworld—but he had so far been unwilling to reveal exactly *what* he was.

Dinner finished, Stephen paid, and followed her out into a quiet, damp night, the yellow glow of the gas lamps dulled by fog. As she stepped up into her carriage, Stephen called out to her a last time: "Diana!"

She turned, and he strode up to her, standing close by. "Please remember what I told you about your allies. You are not alone...as long as you remain on this side of the gateways."

Diana was nodding agreement when he surprised her with a brief kiss. It was just a quick brushing of lips, too quick for her to resist; then he turned and walked away down the sidewalk, disappearing into the fog. Diana almost called after him, but instead she told the driver to take her home and settled back against the cab's upholstered bench.

* * *

The next day she received a brief note from Stephen, a note containing only two sentences that left her quite mystified:

My Dear Diana,
I fear I've done all I can for you at this time, and must depart.
However, we will meet again some day.
Regards,
Stephen

She immediately called her coachman to bring the carriage round, and set out for Stephen's bookstore.

The carriage pulled up before the address she provided, and she stepped out onto the sidewalk. She rang the bell beside the unmarked door, and was taken somewhat aback when it was answered a few seconds later by a young lady wearing a cleaning woman's apron, her brown hair askew about her face. "Yes?" the woman asked as she tried to brush an errant strand back into place.

"I'm looking for Stephen Chappell," Diana informed her.

"I'm sorry, mum" the woman responded, "but there's no one here by that name."

"But this is his bookstore," Diana told her.

The woman said, "Oh, you must have the wrong address. There's no bookstore here."

Diana blurted out, "That's quite impossible. I've been here several times, and I really need to see Mr. Chappell—"

"There's nothing here, mum! I just come in to clean out the space." The woman stepped back, offering access to Diana. "See for yourself."

Diana did push past her, down the familiar short hallway and through the opening into—not a bookstore, but a large empty space, filled not with books but rather decayed wooden crates, cobwebs, and scurrying rodents. A mop, bucket, and pile of rags stood in one corner, testament to the cleaning woman's truthfulness.

As Diana looked around in disbelief, the other woman swept a hand about. "See, mum? There's been nothing in this space for ten years now. The landlord just died, and his son's hired me to clean it up so he can try to rent it again."

Diana walked to a far doorway and looked into a large, dim space, where she'd recently followed Stephen past racks holding countless books, journals and papers; now the room held nothing but a scarred wooden floor and a leaking pipe in one corner. Diana turned back to the front area, mystified, when something caught her eye. She turned and saw a scrap of paper on the floor caught in a single stray ray of sunlight. She crossed to it and picked it up, examining it.

It was one of the missing pages from William's journal.

Although it was as stained and illegible as the other pages from the beginning of the journal, the few bits of writing that could still be seen were undeniably her husband's penmanship, and if the page added nothing to her understanding of William's story it did serve to prove that Chappell and Sons, Booksellers had not been any delusion.

She thanked the cleaning woman, and offered her a pound note and a calling card, asking her to report if she found anything else in the space. The grateful woman curtseyed and thanked Diana profusely as Diana left, returning to her carriage, clutching the one page as if it were a life preserver. Stephen's abrupt disappearance left her feeling somehow weakened, adrift, and she was startled to realize that she'd expected to be able to depend on him.

She was alone again.

Chapter VII

November 1879-April 1880
Europe

Diana did, of course, follow William's trail to the Transylvanian village of Urveri, despite his journal's plea for her not to. She reasoned that when he'd written his request, he'd been unaware of the ability to close the gateway, and would surely have not disapproved of Diana visiting for *that* purpose.

She knew she would be traveling through dangerous provinces at the very worst time of year, but subzero temperatures, freezing winds, snow and ice meant nothing to her in the face of her need to know about William. She also had no interest in journeying to other gateways in Europe (Italy, Greece, Prussia, Brittany); those gateways could wait. They hadn't swallowed up her husband.

The journey was comfortable up until Budapest, and then she began traveling southeast through country that grew progressively wilder and colder. She had to make special arrangements, since the coaches couldn't travel through the mountains at this time of year; she rode as far as she could by horse and carriage, then by horse and sleigh. She traversed the same treacherous passes that William had described in his pages, but they were now made considerably more dangerous, since blizzards assaulted them in the open sleigh. She wore several layers of heavy fur cloaks, scarves wrapped around her face, a fur cap. She was again thankful for the presence of Mina; the little cat seemed to make the journey far easier than Diana, since she spent the worst part curled up on Diana's lap under the fur coverings. Diana would often find herself smiling as she pondered how the cat could breathe beneath all that.

The last civilized inn was in a village called Racovita. She stayed there an extra day, waiting for a storm to pass. The rough Romanian she hired to take her to Urveri, a huge, gruff man named Razvan who spoke no English but understood the universal language of money, had held up two fingers, indicating a two-day journey to Urveri.

It took four. At the end of the first day they stopped in a small house, owned by a family who were fascinated by their English guest, even though they couldn't communicate. Four hours after leaving the quaint house, however, a new storm blocked their way, and they were forced to take shelter in an abandoned barn. Razvan busied himself drinking. Diana and Mina tried to stay warm. They were confined there for the following day as well.

The storms finally let up slightly, and in two more hours they arrived at the village of Urveri in the high mountain valley.

The dead village of Urveri.

From William's description, Diana had expected to find a settlement of hardy peasants hunkering down against the Transylvanian winter; she looked forward to the inn, with inviting blazes lit in the fireplaces, and a savory stew to assuage her appetite.

Instead she was greeted by a ghost town. Doors and shutters swung open to the chill air; snow was banked high up against walls and spilled inside through open doorways. There were no footprints, no smoke from the chimneys, no inviting hearths or aromatic pots simmering.

Via vigorous sign language, Razvan made it clear that he had no intention of spending much time in this haunted place, and Diana was inclined to agree with him. Diana held up one finger, and he nodded, but shook a finger at her in return. She had exactly one hour, then he'd leave with or without her. As Diana stepped into the snowy main street, her boots sinking past the ankles, Razvan hunkered down on the driver's bench with his flask.

She released Mina from beneath her cloaks, and after a few meows of mild dismay ("Yes, Mina, I know it's cold"), the cat began to pick her way through the snow. In a few more paces, she was running, and Diana was struggling to keep up. Mina's lighter weight made it easier for her to manage the snowdrifts, and she was soon lost to sight in the woods just beyond the borders of the abandoned town. Diana couldn't restrain a shiver that had nothing to do with temperature as she strode past the doorway of a house, its inside black as pitch, the opening looking for all the world like a great hungry maw ready to devour any living thing.

As she trudged into the woods, she heard a yowl from Mina and followed the sound. It didn't take long before she found her cat—and the gateway.

As William had guessed, this gateway was nowhere near the cemetery, but rather on the outskirts of the town. Mina sat in the snow, hissing and howling; before her was a small gap in the trees where no snow had piled. The visible ground was black, and the trees ringing the area had slate-colored, gnarled barks that seemed to suggest they held contorted, agonized faces. There was a strange odor, and Diana sensed an eerie, unplaceable tingling in her own body.

In Ireland this would have been a fairy ring; in England, a haunted moor. Wherever anchored, there was no mistaking the unholy influence of a gateway.

The sealing ritual was performed easily and without interruption. The most difficult part came when Diana had to bare her arm to the elements. Her blood had partly frozen in midair before it hit the gateway barrier, but the effect was the same. Mina quieted instantly, and Diana's own senses confirmed the closure.

Overhead, the sun blinked down from moving clouds, but the wind was picking up and Diana feared the approach of another storm. She still had at least half an hour before the sleigh would depart, but she wondered if Razvan might leave earlier, so she and Mina made haste returning to the village center. She was relieved to see Razvan still waiting with the sleigh, and she gestured to the buildings; he responded by pointedly removing a pocket watch and checking the time.

She turned and scanned the few buildings, seeking the inn.It was easy to pick out—it was larger even than Urveri's church—but Diana still hesitated outside before going in. It was an unnerving place, two stories built of wood so weathered that it had turned grey, and the knowledge of what might have happened to William here....

Then Mina ran in as if the place were home.

Diana followed. She waited for a moment while her eyes adjusted to the gloom. She could barely make out the inn's main room by the dim light coming in through the doorway; the windows permitted little illumination to enter, since they were mostly covered by drifts of snow. She spotted a flint on a table and after a few tries managed to strike a light to a small pile of dry twigs, which she used to light an oil lamp.

Her breath clouded in the lamp's amber glow, and she could see that whatever had happened to Urveri had happened quickly. A pot of frozen stew hung forgotten over the hearth; glasses which held nothing now but residue cluttered a long wooden bar top. There were even a few coins sitting forgotten among the steins and bottles.

Although overturned tables and chairs gave mute testament to a struggle, there was no blood anywhere, and no murder implements were visible. Diana found herself staring at the walls above the doors and windows while something nagged at the back of her mind. Finally she had it:

William had mentioned strings of garlic and rowan fastened above them. There was nothing there now.

She peeked briefly into a few of the downstairs rooms—a kitchen, a storage room, the innkeepers' rooms—then she heard Mina meowing plaintively from the top of the stairs, and turned to follow. The old stairs creaked ominously beneath her weight, and she prayed that they wouldn't give way. As she reached the landing, she saw her cat standing before a room which had a ruined door hanging from only one hinge; it had plainly been torn from the other.

Diana carefully maneuvered her way around the door, and stepped into a guestroom that could well have been William's. In addition to the torn-away door, the bedclothes were strewn wildly about, pictures had been knocked from walls, and a chair had been sundered.

And there were bloodstains here.

Mina meowed again, and Diana thought it sounded very much like feline grief. Somehow, both the cat and Diana knew—this was William's blood. Her husband had put up a desperate fight, and Diana had a quick flare of both pride and dread; she felt her love for her husband quicken like skin to a touch, even while she wondered exactly what he'd fought against.

She searched the room briefly, but found nothing more, no shred of clothing, no helpful clue. A quick glance through the remaining upper rooms proved equally fruitless.

And then her hour was gone. She gathered up Mina and returned to the sleigh.

The ride back down the mountain froze tears on her cheeks. She had closed the gateway, but the glimpse into William's final struggle had left her more certain than ever that her beloved was gone forever. Snow whirled around her and she pulled the protective blankets up, clutching them tightly, trying not to remember a ride she and William had once taken in a sleigh, on a snowy Christmas Eve, his heat beside her, a heat that had grown and finally consumed them both in their bed. She wanted to push the memories away, or to take comfort in them, but they brought only suffering now.

She'd never felt so alone.

Two days later, ensconced in a comfortable room in Racovito's pleasant inn, she sipped brandy by a blazing hearth as she stroked Mina and considered her options. She briefly thought of returning to Urveri to locate the evil graveyard, to search for Rákóczi or other revenants, but she suspected it would be a pointless (and difficult) task. The monsters that had taken William and the inhabitants of the village had left Urveri—and probably the earth—forever. There was no point in staying in this savage, desolate country any longer.

She made her way back to Budapest and from there to England; she passed the two weeks of travel despondent, her mood eased only by the presence of Mina. After returning to Hampstead Hall at Derby, Diana spent the next few months assessing her situation. If some_thing didn't want her closing the gateways—a *something* powerful enough to take the life of her courageous and clever husband—then she should simply leave well enough alone. She was still young, and perhaps it wasn't too late for her to find another path for her life.

The library no longer held any attraction for her, and she had her staff reshelve all the volumes she'd cluttered the room with, then she closed the door and didn't revisit. She spent months just wandering the grounds of the estate, sitting for hours among the mouldering stones of the old hall, feeling a strange kind of solace from the ancient wreckage She often longed for the visitations which had come almost nightly before she'd closed their gateway. She tried returning to London, but found the happy bustle she'd once enjoyed was now simply grueling. Howe attempted to elevate her spirits by arranging visits from friends, but she often canceled, or refused to see them. Her low point came when she found herself standing absently before the locked door of the Furnaval family crypt, watching a spider scuttle across the cracked granite and wondering if it comprehended secrets that eluded her.

And then, just when she was certain that her life would be only an endless series of grim, pointless days... the promise of renewal arrived with an invitation.

The Eastern World

Chapter VIII

April 8, 1880
London

"Diana, my dear, how perfectly delightful to see you again!"

Sir Edward Hinton gave Diana's hands a friendly squeeze, and kissed her on one cheek with genuine affection. When he pulled back to look at her, his eyes crinkled merrily, and his great white mustache tilted up on the ends from his broad smile.

She returned the smile, equally happy to see him. Sir Edward had been a dear friend to the Furnavals, and was William's godfather. When William and Diana wed, Sir Edward had instantly treated her as family; since Diana's own parents had died some years earlier, Diana was happy to allow him to assume the role of father figure.

"And a pleasure to see you again, Eddie," Diana responded warmly. Looking at Sir Edward's bulk and obvious wealth, she always inwardly laughed at calling him by the diminutive "Eddie" — which she thought better suited a small boy — but he insisted on it.

They sat down at a lovely antique lacquered oriental table in Sir Edward's vast office, and he poured two cups of tea. "You know, I was dreadfully worried when you took that tour of Europe. In winter, yet! What on earth possessed you?"

Diana sipped her tea and offered Sir Edward a small, rueful smile. "You're right, it was foolish, but...necessary. It had to do with—that *other* business of William's."

Sir Edward nodded sagely. He was the only one of William's friends who had known of the Furnaval legacy as gatekeepers. Although he'd personally never witnessed any of the paranormal activities brought about by the gateways, he had believed William completely. Diana had never told him the full truth of William's death (such as, for instance, the fact that a vampire had been sent home from Transylvania in place of her husband), and so there had been no reason to reveal the full particulars of her recent trip to Europe.

"And you haven't contacted me since you returned," Sir Edward gently chided her. "Antonia's asked about you as well."

Antonia was Sir Edward's only offspring. Diana had only met Antonia (whose name she'd always suspected of having indicated Sir Edward's desire for a male heir) twice previously, and both meetings had been brief; the girl had either been in finishing schools or traveling. But Diana had liked Antonia a great deal—there was a seriousness and intelligence about the twenty-three-year old that Diana encountered far too seldom in other members of her sex, and she always thought that she and Antonia could become good friends, given the chance to spend time together. She also wondered if Antonia had a hand in the running of the family business, the Hinton Company, one of England's largest trading firms. The Hinton fleet rivaled that of the once great East India Trading Company, and kept England well supplied with tea from China. Although she loved Sir Edward dearly, Diana had occasionally wondered how, with his absent-minded manner and more worldly interests (especially those of the alcoholic nature), he could run a substantial business. She suspected that the bright and solid Antonia may have had more than a little to do with the Hinton Company's successful management.

"Please give my regards to Antonia. I'd very much like to see her again. I..." Diana looked away, abashed, uncertain of how much to say. "I'm truly sorry for my absence. You know you both mean the world to me. I've just been...well, there were things I learned recently about William's death that were...greatly disturbing to me."

He leaned forward in concern. "Oh my dear...is it anything I can help with? I have excellent contacts in most major ports of trade, you know."

Although Diana knew little of the Hinton Company's business, she didn't doubt that Edward's contacts were considerable.

"Thank you, Eddie, but there's really nothing you can do. For that matter, there's nothing anyone can do. William is truly gone, and I've spent the last two months trying to come to grips with it."

"I understand." Sir Edward set his cup down, and pulled himself up straighter in his chair. "Perhaps I can offer you a puzzle to solve that will help to divert your mind, then."

Diana set her own cup down. "I'd like that very much."

Edward stood and began to pace before the hearth. "I don't know how much you know of my trade business—you know, tea and silk traded for certain incidentals the Chinese like, that sort of thing. The final destination of our ships is the Chinese port of Canton. England maintains an outpost there, and we deal with an English-speaking chap named Mr. Wong, who holds the job of 'comprador'—basically he ensures that our trading functions smoothly.

"Now recently this Wong chap informed the captains of several Hinton ships that they might wish to consider postponing trade in Canton for some time. When they questioned this Chinaman, he told them that there had been a series of murders and disappearances among the men who worked at the docks, and that there was some difficulty in acquiring new workers."

Diana's mind was already spinning:

According to *The Book of Gateways, Conjurations and Banishments*, there was one Chinese gateway, located in Canton, at something called "Ho-Nam,",although the meaning of that name wasn't made clear.

"Are you quite all right, my dear?" Edward was asking, peering at her, frozen in mid-step.

"Oh, yes, sorry. Please continue."

"Very well," Edward said, resuming his pacing as if he were lecturing to his board of directors. "My captains, who I can assure you are a very capable and trustworthy lot, suggested assembling an armed force of English soldiers to restore order, but Mr. Wong told them it would be useless. He informed them that the culprit was something that sounded like a *goong-si*; he would provide no further translation."

"*Goong-si*," Diana repeated, trying out the strange syllables on her own tongue.

"Yes. It's a damnably strange language these Chinamen speak, if you've never heard it before; it really is like infantile gibberish. Anyway: So my crewmen, bless them, didn't take Mr. Wong's words at face value, but went ashore and met with the British vice-consul and several merchants. Eventually they got together an armed squadron and sent them to the dock warehouses, despite the most vigorous warnings of the comprador. Five men, armed with rifles, pistols and knives, were sent out. They found our docks and warehouses deserted, and no clues as to the whereabouts of the missing workers. They questioned a beggar they found in the streets near the docks, but he just kept repeating that ridiculous word over and over: '*Goong-si…goong-si….*' Finally he scuttled off, and our squad returned, baffled and empty-handed.

"The captains once again met with the comprador, and asserted that he must hire new workers. This time Wong was somewhat more forthcoming in his explanations. He told the seamen that workers could not be found, because the Oriental residents of Canton knew what the Englishmen did not: That a '*kap-huet goong-si*' was a member of the living dead, a creature that preys on men for their blood to survive. What the Chinese fear is an evil spirit in human form, a creature of the supernatural that brought certain doom to those foolhardy enough to approach it."

"A vampire," murmured Diana, already starting to feel both an intense curiosity and a fight blooming in her, neither of which she had felt for some time.

"Oh, yes—vampire, well...." blustered Edward. "Yes, I suppose it could be that...well, that sort of thing."

"Please continue with your story. I'm most intrigued."

"Yes, of course. Mr. Wong said the locals had sent in a priest, but he had fled in terror. Well, the Hinton Company's brave fellows were, naturally, skeptical. They scoffed, and wondered how even a superstitious Oriental like Wong could accept the existence of such a myth. He told them it was no myth, and that they could see the thing for themselves, if they dared venture into the warehouse at night. The captains, thinking that perhaps a night spent successfully at the docks would convince the locals that the *goong-si* was just a fairytale monster, agreed.

"That very night five seamen, including two of the ships' captains, ventured into the docks. Only one man returned the following morning, his senses apparently so badly rattled that he could only utter a high-pitched, hysterical laugh and talk about '*the monster...the thing with claws and burning eyes.*' The English port authorities sent a delegation into the docks, and only one body was found. It was that of one of the captains, Joseph McKay, a burly, strong seaman of thirty years experience. Captain McKay's body was—"Edward broke off his pacing, fingering his watch fob and peering at Diana. "Are you quite sure you should hear all of this?"

"Quite sure," Diana told him.

He continued, somewhat reluctantly, "Very well. Captain McKay's body was found with his eyes open, staring wide in terror, his skin strangely wrinkled and pale—"

"—and bloodless," guessed Diana. "Apparently Oriental and Occidental vampires have the same *raison d'etre.*"

Edward stared at her for a moment, and it occurred to Diana that he might have been less confused by her knowledge of vampirism than her use of French.

At length, he continued: "Yes, well, the poor fellow's corpse was quite bloodless. There was no trace of the remaining three men. And that's as much as I know. I just yesterday received the letter informing me of this somewhat—er, unusual situation. I'd rule it as just more fancies of the Chinese mind—they're superstitious heathens, you know—but for the fact that good British men are dying."

Diana wondered briefly if Edward had ever been to China himself. While she hadn't, she had acquired some knowledge of the land's history and practices; she'd found that many of the herbal remedies she employed against demonic forces had originated in China, and so she had developed a healthy respect for the culture. Unfortunately, Sir Edward's attitude was the norm among westerners, and she saw no point in attempting to correct him.

After a moment, Edward continued: "My ships are still anchored off Canton, waiting, and I don't mind telling you, dear Diana, that this will be a serious blow to the Hinton Company if this crisis is not resolved forthwith. According to the Treaty of Nanking, the British are only allowed into a few ports in China; we can't afford to lose Canton."

Diana set aside her own cup. "Well, this is a very serious matter. I need to proceed to Canton immediately."

Edward's jaw dropped so far Diana was afraid he might injure himself.

He fell heavily into his chair after a moment and leaned towards her urgently. "Diana, that is *not* why I asked you here to discuss this today. China is a primitive and dangerous place!"

"Oh, Eddie," Diana replied, taking one of his meaty paws, "I've heard China is quite a civilized country actually."

"I'm afraid you've been misled, then," he blustered. "We English have managed to transform a few small areas there into something comfortable, but the Chinese themselves are a degenerate race. For goodness sake, their current dynasty, the Ching, is governed by a *child* emperor! Diana, it's simply not possible."

"That's unfortunate," Diana said with a feigned sigh. "Then I'll have to secure passage on some other company's line, I suppose."

He uttered a groan, and shook his large head. "You are impossible!"

"Yes," Diana agreed, then added, "but I know how to solve your problem."

He stopped shaking his head and looked at her in disbelief. "You...know...?"

"Oh yes. I've dealt with vampires before."

"You've...before...." Edward was plainly flabbergasted. "I know better than to doubt your word, but...surely you know how that sounds to a rational mind—"

Diana said, "I assure you, no mind is more rational than mine. I *have* slain vampires before, and I *can* dispatch your vampires, I'm sure. And you would be doing me a favor as well."

"What favor?" he asked.

"Our chat here today has reminded me that I have business of my own in Canton."

Edward's eyebrows inched up before he asked, "*That* business?"

"Yes," she answered simply.

Edward considered. "I will of course recompense you handsomely—"

"Not necessary. I will ask in return, however, that I also be allowed to disembark briefly in Calcutta."

"Calcutta?! What...?" then he groaned and shook his head. "Another of those blasted things there as well, I suppose?"

"Quite."

"Well, I'm sorry, my dear, but our cruise vessels don't go by way of Calcutta. They proceed to Ceylon and then to China—"

"But your cargo steamers do."

He actually spluttered. "But you...you can't...a *tramp steamer*?!"

"You have one leaving soon, don't you?"

Edward sighed deeply, then rose and walked to his desk, where he immediately began scratching out notes with a quill pen. "I'll make the arrangements for your passage. But I want you to know I'm not very happy with this, Diana."

Diana walked over to plant a small kiss on his red cheek. "I know you're not, Eddie, but believe me when I say I'm very grateful to you for allowing me to try."

Edward, his cheeks flushed, didn't look up as he grumbled, "I love you, Diana, but you are a strange woman."

"Yes," Diana agreed, "I am."

Chapter IX

April 10, 1880
Aboard the Althea

Edward arranged an acceptably comfortable passage for Diana and Mina aboard the Hinton steamship *Althea*, which was named after his late wife. Althea had died shortly after William and Diana were wed, and so Diana had known her only for a short time, and felt the poignant tang of regret whenever she considered the ship's name.

Althea was one of the newer steamers, and Diana took a scientific interest in its steel hull (steel being lighter and sturdier than the iron formerly used). The crew were experienced, efficient and amiable, even if they did have a tendency to curtsey and nod to her (who was, after all, a Lady of the Empire) more than she preferred. The ship carried a cargo of English woolens, which Edward had informed Diana was much desired by both the Chinese and the Indians. He also told her they would pick up more cargo en route to Canton.

Edward himself met her at the ship and showed her to her rooms, which were amazingly spotless, and included a tolerable bed and a private head; Diana was surprised to find guest quarters on the ship, but Edward told her that one of the crew had given up his quarters for her. Edward was somewhat nonplussed to see the cat accompanying her, but Diana quickly assured him that Mina was essential to her business. Mina turned out to find the ship utterly fascinating, and when she returned from the cargo hold with a dying rat in her jaws, the crew rewarded her with high praise, dubbing her the official ship's mascot.

After Diana's single trunk had been placed in her rooms (and she'd received Edward's praise for traveling lighter than almost any other female he'd ever met), Edward took her up to the bridge, and introduced her to the captain, and several of her traveling companions:

Captain Terence Hughes was a taciturn seaman whose first words to her were to warn her that she'd clean up after her own seasickness. Diana assured him she'd been on ships before, and wasn't affected by their motion. Hughes had grunted, and then wandered off to check on something in the engine room. Edward tried to assure her that Hughes was very capable and not a bad sort; Diana had merely smiled politely.

Edward had saved his surprise for last: Antonia met them on the deck and told Diana she would also be making the journey aboard the *Althea*. The two women exchanged a warm embrace, but Antonia plainly was more interested in overseeing the crew than exchanging small talk with Diana and Edward. Antonia supervised the loading of the ship's cargo while her father stood in the bridge smoking a cigar and chatting with one of his officers. When Edward left, Antonia offered him a perfunctory kiss and then turned away. Seeing the morose look on Edward's face, Diana made sure she provided him with a long and grateful farewell hug.

After Edward disembarked, Diana returned to her cabin to unpack her trunk and put things in order. Once the tasks were completed, she selected a book and ventured up to the deck with it, planning to enjoy it as the crew completed preparations. Diana knew the voyage would be long and often tedious, and had packed a number of books, including Homer's classic *The Odyssey*, which she thought appropriate for a sea voyage. She improvised a deck chair from packing crates and settled in.

She'd only read a few pages when she looked up from her book to discover a shockingly handsome and very young Oriental man standing nearby, observing her curiously. He wore an officer's uniform, and when he realized she'd seen him he executed a deep bow, doffed his cap and informed her that he was First Mate Leung Yi-kin, "but please you call me Thomas."

Diana laid the book aside and stood to accept his offered hand. He was no more than seventeen, but unusually tall and well-built, with thick glossy black hair (cut short in the English style, not kept in the long queue of the Mandarins), high cheekbones, a strong jaw and thoughtful dark brown eyes.

"Why would I call you Thomas if your name is Leung Yi-kin?" Diana asked, trying not to mangle the Chinese syllables too badly.

The young man was evidently pleased, and offered her a smile of perfect, white teeth. "Many English have problem to say my name, so they call me Thomas."

"Say your name again," Diana asked.

"Last name Leung. Given name Yi-kin," he answered.

"Well, I'd like to call you Yi-kin, if that's all right with you."

Yi-kin nodded, then indicated her book. "You like to read?"

"Very much," Diana answered.

"I also, but my English need work. Maybe you help me?"

"I'd be happy to, but under one condition," Diana told him, and then paused before adding, "teach me your language, too."

"Oh," Yi-kin blurted out, "Cantonese very hard for English people!"

"I didn't expect it to be easy," Diana assured him. "Teach me something right now."

Yi-kin thought for a moment, then offered up: "*Nei ge maau hai ho cheung ming.*"

Diana had never heard Chinese before, and she immediately thought it was a beautiful language, not at all the "infantile gibberish" Sir Edward had called it, but rather musical, with highs and lows quite unlike anything found in English. She also knew better than to try to repeat it before her ear had grown more accustomed to it. "And what does that mean?" she asked.

"'Your cat is very smart'," Yi-kin told her.

"Yi-kin," Diana returned his grin, "I think I'm very glad we're going to be on this voyage together."

That night, after the ship left port and was bound south down the coast of France, Diana shared dinner with Antonia and Captain Hughes.

Despite his gruff manner, Captain Hughes did seem to enjoy regaling Diana with tales of the days when the Chinese trade was conducted by clipper ships that engaged in "tea races", making the China-to-England run around Cape Horn in one hundred days. Hughes turned out to be older than he looked, and had worked "the triangle" (which Diana realized meant the England-India-China trade route) since the days when wind-powered sailing vessels, not steamers, had dodged storms and pirates. When Hughes ran out of sea yarns, the conversation passed largely to the ladies, who chatted over the surprisingly good roast beef prepared by the *Althea's* Scottish cook, Macnaughton.

"Enjoy it while you can," Antonia said, smiling, "because soon enough you'll be quite sick of salt pork and fish."

"Oh dear—perhaps I should have taken your father up on the cruise ship, after all."

Hughes grunted in agreement.

"You know my father thinks the world of you," Antonia told Diana.

Diana smiled and answered, "And he's very dear to me. He was like a father to my husband, and has extended the same affection to me, for which I'm very grateful."

There was a pause before Antonia went on: "Yes, and that's why I'm slightly surprised that he allowed you to accompany us."

When Antonia didn't continue and Diana offered no response, Captain Hughes said, "China's no place for a white woman. Neither of you should be here."

Diana sensed a fight coming, but decided she wasn't going to back down easily. "And why is that, Captain Hughes? If they're all like your man Yi-kin—"

"Who? Oh, you mean Thomas," Hughes said. "And no, they're not like him. He's been around white men long enough to have picked up a few manners."

Antonia also sensed the storm clouds gathering between the captain and Diana, and struggled to disperse them. "What Captain Hughes isn't telling you, Diana, is that Canton could even be somewhat…dangerous."

Diana considered before answering. "I do appreciate your concern for my well-being, Antonia, but I'm probably better acquainted with dangerous situations than you might know. I've had considerable experience dealing with situations which might be thought of as…well, occult in nature. Besides which—how dangerous can it be if you're going?"

Hughes and Antonia exchanged an uncomfortable look, then Antonia spoke. "It's not just the murders at the dockside warehouses. It's also…well, relations between the British and the Chinese have traditionally been rather strained. I'm barely accepted as a representative of the Hinton Company."

"I thought those difficulties were in the past," Diana said, thinking of the last opium war of 1856. "Strained how, exactly?"

"The Chinese," Hughes interrupted, "feel that certain treaties negotiated on behalf of European powers—including England—aren't in their best interest. There are a number of—well, gangs, for want of a better word—that have sprung up around China with the singular goal of ousting all foreigners from Chinese soil."

"Triads," added Antonia.

Diana blinked in perplexity. "'Triads'?"

"Secret societies. China has a great number of them. Apparently they were once quite noble, serving as revolutionary pockets to oust the Manchus from China, but they've devolved over the years into little more than criminal clans. And they think of us as *foreign devils*," said Antonia.

"*Fan-gwai*," added Hughes, and then he spat into a corner.

Diana considered all that, then asked, "Are you saying I'll be in danger simply by being English?"

"The young Chinaman, Thomas," Antonia said, "has he told you what happened to his parents?"

"No," Diana answered. "Why would he?"

"His family worked for English missionaries in a village not far from Canton. One day about ten years ago, when Thomas was only seven, he was at home when his older sister suddenly took his hand and told him to run. The two children hid in the bush, and watched as a group of men killed the missionaries, then burned down the entire village. Thomas and his sister saw the men—who were all members of one of these secret societies—stab their mother and father to death, not fifty feet from where they hid. After that they ran until they could run no more; they lived in the countryside for three days, scrounging what they could to eat and drink. Finally they were found near Whampoa and brought to Canton, where they lived in an orphanage until they ran away two years ago. Thomas's sister married a merchant who took her to Shanghai, and Captain Hughes gave Thomas work on the *Althea*."

Diana, surprised by the notion that the clearly-bigoted Hughes would have hired one of the Oriental heathens, turned to see him staring down at his plate, apparently intent on cutting up a stubborn piece of beef. "Boy had picked up some English from the missionaries, and he has made himself useful."

"So," Antonia said, looking pointedly at Diana, "you see why China could be a land of some risk for you."

"But what of you, Antonia?"

"Well, I've been to Canton before. I know how to negotiate it."

Diana blinked in surprise. "I wasn't aware that you were so widely traveled."

Antonia half-winced. "Yes, well...my father requires considerable assistance in running his company. Once we reach Canton, I shall confine myself entirely to the Hinton Company quarters and the British sector of Shameen, and I'd advise you to do the same. If you are intent on venturing forth to the Chinese areas, Diana, you'll be on your own."

"Well, perhaps I shall have to ask for Mr. Leung to accompany me, then."

Antonia offered a half-nod. "As you will."

After a moment, Diana asked, "What about Calcutta?"

Captain Hughes hesitated in mid-bite, a gesture Diana found curious. He was obviously waiting for Antonia to answer, and Diana wondered why.

"We do dock at Calcutta, do we not? Or was your father wrong?" asked Diana.

Antonia stared at her. "My father wasn't wrong. We do indeed dock at Calcutta, but only for an overnight cargo load. You weren't seriously thinking of going ashore there, surely…?"

"I was. I will. I have business to attend to just outside of Calcutta. Sir Edward assured me it wouldn't be a problem."

"It won't be," answered Antonia, "for *us*."

With some exasperation, Diana said, "Surely you're not trying to tell me both destinations are unsafe? Hasn't India become a popular destination for English who are looking for warmer climes during our winters?" Diana asked.

Antonia shrugged. "Yes. India's fairly safe…."

Hughes muttered under his breath, "…if you don't count the Black Hole of Calcutta."

Before leaving England, Diana had studied some of Calcutta's history, and she was thus knowledgeable on the infamous 1756 incident in which one hundred twenty-three British soldiers were supposedly imprisoned by the cruel Indian *nawab* Siraj-ud-Daula in a cell so small that most of them had perished overnight.

"That was over a century ago, Captain. Surely you can't apply those sorts of conflicts to modern relations?" she asked.

Antonia shrugged. "We won't stop you, Diana, but you must understand we'll only be able to put you in touch with our representative in the city; we won't be able to help you beyond that."

Diana smiled at Antonia, and said, "I quite understand and accept."

Antonia's smile was slow in coming, but its brittleness gave Diana no pleasure when it finally arrived.

Chapter X

April 15, 1880
Aboard the Althea

Captain Hughes may not have provided sterling dinner conversation, but fortunately he was a very competent sailor, and their voyage proved to be overall a calm and pleasant one. They encountered neither human nor natural obstacle, for which Diana was secretly very glad—since she'd lied about not suffering from seasickness. Truthfully, she couldn't stomach storms at sea, and was relieved that so far she hadn't suffered that indignity.

Five nights after they left London—just after docking briefly at Gibraltar before resuming their voyage—Diana had a rare nightmare.

For someone whose waking life was so often invaded by horror, her dreams were surprisingly serene, and in fact she rarely remembered them. When she did, they often involved extraordinarily large buildings in which she wandered, finding interesting structural features or striking details. She always found that fact odd, because she truthfully had very little interest in architecture. She'd once asked Isadora about the dreams, and Isadora had told her that vast buildings were a symbol of a bright and creative mind.

But the dream she awoke from on this night hardly featured extravagant architecture. Instead, she stood before a gateway—which she could see quite clearly as a dark, swirling mass—and heard William's voice, calling to her from the other side. A feeling of immense dread gripped her, and yet she disregarded the ominous sensation and stepped through the gateway—and into the maw of some huge creature. There was a hand that came through the gateway, a friend's hand, that tried to pull her from the thing's mouth, but it was too late. As its great jaws closed around her, she knew she was sealed forever in its hot, dripping insides, and her panic rose until she thought it, not the creature, would consume her—

—and then she was awake, her heart racing, and the humid marine air surrounding her. It was three a.m.

She knew she would sleep no more, and so she arose and dressed; Mina, who slept at the foot of Diana's bunk, gazed at her sleepily before tucking her head back into her paws, and curled into a position that only a cat could attain.

There was a lovely full moon outside and it was a peaceful, warm night, so Diana decided to take a walk around the deck.

At this hour only a skeleton crew would be working—a few on the bridge, a few more in the boiler room—and the decks were empty. The smoke stack in the center of the ship, situated between two of the three masts, puffed out a steady plume, the great engine driving the ship through the windless night. Diana spent some moments drinking in the beauty of the moon's image shimmering in the steamer's wake, and trying to recall certain specifics of the terrifying dream. She was sure William had been saying something to her, something particular that held some deeper meaning, but the words had vanished when she woke. And whose hand had reached through the gateway, trying to rescue her?

She was returning to her cabin, having decided to pass the remainder of the evening in the company of the mighty Odysseus, when she beheld one other figure on the deck, huddled near the light of a single small lantern. Curious, she approached, and saw it was Yi-kin. And he was reading.

She was delighted to see he was reading something she had given him (why on earth she'd brought that old Dickens chestnut *Great Expectations* along, she couldn't imagine, but now she was glad she had).

"Good evening, Yi-kin," she announced.

The young man started, slamming the book shut, then relaxing when he saw it was Diana. He had made himself a sort of nook by arranging some bales of rope, and placing the lantern above his head. He leapt to his feet now, still holding the book.

"Oh, Miss Diana, I do not know you are awake—"

"Nor you," Diana answered. "Are you working the night-shift?"

"Oh no, if I am working I do not read."

Diana smiled. "Do you ever sleep?"

Yi-kin smiled and held the book out towards her. "I like to read. This book is very good."

"I'm delighted you're enjoying it. But why read out here?"

"Oh, I…uh…." Yi-kin looked away, suddenly embarrassed, then finally answered, "I do not have other place to read."

"Don't you have quarters on the ship?" She knew that most of the crew bunked together below deck, while the officers had semi-private or private rooms.

"Yes, I have quarters, but…."

"But what?" Diana asked, prepared for yet some new outrageous display of Hughes's bigotry, or even Sir Edward's.

"You are in my quarters."

Diana was stunned for a second, then blurted out, "Yi-kin, I'm so sorry, I didn't know—"

Yi-kin waved his hands, trying to placate her. "No, *siu jeh*, I am happy to give you my room. I am honored."

He bowed, and Diana felt the blood rush to her face.

"No, please, Yi-kin…don't do that. I'm taking your quarters; I should be bowing to *you*."

He stared at her in frank amazement.

And in that moment, Diana suddenly understood: The hand in the dream, the one that had reached through the gate to save her, had belonged to Yi-kin.

"Yi-kin," she asked, "tell me something: Do you believe in the existence of the *goong-si*?"

Yi-kin shrugged. "I have not seen them. I do not know."

Diana considered that, then went on: "Some of the English say the Chinese are very superstitious."

"Oh," said Yi-kin, "this is true."

"Is it? Tell me about what they believe."

"Chinese people believe in many things. Ghosts. Gods. And *ming wan*…what I think you call…fate."

"Fate...." Diana pondered the word for a moment, and found it suited her. "Fate. Like...perhaps you and I were destined to cross paths."

Yi-kin smiled. "Yes." Then added, "This I believe."

Diana returned his smile. "So do I."

And the *Althea* steamed on across the Mediterranean towards the Red Sea and India beyond.

Chapter XI

May 3, 1880
Calcutta, India

The trip through the Suez Canal and then across the Red Sea and Indian Ocean had been uneventful and smooth; Diana had found the heat during the days occasionally difficult to tolerate, but the nights cooled down and she'd suffered no more strange dreams. Antonia had been busy during much of the voyage with Hinton Company business, but had nonetheless shared many enjoyable meals and conversations with Diana. Although Diana hadn't revealed the full extent of her investigations into the paranormal, she found a happy audience in Antonia, who was especially intrigued by the story of her trip into the heart of Transylvania (a place she, Antonia, had never been, since it was well removed from any waterways or ports). For her part, Diana enjoyed Antonia's skepticism and the breadth of her knowledge; Antonia had obviously excelled in school.

But Diana had shared her most interesting times during the trip with Yi-kin. She attempted to tutor him further in the intricacies of English, and he introduced her to the marvels of the Cantonese dialect of Chinese (Diana hadn't previously realized there were such great differences between the various Chinese dialects, which were virtually separate languages). She was astonished to learn that Chinese had no tense, no articles, and no plurals; on the other hand, it had a profusion of inflections, meaning the same sound could have as many as eight different meanings, depending on whether it was pronounced with high tones, medium, low, or some arcane mix thereof. Her English-bred tongue found such sounds as the Chinese "*ng*" virtually impossible to produce (although she finally managed it by re-creating only the last part of the word "hang"), and Yi-kin suffered through the torturous "th" consonants and verb conjugations of English.

Yi-kin was also interested in her less verbal pursuits, and asked if she herself believed in *kap-huet goong-si*. She told him she not only believed in them, but had met one, and she then did her best to describe her encounter with the vampire in the Furnaval family crypt. Despite his earlier, more skeptical answer as to his belief in the existence of the *goong-si*, Diana was pleased to find that he accepted her story without question.

At last they reached the Bay of Bengal and left behind saltwater for fresh at the mouth of the Hooghly River. Sixty miles upriver they docked in Calcutta and began taking on cargo: Wooden crates, each the size of trunk, stamped with Chinese characters, and heavy enough to require two laborers to lift each one. Diana asked a crewman about the contents of the crates coming aboard the *Althea*, and he matter-of-factly answered, "Opium."

Stunned, Diana could only stare at her friend Antonia, who was busily supervising the loading operations. Antonia noticed the look, excused herself, and hurried over to Diana. "Are you quite all right?"

"Why didn't you tell me what we were *really* carrying to China?!"

Antonia's eyes briefly widened in disbelief. "Surely you knew."

Diana was about to respond, when she thought to herself: *Of course. How could I not know?*

Antonia excused herself to return to her work, and Diana went back to her cabin, lost in thought. How naïve she'd been, believing that *any* British trading company—even her beloved Eddie's—would be content to trade only woolens in exchange for China's fine tea and silk. In London, Diana had read editorials about the evils of opium (London's sharpest writers worried about the drug gaining a foothold in Mother England, given how it had devastated a significant portion of China's population), but she'd never considered that it would be among the *Althea's* cargo.

Diana finally forced herself to remember her own goals, and was gathering what she would need for her brief trip to the gateway located just northeast of Calcutta, when a knock on her door was answered to reveal Antonia.

"I'd like to explain a little more about our trade."

Diana nodded curtly, and Antonia entered, closing the door behind herself. She looked terribly anxious, and Diana felt her anger begin to fade away in spite of her indignation. "I want you to know that I'm not in favor of this particular cargo either. Father would have me believe that a dose of opium is no more destructive to a coolie than a glass of beer is to an Englishman, but I've seen some of its effects on the Chinese people, and it's...well, quite frankly, it's monstrous."

"Then why keep doing it?" asked Diana.

"I'm sorry to have to say this, Diana, but...it's Father's decision."

Diana was literally speechless for several seconds while she struggled to reconcile the image of the benign, slightly befuddled Sir Edward Hinton with that of a ruthless contraband trader.

Antonia continued, "Father told me that we had no choice, that there was really nothing we possess that the Orientals wanted as badly as we wanted their tea—"

"There must be something else," Diana growled.

Antonia shuffled nervously. "I agree, personally. Unfortunately, it's at the base of British trade. We grow it here on our Indian plantations, so it makes our colony in India profitable, and it gives us what we need to obtain tea, which is also profitable. It's been this way for more than a hundred years."

Diana was at a loss for more words.

"I've suggested to Father that we seek other cargo," Antonia admitted, softly. "He wouldn't even discuss it."

Diana finished packing what she would require (including Mina, who meowed in dismay at being forced from the ship, which she'd quite come to love), and said dismissively, "If I'm to make it back by tomorrow I need to go."

She started to push past Antonia, who stopped her at the door with a hand on Diana's shoulder. "Diana, I don't want you to think badly of me."

Diana considered that, then turned back. "No, I don't. I can't say I'm not disappointed, but...well, it's really your father who I'm furious with."

"I understand, but please try not to be, Diana. As I said before, it's been this way for a century now. Truthfully our opium trade has become a rather important part of the British Empire."

"Has it not occurred to you," Diana said, her face burning, "that any empire dependent on this sort of trade is destined to fail?"

Antonia stared at her for several seconds without reply.

Finally she turned away resigned, saying, "I've arranged a meeting for you with our representative here in Calcutta. He's been instructed to assist you in any way we can. Just remember, we sail tomorrow at nine a.m."

With that, Antonia left.

Diana sat for a few moments, stroking Mina and collecting her thoughts. She wasn't pleased with the thought of continuing her trip on a freighter loaded with opium—surely she could book a more luxurious passage either back to England or on to Canton—but she had agreed to help the Hintons deal with the mystery of the *goong-si*, and she would need both Antonia and Yi-kin to help her perform that duty. Once that task was completed, she could return to London and confront Eddie then. Perhaps she and Antonia together could persuade him to discontinue this odious trade. As much as the thought upset her, she decided she must continue her trip aboard the *Althea*.

When Diana appeared on the deck with her bag of supplies and Mina (and dressed in her men's suit), Yi-kin met her and told her he would be happy to lead her on the short walk to the home of the Hinton Company's agent in the Raj. *The Book of Gateways, Conjurations and Banishments* indicated that the Calcutta gateway was located in a temple a modest distance to the northeast of the sprawling city itself, and Diana knew she would require local assistance in getting there.

She was disappointed in Yi-kin's complacency with the drug trade, although less so than she was with Antonia. As they strode down the gang-plank, Diana asked him, "Yi-kin, you've worked on this ship for two years, isn't that right?"

"Yes," he answered.

"And doesn't it bother you that the ship is carrying a cargo of a dangerous drug that many Chinese people are addicted to?"

Yi-kin shrugged. "Chinese government says opium is not illegal, so I do not think about it."

Diana nearly told him, *But it wasn't always that way; it was illegal, until the British won the battles in the last war and forced them to legalize it*; but she thought better of it, and forced herself to let it go.

The *Champaul Ghaut* was a handsome stone esplanade that served as Calcutta's main landing place for the British ships. Yi-kin, carrying Diana's small bag and her cat, led the way up a flight of broad steps, and as they stepped through a triumphal archway atop the stairs, Diana temporarily forgot her anger, gazing about herself in complete amazement:

They were in the fashionable Calcutta suburb of Chowringhee, and it was easy to see why some referred to this Indian port as the "City of Palaces": From where they stood, Diana saw nothing but a broad road fronted by extravagant mansions. Most were three stories high, with colonnades and terraces, built from a local material called *puckha* (brick made from Hooghi clay, covered with cement). Shrubs and trees surrounded some of the estates, while others were graced with low walls running around their perimeters. The wide boulevard was thronged with British in western garb, local Indian vendors, sedan chairs carried by coolies clad only in loincloths, a few horses, and even one man leading a camel. The scent of tuberoses collided with musky animal smells and frying foods, carried on a slight, hot breeze.

Yi-kin spoke again, and Diana realized she was gaping. "We go just a short way there," he said, pointing to their right. "Not far, but maybe Diana *siu-jeh* would like *doolie*."

"I'm sorry, I don't know what a *doolie* is," Diana told him.

Yi-kin pointed to one of the sedans close by, decoratively covered on the sides and top—and attended by four stick-thin carriers. Diana realized several of the conveyances stood nearby, their bearers watching her hungrily.

"No, I'm fine with walking," she declined.

Yi-kin led the way down the broad street to the right, and soon they were passing the lavish houses. All were completely detached from their neighbors, many had Indian servants working on the balconies or in the gardens...and yet despite the tremendous, ostentatious display of wealth, Diana realized that most of the houses were actually somewhat run-down. Paint peeled from the puckha, in some places entire patches of cement had fallen from the bricks, walls were overgrown with lichen, and poor mud huts abutted many of the outer walls, providing shelter for those who serviced the moneyed British inhabitants of Calcutta.

Yi-kin negotiated the way with easy familiarity. "You've been to Calcutta before, haven't you?" Diana asked him.

Yi-kin nodded. "Many times. I sometimes stay on ship, but I also sometimes run errands for captain or Miss Hinton."

They arrived at one particular mansion, and Yi-kin rang a small bell next to a gate set in the surrounding wall. After a few moments the gate was opened by a native Indian who was dressed in the simple robes favored by many of the populace. He eyed Diana (or at least her clothes) strangely, then turned his dark eyes on Yi-kin.

"This *beebee* is here to see Mr. Smythe-Bentley," Yi-kin informed the man.

"Yes," Diana added, handing to the servant a letter of introduction that Antonia had prepared for her, "I believe this will explain everything."

The servant eyed the letter briefly, then smiled at Diana and stepped politely aside. "Please, *memsahib*, come in and follow me. I will tell the master you're here." His accent was very light, and carried a sort of clipped precision, not at all like Yi-kin's slightly slurred use of English.

Diana stepped through the gate, then realized Yi-kin wasn't following. She glanced at him inquiringly.

"I will stay here," he told her, his eyes downcast.

She started to question him, then saw the Indian servant and realized the truth: A Chinaman wouldn't be welcome in this house.

"This shouldn't take long," she reassured Yi-kin, then followed the servant through a small garden and into the house. She asked the servant's name, and he told her he was Goompat, the *khansamah*, or head servant, for Mr. Smythe-Bentley.

She was left in a small waiting room, while the servant conveyed her letter to Smythe-Bentley. The room was open and comfortable, with wide uncovered windows, and settees in the local style. Diana admired the colorful fabrics and fine woodworking, and found they suited her tastes.

She was examining a tapestry when the servant re-entered. "The master will see you now, *memsahib*."

She indicated one particular tapestry, which portrayed the very frightening figure of a four-armed woman with three eyes, a blood-red protruding tongue, and a necklace of human heads. "Excuse me, but I'm wondering...."

The servant saw the object of her interest and smiled darkly. "That is Kali. She is the Hindu goddess of both creation and destruction. She is very much loved in Calcutta, and some here believe the city's name is derived from a very old word, *Kalikshetra*, meaning 'the domain of Kali'."

"I know about Kali—I was just wondering about the artist."

"Oh. I am sorry—I do not know."

She was shown into a room that served as an office, and was greeted by Dennys Smythe-Bentley. He was a dapper, tall man, with a graying, neatly-trimmed beard and only a slight paunch. He wore a suit not unlike Diana's own, and seemed to smile at that as he rose to meet her.

"Ahh, Lady Diana Furnaval, I presume? A pleasure."

They clasped hands briefly, then Smythe-Bentley indicated a lovely lacquered chair near his large desk, covered with papers, pens, bottles of ink, and a hookah. The room was not as open as the sitting room had been, but was cooled by overhead *punkahs* operated by several Indian servants. Diana found it vaguely ridiculous that the man should have servants who did nothing but pull fans for him, and briefly wondered if she had any similarly-employed help back at Hampstead Hall. She hoped not.

"I see you need help with some travel arrangements," Smythe-Bentley said, indicating her letter.

"Yes."

Diana had carefully reproduced a map to the Calcutta gateway included in *The Book of Gateways, Conjurations and Banishments*, and she handed this across the desk to him.

He put on a pair of pince-nez and studied the map briefly. "I see. This location is somewhat northeast of the city; I believe it's still wild there, just past the plantations. Jungle."

He set his spectacles down and stared at her curiously. "It's rather a long way to go just to see another old temple. Are you sure you want to do this?"

"How far is it?"

"Well, no more than a total of three hours travel time—but it might be dangerous." Smythe-Bentley paused to re-light the hookah, then inhaled from it before chuckling and going on: "Traveling through the Black City is bad enough, let alone the jungle."

"The Black City?" Diana asked.

"Yes. The northern part of Calcutta. Where the natives live, you know. We've plenty of temples within the city you could visit, although I'm not sure why you'd want to. Ugly things, if you ask me."

Diana nodded, then chose her words carefully. "Mr. Smythe-Bentley, I appreciate your concern, but it really is vitally important that I see *this* temple, and time is of the essence."

He took another long drag off the hookah, exhaled several perfect smoke rings, then jotted a few notes which he handed to Goompat.

"Goompat, would you arrange these things for Lady Furnaval right away?"

The servant glanced at the list, nodded, and strode from the room.

Smythe-Bentley turned to Diana again. "Are you sure you wouldn't rather simply spend your visit to Calcutta here, Lady Furnaval? I know my wife would greatly enjoy your company, and we can offer you some very fine English food, or an afternoon visit to the local racetrack…?"

Diana smiled slightly, and said, "Thank you, but my business is really very pressing. And truthfully, I welcome a chance to travel through the Black City."

He blinked in consternation. "I see. I take it you're a fan of Lord Ripon, then?"

Diana missed the connection, and Smythe-Bentley went on: "Our current viceroy. Chap actually believes the Indians should have their own representation in the local government. *Swaraj* they call it."

"And you don't?" Diana asked.

"Of course not. Now our last viceroy, Lord Lytton, he understood that these people are little better than apes. The idea of them having a voice in government…preposterous."

Diana couldn't resist. "The last time we refused to give the locals a say in government, we lost America."

He glared at her for a moment, then pretended to busy himself with paperwork. "Yes, well, I'm afraid I'm really terribly busy, Lady Furnaval. Good day to you then."

She rose and left without another word, glad to be out of the man's presence.

Outside, she found Goompat and Yi-kin standing with a sedan chair, four half-naked Indian bearers, and two scowling locals in military garb. "Lady Furnaval, these men are *sepoys*—local soldiers—who will accompany you," Goompat indicated them.

The men looked tough, well-built and scarred, and they carried rifles and long, sheathed knives. "That's very generous, but…are they really necessary?"

"The jungle has tigers," Goompat said.

Diana had no more argument against the involvement of the *sepoys*.

The *doolie* was another matter. Goompat gestured that she should enter, and the bearers immediately moved to their positions, preparing to lift the poles that the covered seat rested upon. "I'd really prefer to walk."

Goompat said, "The chair is more comfortable, my Lady."

When Diana didn't move, Yi-kin stepped closer and added, "And more safe. You are British lady in Calcutta. I can walk."

"Yi-kin, do you mean to say you're going with me?!" she asked.

"Yes. I want to see gateway," he answered, as if stating that he wanted to visit a garden or shop he'd heard about.

Diana considered trying to send him away, but realized he quite intended to accompany her. Besides, he might prove helpful.

"Very well, then."

Reluctantly she turned to the *doolie* and stepped in, seating herself as Goompat closed the small door behind her.

"Be careful, Lady Furnaval," Goompat said softly, and Diana couldn't help but think that he showed considerably more grace and compassion than his employer.

Almost immediately the chair rose and began moving forward with surprising speed. Diana pushed aside the curtains to her right and leaned out, curious about this mode of transportation—

– and immediately regretted the action.

The back of the man directly in her view wasn't just marked by this employment, it was actually mutilated. His right shoulder, which bore the weight of the pole, was so calloused it was actually several inches higher than his left; as she watched, the pole rubbed the skin open and blood began to trickle down the man's side. And yet the man kept up a constant stream of chatter with his co-workers, apparently inured to physical agony.

She saw Yi-kin walking swiftly to keep up with the coolies' pace, and she called to him. He approached the window, and Diana leaned down to ask, "Yi-kin, how much are these men being paid?"

"I do not know. I will ask."

Yi-kin trotted up to the coolie Diana had been observing, and exchanged a few words with the man. He dropped back to the side of the sedan and informed her, "Sixpence each."

"Per hour?"

"Per day," Yi-kin casually answered.

My God, Diana thought, *sixpence per day? That's little better than slavery. No wonder they all look underfed.*

"Tell them there'll be handsome bonuses at the end of the day, when we return to the *Althea*."

Yi-kin ran to the coolie again, spoke to him briefly, and then a cry of joy went up from the four bearers. The pace quickened.

In a few minutes they'd left the "White City" behind, and were heading north on crowded, narrow Chitpore Road. Diana felt as if she were seeing the real Calcutta now, not the faux London suburb the British had tried to impose upon the place. The sedan bearers were astonishingly agile as they negotiated the chair past butcher shops displaying goat carcasses, vendors with carts full of huge, yellow *pumelos*, women dressed in bright yellow, crimson or purple veils, and children who glimpsed Diana's white skin and ran after the *doolie* with outstretched hands.

Mina caused a few heads to turn, as Diana allowed her to peer up out of the sedan, and there was one near-disaster when Diana had to restrain Mina from going after a live cobra performing for a snake charmer. The pursuing children laughed at the cat's antics and pointed, and Diana laughed with them.

At one point Yi-kin disappeared briefly into the crowds, then returned with a small paper-wrapped bundle which he passed through the *doolie's* window to Diana. "Try this. Very good."

Diana pulled back the paper and saw a small dark brown sphere; a heady, sweet aroma rose from it, and her first bite left her senses nearly overcome with a milky sweetness.

"This is delicious, Yi-kin! What is it?" she asked.

"*Ladikani.*"

Diana finished the sweet, then returned to examining the passing scenery.

The chair wobbled from side to side as the coolies deftly traversed the winding road and the traffic, which now included a horsedrawn tram. At one point they came to a halt, and leaning out the window Diana saw a shouting crowd centered around an ox-drawn cart that had tipped over. Her bearers suddenly stopped and looked around, shouting suggestions at each other in Hindi. They spotted an open alleyway to the left and headed for its shadows. The mouth of the alley was narrow, and for a moment Diana felt certain the chair would prove too wide; but the four bearers deftly negotiated the way and soon they'd left the tumultuous bustle of Chitpore Road behind.

Diana involuntarily tensed when she glanced to her left and saw they were passing a row of human arms and legs.

Upon closer examination, she realized the limbs were actually clay, and belonged to hundreds of realistic, life-sized statues that were stacked up against one side of the alley. She saw Christian saints, local deities...and Kali. Everywhere, Kali, with her bloody tongue, third eye and sinuous arms.

Now she saw the makers of these marvels; potters squatted at work in dusty alcoves along the alley, fashioning the figures, molding clay and dressing them in real fabric.

When the alley broadened slightly, Yi-kin edged up to the window again, apparently having anticipated Diana's questions.

"The Indians say this place is called Kumortuli. These people — the Kumors — are very famous."

"No doubt. Their work is breathtaking."

Just before they left Kumortuli behind, they moved past a completely finished statue of Kali, one that had been painted and dressed, and Diana couldn't help but feel that the statue was somehow watching her even as she was watching it.

The ubiquitous presence of Kali was one thing she wouldn't miss about Calcutta.

Not long after the inadvertent side trip to Kumortuli, the landscape changed from urban crush to rural space, *puckha* buildings giving way to lush, open fields. They negotiated a dirt road between two-wheeled carts pulled by cream-colored oxen, and trains of camels bearing crates.

The plantation fields were hot magenta in color, and it took Diana a few seconds to realize what crop would provide that startling hue:

The poppy.

Of course. Poppies, their vivid blooms interspersed with bulging sacs waiting to be harvested and converted into the profitable opium.

"Yi-kin," Diana called, leaning out of the jostling sedan's window. When he'd turned to her, she begged, "How much farther? There's no reason I can't get out and walk now, is there?"

Yi-kin called to one of the sepoys (whose named Diana learned was Amitabh), and conversed with him briefly, then returned. "He say we are almost there, and that please, *memsahib* should stay in *doolie* until we arrive."

Diana surveyed the landscape beyond the road. In one direction poppy fields led off to a distant view of the Hooghly; in the other, they were bordered by thick jungle.

Arrive where? she wondered.

A mere twenty minutes later, her question was answered.

The bearers stopped, and lowered the *doolie* before a rickety building that was set on the edge of one of the plantations. Diana gratefully stepped from the sedan, and examined the exterior of the building.

It seemed to be a sort of way station, not quite an inn, but more than some mere shack.

Most spectacular, however, was the sight of a herd of elephants grazing nearby.

It was the first time Diana had seen this many of the great beasts gathered at once, and the sight was truly impressive. The pachyderms flapped ears and tails lazily in the heat, their trunks reaching up to pluck leaves from tall trees on the edges of the jungle. From Diana's satchel, Mina eyed the elephants, her nose working furiously to parse the strange scents.

Amitabh went into the one-story building, and returned a few seconds later with an Indian man, who took one look at Diana and burst into smiles and bows.

"Welcome, *memsahib*, welcome!"

Diana returned one bow, and the man grinned even wider. "We are honored by your presence!"

"Thank you," she answered, then muttered a quiet aside to Yi-kin. "What are we doing here?"

"Here is where your map say we go into jungle to find temple."

"Ahh." Diana now saw a trail leading from the main road, into the thick growth. "Do we walk?"

"Oh no, *siu je*," Yi-kin answered. "We ride animal."

At first Diana thought he meant a horse...then she realized he was referring to the beasts. "Surely you don't—"

She was cut off by the supercilious Indian man. "These elephants are very good! You will like riding one!"

Diana stared from the elephant rental agent to the elephants to the two amused sepoys and then Yi-kin. "We're actually going to take an elephant into the jungle?!"

Amitabh stepped up and addressed her directly in heavily-accented English. "The jungle has tigers. Tigers do not kill elephants."

Diana could hardly deny the logic of that.

A short time later, an elephant bearing a battered old wooden *howdah* was produced (for which the rental agent apologized profusely, since he was sure a great British lady deserved a better one of gold and jewels). The rental fees were argued and paid, arrangements made for the bearers to wait, and Diana, Yi-kin and the two Indian soldiers climbed a short ladder while the elephant knelt on all fours. The *howdah* was a small platform perched atop the beast, covered overhead and contained two settees, one placed behind the other. She and Yi-kin moved to the front, while the sepoys claimed the rear. A local Indian was hired as the *mahout*, or driver, and he rode bareback atop the elephant's broad neck. As the animal lumbered to its feet, Diana found herself clutching at the arms of the settee anxiously, but then the elephant righted itself, and the ride became surprisingly smooth. The elephant moved forward at a moderate but steady gait, and they'd soon left behind the road and fields and were swallowed by the encroaching greenery of the Indian jungle.

The path was just barely wide enough to accommodate the elephant's bulk, and they often felt vines or fronds brush the top of the *howdah*. The only marks of civilization they saw, besides the trail, were occasional bamboo poles placed near the path, usually topped with tattered old pieces of cloth or shriveled leaves.

"Amitabh," Diana asked over one shoulder, "what do those bamboo poles represent?"

Amitabh said, "Each pole marks a place where a tiger has killed a man."

Diana was suddenly *very* glad they hired the elephant.

Unfortunately the elephant didn't seem very glad to have them, after a short trip. Or, more precisely, the elephant's driver didn't.

They'd ridden perhaps two miles into the jungle when the *mahout* abruptly stopped his elephant, brought it to a kneeling position, and called something to the passengers in the native Hindi language.

Amitabh and the other sepoy shouted something back, and it soon became apparent to Diana that an argument was going on between the elephant driver and the soldiers.

"Amitabh, what's happening?" she asked.

He called something to the elephant driver which only caused the man to shake his head and gesture firmly at the ground, then turned to Diana. "He says he will not go further."

"How far are we from the temple?" Diana asked, suddenly worried.

"Maybe a mile," Amitabh answered.

"Surely he can take us all the way," she pleaded.

Amitabh shook his head. "He says there are *phansigars*."

When Diana looked perplexed, Amitabh added, "Thuggees."

Aaahhh, Diana thought, *now Thuggees I know.*

The books she'd studied on Calcutta and India had described the murderous cult dedicated to worship of Kali, and claimed they had slain as many as two million unwary travelers, using their signature method of strangulation by a length of cloth known as a *ruhmal*.

The Thuggee cult had also been (supposedly) successfully suppressed in the 1830s by a British police organization known as the Thuggee and Dacoity Department.

"I thought the Thuggees were basically dead," Diana said.

"Not dead," Amitabh grunted, and hefted his rifle. "You can walk?"

She nodded.

"We walk, then. The temple is this way."

Diana followed the sepoys and Yi-kin down from the elephant, and they started off down the trail on foot. They'd only gone a short distance when Amitabh glanced back and shouted in alarm.

The *mahout* had re-mounted the elephant, somehow got it turned around on the narrow trail, and was heading back the way they'd come.

The soldiers ran a short distance after them, but the animal was moving quickly and they soon realized they couldn't stop it. They paused in the midst of the jungle trail, anxious and bewildered, and turned back to Diana and Yi-kin.

"Well," Diana said, watching their transportation disappear from sight around a bend in the trail, "that wasn't a very wise investment, was it?"

The Indians grunted and led the way on through the jungle.

Although it was warmer than she would have liked, and steaming, Diana nevertheless enjoyed the trek; free from either *doolie* or elephant, she was happy to stretch her legs and admire some of the spectacular flora and fauna up-close. Mina, likewise, meowed for release, and although Diana was hesitant to let Mina roam free until they got closer to the gateway, she finally gave in to the feline's whining and set her down on the trail. Mina immediately ran to the edge of the jungle to sniff a strange flower, then trotted complacently alongside Diana's feet.

They'd walked perhaps a half-mile when Diana began to suspect they were being followed.

At first she'd dismissed the sounds of rustling brush and the side glimpses of furtive movement as just more of the local wildlife, but she began to realize that what she was sensing was very large and moving upright. And there was more than one.

Amitabh and the other sepoy sensed it, too, and brandished their rifles anxiously. The two Indians actually began to look frightened, and Diana hoped they wouldn't suddenly join the *mahout* and leave she, Mina and Yi-kin alone in the Indian jungle.

They rounded a bend in the trail, crested a small rise, and suddenly discovered their destination awaiting them on the other side:

They faced a small but ornate temple nestled in amongst the trees and vines. Made from stone, its columns, spires and domes had once been gaily painted, but much of the colors had been worn away by time and the destructive natural elements. Brilliantly-hued birds nested in the spires, screaming into the jungle and occasionally taking flight in pursuit of immense insects. Even though the temple seemed to have been abandoned long ago and was fighting a losing battle with the encroaching growth, Diana nonetheless experienced a moment of awed breathlessness at both its beauty and decay.

Without warning Mina darted forward, running directly across a small stream and into the front entrance of the temple.

"What is she doing?" asked Yi-kin.

Diana smiled and started forward. "She's found the gateway."

They made their way over the narrow, muddy creek and hesitated at the entrance to the temple to allow their eyes to adjust. Diana had brought a small lantern, which she removed from her supply bag now. She lit it, then, holding it aloft, led the way inside.

The temple interior was quite long and very low; pillars marched off into the gloom on either side of a central passage. Diana halfway expected the place to be cobwebbed and crawling with vermin, but it was surprisingly clean. In fact, it was possibly too clean.

Her cat had run all the way to the rear of the temple and stationed herself just to the right of what appeared to be an altar. Diana ignored Mina's hissing as she eyed the altar and the wall behind it.

Unlike a Christian altar, this one was plainly not intended to hold a minister, but to strike reverence and fear into the hearts of worshippers, and Diana thought it horribly effective. The wall was painted a bright red, and displayed various scenes of a many-armed monster engaged in acts of destruction. As Diana stepped forward and examined the fresco more closely, she saw that the monster in question was (of course) Kali. Her again, with her four arms and three eyes, black skin and long wild tresses, skirt of severed human arms and necklace of severed heads.

In front of the wall, on a low table, sat a bust of the goddess, with her open mouth and crown-like headdress. The bust was surrounded by what might have been decorations or offerings, including flowers and food.

And they were fresh.

"Miss Diana," Yi-kin whispered near her, "soon someone here."

"You mean 'recently,' Yi-kin," Diana whispered back.

"No, I mean, soon. Please go quickly with gateway."

Diana nodded. *The Book of Gateways, Conjurations and Banishments* had indicated that the proper protection for anything coming through this gateway was a mantra called a *dharani*, to be read aloud. Diana had copied the short chant onto a single sheet of paper, buried in the bag; she hoped she wouldn't need it, but it seemed unlikely that closing this gateway would be a simple task. She held out the lantern and called, "Amitabh, can you take this?"

No one took the bag. She looked around, and saw Yi'kin likewise peering about in confusion. "Mr. Amitabh, where—?"

Yi-kin broke off as they both heard a sound behind them—a cry and a shuddering gasp, coming from the temple's main entrance. They whirled, and made out the silhouettes of their two sepoys outlined in the doorway.

Both men collapsed to the temple floor.

And there behind the fallen men stood their murderers, still grasping lengths of twisted cloth. There were at least four of them visible in the doorway. They were coming in now, stepping over the two dead men.

Thuggees.

Diana backed up until her back touched the altar; next to her, Mina broke off hissing at the invisible gateway and turned to howl at the advancing stranglers, the hair on her back and tail standing straight up.

There were now seven of the Thuggees. They all held deadly garrotes, and looked ready to use them. Diana thought back to what she'd read on the cult, and realized that was all quite useless information.

Her books had said the Thuggees never attacked either foreigners or women.

Diana let her right hand creep into her bag, where she had the iron knife. She was formulating a plan that consisted of hurling the lantern at the cultists, then dodging to one side as she struck out with the knife.

And then Yi-kin was flying and she never had a chance to test her plan.

He was moving so fast that Diana barely had time to see what he was doing. She saw him launch into an astonishing spinning kick, lifting his leg so high that he took out a man easily a full head taller than himself. His hands were hooked into strange claw-like positions, and the second Thuggee fell, scratching at his bleeding face. Yi-kin then spun on his heels, twisting impossibly between two attackers, and then he leapt straight up and launched kicks with each leg that rendered the pair instantly unconscious. The remaining three Thuggees actually pulled back, hesitating before attacking the whirlwind that was Yi-kin, and in that moment of their hesitation he spun towards them, lashing out with low kicks that brought all three men down to the pavement. From there it was a simple matter to knock them out.

He stood in the middle of the seven unconscious men, triumphant, and not the least winded.

Diana was about to express her astonishment when Yi-kin held a finger up to his lips, indicating silence. Diana froze, and he moved silently up to the temple entrance. After a brief hesitation, he leapt through, and Diana saw two more of the Thuggees, who had been stationed secretly just outside, grab for him—before their heads banged together and they joined their fellows at Yi-kin's feet.

Now Diana did cry out: "Yi-kin, that was extraordinary! How did you—?"

And then his reaction silenced her as she saw that Yi-kin was frozen in shock and staring at something to her left.

She turned in time to see Kali materializing as she stepped through the gateway.

There was no mistaking the massive, nightmarish vision approaching Diana: She stood easily seven feet tall, with the top of her elaborate headdress just brushing the ceiling. Her skin was ebon, her hair long and unkempt, her four arms waving (at least only *one* was clutching a sword), a belt of severed arms circled her waist, and shriveled, shrunken heads beaded on an abominable necklace hung over her chest. Her three eyes took in the sight of her defeated and unmoving followers, and then her fiery gaze turned directly to Diana.

Yi-kin ran back from the temple entrance and launched himself at the goddess-demon in a flying kick. His feet impacted with the she-thing's chest...and Kali barely staggered. Two arms swatted the young man aside as if he were an insect, and he flew backward twenty feet to collide painfully with one of the stone pillars. Diana barely had time to glimpse him sliding down the pillar, dazed, before Kali's attention turned her way again.

Kali flung her sword at Diana's heart.

Mina shrieked and flung herself at Kali; the goddess batted the cat aside easily, but her thrust was knocked askew and the sword plunged deeply into the wood altar. In the instant that it took the goddess to wrench the sword free for another attack, Diana upended her bag and snatched the sheet of paper with the *dharani* as it fell. She faced the maddened goddess with a lantern in one hand, the mantra in the other.

"*Namo saptanam samyaksambuddha kotinam—*" she chanted, her tongue struggling with some of the syllables, and she could only hope that incorrect pronunciation would not affect the power of the *dharani*.

Kali had the sword raised again, and this time she brought it straight down. Fortunately her movements were slow, her speed compromised by her bulk, and Diana was able to dodge the blow. The sword hit the stone floor with an explosion of sparks and a clang that made Diana's ears ring. Diana was backed up against the altar again, giving her a brief space to continue the incantation:

"*Tadyatha: Om, cale, cule, cundi svaha.*"

That was the extent of the chant. Diana looked up expectantly, hoping to see Kali stagger back towards the gateway, or shriek in defiance…and instead Kali brought an arm down, her naked fist striking the altar to one side of Diana. Her aim was off, and she smashed her own bust into pieces, which caused her to howl with demonic rage.

So much for the dharani.

Mina leapt at the monster again, but Diana threw the *dharani* aside to catch the frantic feline, packed her under an arm and ran. She went about ten paces, then turned and flung the oil lantern at the monster.

The lantern didn't hold much oil, and only a small patch of Kali caught fire as the glass shattered, but the flames provided the powerful distraction Diana had needed. In desperation she lunged for her overturned bag, released Mina, clutched the iron blade and charged straight at the monster.

Kali was caught by surprise, and Diana buried the knife up to the hilt in Kali's chest, hoping it was near the thing's heart. Diana's effort was rewarded by an agonized shriek—and then a mighty, clawed hand lashed out and clutched Diana's wrist.

Diana tried to wrench away, but Kali's grip was inhuman. The goddess clearly intended to pull Diana in to that gaping, fanged mouth, and there was nothing Diana had strength to do. She was dimly aware of Mina spitting and slashing at Kali's feet, to no avail—

—Incredibly, Yi-kin was there behind the goddess, pulling at the ruhpal he'd wrapped around her throat.

Yi-kin had both feet planted on the nightmare's back, and was drawing back on the ends of the garrote with every bit of strength he possessed. Kali was startled enough to release Diana as she grappled at the ruhpal with all four hands. Rather than flee, Diana reached forward and grabbed the knife, twisting it with both hands and trying to saw it through Kali's chest.

Her exertions were successful, because the creature suddenly stiffened, shuddered, issued a long, foul-smelling exhalation, and then toppled over.

Yi-kin jumped away as the thing hit the floor, and this time Diana heard him panting in the gloom. "Miss Diana, you are fine?"

"Yes, I'm all right, Yi-kin. Are you—?"

"Good," he told her.

Diana scrabbled on the floor for a moment, and located her bag. There were matches inside, and she lit one, looking around. She spotted a torch in a holder on one of the pillars, and held the match up to it, hoping it would catch. It did. She took the torch down from the sconce and thrust it out towards Kali.

The she-demon had turned to stone. Kali looked like nothing more than a toppled idol now.

She'd also fallen face forward, and Diana knew her knife was gone, buried under a bulk weighing more than what she and Yi-kin could probably move.

Mina had returned her attention to the gateway, and Diana thought it would be wise to close the portal as swiftly as possible, lest something even worse than Kali decide to come through and avenge her death. Diana looked around for something else with a sharp edge, and she spotted a shard of the shattered lantern glass nearby.

"Yi-kin, take this," she said, holding the torch out to him.

He did, and Diana pulled off her jacket to roll up her left sleeve, then bent and retrieved the glass shard. As Yi-kin watched, wide-eyed, she matter-of-factly sliced her arm with the edge, waited for a few seconds as the blood began to flow, then faced the area of the gateway and cried out:

"By my will and by my blood is this gateway sealed *forever*!"

Her blood flew through space and then abruptly splattered and smoked as it hit the unseen gateway. Mina yowled a last time—

—and then it was done.

Diana waited, gauging the success of the closure—as always—by Mina's reaction. Mina was already rubbing around Diana's ankles, purring happily. Yi-kin must have noticed the way Diana relaxed, because he asked, "Just now is gateway close?"

"It's closed," Diana agreed.

One of the Thuggees was beginning to moan as he regained consciousness, and Yi-kin said, "We go."

"We go," agreed Diana, pausing only long enough to gather the contents of her bag, pick up her jacket and Mina. She took a scarf from one of the downed Thuggees on the way out, and wound it around her arm; she could bandage that more effectively when they were safely away from the temple.

At the entrance they passed the bodies of the two soldiers. "What about them?" Yi-kin asked.

Diana knelt and felt each man for a pulse. There were none.

"I'm afraid there's nothing more we can do for them."

Another of the Thuggees began to stir, and the fate of the sepoys' remains was sealed, as Diana and Yi-kin fled.

They went back the way they'd come, at a half-jog. They kept up that pace until their exhausted legs could carry them no further, but fortunately they'd nearly reached the edge of the jungle when their strength gave out. Although there'd been no sign of pursuit, they barely spoke until they'd reached the main road again, where Diana noted that the man who had rented them the elephant was conveniently absent.

The *doolie* carriers still waited patiently, and instantly leapt to their feet, but Diana couldn't stand the idea of forcing these men to stagger under her weight again. She gave each of them a pound sterling (much to their astonishment, and voluble gratitude), and dismissed them while Yi-kin stood by silently.

After an hour's rest, they were following after the smiling *doolie* men, walking side-by-side on the return route to the city, trying to avoid camel trains and piles of animal dung.

"Miss Diana," Yi-kin queried finally, "what will happen to Thuggees? When they see goddess like statue?"

"It wasn't a goddess," Diana countered.

"But it look like paintings...."

"It did," admitted Diana, "but the things that come through the gateways aren't gods and goddesses—they're monsters and demons. That particular demon created an army of followers by convincing them that it was a goddess. What I don't understand is why a demon would need a human army. If the things in the netherworld are allying themselves now with human forces in this world...that begins to sound like a true war."

"Not goddess?" Yi-kin persisted.

"Yi-kin," Diana asked with a faint smile, "would we have been able to kill a goddess?"

Yi-kin thought about that, then admitted, "No." Then he asked, "War? We have war with monsters?"

"Maybe," she answered.

"Can we win war?"

"I don't know," Diana mused, gazing off into the poppy fields lining the road. "It won't be easy when spells that are supposed to work against them don't—like the mantra that should have protected us from Kali."

Yi-kin nodded. "Oh, I know mantras. Indian people believe mantras work if they say them many times."

"Ahh," Diana murmured, realizing that perhaps the mantra was supposed to have been chanted *before* Kali had stepped through the gateway. Then she returned her attention to Yi-kin, admiringly.

"But with a few more like you on our side we can. What *was* that back there?"

Yi-kin answered proudly, "My father teach me *Wing Chun* style of *gong fu*. After *baba* die I still practice."

"I wish I'd known you could do that," Diana chided him. "Why didn't you tell me?"

Yi-kin shrugged. "You never ask."

Chapter XII

May 22-23, 1880
Canton, China

The *Althea* completed her voyage to Canton without incident. Diana spent most of the final leg of the trip in her quarters, stroking Mina and reading.

After the events of Calcutta, she discovered her anger at Antonia had subsided, and they resumed their friendship. Diana (and Yi-kin) told Antonia little of what had actually transpired in Kali's temple; they claimed only that the two sepoys had deserted them just after they'd found the temple, and that they'd accomplished their goal there.

When Yi-kin wasn't working or sleeping (a rare activity with him), his time was entirely given to Diana now. Having seen her steely composure in the temple, Yi-kin stood somewhat in awe of her, and she was similarly impressed by the young man's ability in what he called *gong fu*. She considered asking him to teach some of it to her, but she decided to wait until they were on steady land again. They did, however, continue to study each other's language, and Diana found in Yi-kin a hungry and intelligent pupil; she, likewise, enjoyed the way her own mind was energized by learning the Chinese language. Yi-kin soon began to grasp the notion of conjugating verbs and the many tenses of English, and Diana's Cantonese inflections began to provoke less laughter from him.

Captain Hughes and Antonia continued to express their dismay at Diana's plans for going ashore in Canton (or at least in her leaving the confines of the British area, called Shameen) but after the events at the temple of Kali, Diana was more intent than ever on inspecting the Canton gateway. She believed that the Indian Thuggee cult had been led astray by forces from the netherworld that had apparently been intent on creating an army of lethal human allies. She'd never heard of such malevolence before, and felt a renewed urgency to close as many of the gateways as possible. As a result of the attacks on William and herself, and Chappell's notion that there might be some sort of vast war brewing, Diana bore a newfound and immense responsibility.

On the morning of May 22nd, the *Althea* steamed past the island of Hong Kong ("Now *that* is truly a savage place," Hughes told her, with a gleam in his eye) and soon after entered the mouth of the Pearl River at the "Bogue," which had seen heavy fighting during the Opium Wars of four decades earlier. The weather was fine, and the area was really quite picturesque, with rugged cliffs on one side and a broad estuary on the other. Fishing boats and Chinese junks lined the shores, and the water was dotted with smaller islands.

The river was also lined with military forts.

Most were built on high peninsulas that thrust into the river like tall fingers, but they seemed to be largely in ruins, with tumbledown stone walls and no evidence of habitation.

"Why are all these forts deserted, Yi-kin?" she asked the young man, who was working the deck nearby.

He squinted up, saw the one they were just passing, and answered, "Oh, old forts. There are many on the river. Many years ago Chinese use them against British opium ships. Then Chinese say opium is legal, so forts no more need."

"Yes, when the Chinese lost the Opium Wars," Diana said.

It was the first time she'd said anything like that to Yi-kin, and she knew it could have been a test of their friendship; but Yi-kin only glanced at the passing ruin and said, "Because the British are more strong."

She hadn't realized they'd been joined by Antonia, who was watching the conversation keenly. "It's true, Diana."

Diana shrugged. "Well, of course. That, and we weren't afraid to kill thousands of Chinese. I've read that while we incurred losses of five hundred, the number of Chinese deaths may have been as high as twenty-thousand."

Antonia hesitated, then said, "The forts served another purpose, too, after the Opium Wars: They guarded river traffic from pirates."

"Pirates?"

"Oh yes. I have an aunt who was once sailing from Canton to Macau when her ship was attacked and she was taken hostage by pirates. They held her for a week in a small space below decks no larger than coffin. She received a bowl of rice each day, and was beset each night by all manner of vermin—insects, spiders, rats. She thought sure she would die in that horrible, cramped little cell when suddenly one day the hatch was thrown back—she didn't know by whom. She managed to lift herself up, and discovered she was quite alone on the ship. It seemed that the pirates had spotted a British gunship approaching and had all fled in terror. My aunt swore she would never return to China after that."

When Diana didn't answer, Antonia nodded, "That was barely twenty years ago, Diana. You see, the Chinese can be brutal as well."

Diana found her eyes seeking Yi-kin's, but he had wandered away to busy himself elsewhere.

They arrived in Canton that evening.

They steamed up the river past the great island of Macau and the massive shipyards at Whampoa, and docked at a large island which served to house the docks and *go-downs*, or warehouses, of many of the British companies. When Diana heard one of the crewmen mention "Ho-Nam," she stopped the man and questioned him.

"That's the name of this island," he'd told her in his thick Liverpool accent.

Ho-Nam was where *The Book of Gateways, Conjurations and Banishments* said the Canton gateway would be found.

Although Diana was anxious to set foot on Ho-Nam, Captain Hughes and Antonia both told her no one would be allowed to disembark until they'd checked out the location. A messenger was sent to the Hinton Company offices, and returned near midnight with dire news: The comprador, Mr. Wong, was now among the missing.

By morning, Antonia had gathered all the Hinton representatives and ship captains in the area, and made arrangements for a meeting in the company's offices. Without the Hintons' chief Chinese contact, it would be necessary to deal with other local officials, and so Antonia put together a packet of something she euphemistically referred to as "tea money." Then she and Captain Hughes set off down the docks while Diana, Mina and Yi-kin remained behind with the rest of the ship's crew.

Poor Yi-kin was positively champing at the bit; he did miss his native soil more than he admitted, and he peered wistfully toward the mainland, pointing out local landmarks, such as the huge, red, Five-Storied Pagoda, and regaling Diana with tales of Chinese food and festivals. He was particularly sorry to have missed *Ch'ing Ming*, the celebration of ancestors which included visiting cemeteries and cleaning graves (and which Diana reckoned to be similar to the European November 2nd celebration of All Souls Day). They watched the many boats negotiating the Pearl River, many ferried by women, and Yi-kin pointed out the "house boats," opulent *sampans* that served only particular British companies or families.

The sun was setting when Antonia and Captain Hughes finally returned to the *Althea*, with the encouraging news that arrangements had been made for Diana (and for Antonia) to immediately occupy the Hinton family residence in the Shameen district. Diana would have preferred to begin searching Ho-Nam for the gateway, but instead she reluctantly bundled up her things, and a half hour later she and Mina were stepping onto one of the *sampans* with Antonia. She was mildly distressed that Yi-kin would not be joining them (no Chinese were allowed in Shameen, unless employed there as servants), but he assured her he had his own place to stay in Canton. The sun had set as the little boat finally crossed the Pearl, tied up to wooden moorings behind one of the mansions in the Shameen district, and Diana stepped onto Chinese soil.

She was told the British section of Shameen had been reclaimed from river silt by the British at great expense. It surprised (and perhaps slightly disappointed) her to discover that it looked much like parts of Calcutta, which in turn looked much like parts of London. The Hinton family house was decorated largely in Western style, with few touches of local elegance—an exquisite jade carving or vase, a lacquered end table. The few Chinese she saw were servants, and Antonia treated them with a surprising disdain that made Diana acutely uncomfortable.

After a superb dinner of turtle soup and curry roast beef, Diana (and Mina) did take a quick stroll of the small Shameen area, but was dismayed by one scene in particular: An Englishman in a neighboring house was beating a cowering young woman with a bamboo switch. As Diana gaped in horror, peering in through a window, the man was joined by a woman—undoubtedly his wife— and Diana breathed a silent sigh of relief, assuming the woman would stop the beating.

Instead, the woman laughed and Diana overheard the phrase "yellow imbecile" before the beating continued.

Diana nearly stepped forward to stop the abuse, but the man finally seemed to grow tired of the activity. As he dropped the switch, he looked up and saw Diana watching. She tensed, expecting a confrontation—and instead the man smiled and nodded a greeting before following his wife back into another part of the house. The young Chinese girl was shaking badly as she pulled herself to her feet, her dress was torn and bloodied…but she returned to her work as if it were all just part of her regular routine.

Diana was beginning to believe she would truly regret having made this trip to China…but not because of the Chinese.

Chapter XIII

May 24, 1880
Canton, China

Her room was as elegant as any found in a British manor house, only a few touches (an exquisite waist-high cloisonné vase in one corner, a teak dressing table with geometric inlay) of local culture intruding, but Diana's night there was nonetheless uneasy. When she left it in the morning with Mina (who was overjoyed when Diana let her scamper briefly in the small courtyard near the house), Diana breakfasted with Antonia, who told her that after the meal she needed to attend to Hinton Company business. She then informed Diana that she'd arranged for her to take a tour of Canton with a famous local guide named Ah Kam. Diana would have preferred to head back to Ho-Nam, but she knew it would be unsafe to go without Yi-kin, so she agreed to the tour.

She found Ah Kam awaiting her just past the heavily guarded bridge that spanned the small inlet separating Shameen from the rest of Canton. Ah Kam—who had accrued a small fortune acting as guide for at least two generations of visiting foreigners—was an older Chinese man dressed in elegant silk robes and knobbed cap, and with three-inch long nails on the fourth and fifth fingers of each hand. Diana had read in her studies that the long fingernails were a Chinese sign of status, since their owners were capable of very little manual labor.

"Ahh, Lady Furnaval, welcome," he greeted her, bowing and smiling. "I will show you best parts of Canton."

He gestured behind himself, and with some horror Diana saw that he had two sedan chairs and coolies ready.

"Thank you, Ah Kam, but I'd really prefer to walk."

The elderly guide put up a brief argument, but decided to let the headstrong *fan-gwai* have her way, although he insisted upon a sedan chair himself.

And so, Diana had a walking tour of Canton, as Ah Kam leaned out of his sedan chair, pointing out the sights and offering explanations in his pleasantly-accented English. He showed her the narrow streets of the merchant district, barely six feet wide and extending up three stories through a proliferation of carved wooden signs. They visited a jeweler's where Diana gasped in delight as the proprietor worked actual insect wings into his designs, and they rested at a tea shop where Diana sampled a luscious *oolong* that smelled of orchids and was completely unlike any other tea she'd ever tasted. Ah Kam showed her *Tung Wu Ti-low*, Canton's famed water clock (a contrivance of four copper jugs that dripped water at such a precise rate the clock was said to have been accurate for hundreds of years), and the "Factory," which had housed workers with the East India Company a hundred years before, but was now only a pathetic Chinese tenement.

Diana was enthralled by the city. She loved its bustle and speed, she adored the clash of silk-clad merchants and bare-chested laborers, of adolescents happily gambling on street corners while accountants sat behind them figuring sums on their abacuses. Canton was no more or less crowded than her own London on a week day, but London had never sounded or smelled like this. Open barrels of dried herbs exuded scents that were completely new to her; large metal pots full of simmering wontons set her mouth to watering. Her ears picked out the strains of a two-stringed *erhu* issuing from a second-floor salon, sounding like the love song of a dying heron.

Most of the Chinese simply ignored her; a few strangely eyed her Western dress and features, and gave her a wide berth; children occasionally ran after her pointing and shouting *"Fan-gwai!"* A few (especially the merchants) bowed to her.

She tried to remember some of the Cantonese Yi-kin had taught her, but found she couldn't correlate it to the fast, heavily-slurred language that whirled around her. She yearned to try the tantalizingly-spicy local foods she scented around her...until she found herself next to one street vendor hawking rats, their tiny bodies impaled and cooked on long spits. Apparently rats were considered something of a delicacy, much favored by Chinese men who believed they aided in growing hair. Diana thought she already had quite enough hair, thank you.

Ah Kam seemed most excited to show her Canton's infamous execution grounds, which were located just outside the city walls near the river shore. En route, he proudly told Diana that they carried out some fifteen-hundred executions per year at the place; when Diana asked about their crimes, Ah Kam leered and told her they were murderers, rapists and traitors. Diana knew little of the Chinese system of justice and wondered what a trial must be like, or how much evidence was required to sentence a man to death. Her guide explained how prisoners were carried in baskets through the streets of Canton before arrival at the execution grounds, where they were lined up in rows of fifteen or twenty, and then swiftly beheaded by swordsmen who were so experienced that each decapitation took only a single stroke. When they arrived at the accursed place, Diana noticed the ground was permanently stained dark red, a testament to the thousands of killings. When she asked Ah Kam about some large earthenware jars lining a far wall of the grounds, he laughed and had a coolie remove the lid from one of the jars. Diana looked in, and saw the jars were packed with severed heads; the smell of quicklime made her flinch and pull sharply back. Ah Kam giggled at the look of disgust on her face, and Diana agreed that perhaps one commonly held western belief about the Orient might be true: Death held little terror to the Chinaman.

The last item on the tour was a larger horror.

Ah Kam's bearers stopped before an ordinary-looking brick building, which Diana would have taken for a hotel, or apartment house. Her guide alit from his sedan chair and led the way down a short corridor into a large, dark open room.

The smell assaulted Diana before her eyes had adjusted to the gloom, and she grimaced at the combined scents of musky opium smoke and unwashed human bodies.

Then a small light flared as another pipe was lit, and she saw them.

There were a dozen men in the room, all reclining on filthy bunks. Some sucked languidly on long pipes; other simply lolled, motionless, eyes half-open. All were thin and wasted-looking; none were older than early middle-age.

Ah Kam seemed to think Diana would find the den scandalous. "See this man?" he said, pointed at an addict who couldn't have been older than thirty, and who gave no sign that he was aware of their presence. "His family very famous merchants. He is supposed to take over business, but he end up here."

Diana turned away, sickened. "I'm sorry, Ah Kam, but this isn't what I wanted to see."

As Diana strode back towards the exit, he followed, genuinely puzzled. "But British gentlemen and ladies always like to see opium dens—"

"No doubt they do…but this one doesn't."

It was sundown when Ah Kam finally led them back down Factory Street to the Shameen bridge. He stepped down from his sedan chair, his coolies puffing as he did so, and he bowed deeply to Diana. She paid him with a liberal tip (which produced another bow), and then without a word she returned through the gate to the Hinton house.

She was surprised to find that Antonia had not arrived yet. She dined alone (on an excellent meal of crab, with local mangoes for dessert), and by the time she retired there was still no sign of her host. Diana wondered what business could have kept her friend out overnight. She only hoped her suspicion, that something bad might have happened, was wrong.

It wasn't, as she discovered the next day, when Antonia could barely choke out words through a throat constrained with terror.

Chapter XIV

May 25, 1880
Canton, China

It was the morning of her third day in China when Diana, who was relaxing with an excellent cup of a local "gunpowder" tea and reading a book on Chinese history, looked up from her chair in the sitting room to find Antonia in the doorway, shaking badly and ashen-faced. Diana poured her a cup of tea and waited while Antonia tried to collect herself. Mina helped, seating herself at the young woman's feet and staring up at her with such obvious feline concern that Antonia finally exhaled hugely and stopped trembling.

"I did a foolish thing, Diana," she admitted, gazing down into her teacup as if searching the unfurled leaves for omens. "I went to the docks yesterday."

"The docks at Ho-Nam?"

Antonia nodded, and Diana knew then that something terrible had come through the Canton gateway.

"Oh, Antonia, why didn't you tell me? I should have been with you."

Antonia ran a hand through her disheveled hair. "I thought...it was foolish, as I said...but I just felt as if this was company business, and it was my duty to investigate the situation before allowing you into it."

Diana felt a surge of affection for her, and reached across the small table between them to take her hand.

Antonia returned the gesture, as if hanging on to Diana for her life. "Truthfully, Diana...I didn't believe the stories. I thought they were surely naught but the imaginings of superstitious men, some oriental fantasy...."

"You learned it was no fantasy, I take it," Diana said.

"No fantasy," Antonia concurred. Mina leapt into her lap just then, and Antonia seemed to dissolve into blankness, absent-mindedly stroking the cat.

After a minute of silence, Diana gently prodded: "Antonia, can you tell me what happened? It's important I know."

It took the entire night and well into the following day for Antonia to gasp out her story, between choked reactions and shudders. Diana stayed with her the entire time, even when Antonia finally slept, moaning softly. She was able to finish the story in the morning light, but even then she half-whispered parts of it, looking away. Diana almost thought she could see Antonia physically *age* during that night, and she regretted forcing her friend to relive the horrors she'd endured—

Antonia had gone back to the *Althea* just after their breakfast the morning before, and gathered a small troop of the strongest crewmen. She'd also taken a pocketful of cash, which would be useful should she need to bribe her way out of a predicament, and a pistol, which she had some skill with.

Accompanied by her six crewmen, Antonia set out for the Hinton godown on Ho-Nam, a short distance from where the *Althea* was moored. Her plan had been to search the warehouse thoroughly, and then occupy it for an entire day and a night, proving to the Chinese workers that their fears were baseless.

An inspection of the warehouse revealed nothing but tarpaulin-covered crates, rusting pulleys and hooks, and a few side storerooms; the empty warehouse was like those to be found anywhere in the world, except that the writing on the crates was mostly in Chinese. The day passed quietly, the men patrolling or conversing while Antonia perused some ledgers she'd found, which turned out to be thoroughly unremarkable. At dusk they lit several lamps and seated themselves in the center of the large building, the crewmen squatting on crates and lighting pipes.

Sometime after midnight they heard the first sound—a rhythmic thumping or pounding coming from one of the storerooms. Antonia ordered two of the men to wait, while she went with the other four to investigate. They easily located the sound, coming from a storeroom. The sailors formed themselves around the door leading in, and she stood off several feet, raising the pistol. The door was opened, and at first there was nothing, only darkness. The pounding noise stopped, and one of the men was just raising a lantern to look within when something lurched out. They all leapt back in surprise, and one man thrust forward with a long knife.

Only then had Antonia clearly seen the thing: It was one of the missing Hinton ship captains. He still wore the company uniform, but tattered and stained; even his hat was in place.

But there was no hint of humanity whatsoever in that face; it was pale and withered, the eyes were shrunken, fallen in, and the lids had wrinkled shut around them. And yet even apparently sightless, the thing (for it was surely not human) had sought them, hands extended, clawing as they leapt back in shock. The man with the knife withdrew his weapon, plainly expecting his foe to fall—and instead the thing fell on *him*. The hands, with nails that seemed impossibly long, clutched at his throat and drove him back against a crate. The poor man grappled in vain, but his strong, heavy fingers were unable to pry off his assailant's deadly grip.

Antonia had fired her pistol then, and a large section of the captain's uniform blew away, but the thing was otherwise unfazed. It completed its horrible task of killing the man it held with a clean wrench of his neck, then it turned its hideous visage on Antonia and hopped towards her—not walked or ran, but rather *hopped*.

One hop—two hops—and the nightmarish creature was nearly upon her when one of the crewmen intervened, swinging a long knife up and bringing it down, so that he cleaved one of its arms off. It turned towards him and he backed away, beckoning it. The man had clearly gone mad.

Antonia had sensed movement behind her and turned to see another of the creatures. He still wore the elegant, embroidered silk robes he had favored, and the western-style patent leather boots. But, like the other monster that was once a ship's captain, this thing was also long dead, desiccated and wan, and hopping in that preposterous but terrible fashion. It accomplished a leap which took it ten feet forward and into the knot of the men; it slit one's throat with its talon-like nails and turned to another man who was screaming; screaming in a way that a man—especially an armed and trained man—should never be able to.

The horrors had continued, as Antonia sensed something else there, something in the dark, atop a pile of crates set against a far wall. In the shadows, she saw eyes that gleamed red like hellfire coals, and as this ultimate monstrosity had swooped down to fix on a newly-slit throat, she'd fled. Preoccupied with their feast, the monsters had allowed Antonia to escape.

She made it alive to the streets and ran blindly in the direction of the *Althea*. It was late, and the streets were empty. She passed only three astonished British guards, one of whom accompanied her back to the ship. It was only then that she realized—she was the only one to return from the docks. All six of the crewmen were undoubtedly dead—or worse.

Antonia knew she would spend the rest of her life not only reliving that horror, but believing that she had been at least partly responsible for the deaths of six dedicated men—

Antonia slept again after breakfast, and Diana spent the next few hours in thought. William's journal had recounted the attack by a group of vampires, and yet all the folklore of past vampires described them as single predators, creatures that moved alone under the shadow of night. Now they were converging in packs? Like the alliance of the Thuggees with Kali, hunting packs of vampires presented a terrible new challenge in regards to the gateways—and it wasn't something Diana wanted to face.

At least she now knew the precise location of the Canton gateway.

In the afternoon, Antonia seemed more composed and Diana asked her the question that had been troubling her for hours. "Antonia, did you take Yi-kin—Thomas—with you to the godown?"

Antonia shook her head. "No. He was on leave, visiting friends in the city."

"Thank heavens."

Antonia suddenly understood why Diana had asked about her Chinese friend. "Diana, you mustn't go there—!"

"I know you feel that way right now, Antonia, but it's why I came—"

Antonia cut her off again, urgently. "Why you came doesn't matter. Just promise me you won't go there, Diana—please!"

Diana looked into her friend's eyes for a moment, then finally said, "I'm sorry, Antonia, I can't promise that. I have to go. And I can destroy these things. Isn't that what we all want?"

Antonia stared at her in disbelief. "You can't kill these things, Diana. I saw them murder six strong men—they tore them apart as if they were paper dolls! I know your life isn't ordinary, that you have seen things the rest of us don't even know exist...but you can't stop these things. You can't."

Diana opened her mouth to answer—and found she couldn't.

Chapter XV

Had Diana needed any confirmation of Antonia's story, she received it later that day, when the body of the one of the vanished sailors was found floating in the river near the docks. He was hauled aboard a Chinese fishing junk, identified by his western garb, and turned over to the British authorities. The Hinton Company was notified shortly thereafter.

Diana had arranged for a local practitioner of western medicine to give Antonia something to calm her nerves, and when she awakened the following morning she seemed much improved. She was pale and drawn, but anxious to proceed with Hinton Company business.

Together they went to the offices of the British consul, where they viewed the body. Diana experienced a small thrill of recognition upon seeing that the man had plainly been drained of all blood. His skin was so white it nearly shone, and seemed to have lost some of its elasticity. While Antonia went over paperwork with the officials, Diana examined the dead man's neck, then wrists, hoping to find the signs of the traditional vampire, but the corpse was curiously free of any puncture or bite wounds. The Chinese fisherman who had brought the body was still present, and murmured the same phrase (*kap-huet goong-see*) which Yi-kin had told Diana translated to something like "blood-breathing corpse."

She was quiet after they left the consul, mulling over the meaning of the bite-less body. Was this a trait peculiar to the Chinese vampire, or was this a completely different form of revenant altogether? And if it was not a traditional vampire, would she know how to fight it? Would a crucifix or holy water affect a creature that had probably never even heard of Christianity?

It was mid-day when they returned to the Hinton Company offices, and Diana was about to bid her friend farewell (she was anxious to return to her room and go over *The Book of Gateways, Conjurations and Banishments* for any hints on dealing with this new menace), when a clerk entered the office and announced that a Chinese priest of some sort had requested a word. Curious, Diana asked if she might stay for this audience, and Antonia assured her that she would very much like her present.

The clerk returned shortly with a most curious personage: The man admitted into the office was Chinese, middle-aged, wearing a somewhat garish yellow robe emblazoned with exotic signs and symbols, and a tall black hat likewise ornamented. He bowed to the two women, and began to speak in Cantonese. Antonia motioned for him to pause, then called for an interpreter. A few moments later Yi-kin entered, and gaped briefly at the sight of the yellow-robed man before bowing to him and exchanging a few words.

They soon found they were in the presence of one "Master Li," a highly-skilled practitioner (actually Yi-kin used the word *sage*) of the local religion known as Taoism; he claimed to come from "the mountains," and had been sent for by the terrified Cantonese. Master Li assured them he was skilled at dealing with monsters, including that known locally as the *kap-huet goong-si*. He stated that only a Taoist master such as himself could seize this kind of monster, and return it safely to Hell.

Antonia listened politely, but then cautioned him, "There's more than one monster at work here."

Yi-kin translated, listened to the Taoist's reply, and then told them, "He say that what you see is only the *goong-si* servants. The *kap-huet goong-si* turns people into *goong-si*—"

"Those were the hopping predators I saw?" asked Antonia.

Yi-kin puzzled over her words for a moment, then turned to Diana helplessly. "Hopping," Diana said, then explained by hopping two fingers across Antonia's desk.

Yi-kin brightened. "Yes, hopping! That is *goong-si*."

The sage said something else, and after a moment Yi-kin relayed the message: "Master Li say *these* are easy to control. He say he can stop them and bury them with proper…uh…*feng shui*."

"What is *feng shui*, Thomas?" Antonia asked.

"Meaning is…very hard…like…correct way to place things…."

Yi-kin finally shrugged and threw up his hands helplessly.

Master Li added something else, then waited impassively. Yi-kin's jaw dropped at whatever had just been said, then he turned back to Antonia. "He say he want five hundred pounds to clean out *goong-si*."

Antonia burst out laughing.

"Are you sure you translated that correctly, Thomas? Because otherwise the man is surely mad. Five hundred pounds is a small fortune!"

Yi-kin reddened, and addressed a question to the Taoist. To Diana, it sounded something like, "*Nei jaan yiu pounds ng baak ma?*"

The Taoist merely nodded, impassive as ever.

Antonia smirked. "I'm sorry, but I know when I'm being hoodwinked. Please show him out, Thomas."

Diana started to object, but Master Li had clearly understood both Antonia's tone and expression; he bowed and turned to go.

"Wait, please," Diana blurted out, before turning to Antonia. "He might be useful to us—"

"Please, Diana. He is clearly a charlatan. Have you ever heard of a genuinely religious man demanding such a sum?"

Diana knew she had, but didn't bother to tell that to her friend.

Yi-kin was looking guilt-stricken, and fortunately Antonia noticed. "Thomas, no need to translate any of that. Just show him out, please."

Yi-kin bowed and gestured towards the door, but the movement was unnecessary, since Master Li was already halfway out the door.

Diana considered for a moment, then jogged out after him. She caught up to him in the hallway outside, and threw out a Cantonese plea, hoping she didn't mangle the words too badly. "*M'goi, cheng dang.*"

Master Li turned to her with one eyebrow raised in amusement. She'd made *some* kind of point, at least.

Diana turned urgently to Yi-kin. "Please, tell Master Li that I'll gladly pay him the sum he asks."

Yi-kin's eyes widened, then he recovered and relayed the information. Master Li uttered a few words, offered a bow to Diana, and then turned and walked away.

"Yi-kin," Diana said, disappointed, "what happened? Why did he walk out?"

"He say good. He say at two p.m. today go to dock."

"Oh!"

Diana returned to Antonia's office, who seemed to have already forgotten the matter, as she was now poring over a sheaf of documents. "Well?" she asked without looking up.

"I've hired Master Li instead."

"It's your money, I suppose, but I think you've just spent it foolishly. After all, you said you've slain vampires, so even if he was genuine, what could he do that you couldn't?"

Save my life, thought Diana.

A few moments later, she found Yi-kin in conversation with several other Chinese workers in a storage room behind Antonia's office. As soon as he spotted her, Yi-kin excused himself from the other men and joined her.

"Yi-kin, I need to talk to you very seriously."

They moved off to a quiet corner, standing near a dusty window that let in some of the hazy midmorning sunshine. "You know why I made this trip," Diana said to the young man.

He nodded. "To fight *goong-si*."

"Yes," Diana said. "And I intend to be at those docks today with Master Li to do just that."

"I go, too," Yi-kin said.

"There's something you may not know, though, Yi-kin. Miss Hinton went to the docks with six crewmen—"

"—and they all die there. I do know," Yi-kin finished.

Antonia gaped for a moment, "How?"

"Everybody here know that. Sailors leave with Miss Hinton; they do not come back. They find one dead in water."

"Yes."

"Miss Hinton see *goong-si*?"

"Yes," Diana said, then hesitated before adding, "There's more than one."

He nodded soberly.

"Yi-kin," Diana said, "do you think Master Li was genuine? Could he stop the *goong-si*?"

Yi-kin looked away, then answered softly, "Maybe. Taoists are very strange. They know many strange thing."

Diana realized she knew too little about the religions of China, and virtually nothing about Taoism. "Do you know much about what they believe?"

"I know little. They believe in many, many gods. They believe in eight immortals. Taoists believe Heaven and Hell have generals and they sometimes pray to them. They believe they can live always."

"Yes, immortality," Diana nodded. "I think all religions believe in that—"

"But Taoists are different. They believe *body* can live always, not just...."

"Spirit," Diana filled in.

"Yes," Yi-kin affirmed.

Physical immortality, Diana thought. *You'd think that would be easy to prove, wouldn't you? Perhaps the man is just a charlatan, after all.*

"Well, I haven't paid him yet. If he is lying and can't stop them—" Diana broke off, realizing the next part of the sentence would have run, *then I probably won't be alive to pay him.*

"You should not go to dock," Yi-kin said, having evidently surmised her thought.

"I have to. I have to close the gateway, for one thing."

And I need to see Master Li slay the goong-si *with my own eyes, especially if I'm paying him,* she thought. Instead she said:

"But you do not need to accompany me, Yi-kin. This will be far more dangerous than what we faced in Calcutta."

"Badder than Thuggees and Kali?"

"Not 'badder,' Yi-kin; in English we say 'worse.' And...well...I didn't know we'd be facing Kali and the Thuggees, or I would never have had you join me."

Yi-kin considered that for a moment, "Worse. I remember that."

"Yi-kin," Diana said with more anger than she wanted just then, "do you understand what I'm saying to you?"

"Use worse, not badder. Also, at docks we maybe die and become *goong-si* ourselves."

Diana blinked for a moment, then stammered, "Very well, you do understand. I suppose I don't need to give you the speech then, about how you really shouldn't come...?"

"Like we say in Cantonese, Miss Diana—*m sai.*"

"Not necessary," Diana translated.

"Correct."

Diana had already told Antonia of what she planned to do, and so they took only enough time for Yi-kin to jot a quick letter before leaving the Hinton Company. Yi-kin told Diana the letter was for his sister, Leung Mei-yi, who lived in Shanghai and who had spirited him away after their parents had been murdered. The letter was to be mailed to her in the event of his death. Yi-kin also changed out of his uniform into local clothing, reasoning that it would be easier for them to move through Canton if he didn't look like a British sailor.

Diana seized on Yi-kin's cast-off uniform, and left her young friend quite proud when she reappeared in it a few moments later. With her hair tucked up and the cap pulled down low over her face, she thought she could pass for a man, and hoped the uniform would both disguise her gender more successfully and ease any fighting that she might be forced to engage in. Next, she gathered up supplies: She felt fairly sure that the weapons purported to work against the western vampires—garlic, crucifixes, holy water—would prove useless against the *goong-si*, and she assumed Master Li would have his own arsenal; but she hoped that other traditional demon-fighting tools—sprigs of rowan and ash, rosemary, an iron-bladed knife—would work. She also packed the copy of *The Book* and, of course, Mina, who seemed to meow her approval as Diana placed her in the traveling bag.

At slightly past noon she met Yi-kin at the Shameen bridge, and they proceeded towards the river. Canton was famous for its temples (it contained over eight hundred in its mere six-mile circumference), and their route took them past one in particular that gave Yi-kin pause. Like most everything else in Canton, the temple—which had once been glorious and ornate, with its curving roof and heavy blocks of stone and gilt trim—now seemed somewhat rundown.

"What is it?" Diana asked.

"Temple of Five Genii. These were five men who start Canton. They ride here on rams, and say they will always protect us. I want to go in."

"Then do, please," Diana told him, thinking it probably wasn't a bad idea.

They passed through an outer courtyard, filled with lovely blossoming jasmine and cherry trees, and the sweet aroma of petals and incense wafted around them. Diana was suddenly glad they'd made this detour; she felt her spirits both soothed and emboldened by the lovely scents.

They walked up a short run of wide steps and in through the temple entrance. Immediately ahead were five colossal statues, each seated, each with an upraised right hand offering benediction. The temple was quiet at the moment, although there were a few other supplicants bowed near the altar before the statues, and Diana caught a glimpse of a priest off in the shadows to the side.

She waited near the entrance, and watched as Yi-kin stepped forward, took three joss sticks from a large container, lit them and then bowed three times to the five figures. After a moment of silent prayer he placed the smoking sticks in a large sand-filled pot, bowed again and then reached for a long bamboo cylinder in front of him. He shook the cylinder vigorously, then tilted it downward, and Diana saw that it contained long, thin strips of wood. Yi-kin grasped the one that had slid out the farthest, then returned the cylinder to its place.

He took the strip of wood to a man seated near the entrance. The man examined the strip for quite some time, then turned to Yi-kin and spoke to him in low tones. Yi-kin listened, then dropped some coins in a plate near the man and rejoined Diana and Mina.

"What was that you just did?" Diana asked, as they walked from the temple.

"First I pray to Five Genii for protection, then I use sticks to tell fortune."

Diana had already discovered that the Chinese had a penchant for fortune-telling. It was a significant part of their religions, of their festivals, and even of their languages; with their many different tones and inflections—Cantonese was rich with homonyms and provided the basis for considerable belief in numerology. Back on the *Althea*, Yi-kin, for example, had told Diana that his people believed the number four to be bad luck because the word, *sei,* was a homonym for the word for death.

Although Diana personally found the notion of fortune-telling quite absurd, she supposed it was still easier to believe in than the existence of *goong-si.*

"And what did your fortune reveal?" she asked.

"*Ha ha.*"

Diana glanced over at Yi-kin, uncertain whether he were joking or saying something in Cantonese. "What is *ha ha?*"

"Very bad luck. We probably die."

Not very funny at all, Diana thought.

They were almost to the docks and about to hire a sampan to cross the river to Ho-Nam when they heard the sounds of commotion behind them—shouts, trampling feet—and suddenly Yi-kin tugged her urgently into a small shop.

"Yi-kin, what—?" she barely got out before Yi-kin held a finger to his lips, and guided her to the back of the lacquerware store.

Looking anxious, he took her as far to the rear of the shop as he could, and feigned interest in a low chest of drawers. The merchant approached, smiling, and bowed. "Welcome!" he offered.

"Do not move," Yi-kin whispered in Diana's ear, then moved to place himself between her and the entrance to the shop.

"Yi-kin, what—"

"White Lotus Sect."

Diana remembered something she'd read once, an article buried on the back page of a London newspaper: The White Lotus Sect was a secret society—a triad—that was vehemently opposed to foreign intervention in China. So vehemently opposed, in fact, that they had supposedly murdered a number of British missionaries in rural parts of China, and had recently stirred up trouble with demonstrations in several major Chinese cities.

Including Canton.

Diana risked a look past him and out into the street, where she saw a large parade of people passing. Many were dressed as coolies, some as farmers, but they all wore red bandannas, red sashes, and, about their necks, lengths of red cloth inscribed with characters. They were handing out small booklets to onlookers, who were handing them coins in exchange, and they chanted a slogan over and over.

"What are they doing?" Diana whispered to Yi-kin.

"They sell anti-European literature. Anyone not pay them get beaten."

Nice chaps, thought Diana.

"They say 'force out all foreigners'," Yi-kin added.

"Oh dear," Diana said, and attempted to make herself as small as possible.

Then several members of the group entered the shop.

Yi-kin saw them, and immediately began calling out, "*Ni jeung toi gei chin a?*"

The merchant, startled, turned to Yi-kin, but he was plainly also keeping one eye on the White Lotus Sect men—and on Diana.

Yi-kin spoke in an abnormally loud voice, and Diana realized he was trying to let the White Lotus Sect know they were natives. "*M goi, ngoh seung maai ni jeung toi.*"

Diana dropped to the floor, pretending to examine the legs of a dresser.

Yi-kin leaned down over her and whispered urgently, "Do you have money?"

She nodded, dug briefly into a pocket, and produced a handful of local *taels*.

Yi-kin took them and shoved them at the merchant, whose attention was instantly diverted from the triad members.

"Ahhh, *do jeh!*" the merchant responded, bowing.

At the front of the shop, another customer was buying some of the booklets. As the Sect completed the transaction and were turning to look back towards them, Diana hugged her satchel to her tightly, praying Mina would stay quiet while her heart beat a tarantella.

After what seemed an eternity, she heard two loud thumps on the table above her. *This is it,* she thought. *Not a very heroic way to end.*

And then Yi-kin's smiling face appeared beneath the table as well, and he said to her, "You just buy this table."

Diana straightened up, and saw instantly that the Sect had left the shop and moved on down the street. The merchant stood nearby, making notes on a paper.

"I ask him to deliver table to Hinton house," Yi-kin informed her.

Diana felt a rush of relief that left her weakened, and she actually had to grasp her new table to remain steady. She glanced down, and saw that it was a very beautiful thing indeed, and made an instantaneous decision.

"No, I'll give him my address in Derby."

She managed to leave both the merchant and Yi-kin quite astonished, but she thought the table would serve as an attractive reminder of the fact that her most dangerous enemies could still be quite human.

After they completed the shipping instructions and left the shop, they reached the river's edge and hired a sampan, rowed only by a silent, sturdy woman with a baby strapped to her back.

The sampan deposited them on Ho-Nam, and a short walk brought them to the Hinton Company's go-down. It was a dank, foul place, with weathered, dark wood and the smells of fungus and decaying fish. But Diana detected another scent in the air as well: It was the stench of the thing she'd slain in the Furnaval family crypt. It was the smell of death.

Yi-kin was clearly unnerved by the scent, and halted his pace, grimacing.

"Yi-kin," Diana told him, "you don't need to do this."

Yi-kin glanced at her, then held one of his sleeves up over his nose; his voice was muffled when he said, "I will not leave."

"*Doh jeh*," Diana told him, and she was genuinely grateful to have him with her.

"*M sai.*"

They entered the warehouse wherein Antonia had suffered her terrible experiences. It was easily identified, both by her description and by the flags of the British Empire and the Hinton Trading Company flying above its doorways. Even though it was early afternoon, it was gloomy inside the large building, and their eyes took some few seconds to adjust. They made out stacks of crates, some balanced precariously, and a few grimy windows set near the ceiling.

"Master Li?" Diana cried out, her voice bouncing off of cargo chests and rotting wooden walls.

There was no answer.

Mina mewled for release, and Diana set her free. The cat walked scarcely a few feet, then set up her characteristic hissing at the air.

"Cat find gateway?"

Diana nodded.

There was no immediate sign of either the Taoist or *goong-si,* and so Diana decided to seal the gateway immediately. She was just preparing for the ritual when she heard Yi-kin gasp, and then cry out, "*Siu Je....*" She joined him.

He'd found streaks of blood and one of the sailors' knives on the floor. The blood had also spattered nearby crates and the splintering walls, and left its own acrid, coppery tang hanging in the air.

"We have to close that gateway *now*," Diana told him.

She strode back to where Mina was hissing, and felt some of the distinctive unease she knew the cat must experience; the small hairs on the back of her neck rose, the very air around them charged with dark energy. She wasted no time in sealing this gate, and had accomplished the act less than one minute later.

Even though the sense of surrounding menace ebbed for Diana, Mina didn't curl happily around her mistress's ankles as usual;. Instead she ran to the closed doorway leading into a side room, and began to scratch at the wood.

As Diana bound her new cut, she pondered the cat's actions. Nothing would be able to come through the gateway, but she thought that the creatures Antonia encountered were certainly still present, and nearby. And she had mentioned that the monsters had come from within one side room in particular. Diana knew she should wait for the arrival of Master Li, but curiosity got the best of her (a trait she shared with Mina).

Although she'd already considered that the usual vampire protections might be useless here, she nevertheless gave a strand of garlic cloves to Yi-kin, and instructed him to place them around his neck; a second string of cloves went around her own throat. She prepared and passed to Yi-kin a lantern, guessing the smaller storeroom might be windowless and dark; then, still holding the iron knife, she cautiously opened the door.

Mina immediately disappeared into the room, but Diana and Yi-kin were staggered by a redoubling of that nauseating scent of death; Diana knew with certainty that there were dead things present somewhere in the warehouse.

The room was small, and as Yi-kin raised the lantern they spied only more crates of varying sizes. Moving carefully, they peered around the stacks of boxes, but found nothing. In one corner stood a large shrouded object; as Diana tensed, Yi-kin pulled the tarpaulin aside, but nothing more than a heap of rice bags was revealed underneath. Some of the canvas bags had split open and Diana saw squirming maggots mixed in with the white grains.

They were about to examine the roof overhead when they heard the sound of Mina's tiny claws on wood. Diana turned, and saw that the cat had indeed led them to what they sought: About ten feet in a straight line from the doorway was a handhold carved into the wood of a trap door laid into the floor.

"*Maau ho lek,*" Yi-kin noted, complimenting Mina's talents.

Diana still had to smile at the Cantonese word for cat (*maau*), then she motioned Yi-kin over with the lantern. Now she could plainly make out a trapdoor large enough for a man—or something that had once been a man—to pass through. She knelt down and grasped the handhold to give it a slight tug. The trapdoor gave an inch; it wasn't bolted from the other side.

She hesitated long enough to exchange a look with Yi-kin, who nodded back to her, tensing himself. Holding the knife ready she wrenched the trapdoor open.

If the noxious odors had been bad before, now they were intolerable, striking Yi-kin and Diana with an almost physical force. He struggled briefly, then turned aside to retch. Even the cat backed away from that loathsome smell.

Diana forced her own gorge down, waiting, every nerve tingling…nothing but the vile odor came up at them. As Yi-kin struggled to recover, Diana gently took the lantern from him and tentatively bent forward over that hole in the floor, trying to peer down.

At first she saw nothing but a ladder descending; Diana figured this space was part of the warehouse's system of handling contraband, although now it had been put to a more malevolent use. The lantern's yellow glow seemed to barely penetrate the miasma of rot, and Diana could make out nothing but blackness a few feet down. She glanced around and spotted a rusted pulley close by on the floor, she picked up the heavy device and tossed it into the hole. It fell about twenty feet, but Diana couldn't tell what it landed on—the noise had been muffled, without the splashing sound of water. She considered the dangers a moment further, then made her decision to lower herself into the hole.

"No, *Siu Je*, no!" Yi-kin cried out, when he saw that she intended to climb down the rickety algae-covered ladder into that darkness. "Wait for Master Li!"

Diana glanced at the pocket watch she always carried. "It's well after two. He's not coming."

Yi-kin wouldn't give up. "Then we leave. Gateway is closed—"

"But the *goong-si* are still here," she cut him off. "If we can stop them as well, we must do it."

"And if you cannot stop *goong-si*, we die and become *like them*," he whispered to her.

She did hesitate, considering Yi-kin's words. She could rationalize that the *vampires* would spread if she didn't stop them, that she was striking a blow against the forces of darkness, but, there was another, more delirious truth as well: She *wanted* to see them. She'd traveled around the globe to confront them, and she wouldn't be stopped now.

"That won't happen," she told Yi-kin, then started down.

He moved to follow her, and Diana stopped halfway down the ladder. "Yi-kin, I want you to stay up there."

"But—"

She cut him off. "Stay up there, and if anything happens to me, I want you to run. *Ming baak?*"

Reluctantly, he moved back away from the ladder. "I stay."

She knew he was lying, and that there was every chance she might get them both killed.

She secured the knife under the belt of her Hinton uniform, then reached up and took the lantern Yi-kin held down to her. She lowered herself down about fifteen feet before her feet touched the sodden bare ground, not unlike the marshy soil she'd stood in during last October's efforts at the Hertfordshire cemetery. She made sure her footing was solid, then she moved the lantern around—

—and her heart nearly stopped at what she saw.

Around her lay at least a dozen bodies. She saw the *Althea* crewmen; she saw two men she didn't know, both dressed as officers; she saw local workers in tattered Chinese clothing. That they were all clearly dead, there could be no question; for one thing, no living man could repose on this fetid swamp. When she looked closer, she saw that some of these men had clearly suffered grievous wounds, wounds now long since dried and caked over. The skin of the cadavers was ashen and shriveled, and there was even one figure partly covered with the same awful moss that grew on the slick stone sides of the room.

Diana was looking up to tell Yi-kin her discovery when some movement caught her eye. Above her, Mina let out a sharp hiss, and Diana held the lantern higher, but saw nothing. Then she heard the obvious scraping noise of movement behind her, and she turned just in time to see one of the abominations rise to its feet. Impossibly, it rose puppet-like, never bending its knees or hips. It was one of the sailors, a particularly fearsome-looking brute in life whose long beard was now matted with clots of gore.

Then its arms swiveled upward and it leapt towards her, its limbs too frozen by rigor to allow for any other motion. For a moment Diana could only gape, paralyzed; then she tore the garlic from around her neck and thrust it out at the thing.

"Diana *Siu Je*—!" Yi-kin cried out.

The *goong-si* took another of those terrible leaps towards Diana, and its claw-like fingers connected with the garlic, ripping the strand out of her grasp and flinging it aside.

She backed away, but not quickly enough, as it lunged towards her again. Before she could react, its icy cold hands were clutching her throat, with a grip like steel bands. Diana struggled to cry out, to tear at the thing's arms, to jab with the knife, to do anything, but all she could manage was a choked gasp as her vision began to darken.

I'm so sorry, William, she thought.

And then the pressure was gone and she fell to her knees, her strength taken but not her life. She looked up to see someone between her and the *goong-si*—a man in yellow Chinese dress. Her brain still reeling from the attack, it took her a moment to place the distinctive canary colored robes:

Master Li, the Taoist monk. He really had come.

Li turned calmly away from the revenant to Diana, and she looked up to see that the monster stood completely frozen. Blinking with surprise, she saw not a stake nor crucifix nor garlic, but a strip of yellow paper inscribed with Chinese pictograph characters affixed to the creature's forehead. The thing was completely motionless, its hands still stiffly extended; hands that had held her in their deathgrip until this monk had intervened.

Li quickly gestured to the ladder, and Diana, still weak, tried to climb; she was grateful when Yi-kin pulled her up. Once she was safely out of the hole, she collapsed onto a nearby crate. She expected to see Master Li follow her up, but he didn't. For several minutes she and Yi-kin waited breathlessly, half expecting one of the monsters to come vaulting up out of the trapdoor; they heard nothing at all from below, neither screams nor moans nor sounds of fighting.

But Master Li did reappear, climbing slowly up the ladder and appearing completely unfazed.

As he stepped out onto the floor, the Taoist spoke rapidly in Chinese, which Yi-kin translated. He told them he had secured all the corpses by placing a sacred *sutra* on them, and that the bodies of those innocents could now be safely transported to their final resting places.

"Tell him about the gateway," Diana requested.

He uttered a lengthy speech, occasionally gesturing at Diana's bandaged arm or the cat, who now curled herself happily at Diana's feet. At the conclusion of the speech, Master Li turned to Diana and bowed with a curious gesture, with both hands held out before him, the left hand cupped over the right fist.

Yi-kin smiled and told her, "Master Li offer you sign of great respect."

Diana stood and attempted to repeat the bow, offering it to the monk. From the look of pride she saw on Yi-kin's face, she assumed she had done the right thing.

The Taoist and Yi-kin exchanged a few quick words, then Master Li swept hurriedly from the room. Yi-kin turned to Diana and explained, "Master Li invite us to return tonight to watch *him* fight *kap-huet goong-si.*"

"But I thought...." Diana trailed off, perplexed.

"He stop only these, they are like…what is English word for...." Yi-kin suddenly moved in a jerky fashion, his arms held at strange angles.

"Puppets," Diana supplied.

"Yes, *goong-si* like puppet. Now he must kill one who *make* puppet."

They left the warehouse and hurried to the English Consul, where arrangements were made for Diana to cash a large check. It took some time (and the bureaucrats at the consul gave her sideways looks and wrinkled their noses at the scent of death on her), but eventually she left the Consulate with an envelope full of hundred-pound notes. After that, Diana asked Yi-kin to wait at a tea shop while she changed out of his uniform, and deposited Mina. She returned in a tidy suit, and they relaxed beneath cages of singing birds while around them merchants conducted business over tea and *dim sum*. As they consumed buns stuffed with tangy pork (which Yi-kin called *chau siu bau*), Diana asked him if he understood what Master Li had done.

"Taoist have strange magic. I do not understand."

Four hours later they returned to the warehouse and were surprised to see what Diana could only think of as an altar, now erected in the middle of the space. Long tables were arranged on an elevated platform, and they were draped with vivid red cloth. Incense was burning, only slightly masking the odor of decomposition with a musky aroma; there were bowls, strips of paper, calligraphy brushes, idols, and, strangest of all, a live chicken tied by its feet and squawking noisily (which caused Mina to strain against Diana's hands and mew hungrily). Standing over a table nearby, Master Li muttered a chant while making exotic gestures with his fingers.

As Diana watched, intrigued, Yi-kin listened closely to the chant, then leaned to her ear and whispered, "Master Li call on generals of Heaven to seize *kap-huet goong-si.*"

Li, while still chanting, lifted the poor fowl, picked up a blade and quickly slit the bird's throat, making certain its lifeblood drained into the bowl. He flung the twitching corpse of the chicken aside, added some sort of powder to the bowl, and mixed it swiftly with one of the brushes, which he then used to inscribe yellow paper talismans similar to the one that Diana had seen him use earlier to save her.

Diana could not help mulling over the ramifications of what she was watching. Although she'd never strictly been a Christian, she was still a modern European, and at first she thought this bizarre ritual rather primitive. Animal sacrifice had been extinct in western religions for hundreds of years, and surely if she found belief in one god impossible then how was she to accept an entire pantheon? And yet the Taoist's magic had prevailed where her own attempts failed, so who was really the primitive here? Was she learning that each culture had its own good and evil, and that the western crucifix was no stronger than the eastern *sutra*? Was she witnessing a universal force for good that operated through the symbols of different beliefs?

Diana's thoughts finally circled back to the one constant she accepted wholeheartedly: Evil existed everywhere on the globe, and everywhere was a murderous, destructive force that must be stopped…by whatever means necessary—and her methods might need to be different each time.

Her concentration was interrupted by a shocking clap of thunder. Next to her, Yi-kin grinned.

"I think Thunder General come," he whispered to her.

A mighty gust of wind suddenly blew the warehouse doors wide open and there, framed by an intensifying night storm, stood the vampire. The *kap-huet goong-si.*

The creature was the size and shape of a man, dressed in tattered robes that indicated a Chinese who had once owned considerable wealth, perhaps a warlord or land baron. What had once been a human face was now little more than patches of yellowing bone showing through strips of browned flesh; the most arresting feature of the thing was the eyes, glowing red with tangible malevolence.

Diana shivered, not from the storm but from the presence of an evil so old and all-consuming that no heat could exist in its presence. The thing began to glide forward, not walk, not hop like its ghoulish minions, but simply glide along the floor towards them. Master Li had assured them they'd be safe, but she felt less certain of that now.

Master Li, however, gracefully hefted a long, ornately-carved sword and advanced, still chanting, and moving in a very curious way. At first Diana wondered if the man was drunk, but then she watched his feet carefully, saw the look of concentration on his face, and realized that he was dancing, moving around the vampire in a very specific pattern, and thrusting his sword at it while not actually making contact with it.

"Do you know what he's doing?"

"He say he 'dance stars'."

Diana continued to watch Master Li's feet (while Master Li reiterated his chant)—seven steps repeated over and over, first one direction then the other, four steps in a square, three steps in a broken line…and she understood.

"'*Dance stars*"…Li was outlining the shape of the constellation known as Ursa Major—the Big Dipper.

The vampire stopped before Master Li and opened its skull-like jaws, as if trying to inhale. Master Li stumbled, and it swiftly became apparent that he was involved in a titanic struggle with the monster; his chanting became louder, more forceful, his thrusts at the monster more violent. The very air between them began to fill with a reddish mist, which Diana realized with astonishment was actually emerging from Master Li; the vampire was sucking his blood simply by inhaling, pulling it out through the man's very pores. Now she knew why she'd seen no bite marks on the victim she'd examined.

This abomination is so powerful it need not even touch its victims. She shuddered.

Master Li redoubled his efforts, screaming his chant and slashing with the sword, and the vampire was the one falling back now. The monk reached behind himself with the swordtip and neatly stabbed the talisman he had created earlier, then turned to the vampire; the monster's jaws snapped closed as the air between them cleared of that horrible moisture. With a final invocation Master Li thrust both sword and talisman at the vampire's chest, pinning it before it could react. Outside there was a clap of thunder like a hundred cannon-shot, and suddenly the fiend was simply gone. No finally hellish screech, no fountain of stolen blood; it had just winked out of existence.

Outside the storm faded, rolling off into the eastern night. Master Li looked pale and spent. After a moment to regain his breath, the monk turned to Yi-kin and spoke a few words in a soft, weakened voice.

"He say heavenly general have seize *kap-huet goong-si* and take it to Hell," said Yi-kin. "He say docks are again safe."

Diana reached into her satchel and withdrew the envelope of pound notes, which she offered to Master Li with a bow and the gesture of respect. Master Li accepted the envelope, returned the bow, and gathered the few of his things (brushes, bowls, red cloth). Before he left, however, he turned to Diana a final time and stared directly— unnervingly—at her as he spoke. Yi-kin listened, and was apparently rendered speechless by whatever he'd heard. The Taoist offered a final brief bow to Diana, and then left.

"What did he say, Yi-kin?"

When Yi-kin turned to her, his eyes were haunted. "He say demon on other side of gateway have your husband."

Diana's knees nearly gave way. Fortunately Yi-kin caught her, and after resting on the sturdy young man for a moment she composed herself and led them away from that awful place.

Chapter XVI

May 27, 1880
Canton, China

On the day following the exorcism of the vampire, Diana reported to Antonia that the docks were quite safe again (although someone would need to collect the bodies found beneath the Hinton's go-down, following Master Li's instructions for burial). She didn't elaborate on what had transpired, and to her credit Antonia didn't ask.

The next day Diana found out that British troops outside a small portside Chinese town had just killed several peasants who had protested opium importation. The British had thus far refused to hand over any of the soldiers involved in the incident, and Diana knew they never would.

It was of course news throughout Canton, although Diana was quite sure it would never reach England. Even if it did, it would be dismissed as a simple "disciplinary action," something designed to keep "John Chinaman" in line.

Diana began to hate the British.

Although she'd become very fond of both Yi-kin and Canton, she felt increasingly that she didn't belong there; in fact she felt that *none* of her countrymen belonged there. But she also felt repulsion at the idea of returning on a British ship, via more examples of arrogant imperialism (as in India), and so she made a startling decision:

She would return to England—which was still her home—by way of the Pacific and America.

Besides, there were two gateways in America, and she was impatient to get to them. She desperately wanted more news of William.

If he were truly being held captive by a demon in the netherworld, she wanted to know the name of that demon. She wanted to know how to reach it—and she wanted to know how to kill it.

And she'd always had a curiosity to see the United States.

She informed Antonia that she would not be returning home on a Hinton Company vessel. Antonia reacted coolly, and Diana suspected that the young woman was embarrassed at breaking down in front of Diana after her experience with the *goong-si,* and she was likely stung by the Taoist's triumph after her refusal to meet his price. Diana mentioned that she wanted to go to America, and Antonia said she would arrange passage for her out of Hong Kong on an Occidental and Oriental Company steamship, bound for San Francisco. Antonia seemed somewhat eager to make the travel arrangements, and Diana thought— sadly—that her friend would probably be happier to see her go.

Diana sought out Yi-kin before she left. She found him in an office, looking over a number of documents. He looked up, smiling, and she had a pang at the thought of leaving this young man behind.

"Yi-kin, I just wanted to tell you that I'll be leaving Canton soon."

He stared down at the floor, his voice low. "I am also leaving."

"Yes, you'll be bound back for England, I expect—"

"No," he blurted out, cutting her off. "I am leaving Hinton Company."

"To go where?"

"I do not yet know." Finally he looked up at her, and his handsome young face was creased in pain. "When we are in Calcutta, you ask me about opium. And I say it is legal, so I do not think about it. But now...I do think. You are right, *siu je.* Opium is very bad. I cannot do this work. I will find another job."

And with that Diana had a sudden inspiration. She didn't stop to think about the ramifications, or the difficulties built into the idea; she simply asked:

"Yi-kin, would you like to work for me? I'll pay you more than whatever you've earned here. I promise you'll never have to transport opium."

Yi-kin's face nearly split apart from the resulting grin, and he literally leaped over his desk to bow to her. She waved at him to stop. "Yi-kin, really, that's not necessary—*m sai....*"

He happily pulled off his Hinton Trading Company cap and jacket and hurled them onto the desk. Then he asked just one question:

"When we leave?"

The New World

Chapter XVII

June 20-21, 1880
San Francisco, America

Diana, Yi-kin and Mina arrived in America three weeks later, on the date of the summer solstice.

They'd left Canton on a ship belonging to the Hong Kong and Canton Steam Packet Company, and arrived in Hong Kong that evening. Captain Hughes had been right—although a British colony, compared to Canton, Hong Kong felt primitive and dangerous, and Diana was hardly unhappy to leave it behind. Their Occidental and Oriental steamer was a comfortable vessel that had crossed the Pacific without a hitch in a speedy twenty-two day voyage that was warm and pleasant. Diana enjoyed strolling the deck, and was somewhat alarmed to realize that she was acquiring a brownish tone to her face and arms; although she secretly thought it rather becoming, she also knew it would be frowned on back in London. Englishwomen were simply not supposed to expose themselves to the elements.

Yi-kin and Diana continued their mutual language studies, each becoming more fluent in the other's tongue, and Diana also taught him more about the lore of the gateways and fighting spirits that came through them. Yi-kin asked about the American gateways, and Diana told him there were two. The closest was in the Pacific Northwest, which she reckoned to be not far from a town called Tacoma that she'd located on a map; that gateway supported not only ancient Indian legends of a mythical Thunderbird, but also more recent whisperings of a tall, hairy, lumbering beast much larger than a man. The other gateway in the United States was located in West Virginia, and was the center of a number of tales of a winged, moth-like man.

Their boat docked in San Francisco, and after collecting their baggage and checking themselves through customs, Diana was happy to discover that San Francisco was not unlike her beloved London in many ways. It was summer but there was a hint of chill and fog. Around them the streets were bustling with activity and handbills were posted everywhere for various artistic events, and there was a charming layer of industrial grime laid across everything.

On their voyage over Diana had read that one thing San Francisco possessed, which London did not, was an instant feeling of wealth. The 1870s had been the "silver age" for San Francisco, and the city now supported a large and active wealthy class. They were easy to spot all round them now on the streets, the men with their gold-knobbed canes and silk top hats, the women with their colorful parasols, Watteau half-shoes laced up the front, and silk stockings. A scandalous new accessory, the "garter" (or, as one advertisement Diana had read coyly referred to the leg accessories, "g.rt.rs"), was everywhere in shop windows, some pairs selling for as much as one hundred American dollars.

They hired a cab, and asked for a hotel recommendation. Their driver asked Diana what her price range was, and when she assured him that price was no object he recommended the new Hotel del Monte for her—but said Diana would have to drop *her boy* off elsewhere, since the del Monte was "an upper class place that won't take no Chinee." Diana politely informed the driver that she had no interest in staying at a place that would not accept Yi-kin, no matter how *upper class* it might be otherwise. The driver frowned, but suggested a place called the Powell Arms, and off they went.

There was such a boisterous quality to the city; live music emanated from bars, placards announced stage productions, and newspapers trumpeted arrivals by European and Asian princes, celebrities and scholars. Quaint carriages called cable cars took patrons up and down some of the steep hills, and Diana saw mansions that easily outshown her old estate manor in Derby, what with their parquetry, cloisonné ornaments and tapestries.

The Powell was an acceptable hotel, somewhere in between middle and lower class, but they were reluctantly willing to provide a room for Yi-kin, only so long as Diana paid in advance. She'd hoped to find that she'd left the ridiculous prejudices of the British behind in Canton, but apparently they were just as prevalent in America.

After all, this did begin as another British colony, she reminded herself.

Their rooms at the Powell Arms might have been less than what Diana was used to, but they were clean and tolerably comfortable. After getting settled, they exchanged money, did some shopping for a few supplies, and bought Yi-kin a western-style suit, complete with a new hat called a Homsher, which they were told was popular here in the States. Diana thought her assistant looked quite charming in the suit, but she had to tip the tailor extravagantly before he would serve "John"—as he insisted on referring to Yi-kin (and apparently all other Chinese men).

They learned the city had a thriving Chinese area, and after a delightful search Diana was happy to enjoy a Cantonese dinner with Yi-kin in a restaurant where neither of them was treated to mutterings or sideways glances. The restaurant, with its beautifully-carved teak tables inlaid with mother-of-pearl, and superb wait-service, almost made up for the bare-amenities of their hotel rooms.

After a restful night, they spent the following day making travel arrangements; Diana was intent on sealing both of the American gateways. Unfortunately reaching the Washington state area would be somewhat difficult, involving a combination of ship, rail, and carriage. After attending to that gateway, they would need to return to San Francisco by similar fashion, then venture east by rail. Diana had read exciting accounts of rail travel in the United States aboard the fairly new Southern Pacific and Central Pacific lines, and so she looked forward to heading east; she was quite sick of sea travel, and didn't relish the boating part of the trip to the Pacific Northwest.

By late afternoon they had secured reservations and purchased tickets, and would be departing for Washington the following day. Diana would be sorry to leave San Francisco so soon, but she would not be sorry to bid farewell to the treatment Yi-kin was receiving, where he was universally referred to as "John" and laughed at, ordered about, or (once) threatened with stoning. Yi-kin accepted the various slurs with astonishing grace and reserve, an attitude which both impressed and frustrated Diana.

They left their rooms in the early evening in search of a new restaurant; Diana was determined to find a fine western-style establishment that would allow Yi-kin entry. As Diana exited her room, Mina was curled up in a sweet, warm ball on the bed, sleeping soundly. Diana ruffled her fur, promised to return with a lovely piece of fish or chicken for her, and received one small purr of contentment before Mina resumed her nap.

Their search for a non-Chinese restaurant that would accept Yi-kin's presence proved fruitless, and so they enjoyed another meal at one of the excellent Chinatown eateries. It was nearly nine p.m. as they returned to their rooms at The Arms.

Their accommodations were on the second floor, and could be accessed via either a staircase or a wrought-iron elevator. They heard Mina clearly from the bottom of the staircase.

"Madame, you'll have to silence that animal," the desk clerk told her as she raced by him. "Madame—!" he called after her.

She didn't stop to answer...because Mina only howled like that in the presence of a creature of the Netherworld.

They rushed up the stairs, Diana cursing her voluminous skirts. Yi-kin reached the landing well before she did, but waited, bouncing on the balls of his feet as Mina's wild screams continued assaulting their ears. Now there was another sound, too—a low, ominous hissing.

Diana finally reached the top of the stairs, and together they ran down the hallway. She already had her keys out by the time they reached the door, and they hesitated as she inserted the keys in the lock.

Then Mina's sounds were abruptly silenced.

With that Diana threw a look to Yi-kin, then pushed the door open. He leapt into the room—and was promptly flung back out, hitting against the far wall of the hallway.

Diana looked from Yi-kin, sliding down in a dazed heap, into the doorway of the room; it was dark within, and she caught only a glimpse of a man-sized figure ducking out of view. Mina shot out of the room as if spring-loaded, and Diana looked at her just long enough to ascertain that the cat wasn't harmed. Mina ran a few feet down the hallway then stopped, snarling and spitting at whatever was in Diana's room.

Diana smelled a strange odor, something acrid and unpleasant that she couldn't quite place, slightly fishy but mixed with a scent that seemed inorganic, chemical. She could hear something breathing with sussurant exhalations, but could make out nothing beyond the doorway. She needed to get light into the room, but the fixtures in the hallway were gas, and it was obviously impossible to reach a lamp in the room.

Her mind raced through the possibilities, and she rummaged through her purse, then her fingers fell upon a large brochure of time tables and fare schedules they'd collected from the Southern Pacific railway offices. She pulled the brochure out, dropped her purse, rolled the booklet up tightly, and then held it up to one of the gas torchieres in the hallway. It caught flame instantly, and she thrust her little torch into the darkness of her room.

And was greeted by the sight of a man-sized reptile's head hissing back at her.

She jerked back instantly. She wasn't aware Yi-kin had regained his feet and was standing by her side, equally shocked. "What—?!"

Diana swallowed hard, then thrust the flaming booklet into the room again, and this time held it there. She could see it more plainly now: A greenish, scaly reptilian face with yellow eyes and slitted pupils, like an impossibly oversized lizard head, set atop a human-like body with two arms, two legs and a tail trailing behind it. The thing hissed again, flicking its long reddish, forked tongue, and reared back, and Diana suddenly understood:

It was afraid of the light.

Diana realized her little torch was about to reach her gloved fingers, and without thinking further she thrust it straight at the lizard thing. It recoiled backward, glared at her a last time, and then leapt out through the open window.

Diana and Yi-kin ran to the window and bent out over the sill. There was just enough of a glow from a nearby street lamp that they could make out the thing crawling effortlessly down the side of the building. It reached the street and slithered down into a manhole cover that had been left open, and Diana thought she made out the distant sound of a splash from somewhere down below.

Diana yelped as the flames did reached her fingers, and she flung her torch out into the street, where it fluttered down to the wet pavement and sputtered out. Behind her, Yi-kin had already lit a lamp, and was moving about the room lighting more.

"That thing didn't injure you, did it?" she asked in concern.

"No, I am fine," Yi-kin answered, then asked, "how about Mina?" He had become very attached to the cat.

Diana stepped out into the hallway, and gathered up Mina, who relaxed in her arms and allowed herself to be carried back into the room, although a tiny growling in the back of her throat told Diana she was still frightened.

Diana couldn't blame her.

Yi-kin moved hastily, lighting every lamp in the room, before turning to Diana. "Miss Diana, do you know what that thing is?" he asked.

"I haven't a clue, Yi-kin. It looked like some kind of reptile—a lizard, specifically."

"*Seh.*"

"What?" asked Diana, still scanning the street below. She thought it unlikely their intruder would pay a return visit, but she was on edge now and in full defensive mode.

"*Seh.* How do you say in English...." Yi-kin put his arms together and wiggled them through the air, while darting his tongue in and out.

"Snake," Diana supplied.

"Yes, snake. In China we have stories about snakes who want to become people. Two become beautiful women, get married and even have baby. Maybe that was like *ching seh*—green snake."

Diana nodded, and finally turned away from the window, closing it behind her.

"Maybe." Diana dropped into a chair and Mina huddled against her, still anxious. "It doesn't make sense—we're nowhere near a gateway. Where did that thing come from?"

Yi-kin paced before the fire he'd started in the room's small stove. "If there is no gateway around here, then it come a long way."

"Why?" Diana pondered.

"To kill us."

Diana admired his bluntness.

He continued: "Things in netherworld don't want you to close gateways any more, so now they send monsters to kill you. And they must have human help, since they know exactly where you are."

A chill ran down her spine—everything he said made sense. On one level she was pleased—Yi-kin was proving to be not only hard-working and physically adept, but a fine strategist as well. But her pleasure with her assistant didn't dispel her growing unease at the notion that they were now prey.

"One thing, though," Diana said after a brief consideration, "that thing was afraid of light. How far could it travel, being unable to move in daylight, or in well-lit cities?"

"True. It maybe can travel hiding in ship, or in trunk."

Diana nodded, then said, "We need to know what it was, and exactly where it came from."

"How we find that out?"

They were in a foreign city, and although at least it was a sophisticated city where English was spoken, Diana knew she would have access to none of her usual information sources. "Perhaps we can try…a library, a museum…."

Yi-kin noted, "We tomorrow have a little time before boat leaves. We can try then."

"*Ho yeh*," Diana told him. (He no longer laughed at certain of her Cantonese pronunciations, so she assumed she was starting to grasp the difficult inflections.)

"In the meantime," Diana continued, "we will apparently need to exercise caution at all times now, no longer simply when we're near gateways."

"I know," Yi-kin said, then added, "tonight I will sleep with all lights on."

Chapter XVIII

June 23, 1880
San Francisco, United States

Diana slept little that night, what with the unnerving attack and the way it sent her mind spinning.

She was no longer safe anywhere.

That thought disturbed her at first, then made her angry, and finally fueled her with a furiously renewed determination. Now she was no longer sealing the gateways only out of vengeance for what had been done to William, nor even to halt a potential incursion; now she was also doing it to save her own life.

It also gave her a small thrill of pleasure to know that she was apparently causing some disturbances of her own in the Netherworld.

She did manage to drift off just before dawn, but her brief sleep was troubled by nightmare visions of fanged snake heads darting down at her from dark corners. Even though she was greatly fatigued, she was nonetheless grateful to be awakened by a soft knock on her door around nine a.m. She heard Yi-kin calling, and she rose and moved to it. She asked him to wait while she prepared herself for the day.

After a quick wash in the room's basin and a change of clothing, she hurried out to meet Yi-kin and found him awaiting her in the hotel's main lobby. He looked very smart in his new suit; he also looked bright and well-rested, and Diana found herself envying his apparent abilities to sleep off their terror of the night before.

"Where do we go first?" Yi-kin asked her.

By way of answer, Diana went to the main desk clerk and asked if he could suggest libraries, museums, or universities in the nearby vicinity. He smiled and jotted down a brief list on a sheet of paper, which he passed to her. She thanked him, and then returned to Yi-kin. "Let's find a cab," she told him.

They stepped outside the hotel's doors and Yi-kin was just walking down towards a busy intersection in search of transportation when Diana stopped, frozen, staring at something across the street from the hotel:

A sign on a building there read, "Chappell and Sons Booksellers, 2nd Floor."

Yi-kin rejoined her, and looked to see what she was staring at. "What is it, Miss Diana?"

It took her a few seconds to find her voice. "Don't bother with the cab, Yi-kin."

As she started across the street, he finally saw the sign. "Bookstore...strange. Yesterday I do not see this sign."

Diana answered, "That's because it wasn't there yesterday."

Yi-kin didn't ask, he just followed her through the small door next to the sign, and up the stairs inside.

On the second floor landing, they found a door with a frosted glass window and a stencilled name, "Chappell and Sons Booksellers." Beneath that was a smaller notice, "By appointment only."

Yi-kin, whose reading of English was still coming along considerably better than Diana's reading of Chinese, tried to sound out the bottom line. "By...what is middle word?"

"By appointment only."

"Oh," Yi-kin, muttered, dismayed, "we do not have appointment."

"I believe I have a standing invitation," Diana answered as she opened the door.

They stepped into a small room that was a virtual duplicate of the one Diana had visited in London. Diana even recognized particular books, in exactly the same places they were previously.

Then Stephen Chappell entered the room.

He, too, looked just the same as when Diana had last seen him, and she felt an almost inexplicable rush of warmth flood through her. He smiled at her for a few seconds before either of them said anything, then he said to her, "I'm happy to see you again, Diana."

"And I'm happy to hear that, Stephen," she told him. Then, seeing Yi-kin gaping in perplexity, she set about introductions: "Yi-kin, this is my friend Stephen Chappell. We know each other from London. And this is my assistant, Leung Yi-kin."

Yi-kin bowed to Stephen, and was noticeably pleased when Stephen returned the gesture perfectly. "A pleasure to meet you, Mr. Leung. If Diana has seen fit to hire you, you're undoubtedly a man of many rare talents."

Yi-kin bowed a second time, and more deeply.

Diana said, "I had no idea that Chappell and Sons had American branches."

"Ah...well," Stephen said, "it's a new venture for us. In the new world, as it were."

"Quite," said Diana. "Now, suppose you tell me why you're really here."

Stephen nodded to her, once, then turned away, searching his shelves. "I understand you're in need of some information."

"Of course you know about our scaly visitor last night."

"A good bookseller always tries to ascertain the needs of his clients," Stephen said, and then handed her a book.

Diana looked down at the title, and blinked in surprise.

American Indian Mythologies and Legends: Being an Investigation into the Curious Lore and Beliefs of the Savage Tribes. The author was listed as Dr. W. Augustus Raphael, and the publishing date was 1875. At least it was somewhat current.

"I think you'll find the section on stories of the Hopi people particularly enlightening," Stephen added.

Diana restrained the urge to open the book right then and there. "Thank you. How much do I owe you for this?"

"No charge," Stephen told her, then added, "or rather, I should say...your expenses on this matter are being covered by a...patron."

Diana nodded slowly. She knew better than to ask who that "patron" was, since Stephen would undoubtedly provide no firm answer, only more metaphysical meanderings about the "good forces" on her side, etc. etc.

"Is that all?" she asked, reluctant to leave.

"I'm afraid it is," he told her.

Yi-kin started to turn away, but Diana didn't follow. Instead she fixed Stephen with a hard look. "There is one other thing: A Taoist monk in China, Master Li, told me that my husband William was being held by a demon in the Netherworld, and yet you told me William was dead."

"Yes," Stephen responded, adding nothing more.

"Which one of you is lying?" she asked.

Stephen considered for a long time, then answered with another single word:

"Neither."

Diana wasn't going to let it go so easily this time. "What does that mean? Is William dead until he leaves the Netherworld?"

"Diana," Stephen said, and he shocked her by suddenly taking one of her hands, and even through the fine leather of her glove she felt his touch like an electric vibration, "you mustn't ever try to step through a gateway and cross over into the Netherworld yourself. In this sphere you are provided with certain protections, whether you are aware of them or not. In that place, you would be completely unprotected."

Diana pulled her hand from his. "Were those protections helping last night when we were nearly attacked by some lizard creature?"

Stephen had no answer.

She surprised herself by leaning forward and offering a small, quick kiss to Stephen's cheek. When she pulled back, he was looking at her wonderingly. "Will we meet again?" she whispered.

"I trust we will," Stephen murmured back.

As they stepped out of the bookstore, Yi-kin leaned in close to Diana.

"Do English people always kiss book merchants?" he asked.

They left Chappell and Sons, had a quick meal at a bar that was willing to serve Chinese (and where Diana had to foist off not a few undesirable advances), and then returned to their rooms at the Powell Arms. Diana fed Mina the fish she'd kept over from lunch, then sat down to peruse the book.

The day was warm, and she was happy (with the bright sunlight streaming down) to throw her windows open and let the cool breeze blow into the room from off the nearby bay. The breeze smelled of salt and smoke, and it cleaned the last of the lizard thing's foul scent from the room.

She found the section on the Hopi Indian tribe, and scanned a few pages until she came to what she sought. Yi-kin had gone out to do some shopping, and when he returned lugging a few wrapped packages, she exclaimed excitedly:

"Listen to this, Yi-kin: 'The elders of the Hopi tribe tell weird tales of a race of lizard people, who were descended from the gods and lived on the earth before men. They built a great city and they amassed an astonishing fortune in gold, but their city was destroyed by a conflagration of some sort. Anxious to leave behind the cruel surface world, these enigmatic beings moved underground and built three cities along the Pacific Coast.

"'One city was said to have been constructed beneath the prominence now known as Mt. Shasta; the location of another has never been revealed, and is now presumed to be long dead; but the capital of their empire was built beneath a small community in the southern part of California called Los Angeles. The Lizard People, who were described as walking upright like men but having the head and skin of reptiles, carved out an intricate system of tunnels beneath Los Angeles; the underground city eventually held a thousand families, and vast amounts of gold, which was a symbol of long life to these creatures. The tunnels, which also held elaborate temples and golden tablets recording the history of this peculiar race, was built in the shape of a lizard, and covered more than thirty miles in length.'"

She finished reading and looked up excitedly at Yi-kin—only to see for the first time that he was wearing smoked spectacles that shaded his eyes.

"What on earth are you wearing?" she asked.

"I think maybe with these, people cannot see my eyes and so cannot know I am Chinese," he answered.

Diana tried to tell him there was nothing wrong with his heritage or features, but he wouldn't relent; he told Diana that he would not inconvenience her any longer, and he thought this disguise would work. Diana finally gave in, but asked that he at least remove the glasses in her presence.

He did, and then sat down to discuss her new findings. "So these lizard people live in...."

Diana checked the book again. "A place called Los Angeles. It's quite some ways south of here, I believe."

"But have you not said gateway is north?" he asked.

"Yes, it is," Diana acknowledged, as the full impact of that question hit. An entire city of demonic reptilian beings, hell-bent on her demise...and they were located a thousand miles from the nearest gateway? It ran completely counter to everything she thought she knew or understood about paranormal activity. Things simply didn't work that way.

"We're going to Los Angeles," she declared.

"But we have tickets to north—"

"Cancel them. Make new ones."

Yi-kin rose, already looking weary at the thought of wrangling with lines and ticket offices again. Diana saw his reluctance and smiled at him. "I know, Yi-kin, but this is a dilemma that demands answers. *Ngoh dei yiu hui.*"

We must go.

Yi-kin nodded and waited while Diana gathered her things to head out.

Fortunately arranging travel to Los Angeles turned out to be easier than setting up the northwest venture had been. The Southern Pacific rail lines had begun running from San Francisco to Los Angeles a few years before, and the trip would take only two days, on comfortable passenger trains. The trains also left frequently, and so two hours later they were in a first class section of a coach, leaving behind San Francisco and heading south.

Chapter XIX

June 26-28, 1880
Los Angeles, United States

Diana thought Los Angeles quite possibly the strangest place she'd ever been.

The trip down had been uneventful, even a bit dull. The train lacked any trace of the ornate luxuries of the European trains–there was no food car with finely-dressed servers, no crystalline fixtures or gold trim–and the stops during the first leg of the trip were frequent. Then the train entered a long, flat valley that apparently comprised much of the length of California, and speed picked up considerably; given the complete lack of scenery, she was glad. They dined at train stations, which offered plain meals, and at one point Diana nearly suffered a small disaster when Mina scampered off away from the train just as it was about to depart. Fortunately Yi-kin captured the mischievous feline and literally had to run with Mina in his arms to catch up.

At one point they'd wound around a fabulous concatenation of tunnels and curves, which they were told was the Tehachapi loop. On the other end of the long valley, the scenery at least became slightly more interesting, as they entered a wild region of high chaparral and rocky cliffs. Diana began to wonder what Los Angeles would look like, if this were where it was located.

But, as the sun set on the end of their second day aboard the train, they passed through a final, mile-long tunnel and descended from the desert hills into a long, low plain that was unexpectedly lovely: Luxurious orange groves, their boughs positively sinking with fruit ready to be picked, stretched off into the distance. Sprinkled in among the orchards were sprawling mansions, many of which seemed to be less farmhouses and more castles, with turrets and gingerbread trim and wrought iron ornamentation. The few hillsides not covered with orange trees sported huge flocks of sheep, grazing peacefully beneath an uncannily blue sky.

The temperatures were uncomfortably high for Diana's English nature, and even after the sun had completely sunk below the horizon and the train had pulled into the Los Angeles station, Diana felt sweat popping out all over her body. She was also surprised by the mélange of races she saw around the station: There were sturdy, brown-skinned Mexicans; indigenous Indians, with skin similar in hue to the Mexicans', but different facial features; Orientals like Yi-kin, dressed as their kinsmen in San Francisco and Canton were; and peoples of European blood like herself, with pale skin and blue eyes.

Downtown Los Angeles looked like a slightly bigger version of a few of the smaller western towns their train ride had taken them through. A muddy main street ran between rows of two and three-story buildings that housed merchants, hotels, businesses, restaurants, and a number of saloons. Many of the buildings featured false fronts (which Diana personally found quite ridiculous), and even now at night the streets were thronged with pedestrians and horse-drawn trams and buggies.

The most highly recommended hotel was something called Pico House, and as they checked in the desk clerk indeed eyed Yi-kin somewhat suspiciously; however, finally they were both registered, and for the first time Diana had to admit to the wisdom of his dark-colored spectacles. Later, she found out that, despite the seeming tranquility of the racial mix in Los Angeles, the city had a long history of suppression and riots, especially surrounding the local Chinese population.

They awoke the following morning (after another night spent trying to sleep under numerous lights), and over breakfast in the hotel's restaurant (which was much better than their fare on the train trip, but not as good as the meals in San Francisco had been) they discussed their options. Los Angeles turned out to occupy a much greater geographical area than Diana had counted on; she'd heard that it resided on a verdant plain set between mountains and the Pacific Ocean, and somehow she'd pictured that as a matter of just a few miles. Now that she saw it, she had absolutely no idea of where to start looking for entrances to these underground tunnels. For that matter, she realized at one point that the book she'd acquired from Stephen made no mention of actual entrances;

perhaps the Lizard People had constructed their underground city and then sealed off the entrances, for safety.

And would they find a renegade gateway somewhere in this City of Angels? Mina had so far shown no inclination to the usual discomfort she manifested when in the proximity of gateways; in fact, she seemed quite taken with Los Angeles, and spent much of her time curled up asleep in the direct sunlight coming through one of the open windows. Diana thought it must be at least ninety degrees in that spot, and she wondered how the little feline could stand it, let alone adore it.

Their conversation at the morning meal seemed painfully solipsistic, always circling back to the idea of locating the tunnel entrances without offering any solutions. They considered researching the area's newspaper archives to see if there were any strange attacks or sightings on record; crawling down into the sewer system to see if it might join any tunnels at some point; hiring some sort of local guide who might know the locations of mine or tunnel entrances around the area; or creating some sort of scene to draw attention to themselves and let the Lizard People know they were here.

Actually, Diana had the uncomfortable notion that the creatures already knew they were here.

What she really wished, of course, was that Chappell and Sons Booksellers would suddenly manifest a Los Angeles branch. However, a brief walk through the muddy downtown after breakfast swiftly convinced her that it was quite unlikely she'd find a sophisticated bookstore in this environment. She did visit a local tailor, and although she was disappointed by the somewhat drab gown he recommended, she also purchased a man's riding outfit, complete with leather chaps, long black coat, and a rugged, wide-brimmed hat that was called (quite charmingly, she thought) "Boss of the Plains."

Their first few inquiries (of the tailor, the hotel desk clerk, a carriage driver) turned up virtually no useful information. They discovered there were no caves to speak of in the area, and no strange phenomena or inexplicable deaths. Diana's accent invariably elicited the assumption that she'd come to Los Angeles for health reasons; apparently its climate was thought to be a cure-all for everything from tuberculosis to infertility, and over the last ten years, as the new railroads had made it easier to reach the area, it had drawn hundreds of residents looking for healthier living. Its population had swelled to over fifteen thousand at one point in the mid-Seventies, but now it was down to a mere eleven thousand.

None of this proved particularly efficacious in trying to locate a race of underground reptilian beings. She even found and visited a local medium, whom she realized within minutes was a charlatan.

On their third day in Los Angeles, they bought papers from the newsboys calling out headlines on two different corners. One paper, the *Los Angeles Daily Herald*, was small by comparison to London's (and even San Francisco's) papers, but it was at least well laid out and easy to read. It contained mainly stories of global news, national news, a few local items, and ads. The second paper was a weekly, curiously titled *Los Angeles Porcupine*, and true to its title the stories were mainly barbed and/or satirical reports on both national and local personages. The editor, a "Horace Bell," wrote virtually all of the stories in an amusing and curmudgeonly style, and many of his pieces contained autobiographical anecdotes. Apparently Mr. Bell enjoyed talking about himself.

Diana obviously chose the *Herald*, and she and Yi-kin proceeded to the address given in the paper for its offices. They found a large, new building of three stories and bustling with activity. Diana was relieved to see something in the town that looked like real industry and didn't involve sheep or oranges.

A desk clerk assured them they'd be welcome to examine the archives, and they were shortly led into a dusty room lined with wooden shelves upon which were piled newspapers by month and year.

The *Herald* evidently had been in business for some time, since there must have been ten thousand papers there.

Diana and Yi-kin gaped for a beat, then he asked, "Tell me again—what do we look for?"

Diana was starting to wonder herself.

Still, she went to the nearest shelf—March 1879—and pulled down a stack of the papers, grimacing as dust rose into her face and ink rubbed off onto her hands. "Anything about disappearances, or strange happenings, or caves."

Yi-kin, looking somewhat confused, also took down a stack, and they both sat at a small table, then began reading.

They spent six hours in the archives and found nothing but stories about horse thefts, unseasonal frosts and corrupt officials.

The sun was already heading for the western horizon as they finally gave up and left the *Herald's* offices behind. They were both hungry, and found a saloon which also served food. It struck Diana as a rather unsavory place—it was already filling up with grimy men who spat into brass spittoons and eyed her too plainly—but she was in no mood to search for something better. Their meal was quick and silent, and Diana left with a bit of mutton wrapped up in a handkerchief for Mina.

As they returned to their hotel, Yi-kin hung his head and said, "I am very sorry we did not find something."

"It's not your fault," she told him.

"I am not happy with this place," he suddenly announced. "In paper I see mention of Americans killing Chinese. Nine years before, they murder nearly twenty Chinese."

Diana's own jaw tightened in frustration. "So much for paradise. Apparently health cures don't pertain to prejudice."

Yi-kin nodded, then went on: "Chinese people are ones who make railroad and tunnels for railroad, but American people say they take jobs and then they kill Chinese people."

Diana suddenly froze. "Yi-kin, what did you say?"

Yi-kin considered. "American people say Chinese people take their jobs—"

"No, before that," Diana urged.

"That Chinese people make railroads and—" Yi-kin's eyes suddenly went wide as he remembered. "—and tunnels!"

Yi-kin and Diana looked at each other, with slowly emerging smiles.

The next day Yi-kin traveled alone to the Chinese sections of Los Angeles.

He and Diana had agreed that it was probably the best course of action; the local Chinese would be likelier to trust him alone than if he were accompanied by an Englishwoman. In the morning, she gave him fifty American dollars that he could use as bribes, if necessary, and told him she (and Mina) would await his return in the hotel.

Truthfully, Diana was coming to appreciate the local weather more and was not unhappy to have a day of rest. Their hotel overlooked an orange grove, and the air was fragrant with the deliciously tangy scent of the fruit. In the morning she enjoyed tea and fresh fruit on one of the hotel's spacious terraces, and in the afternoon she relaxed in her well-appointed room with Mina and one of the books she'd brought all the way from home.

Home. She did miss it. She missed London and Derby; she missed Howe and her house and her lands. She missed the rambunctious energy of London, its industry and culture.

Still, she supposed, if she had to be away from home, enjoying just-picked oranges under a flawlessly blue sky and warm temperatures wasn't so bad. And she still had Mina, after all.

It was just before dinner when Yi-kin finally returned. He knocked politely on her door, then entered her room, sat in a chair in her drawing room, removed his dark spectacles, fanned himself with his hat—and looked utterly downcast.

"Well, Yi-kin? What is it?" she asked, genuinely concerned.

"I do not like this place, this America."

And then Yi-kin told his tale:

He'd taken the horse-drawn tram across Los Angeles to Chinatown. There was no question when one had entered the city's Chinese section; aside from the differences in architecture, every other shop was a laundry, with steam pouring from doorways and chimneys. Yi-kin had been relieved to remove his disguising glasses and speak in his native tongue (fortunately the Chinese immigrants were almost all from the Southern parts of China and so spoke Yi-kin's Cantonese, rather than the Mandarin dialect of the north). Even though he lacked the robes and long queues of the Chinese men, the people treated him casually and politely.

He talked to people in restaurants and shops and laundries, and soon received a very different picture of Los Angeles than that painted by the newspapers: The Chinese told him the city had been built on their sweat, that they'd built the railroads and picked the fruit and washed the clothes, and yet they were still despised and treated with contempt by the white men. They told him of the massacre of 1871, when the accidental shooting of a white police officer had led to the murders of twenty Chinese, in a two-day long riot. In the newspapers, the white people accused the Chinese of taking away their jobs.

Yi-kin wondered aloud how many of the whites would have labored on railroads for little more than a bowl of rice and a few cups of tea a day, but he continued his tale.

In 1876, the Chinese laborers had built the final portion of Southern Pacific's San Francisco-to-Los Angeles railway, by constructing a 6,975-foot tunnel that ran under the local mountains. A few inquiries brought Yi-kin to a young man named Wu who now ran his own import/export business, but who had worked on those railroad crews. Yi-kin queried the man extensively, and although Wu provided some hellish descriptions of poorly-lit and unventilated work under the mountains, with frequent cave-ins, none of it involved anything supernatural.

Yi-kin finally thanked Wu and offered him a five-dollar gold piece. Wu's eyes widened as he took the coin and examined it, apparently to be sure it was real; then he called Yi-kin back and told him that, for another ten dollars, he might be able to give him what he sought.

Yi-kin gladly paid, and Wu promptly led Yi-kin through his store to a dingy backroom-cum-warehouse. He made his way through stacks of crates and rows of barrels, until he finally spotted a barrel marked with the character was for *ni doh*, or "here."

Wu pushed aside the barrel, exposing a trapdoor in the wooden floor beneath; it led to a rickety wooden stairway, and Yi-kin could just make out red brick lining either side of the narrow passageway down. Wu paused long enough to light a paper lantern suspended from a stick, and then led the way down the steps—Yi-kin following carefully.

At the bottom of the steps, they turned a corner and Yi-kin was astonished to find they were in a long tunnel that ran off into darkness on either side of them. The walls were completely lined with more of the red brick, and a few more boxes were stacked here and there against the walls.

Wu then told Yi-kin that when the Chinese had originally claimed this area of Los Angeles for themselves, one of the first things they had done had been to build this intricate network of strong tunnels, running the entire length of the Chinatown district. The tunnels served to move goods more easily between stores, but had a second and far more vital purpose: Because they remained unknown to the white men, large numbers of Chinese could hide safely and comfortably in the tunnels for as long as necessary. Wu said that many Chinese had hidden down here during the riots of 1871, and so the tunnels had already saved many lives.

Yi-kin was deeply moved by Wu's explanation of the tunnels, but he was also dismayed to realize that, just as with the railroad tunnel, there was nothing supernatural at work here. He attempted to broach the subject of *gwai*—of monsters or ghosts—but was met with silence and strange looks. Yi-kin guessed that Wu truly was unaware of any Lizard People, and not that he was hiding some greater knowledge.

And so Yi-kin had finally left Chinatown behind, sadder and no wiser.

The following day, with their options running out (and anxious to avoid the one that involved rummaging about in the Los Angeles sewers), Diana decided they should pay a visit to the offices of the *Los Angeles Porcupine*.

Their cab dropped them off before a small storefront, featuring wide plate glass windows with the gilt legend:

LOS ANGELES PORCUPINE

Horace Bell, Editor and Attorney-at-Law

They stepped through the front door, a bell jangling above their heads as they did so, and walked the few feet to the wooden counter that ran the length of the space. Behind the counter was a printing press, currently unmanned and somewhat disassembled; nearby were shelves holding reams of paper, metal plates and type. A large worktable was on the opposite side of the room, as was a small desk covered with rows of type. A wooden partition partially enclosed one far back corner of the single large room, and Diana could just glimpse the corners of a messy desk, with various articles and letters pinned to the wall above it.

"Frank!" shouted an older male voice from behind the partition.

"What?" came another voice in response, and Diana blinked in surprise when a man's head popped up from behind the press—a head almost completely covered in black ink.

"Oh never mind, Frank, I'll get it," came the original voice, and then its owner hove into view from behind the partition.

Horace Bell was fifty, big and beefy, with a long waxed and twirled mustache and ruddy complexion. He lumbered up to the front counter, slapped his steak-sized hands down on the wood, and demanded, "What in hell brings you folks to the Porcupine?"

Diana was so taken aback that at first her mouth just hung partway open without actually making any sound; then she saw a hint of amusement in the man's face, and she affected her most persuasive charm. "You wouldn't by any chance be the editor, Mr. Bell, would you?"

Upon hearing her accent—and possibly sensing a story—Bell's glower faded away, and was replaced by an equally-unnerving expression of keen interest. Diana was reminded of a bird-of-prey.

"I would, indeed, Madame, I would indeed. And to whom do I have the pleasure of speaking this fine morning?"

Diana offered her hand, which she'd left ungloved because of heat and only now stopped to think that she might be violating custom. "Lady Diana Furnaval, of Derby, England. This is my assistant, Leung Yi-kin."

Apparently Bell wasn't especially violated, since he took her hand and kissed it, completely ignoring Yi-kin. "Well, I had no idea we had visiting royalty in town. What can I do for you?"

Diana had realized, as soon as she saw the interior of the *Porcupine* offices, that asking for archives here was useless, but perhaps it wouldn't be necessary; after all, she hadn't had access at the *Herald* to the editor.

"Mr. Bell, I'm here on behalf of my work with the Royal Museum in London," Diana began, doing her best to ignore Yi-kin's raised eyebrows, "and we're hoping you can help us to track down some information. We're investigating some reports from this area of an ancient tribe of Indians who may have been involved in any sort of lizard or reptile worship."

"Huh," Bell murmured, his eyes wandering off as he stroked his mustache and mulled it over. "Injuns worshippin' lizards. Well, that's 'bout the strangest thing I've heard since Pegleg Pete claimed to have seen El Dorado."

As Bell continued to think, Yi-kin stepped up to Diana and whispered, "*Gam.*"

"Right," she whispered to Yi-kin, then turned to Bell and added, "this tribe had supposedly amassed a great deal of gold."

"You don't say," Bell said. Then suddenly he snapped his fingers and shook a finger excitedly at Diana. "Come to think of it, there is somethin' ringin' a bell there…'scuse me just one sec."

He turned and went back behind the partition, and they could hear the sounds of papers being flung madly about. After a few seconds the busy sounds were replaced with a loud and hearty, "Aha!"

Bell re-emerged and strode to the front counter, presenting an old issue of the *Porcupine* to Diana. He laid it out flat for her, then jammed a finger down on one story. "Take a look at that. Maybe that's what you're lookin' for."

Diana read the headline first:

LOCAL MINER FINDS
DIFFERENT KIND OF GOLD

Then she scanned the article, with growing excitement. Although only two paragraphs long, she thought they might finally have found their first clue:

> Local miner and general all-round eccentric Hugh "Crazy Mac" MacLean recently showed up in town with the strangest gold find ever made in these parts: A gold nugget, roughly the size of a man's fist, and in the shape of a lizard. Those who saw the gold were unanimous in believing it to have been manmade, although by whom no one can guess. Crazy Mac, who came to town in 1835

to work the placers but refused to leave with the other prospectors when more gold showed up in Northern California, stated he had found the gold in a creek running through his claim in the Santa Monica mountains some ten miles northwest of Los Angeles. Although the find paid off handsomely, Crazy Mac said he had no plans to relocate. He hopes to find gold in the shape of coyotes, horny toads, and possums, too, we reckon.

Diana's pulse had quickened considerably by the time she finished reading the article. She scanned the date and saw it was 1874.

Good, not that old, she thought.

She looked up at Bell and asked, "This is exactly what we're looking for. How would we get in touch with Mr. MacLean?"

Bell burst into howls of laughter. "Well, Lady Furnaval, that makes you 'bout the first person ever wanted to see Crazy Mac, not get away from him! It ain't gonna be easy; first you'll have to find him."

Diana glanced back down at the article. "It says here he lives in the Santa Monica mountains—is that far?"

Bell said, "No, ain't far…but you gotta understand, Crazy Mac's up there on some little bit of land he's claimed, way up in the hills. This ain't no city street you can just ride up to; it's probably gonna take a while just to find him. If you're lucky, there'll at least be a path heading to his place."

A path?! Diana wondered how these Americans could live the way they did.

Before she could ask anything else, Bell continued, "And you might end up wishin' you didn't find him—they don't call him 'Crazy Mac' 'cause of his personal hygiene, though that's none too sane, neither. He's as likely to meet you with a shotgun as a 'hello'."

Diana exchanged a worried look with Yi-kin, then pushed away from the counter and reached for her purse. "Thank you, Mr. Bell, you've been very helpful. Perhaps I can recompense you for your time?"

Bell motioned away her offer of money. "No need, I'm just happy to help. But keep me in mind if you do any socializing with the upper crust 'round here and pick up any juicy tidbits!"

Diana assured him she would. She didn't bother to add that the only people she expected to be socializing with had lizard heads.

Chapter XX

June 29-July 1, 1880
Los Angeles, United States

They spent the rest of the day deciding on a plan for seeking out Hugh MacLean. First, they needed their own horses; Diana, who had ridden in a number of hunts and cavalcades back home, adored horses and was very impressed with the local breed. They were large, muscular animals, bigger than what she was accustomed to but equally beautiful, and she was only too happy to take charge of this purchase. Yi-kin, it turned out, had never ridden, but fortunately he was a natural, being already possessed of exceptional agility and strength.

Next they needed a guide. A few inquiries at the stable produced a quiet young man of Mexican heritage, Manuel Navarro. Manuel could ride, shoot, and even cook, and he knew the area very well; he'd even heard of the *loco gringo* in the hills, and thought the prospector could be found without too much difficulty. Diana paid him an advance, and promised him a considerable bonus once they'd found Crazy Mac.

Yi-kin was mildly upset at first by the addition of Manuel to their little party ("I can do everything he can do!"), but Diana convinced him without too much struggle that they would never find their way around Los Angeles's dirt roads and trails on their own.

Besides, Diana had another plan for Manuel. Although she hadn't told him exactly why they sought Crazy Mac, once they'd found him—and provided they found an entrance to the Lizard People's tunnels nearby—she planned to offer Manuel a considerable amount of money to join them underground. Despite Yi-kin's claims, Diana knew he'd never touched a gun in his life, and Manuel had his own pistols. Besides, she liked and trusted him.

Manuel and Yi-kin assembled their supplies, anticipating spending several days in the wilderness to track down Crazy Mac (a prospect which most certainly did not delight Diana). Finally, early on the morning of the thirtieth they headed west, each mounted on their own horse, with one extra mount for supplies. Diana, dressed in her new riding clothes and broad hat, seated Mina in a traveling case directly in front of her; although she didn't anticipate needing the cat's talents for discovering gateways, she wasn't about to leave her behind in the hotel.

The area west of Los Angeles was a quilt of orange groves, sheep pastures and wilderness, with fewer and fewer buildings to be seen. Diana had heard there were a number of small communities further west, along the area's lush beaches, but they wouldn't be going that far. After a few hours at a mild trot their way began to wind uphill, through oak and sage. Manuel led, and Diana had absolutely no idea if they were actually following some kind of path or simply picking their way through the brush. Still, the ride wasn't without its distractions—the air was perfumed with herbs, and the mild buzz of insects reminded Diana of her garden back home on a summer afternoon.

Manuel had spoken very little since they'd left Los Angeles, and so Diana jumped when he pointed at a small stream just ahead of them and said, "This is Watson Creek. The crazy man is said to live near it."

They'd passed several such creeks, and Diana was baffled as to how he could tell one from another.

They rode their horses across the ten-foot wide stream, and found what did seem to be (at last!) a clear trail on the other side. It was late afternoon by then, and the streambed became a small canyon, angling slightly uphill between sandy cliffs on either side.

It was the perfect place for an ambush.

Diana could tell Yi-kin had the same thought; he glanced at her, and she saw him flex his shoulders and glance around uneasily. Manuel, however, seemed unconcerned, and so Diana tried to relax.

She was mildly successful—until a man stepped into their path with a shotgun pointed directly at them.

"Y'all just hold it right there!" the man yelled.

He was at least eighty, with a heavily lined face and gray hair and beard down to mid-chest, but he carried himself with the vigor of a much younger man, and the shotgun leveled at them was unwavering. The man's clothes—a cowboy hat, flannel shirt and blue denim work pants—were all ancient and ragged, and he was missing most of his teeth. Diana could tell the latter fact because he was grimacing at them.

"Y'all are trespassing. Ya got ten seconds t' turn them horses around and git off my land."

It was Diana who answered him. "Are you Hugh MacLean?" she asked.

That did at least cause the grimace to twitch. "Maybe you didn't hear me right, girly—just git!" he screamed again.

None of them budged. Diana said, "Mr. MacLean, we've come a very long way to see you. Please just talk to us."

"Got nothin' to say," he growled.

"So you don't know anything about lizard people?" she asked.

It was a risk that paid off. The old man—who could only be Crazy Mac—lowered the gun a few inches. "Lizard people?" he said back to her. "And they call *me* crazy."

Diana tried another gambit. "Mr. MacLean, if you'll just talk to us for a few minutes, we can make it worth your while."

"I don't need your money—"

And then he was interrupted as Mina picked the inopportune moment to poke her head up out of the satchel and meow loudly.

Mac squinted in perplexity. "What the hell...you got a cat in there?"

Damnation, Mina! Diana put a protective hand on Mina's head, and the cat immediately began to purr. "Yes. This is Mina," she admitted.

And then, to everyone's absolute astonishment, Crazy Mac lowered the shotgun and grinned. "Always had me a weakness for felines. I reckon you must be decent folk after all."

Mac suddenly turned around and motioned forwards with the shotgun. "C'mon. Just be sure to bring the cat."

Diana, Yi-kin and Manual all shared a look with an obvious collective meaning:

Crazy Mac, indeed.

Mac led them another few hundred yards up the trail, until they came to a ramshackle one-room cabin, not far from the small stream. The cabin, made from rough-hewn planks, had a dirt floor, a small woodburning stove with a pipe leading up through a hole in the roof, and a clutter of old junk—bent and useless tools, old newspapers, utensils with missing parts. One corner was devoted to prospecting tools, which included several dinged gold pans, a pickaxe, and a wooden crate alarmingly labeled DANGER EXPLOSIVES.

"Do you often blow things ups, Mr. MacLean?" Diana asked.

The old prospector opened the crate and pulled out a paper-wrapped stick stamped DYNAMITE on one side, with a long fuse dangling from it. "Sure. I could show ya right now," he said, as he nonchalantly tossed the stick from one hand to the other.

"That won't be necessary."

Even before the aging eccentric had juggled high explosives before her, Diana had been loathe to stay in the cabin, which exuded much of the same scent that he himself gave off, and so she was hardly unhappy when Mac told them they could camp outside, if necessary.

It *would* be necessary: Mac told them that he had dug the lizard-shaped gold piece out of a placer in the stream in front of his cabin one morning, and had no idea where it had come from. He swore that the stream's source—a spring several miles further up—was nowhere near any cave opening, and in fact he'd never seen any cave openings in this area. "Land's too dern sandy in these parts," he claimed.

Still, Diana insisted on exploring the area further, but knew that any such exploration would have to wait until morning, since the sun was already setting.

Manuel set up an efficient camp for them, one ringed in the half-dozen lanterns they'd brought, and centering on an aromatic, cheery bonfire. The night was chillier there in the hills than down in the town, and Diana was none too keen on trying to sleep on the ground, but she supposed it could have been far worse. Fortunately her American garb kept her warm.

And Mina was happy. She romped in the nearby trees and at the edges of the stream, and returned to Diana at one point to proudly display a squirming lizard in her jaws.

"I feel safer already," Diana told her.

"Miss Diana…wake up…."

She came swimming up out of a troubling dream of hearing William's voice calling to her from a thick fog, and although she searched and searched she could never find him. Then she realized it wasn't William bending down close to her, but Yi-kin, and she blinked the last of her sleep away.

"Yi-kin…*mat yeh a?*"

She sat up, and from the chill in the air and the jet-black sky overhead, she knew she hadn't been asleep long.

Yi-kin was wide-awake and gesturing in the direction of Crazy Mac's cabin. "Crazy Mac just now go out."

She reached over to her jacket, which had her pocket watch within. It was just after two in the morning.

Diana looked around, and saw Manuel watching them carefully from within his bedroll. He evidently wasn't concerned enough to sit up, and Diana took that as her cue. "Well, I'll admit it's odd, Yi-kin, but…."

"I do not trust him," Yi-kin said, with a hooded look.

"Of course not," Diana answered, "he's crazy. But that's probably why he's up at two in the morning. I, however, am not crazy."

She lay down again, pulling her blankets up snugly over her shoulders. Yi-kin crab-walked backwards a few paces, then sat cross-legged on a blanket, looking completely alert.

"I keep watch," he declared.

"Very good," Diana mumbled, already drifting off.

Mina crawled into Yi-kin's lap and meowed her own approval.

When they awoke at dawn, Crazy Mac ambled out of his shack, stretching and yawning, then joined them for breakfast. They invited him to share their provisions of salt beef and a local Mexican bread called *tortillas*, and Diana took the opportunity to question him, as off-handedly as possible.

"Yi-kin thought he saw you up and about during the night," she said in between mouthfuls of Manuel's spicy beef and hot black coffee.

"Oh, I reckon he did. Old-timer like me, joints start to ache, 'bout all I can do is get out and walk it off."

She shot Yi-kin a look, but he seemed unconvinced.

After breakfast, they started up the trail on foot, following the stream. Mac led the way with his shotgun, cackling as he told them they might encounter coyotes, rattlesnakes, or even mountain lions in these parts. Within an hour temperatures had risen dramatically, and they all started removing their outer coats.

After several hours of walking, often clambering over rough rocks, climbing short cliff faces or pushing through brush, they came to a wide pool nestled into a flat area near the mountaintop. Approximately thirty feet wide and perhaps five feet deep, it was the spring opening that Mac had described. Diana supposed that it would have been a lovely place to relax or even swim, but she wasn't here for her own amusement. They searched the area thoroughly, looking behind boulders and around overhangs, but the old fellow had been right—there was absolutely no sign of any sort of cave opening, and it did seem an unlikely place to find one.

They decided to stay by the inviting pool long enough to have a brief meal, then started the trek back downhill. At least the going would be easier.

This time they looked more carefully for any sort of feeders or tributaries, although Mac had assured them there were none.

He was wrong.

They were only a few minutes from camp when Yi-kin cried out excitedly, "Miss Diana—!"

She spotted him by a corner of the stream, holding back a thick growth of cattails on one side. She ran up to join him, tilted her hat up, and saw what could have been a smaller creek winding through the cattails to join the larger one.

"Excellent, Yi-kin," she commended him. "Now let's just see where it comes from."

They began pushing through the tall, thick cattails, up to their knees in water and feeling insects scuttle across their faces and hair. Diana heard the old man mutter behind her: "Well, I'll be goshdarned...never knowed that was here."

The cattails finally thinned out, and they were able to follow the small creek along soggy banks for perhaps fifty yards or so. It narrowed to no more than two feet wide, and disappeared beneath a tangle of brush growing against one wall of the ravine. Yi-kin pushed aside the brush, and there was what they sought:

The small creek flowed from a cave opening in the side of the cliff.

It was a small opening, no more than three feet wide and two feet high, but it was undeniably there. Manual joined them, and he shared a smile with Diana. They both turned to watch as Yi-kin tore away some of the brush, then kicked experimentally at the dirt around the edges of the opening.

It crumbled away easily, and there was no doubt that there was a much larger cave behind the opening.

"Manuel, see if you can find us some sturdy branch, something we can use as a lever."

Manuel said, "*Si*". He started to turn around—

—and flew backward as a shotgun blast struck him.

Diana whirled, and saw Crazy Mac standing five feet away, smoke still curling out of the barrel of his raised shotgun. "S'pose you did save me the trouble of havin' to drag ya here," he said.

Diana looked down at Manuel, who had fallen into the brush, blood and clumps of gore protruding from a foot-wide hole in his midsection. Diana knew he was dead.

"You killed him!" she cried out.

"Yep. They didn't care squat 'bout no Mexican—it's *you* they want."

Diana wanted nothing so badly at that moment as to see Crazy Mac fall over dead. "My god...you're helping them...."

Mac giggled. "Working for 'em, more like. You oughta hear how much gold they promised me if I brought you to 'em alive. Dead was okay, too, but it's more if you're alive. I reckon they got somethin' big planned fer you. Nope, wouldn't want to be in yer shoes right 'bout now, little lady...now I 'spect we'll just sit here quiet-like 'til nightfall, then they'll be round to collect ya, and I'll be rich—"

Just then something flew into the branches of a tree over Mac's head. Startled, he jerked the barrel of the gun up, and in that split-second Yi-kin seemed to literally fly from behind Diana, his legs extended before him. The shotgun went off as it was kicked from Mac's hands, then, as Yi-kin landed perfectly, one of his fists ploughed into the side of Mac's head, and the old man crumpled. Yi-kin stood over him for a second, fists still clenched, making sure he was unconscious; when he was certain, he picked up the shotgun and turned to hand it to Diana.

"Here, Miss—" and then broke off, his eyes going wide, as he saw the torn fabric and blood on Diana's left shoulder. "You are hurt—!"

Diana's hand was already clamped over part of her shoulder, and her face was white, but she tried to sound casual, "Really, it's not bad. A few grains of the buckshot caught me, that's all. Let's get him tied up."

Manuel had been carrying a length of rope, in case they'd needed to do any serious climbing, and now they used it to bind the unconscious prospector to a nearby large tree. Yi-kin wrapped him up so tightly that Diana wondered if they'd ever be able to free him.

Just then, she didn't really care.

Before returning to camp, Diana pulled away the shoulder of her shirt to discover five small wounds. Fortunately none was large or deep, but they would need quick attention. Holding her wadded vest up to staunch the bleeding, they finished making their way back to the camp. Yi-kin turned out to be surprisingly squeamish, and had to look away as Diana swabbed wounds with whisky, then heated a knife blade over a fire and used the tip to pry out the tiny balls of buckshot. When Yi-kin heard her cry out a second time, he overcame his reluctance, knelt beside her and finished prying out the last three pieces.

When it was done, she washed the injuries with water and whisky, then used the remains of that shirt to bind her shoulder. She was almost too exhausted and weakened to stand, and the sun was sinking.

"I think maybe tonight we must stay in house," Yi-kin nodded, helping her to her feet.

"As much as I dislike the idea, I agree," she said, leaning on him as they walked towards Crazy Mac's foul little shack.

"I will set up lanterns. I think lizard people might be out tonight," he said, already glancing about nervously even though the sky was still blue overhead.

"Looking for me," she added.

"What about Manuel and Crazy Mac?" queried Yi-kin, as he led her into the shack's single room.

Diana sank down into a corner near the stove; she refused to go anywhere near the old man's bedding. "Manuel's dead," she answered, "and as for Crazy Mac...well, perhaps he can work out something new with his masters."

Then she passed out.

She regained consciousness briefly in the night, and it took her a moment to realize what had brought her back around, then she identified it:

It was the sound of someone screaming not far away, great, incoherent shrieks of pure terror and agony.

"What's that?" she muttered.

Yi-kin, who was seated in the middle of the shack, tense, Crazy Mac's shotgun laid across his lap as he faced the closed doorway, answered, "That is Crazy Mac."

Then Diana was out again.

She awoke in the morning, and at first was unsure where she was. She felt Mina's reassuring weight on her feet, and then she was flooded by pain. When the pain subsided, she raised herself up and looked around.

Yi-kin was asleep in the middle of the floor, Crazy Mac's shotgun still clenched in one hand. Although they were ringed by their lanterns placed around the cabin's interior, light was seeping in through the cabin's cracks, and so Diana knew they'd made it through the night.

She sat up, wincing, and looked down; the wounds hurt, but she was pleased to see the bleeding had ceased. She changed the dressing and then staggered out over the sleeping Yi-kin into the cool, welcome morning. Kneeling by the edge of the stream, she let handfuls of cold water pour over her, and then changed into the extra shirt she'd brought with her. After a few bites of some of their salt beef, she actually began to feel better.

Yi-kin appeared in the doorway, looking panicked until he spotted her. "You scare me, Miss Diana!"

She smiled to reassure him. "I'm really quite all right, Yi-kin. Much better today."

"Oh, good. But do not leave again!"

They were pleased to find their horses were still where they'd left them; they loaded them up with their supplies (including, especially, the lanterns), but before they left, Diana went back into the shack. She pried the lid off the crate marked DANGER EXPLOSIVES and saw three sticks of dynamite left within, all with long fuses attached. She wrapped each of them carefully in pieces of a threadbare blanket, put two in one of the horses' packs, and one in her bag.

Yi-kin watched. "Explosive?"

"I prefer to think of it as precaution."

Ready at last, they led the horses the short distance upstream to the cave opening.

And then found Crazy Mac, still tied to the tree.

Of course pieces of him were also in the branches, on the ground, on the cliff face, on the brush and in the stream.

Yi-kin went green, and for a moment Diana feared he might faint, then he gulped and looked away. "What about Manuel?" he asked.

Curiously enough, the creatures had left Manuel alone. She thought perhaps they just weren't carrion eaters.

When Yi-kin learned of her plan—to enter the cave beyond the opening immediately—he initially objected. She wasn't well enough; there were only two of them; they'd surely be killed.

"And if we don't, they'll keep coming after us, and some night we might be careless—"

"We will not!" he answered, taking a step towards her. "We will always keep light. We will fight them—"

"Then let's fight them now. And this way perhaps we can answer some questions as well."

"But you are hurt."

"I'm quite fine, Yi-kin, really. We'll take plenty of light with us, and we'll be fine."

Or at least she hoped so.

Yi-kin knew better than to argue further with her. He lit one of the lanterns, and prostrated himself before the hole. Flinching as if expecting to share old Mac's fate any moment, he slowly pushed the lantern into the cave and squinted to look inside.

"Very tall inside. We will not have to crawl," he pronounced, withdrawing.

"Good."

They spent a few moments assembling what they'd need and finalizing their plans, while desperately trying to avoid stepping into pieces of the dead prospector. Yi-kin would carry rope, chalk (to mark their way), a pack filled with extra oil, some branches they'd fashioned into crude torches, and two lanterns. Diana would carry one lantern (her left arm was too weak to lift a second lamp) and her bag, and walk behind Yi-kin. They briefly debated whether to carry Mina or not, then she decided for them by scurrying into the cave opening.

Finally they were ready, and he crawled in first. "Is good," she heard him say on the other side. She removed her hat and left it with the horses, then knelt at the mouth and scooted through.

The other side of the entrance was a tunnel at least eight feet tall and equally wide.

Yi-kin looked at her, adjusted his lanterns so they were held out well before him, and then asked, "Ready?"

She told him she was.

And they began the descent into the world of the lizard people.

The first thing Diana noticed, as their route sloped gently downward, was that the sides of the tunnel were remarkably even.

"This isn't a natural cave," she noted.

Yi-kin didn't reply; he was too busy scanning the darkness ahead of them.

At one point the descent became far steeper, and Diana checked her watch—their descent from the cave mouth had taken them about thirty minutes. Here, a series of wide steps had been hewn into the stone, and they found it amazingly easy to continue downward. At the bottom of the limestone staircase the cave broadened, and they heard the sounds of water. The sides of the cave opened onto an underground river, stretching off into the darkness. Strange luminescent fish darted about in the black waters, and Mina reached a paw down, trying to swat at them until Diana pushed her away. She wanted Mina nowhere near those nightmarish depths, which uncomfortably brought to mind the River Styx, the final river crossed by the damned in ancient Greek mythology.

Diana guessed they must be at least three hundred feet below the surface now, and the air had taken on a weird quality around them, being colder but more humid than on the surface. There was also a faint odor that it took Diana a few seconds to place, then a chill that had nothing to do with the temperature passed through her:

It was the smell that had been left in her San Francisco hotel room after the attack by the lizard thing.

At one point the river curved, and Diana nearly ran into Yi-kin as he stopped just beyond. They were facing a huge open archway, perhaps fifteen feet tall and twenty feet wide, carved into the very stone of the cave itself. The arch was sculpted with bas-relief images of lizard-headed beings, engaged in a variety of practices—Diana picked out what looked like trade or merchant activities, a king or priest with hand extended in blessing…and armies.

The arch was also trimmed in gold.

There was no mistaking its glitter in their lanterns; great strips of it outlined the edges, and the interior of the archway was covered in it.

Diana guessed she was probably looking at enough gold to set up her own small country.

"This is the entrance to their city," Diana said.

Yi-kin examined the area, then asked, "Why no guard?"

Diana had been wondering that herself. She had expected to encounter her opponents before now. "I suppose we'll find out."

She nudged Yi-kin ahead; he gulped and stepped forward reluctantly, but seemed to gain strength when Mina ran on ahead of him.

Beyond the arch the cave ran a short distance before opening to an intersection of nearly a dozen new tunnels. Golden plaques, displaying messages in an indecipherable pictographic language, were mounted above each opening. In the center of this area was a fountain decorated with great carved stone lizard heads. The fountain was dry and cracked, and looked as if it hadn't worked in decades.

Yi-kin peered around in perplexity. "Which way? What do we look for?"

She saw Mina take off down the second opening from the left, and she pointed after the feline. "We need to know why they're here, which means we may be looking for an unknown gateway. So we follow her."

He nodded, but hesitated just long enough to chalk an X beside the exit tunnel before heading after the cat.

Diana was about to follow him into the side tunnel when something odd caught her attention. As she stepped into the new cave, she momentarily covered the light from her lantern, and saw the intersection they'd just left was bathed in a faint, phosphorescent glow. She ran her hand over the stone wall, then held it up in the darkness, and saw that her glove now radiated a green light.

The walls were covered with a luminescent moss of some kind. It must provide just enough light for the sensitive lizard people to see by, but not enough to offend their delicate senses, apparently.

She turned to follow Mina and Yi-kin down the side tunnel, and saw that this new cave was the most astonishing they'd seen yet. The walls were ornately sculpted with writhing lizard forms and geometric designs. Some had been painted, mainly in hues of red and green. Somehow the carvings reminded Diana of religious tableaux.

Her suspicion was confirmed when lanterns illuminated a gruesome scene of lizard people plainly sacrificing a struggling human being. The scene was complete with crimson accents.

"Miss Diana...." Yi-kin muttered, fearfully eyeing the horrible mural.

"I think this is leading to some sort of temple, Yi-kin."

He reluctantly moved forward, skirting the depiction of sacrifice with as much distance as possible.

They continued on, only glancing at the murals surrounding them. They passed branching avenues, but many of them seemed blocked or unusable. They saw cracked archways and piles of shards that might once have been ceramics, and Diana realized that this civilization, which may have been grand at one point, had crumbled into ruin.

The tunnel opened onto a ledge that wound around the inner wall of a large chamber, a hundred feet above the floor. Below, they could just make out half-ruined walls and rooms, with a few decaying mounds of wood scattered about.

"I think this was a market of some sort," Diana whispered.

"Their world die."

Diana nodded. "That's why we haven't seen any of them yet—I suspect there are very few left."

Their path left the open chamber and became a tunnel again, they rounded one last curve, and stepped out of the cave into what was apparently a temple. The large cavern was supported with redwood-sized stone columns, which extended beyond the light of their lanterns. They stepped to the far wall (for a moment Diana was reminded of the temple of Kali outside Calcutta), and saw a huge stone table resting there.

It was unquestionably covered in ancient, dried blood. Human blood.

Yi-kin stared at the altar stone, horrified; but Diana moved around it, her attention captured by something she saw glittering just beyond:

The back wall of the temple was lined with great golden tablets, each about seven feet tall and four feet across, covered with more of the pictographs and friezes, highlighted with fading, chipping paint to bring out the illustrations. There were a total of twelve, and she swiftly realized that they told a single complete story. She guessed they read from right to left, and showed the history of the Lizard People.

On the one farthest to the right she saw scenes of the reptilian figures cavorting with a variety of other oddities: There were wolf-headed creatures, winged humanoids, dancing skeletons, huge spiders—

—and a tall horned man who too plainly represented the demon she'd once fought in the woods near Derby.

The story told by the tablets seemed to begin with the Lizard People in the Netherworld.

In the second tablet, they appeared to be stepping through a large hole and disappearing, and she knew she was witnessing the Lizard People using a gateway to leave their realm.

She moved to her left, and saw that the third tablet showed the reptiles stepping out of black circle and appearing among tall trees.

"They come through gateway," Yi-kin murmured.

"Yes. Look at those trees...I understand the one to the north of us is in a thick forest, so it's probably that one."

"But how do they come here?"She didn't answer, but proceeded to her left again, and was examining the fourth tablet: The Lizard People were sacrificing humans, and offering prayers. Red paint trailed down parts of the frieze, and her stomach churned as she thought of the altar behind her. She felt Mina brush her leg and picked her up, cradling her protectively.

The following three tablets showed an exodus: The Lizard People had traveled by land, beneath a glowing moon, and then they'd completed their journey south in boats they'd fashioned.

The eighth tablet showed them landing their boats, and digging out their tunnels. In the ninth tablet the Lizard People sacrificed to their gods, in this very temple.

The final three tablets were empty.

"They didn't finish," Diana muttered. She thought back to the parts of the city they'd passed through, and realized now that what she'd taken for ruins might have been structures that had never been completed. "Something happened to them not long after they arrived here...but what?"

When Yi-kin didn't respond, she called out, "Yi-kin?"

"Here," he called from the darkness, but something about his voice chilled her instantly.

She walked off to where she thought she'd heard him, and rounded one of the huge pillars to find a twenty-foot tall pyramid obscenely crafted of human bones. They were all very old, decaying, although a few were mummified and still bore shreds of papery skin or wispy hair. There were arms, legs, torsos, and heads, all piled neatly to create a four-sided pyramid.

"There is opening back here."

She followed Yi-kin behind the abominable pyramid to a carved entryway. Although not as large or elaborate as the main archway leading into the city, this nonetheless led to something special. Diana set Mina down, thrust a lantern in, and saw a narrow hallway that stretched off well beyond her light. It was lined on both sides with stone shelves that held corpses. Those nearest were little more than skeletons, but a quick inspection revealed they weren't human.

"It's a catacomb," Diana breathed out.

"Many thousands dead," Yi-kin said as he peered in beside her. "Why?"

She shrugged. "Plague? Perhaps they caught something from the very humans in that pyramid. That would be a rich irony."

"What is 'irony'?"

Diana was reaching affectionately to Yi-kin's shoulder when Mina yowled. She stood a few feet away, back arched and tail puffed out.

They heard the hissing then.

In the temple entranceway, she could make out the shapes of lizard men. The creatures were hesitating, just out of range of the light they so feared.

Diana and Yi-kin exchanged a look of dread, then she moved carefully towards the entrance. She held the lantern up, Yi-kin came just behind her. As she reached the edge of the archway that led into the tunnel beyond, she girded herself, then stepped into the opening, holding the lantern out before her.

There were six or seven of the creatures waiting. They fell back from the light, snarling and hissing, covering their eyes, stumbling into one another.

Yi-kin was beside her, staring wide-eyed in horror, while Mina hissed at her feet.

"What we do now, Miss Diana?!" he cried out.

Diana thought furiously for a second. The catacomb was the only other way out of this temple that they'd found, and it obviously led farther into the city, so they'd have to go back out the way they'd come in. They might be able to force the lizard people back for a while with the lanterns, but when they reached the point where the many tunnels intersected, they'd be vulnerable to attack from every direction. Diana could only hope she was right and that there were very few of them left.

"Keep those lanterns up!" she commanded, then set her lantern down to rummage furiously through the pack on his back praying the creatures feared fire more than they did the light.

She pulled out several of the handmade torches and removed the glass of her lantern long enough to set flame to the ends. They caught fire easily, and the amber light around them increased greatly, causing a collective hiss of fury from their adversaries.

"Hold these!" she commanded Yi-kin. She took the lanterns from him (wincing at the pain in her left shoulder) and passed him the flaming branches, then she scooped up Mina and deposited the cat in the backpack.

Yi-kin grinned as he saw the lizard things snarl and stagger further from the torches. "You take lanterns, I go first!" he called out over his shoulder.

Diana was only too happy to oblige him.

Yi-kin began pushing his way through. The lizards pulled back from him; occasionally one would attempt to rush forward, but Yi-kin wielded the torches like swords and more than one monster pulled back a burned arm. Sometimes he thrust forward, startling them, leaving one or two screeching in terror.

They made good progress and reached the intersecting area but were forced to hesitate in the mouth there. Diana pushed up to peek around Yi-kin:

Three more lizard creatures awaited them there, clawing, widening jaws to bear fangs, and darting narrow forked tongues at them.

Yi-kin thrust forward again and again, sending the first attacker reeling back with scorched tongue and hands. Diana knew that, even as talented as he was at fencing with those torches, they'd never make it across that chamber, around the central fountain and out the far archway, unless....

"The lanterns, Yi-kin!" she shouted.

He instantly intuited her meaning, and stepped slightly to the side.

She hurled the first lantern to her left. It struck one of the lizardmen, who was instantly covered in flaming oil and glass shards. The creature let out an eardrum-shattering shriek and wheeled around madly, while his fellows cowered back.

Diana hurled the second lantern in the tunnel behind them. This one fell to the stone floor and created a wide, fiery puddle that none of their pursuers would come near.

Diana shoved Yi-kin from behind. "GO!"

He leapt into the chamber, whirling the torches at shoulder height. Diana ducked beneath his arms and ran for the way out. She reached it— but cried out as talons sank into her injured shoulder from behind.

And then Yi-kin was there, jabbing a torch over her shoulder. She heard a screech, and felt something hot splatter her skin. Yi-kin pressed one of the torches into her hand, and by its light she saw one of the lizards clutching at one burned and now-useless eye socket.

Two more of the reptiles stood between them and the main archway. Behind them, they saw several more emerge into the central intersection and begin to edge toward them.

With Yi-kin guarding the rear and Diana pushing forward, they began working their way out back-to-back. Fortunately there were more of their opponents behind them, and Yi-kin was very effective indeed at dispensing those. Diana swung her torch wide and got them past the two guarding the archway, and she felt relief when she saw the underground river, with the path beside it clear.

They ran to the bottom of the steps and Yi-kin called a halt. "I need last torch."

Diana dug it from his backpack, lighting it from hers, and Yi-kin laid one torch down at the bottom of the stairs. He was rewarded with a few of their pursuers rearing back and cover their eyes before he turned and ran up the steps after her.

Diana knew they had thirty minutes from the top of the steps to the surface, maybe less if they ran. She'd lost track of time in the underground world, and hoped it would still be light outside when they reached the top. But the torch Yi-kin had placed at the bottom of the steps was sputtering out, and the lizard men were coming. They seemed to be growing bolder, perhaps desperate to not let their prey escape. "Hurry!"

Diana was panting as they reached the top of the steps. Yi-kin had rushed on ahead of her, but she shouted after him, "Wait, Yi-kin."

He paused and turned back as she unslung her bag from her good shoulder and dug out the stick of dynamite.

Yi-kin saw it and stopped. "Here?"

She nodded toward the bottom of the stairs, where the lizard men were coming up. "Down there, to be precise."

"It not blow us up, too?"

"It might. But I'd rather die in a cave-in than on their altar."

She waited no longer. She pulled the fuse out as far as she could, prayed the explosive hadn't been in Mac's possession so long that it had degraded to uselessness, lit the end of the fuse and threw it down the staircase.

"Go!" She pushed Yi-kin ahead of her.

They ran up the stairs, Diana unconsciously counting. *One...two...how long is that fuse?...three...the dynamite has gone bad...*

The explosion deafened them, and a second later a shock wave threw them to the ground. They waited for a second as rubble rained down, half-expecting to be buried any second, but finally the echoes of sound died away. They picked themselves up hesitantly; pebbles continued to pelt them from overhead, and a dust cloud showed in the gloom behind them.

The opening to the staircase was gone. There was nothing there now but a solid wall of boulders and dirt.

Diana turned and saw Yi-kin saying something; she couldn't hear him, but his grin made his meaning clear.

She choked on dust then, shook some out of her hair, and motioned him forward.

The way ahead of them seemed blessedly clear, and soon they were in the final passage before they could make the opening.

Suddenly one of the things stepped from around a shadowed corner and clutched at her arm, wrenching the torch from Diana's hand.

Taken by surprised, she instinctively lashed out and felt a fist connect with scale-covered tissue. She screamed, but couldn't hear her own voice and knew Yi-kin, who'd been in the lead and unwittingly gone past the thing, was deafened as well. It hissed and fell back long enough for Diana to duck and roll under its arm and recover her torch. As it hissed and recovered, she swung upwards with the torch, and thrust it into the creatures mouth against the long, thin tongue. The thing screamed inhumanly as its tongue caught fire, becoming a flaming whip in the dark cave.

She ran past it, and saw a spot of sunlight at the end of the tunnel, Yi-kin silhouetted before it.

Just a little farther.

They flung their torches down and stumbled into the sunlight. But, it was late afternoon already, and there wasn't much time before darkness would be upon them.

Diana was blinking in the sunlight, and it took her a few seconds to realize Yi-kin was saying something and looking at her shoulder. She just made out the words, "...you are hurt!"

She was, but there was no time for that now. She wanted to be sure this cave became a tomb for the Lizard People; she knew she had to seal this entrance.

She went to the horses, and dug the two remaining sticks of dynamite out of the satchel. Yi-kin watched her, and she saw the question on his face.

"We have to seal that cave."

"You not have to shout."

Together, Yi-kin took the sticks and placed them just inside the cave mouth. He straightened out the fuses, dug a matchbox out of a pocket, and turned to Diana. "You get on horse now. These fuses not long."

She nodded, and climbed onto her horse.

Yi-kin crouched to light fuse—and fell back as a clawed hand darted out of the cave opening.

"Yi-kin, light the fuses!"

He recovered, struck the match, and placed the flame to each fuse. The fuses started to spark and sizzle, crawling toward the dynamite.

Yi-kin ran to his horse, leapt onto it, and screamed, *"Jau la!"*

They rode like hell, hoping the fuses didn't go out. Hoping they would kill the last of the Lizard People. Hoping they wouldn't die themselves.

They were a good distance away when the ravine thundered and crumpled in on either side of them. Their horses neighed wildly and drew up short, pawing frantically, but they were far enough away that only dust came down on them. When it had settled and the horses had calmed, they looked at each other.

"Miss Diana…?"

"I'm fine."

Mina poked her head out of Yi-kin's backpack and meowed.

They rode back a short distance, but couldn't go far—the entire cliff face around the cave mouth had tumbled down and blocked the stream and the ravine. Yi-kin nonetheless dismounted, to make sure the way was completely blocked. He passed the backpack to Diana, who made sure Mina was uninjured. As Diana stroked her reassuringly, the cat vibrated with pleasure.

Yi-kin soon reappeared. "No cave now," he said.

"Mat ye a?" Diana asked, then looked at his face, covered in light brown dirt, his hair wildly spiked, his clothes shredded…and she burst into laughter.

Chapter XXI

July 2—July 17, 1880
Los Angeles, United States

By the time they'd returned to the hotel their hearing had come back, but Diana was in the grip of infection-induced fever. They found new puncture marks in her shoulder, apparently made by the claws of a lizard demon, and she reckoned that as the source of her toxins, rather than the buckshot wounds. She wasn't sure if they'd truly destroyed the last of the Lizard People or not, but either way they'd nearly killed Diana in the end.

The fever was virulent, and her temperature was a few points above a hundred for well over a week. The hotel was able to send for a fine doctor, who gave Yi-kin specific instructions on caring for her.

During that week, she decided that she desperately wanted to be home; she had wearied of travel and hot weather, and absurd prejudices, and illness without the comfort of her own bed; she felt weakened and drained of fortitude. She informed Yi-kin that they would skip the northwest gateway, in favor of heading east across America as quickly as possible, where they would catch a ship bound for home across the Atlantic. However, there was that gateway in West Virginia, and she reckoned since it wouldn't take them far out of their way, they would stop long enough to seal it.

While Diana continued her recuperation, Yi-kin made their travel arrangements, which would involve a combination of rail and stagecoach. The railroads would take them east from Los Angeles as far as New Mexico; from there it would be horse-drawn coach through various Indian territories, with occasional short journeys on smaller rail lines. They would cross the great Mississippi River on a steamboat, and eventually arrive in the small town of Cedar Grove, West Virginia, where the gateway was said to be located "near the frog rock by the river's side."

On July 17, with Diana's recuperation accomplished, their tickets purchased, and absolutely no sign of the lizard people whatsoever, they gladly left California behind and journeyed east.

Chapter XXII

July 17—August 3, 1880
Los Angeles—Cedar Grove, United States

The trip east proved to be both happily uneventful and surprisingly interesting. They passed through the savage Western frontier, with its peeling wooden towns and breathtaking natural vistas; they traversed the mighty Rockies, whose upper peaks were snow-covered even in the height of summer; they rode the coaches across the Great Plains, which Diana knew had once been covered by herds of shaggy buffalo and handsome Indian braves on bare horseback. They gambled on the Mississippi steamboat, and Yi-kin actually won. They got kicked off the steamboat when the white gamblers realized they'd been beaten by "John." They passed one-time great plantations, now divided up and farmed by the black men who, not long ago, had worked the same fields as slaves.

At last the trip brought them to their destination, a tiny town in the West Virginia countryside called Cedar Grove. The town, which consisted of little more than a general store (which also served as the coach stop), a saloon, a church and a few houses, lacked even an inn; Diana was told by the proprietor of the general store that a Mrs. Mills on the outskirts of town had a big old farmhouse and was always happy to rent a few rooms.

They stored the luggage in town and walked to Mrs. Mills' place, which turned out to be a very comfortable and clean two-story house adjacent to a large barn and small garden. Mrs. Mills was a kindly woman in her fifties, who lived only with her ancient hound dog, Josie, and she seemed as happy to have company as to take Diana's money for two rooms. Josie and Mina sniffed each other briefly, then Mina strode haughtily off to Diana's side, while Josie's head dropped back to drowsing on the rug by the fireplace. As usual, Yi-kin tensed when attention turned to him, and she asked what kind of "Injun" he was. When informed that he was Chinese, not Indian, Mrs. Mills was genuinely thrilled; she told him she'd never met a real Oriental before, and she deluged him with questions about his country—how big it was, what the people ate, how they dressed, if they liked music (she did). He was pleased to find an American at last who didn't wonder why he wasn't working with the other coolies on the railroads, or running a laundry in one of the cities.

After getting settled into the rooms (which were plain and simple, but very clean and spacious), Diana and Yi-kin enjoyed a farm dinner with their host, who celebrated their arrival by killing a chicken, and preparing a fine repast of roast chicken, potatoes, corn, bread, and apple pie for them. Mrs. Mills was also an excellent cook, and Diana thought it easily the best meal she'd had in the United States.

While they ate, she regaled Mrs. Mills with questions of her own, and received some most interesting answers: Mrs. Mills was a widow who'd lost her husband in the Civil War fifteen years earlier, and they never had children; now she survived by her garden and renting the occasional room. Yes, she'd experienced many strange goings-on in the area, and yes, she'd personally encountered the huge insect-man mentioned in connection with the local gateway.

"One night," she told Diana, "I'd been down to my sister's place and I was comin' home on my horse, Bonnie. It got to be late—I figure it for 'bout two in the morning—but I didn't want to stop nowhere else, and anyway I wasn't far from home then, maybe fifteen minutes. I was ridin' Bonnie 'long a road not far from here, when I heard this sound, like big wings. Well, I look up overhead, and I 'bout died right there—not ten feet above me is this thing soarin' along, keepin' pace with Bonnie. At first I thought, That's the biggest dern bird I ever seen, but then I saw it had arms! I know it sounds crazy, but I swear, this thing had arms just like you or me! And the eyes...I'll never forget the eyes: Bright red, glowin' in the night they was, and huge, big as my fist."

She held up her hand for comparison, then continued:

"Well, it flew over me for a few seconds, and I don't mind tellin' you I was scared putnert to death. So I spurred poor Bonnie on harder, but that thing had no trouble keepin' up, no matter how fast Bonnie ran. I thought sure it would try to grab me right off the saddle, but then we came in sight of the house here, and Josie ran out barkin' up a storm, and that flying thing just turned away and disappeared. That was five years ago this October, and I ain't seen it since...and I hope I never see it again!"

Diana and Yi-kin offered their sympathies, then asked Mrs. Mills if she could identify the frog rock described in *The Book of Gateways, Conjurations and Banishments*, and she nodded enthusiastically. "Oh, land, yes, everyone hereabouts knows that place. It's maybe fifteen minutes walk from here."

Yi-kin and Diana exchanged a look of both triumph and anxiety—it was evening now, too late in the day to venture out to the spot, which meant spending the night in an isolated farmhouse nearby to a gateway.

They helped Mrs. Mills clean up after dinner (despite her protests), and then she retired to her own room; she was an early riser, she told them, but they were welcome to stay up as late as they liked and sleep in as long as they wished.

Diana and Yi-kin sat in the homey living room by the hearth after she left, discussing their options. They finally decided to prepare their own rooms, and dress them with whatever protections they could—lamps left burning (some voice deep inside her warned—*to protect against demons*), garlic, rosemary twigs. They left their doors slightly ajar, so that calls for help could be heard. Diana took the iron-bladed knife and set it carefully by her bedside, and Mina positioned herself at the foot of the bed.

Diana was certain she'd never be able to rest, but the enticements of Mrs. Mills' crisp, sweet-scented sheets and the comfortable mattress proved too much, and she was soon fast asleep.

When she awoke, she knew someone else was in the room with her.

She was very tired, and it was difficult to even open her eyes. The first thing she noticed was the fire had burned down to embers in the fireplace, so she knew she'd been asleep for several hours. Some inner alarm was ringing in her skull, and her stomach was clenched in anxiety—and yet Mina slept soundly on a nearby chair, curled up on Diana's cast-off clothing. The house was quiet, and she was certain she'd awakened from a bad dream—

—when she saw the figure in the corner.

She didn't stop to examine it, she merely opened her mouth to cry out for help, and in the split second it took her to draw in breath, she heard a voice say her name:

"Diana."

Any breath she'd taken froze in her throat. She knew that voice. It couldn't be. It wasn't possible. And even if it was—why here, in a farmhouse in West Virginia?

No, it couldn't be—

"It's me, William."

Diana's breath suddenly left her in a rush, coming out as a choked sob. "William—"

The figure stepped into the dim light from her bedside lamp, and there was no question—it was her William, looking just as she had last seen him, young, strong and so beautiful. He stepped closer and Diana saw his own features quivering with emotion.

She wanted to jump from the bed and embrace him, smother him with kisses and questions, hang onto him so tightly he could never be taken from her again...and yet a paralysis gripped her limbs, leaving only her eyes able to move. She watched, immobile, as he bent down and then sat on the edge of the bed. Tears streamed from her eyes at the sight of his tousled hair, his white shirt, his sweet smile.

"Oh Diana, how I've missed you," he murmured, and then he lowered his face to hers, and she thought she would surely swoon from the feel of his cheek, his slightly roughened skin on her smooth face, his lips brushing hers.

The kiss was long and deep, and Diana felt it with every fiber of her being. Tender and yet forceful, the kiss filled Diana with something she hadn't even realized she'd been missing—or hadn't been willing to acknowledge. Heat flooded her as William's lips moved down her cheek, to her ears, to that small cleft in her throat; she felt desire such as she hadn't experienced in years. She suddenly wanted all of William, his lips, his hands, that part of him that could fill her completely. She moaned softly as his hands moved down her body, pulling at her undergarments, tearing at the cloth—

—and that was when she knew something was false. William had never been rough; in fact, Diana had once or twice wished he'd been more aggressive. He'd always been a fine lover, but if anything he was slightly timid.

But now he was making small, animalistic grunts and ripping at her clothing.

And, perhaps more alarming, Diana turned her head, allowing William to nibble the skin of her throat—and she realized Mina hadn't stirred. She slept peacefully on, as quiet as the rest of the house.

This was not William.

Even as that realization overrode her desires, extinguished them abruptly, she found herself unable to move. Whatever *thing* had taken William's form—was now undoing its own clothing, with great haste. It lifted its bulk off her, and still she had to struggle to move even her head or flex a finger; she could make no sound, nor curl fingers into a fist.

The William-thing was leering at her now, as it pulled down its trousers. What sprang free was definitely not part of her husband; it was too large to be human, and she knew she only had seconds to break the paralysis that gripped her.

She summoned all of her willpower, and concentrated on moving only her right arm. It was already free of the covers, and only two feet from the bedside table—where the iron knife waited. She focused on moving the arm, gritting her teeth, feeling sweat pop out on her face with the effort—

—and just as the William thing was lowering himself onto her, she overcame her paralysis, thrust her hand out to the knife, gripped the hilt and plunged it into the monster's thigh.

There was a horrific, deafening screech, and suddenly Diana found she was completely free. She pushed the filthy thing back and bolted up from the bed, instinctively clutching her clothing more tightly around her. "Yi-kin!" she shouted.

She knew she couldn't wait for help; she didn't want this thing to escape, and although the knife had wounded it badly, it was already crawling across the floor towards the open window. Diana looked frantically around the room, and saw the lone decoration was a large old tintype photo, mounted in a wrought iron frame. She grabbed the piece down from the wall, muttering an apology to Mrs. Mills, clasped both sides of the heavy frame and then smashed it down over the demon's head and shoulders. It came to rest just above the elbows, effectively binding the demon from using its hands.

Diana stumbled back, baffled. *The frame wasn't that big—barely the size of a man's head...?*

The thing screamed again, writhed around to face her, and she saw it no longer bore any resemblance to her husband. It was now a small, withered creature of dead-white hairless skin, glowing yellow eyes and rotting, pointed teeth; it seemed to have shrunk to the size of a child, and was hopelessly trapped in the iron frame.

"Yi-kin!" Diana shouted again, and then realized there'd been no response from *anyone* else in the house. She risked a quick run down the hallway to his room, where she saw him peacefully slumbering by the light of his lantern. Even Mina hadn't so much as twitched a whisker.

Very well, then; whatever spell the thing had cast had paralyzed the entire household, and only Diana had managed to throw it off.

Then she would see the rest of this night out alone.

While the thing in her bedroom continued to screech, she proceeded calmly downstairs and located a small storage room off the kitchen where she found a coil of sturdy rope. She took the rope upstairs, and bound it around the struggling demon and the iron frame, securing it to continue working as a charm against the creature's magic.

Diana was startled, when the creature's incoherent shrieks turned to intelligible words. "Let me go," it pleaded in a high, grating voice.

"You can speak?"

"Yes, yes. Let me go and I'll answer one question for you," it told her.

"Oh, I'm after more than one answer from you."

She grasped the iron knife in the demon's thigh, and twisted; its black ichors splattered her as it shrieked and struggled. She disregarded both the blood and the agony; she dressed quickly in her heavy coat, and picked up one end of the rope. She gave it a tug, and discovered the creature was light; in fact, she doubted that it weighed even as much as a child.

She began to drag it from the room.

"What are you doing?!" it screamed at her. "Where are you taking me?"

Diana didn't answer. She tugged it out into the hallway, and then headed for the stairs.

"No, don't—" it had just enough time to beg, before she hauled it, bumping it painfully along, so that it moaned and cried the entire length of the staircase. She paused once, halfway down, to make sure the iron frame was still tightly bound.

Diana hauled it across the main room of the house towards the front door. She paused only long enough to light a lamp. Her prisoner continued to demand to know where they were going, and Diana continued to tug it silently—

—towards the barn.

She reached the barn, and by the lantern light spied what she wanted: Overhead was a pulley, with rope and hook attached. She dragged the demon to the center of the barn and secured it to the hook. She pulled the demon into the air until its feet dangled several feet above the floor, and it swung helplessly back and forth. After securing the rope, Diana glanced about the barn until she found the things she wanted:

A small hand-scythe.

A branding iron.

A coal bucket.

She began heating the coals while the demon's pleading rose to fresh heights, as it realized her intention. "You don't want to do this! I'll answer anything you want, really I will—"

Diana stuck the branding iron down into the coals. "Oh, I trust you will. Tell me what you are first."

"I thought that was obvious," it answered.

When Diana didn't respond, it supplied, "I'm an incubus."

"An incubus," Diana considered, nodding, remembering what she knew of incubi: Demons that seduced human women during sleep; they induced a paralysis that supposedly rendered their victims helpless. They took on the form of a particularly attractive human....

"How did you know about William?" she asked.

The incubus looked away furtively. "I can't...I can't answer that—"

"Why not?" she asked.

"Because," it told her, "I'll be killed when I return."

Diana used a heavy glove to pull the branding iron from the bucket of coals. "No, you won't—because I'm going to kill you here tonight. Your choice is whether to answer my questions and die quickly, or not answer them and die very slowly and very, very painfully."

The demon turned—if possible—even paler.

Then it abruptly tried a new tact, raging at her. "I have very powerful friends on the other side! If you kill me, their wrath will fall on you—"

Diana twisted the branding iron, which bore a stylized 'M' logo. "Their wrath is already on me."

The incubus cried out, "You won't do it."

Diana set the iron aside, and the demon's expression showed its relief—until it saw her pick up the hand-scythe instead. "You're only partly right: I won't do it with the iron, because it'll take too long to get red-hot."

"You won't torture me. I know about you."

Diana looked the incubus directly in the eye as she hefted the curved, sharp blade. "You don't know me, then. Because if you did, you'd know that there are no words to describe how much I despise you for using my husband to trick me. William is a sacred memory to me, and you've tried to pervert that memory. I would very, *very* much enjoy torturing you slowly for the duration of this night, but if you tell me what I want to know, I'll try to force myself to simply kill you at some point."

The demon stared at her in stony, tightlipped silence.

Until she drew the scythe tip across the bottom of one its feet.

More of its acrid blood gushed out, but Diana was beyond disgust, beyond feeling, beyond most human sensations. She was intent only on making this thing suffer. She swung the scythe and nearly severed the toes on that same foot.

It screamed.

"Aeshma sent me—he has your husband!"

Diana flung blood from the scythe blade and asked, "Who is Aeshma?"

"He's a great general in the Netherworld—a prince," the incubus sobbed.

"Is he planning to launch an attack on this world?"

"Yes—" and then the incubus broke off, gasping as it saw Diana raise the hand-scythe again. "No...enough, woman!"

"I think not," Diana said, and hacked off the creature's hand at the wrist.

She flinched as she was splattered by more of its black blood. The demon renewed its struggles, and hissed at her. "You'll pay for this, and your sufferings will make mine look meager, whore!"

"When will this Aeshma attack? What is he waiting for?" she asked calmly.

"Cut off whatever you like, I'm done answering anything for you," it spat at her.

Diana moved the scythe to its tiny, shriveled penis.

"I'll answer!" it screamed, its eyes huge as it stared down. "He has been building his army for two hundred years, since the guardians of most of the gateways vanished—"

"Guardians? What guardians? Why did they vanish?" demanded Diana.

"I don't know, I swear I don't know!"

Diana weighed the fiend's words, then motioned with the scythe. "Go on."

"His army will soon be ready, and so he decided to destroy Lord Furnaval, who was the last guardian—"

Diana felt that news as almost a physical blow. "William was the last...."

"Or so we thought," cried the demon. "We didn't know about *you*. And now you, you've begun *closing* the gateways, forcing Aeshma to change his plans. He has now moved up the attack to midnight on All

Hallows' Eve. Because, you see...you can't possibly close all the gateways by then."

The incubus uttered a wracked, fitful laugh.

And it was right. October 31st was just over two months away. Diana would have just barely enough time to make it home. And then....

She thought for a moment, and then realized there was still one last thing she wanted to know: "Why were you sent?" she asked, thinking this weak, one-armed thing hanging before her wasn't much of an assassin.

"You've managed to defeat the others—Kali, Cernunnos, the lizard people—"

"The lizard people are dead?"

The incubus added, "They were dying anyway, but you finished them off."

"That still doesn't explain why they sent you."

The incubus mocked her, and more of its black blood trickled down from the corner of its thin-lipped mouth. "Aeshma thought if we couldn't kill you, maybe we could trick you. With William."

Diana was still confused. "But what good would that do?"

"Maybe I couldn't kill you myself," the incubus answered, and suddenly the horrible thing was leering at her again, "but I could impregnate you."

Diana nearly retched as she understood their plan. "A demon child. I would have...it...."

"You wouldn't have survived the pregnancy," the incubus confirmed. "But my child would have."

This time Diana didn't hesitate with the scythe, and the demon's shrieks were noticeably higher.

After an hour the dawn arrived, and Diana lowered what remained of the fiend to the ground, and then dragged the pieces out into the morning light. As the sun's rays hit them, they sizzled like meat on a fire and began to smoke. Within a few seconds there was nothing left but a small black puddle on the ground.

Diana returned the borrowed instruments to their rightful places in the barn, and then went back into the house, intending to make thorough use of Mrs. Mills' fine bathtub. As she trudged up the stairs, a weariness suddenly descended on her that made every step a great effort. At the top landing she met Yi-kin, yawning and trudging toward her, already dressed.

"Good morning, Miss Diana—" he started, and then broke off, staring at her. "What is all over you?"

Diana realized she was almost completely covered with dried, black blood from the incubus; it apparently hadn't steamed away with the rest of the monster. Yi-kin wrinkled his nose and it suddenly dawned on Diana how foul its stench was.

"Oh, this?" she said, indicating her stained coat. "I thought I'd do Mrs. Mills a favor and collect some eggs for her, but instead I tripped and fell right into a mud puddle."

"Stinky mud," mumbled Yi-kin.

Mrs. Mills appeared in the hallway, looking chipper and cheery. "'Morning," she sang out, "can't imagine how I overslept so!"

Chapter XXIII

August 4, 1880—August 10, 1880
Cedar Grove—New York, United States

After cleaning the demon's putrescence off her (in two baths), Diana had Yi-kin burn the clothing she'd worn. She apologized profusely to Mrs. Mills for her "clumsiness" in destroying the portrait of the late Mr. Mills; she was genuinely sympathetic to the woman's pain and commiserated with her about losing a cherished commemorative of her late husband. Fortunately, Mrs. Mills liked Diana a great deal, and was willing to forgive her.

In the afternoon, Diana and Yi-kin found the gateway and sealed it without further incident.

Diana was exhausted afterwards, and so they stayed with Mrs. Mills one more night. Diana slept for nearly twelve hours; the next morning she paid Mrs. Mills twice the amount they'd agreed upon, exchanged an embrace with her new friend, and then she and Yi-kin departed.

It took them another three days to cross Maryland, Pennsylvania, and New Jersey on a number of small railways before they arrived in the great city of New York. During that time, Diana was somber, answering Yi-kin's questions with only "yes" or "no."

When he finally asked if something else had happened at the farmhouse she answered "yes." She elaborated enough to tell him it was vitally important that they return home as quickly as possible.

In New York, he was fortunate enough to secure them passage on a steamer leaving for England two days hence; they spent their day in New York purchasing a few new items of clothing for her, to replace what she'd had Yi-kin burn back in Cedar Grove. During meals they said practically nothing to each other, and Diana's gaze was haunted and turned inward. Even Mina was little consolation to her.

Finally, on the morning of Monday, August 10th, they boarded the steamship *SS Celtic*, and left the United States behind.

And Yi-kin admitted that he was very glad.

The Netherworld

Chapter XXIV

September 2-4, 1880
London, England

Two weeks later the *Celtic* arrived at the British port of Liverpool, and upon landing Diana cabled Howe of her return, but also warned him that intended to visit London before returning to Derby.

By late that evening, Diana, Yi-kin and Mina were relaxing in her comfortable London apartments. The staff was delighted to have her home, and Mina was treated to scratches and treats. Her introduction of Yi-kin as a full-time "secretary" raised a few eyebrows, but he soon found himself at home, treated with more friendliness and courtesy than he'd known since their few days with Mrs. Mills in West Virginia.

Diana slept late the next day, and when she rose she seemed to have at last regained some of her easy strength. After going through piles of waiting correspondence and a few matters regarding the management of the Furnaval estates and businesses, she excused the rest of her staff and requested a private meeting with Yi-kin.

She showed him into her sitting room, with its wide windows overlooking her courtyard, its small hearth, the tasteful leather chairs, and the table she'd purchased in Canton. She asked him to close the door and take a seat across from hers, before the fire. Yi-kin paused long enough to stroke Mina, who lay curled up at Diana's feet, then he accepted the cup of tea she handed him. She took a sip from her own cup, then set it aside and looked down at her fingers, as they fidgeted in her lap.

"First off, Yi-kin," she finally began, not looking at him, "I apologize for my behavior these last weeks."

"*M sai*—" Yi-kin started, but she cut him off.

"Yes, it is necessary—you deserve more than my sullen silence. You've saved my life, and I owe you more than a weekly salary."

Yi-kin bowed.

"It's time I told you the truth about what happened in West Virginia," she said, still not looking at him. "That first night a demon called an incubus visited me—"

Yi-kin sat forward in his chair so quickly he spilled some of the hot tea into his lap, and hissed in pain, "Why did you not call me—?!"

"I couldn't. You were under a spell. We all were. Even Mina."

Yi-kin looked away for a minute, then went on excitedly: "But you kill demon? Your dress I burn—"

Diana nodded. "I killed it. But first I...." She hesitated, then finally went on: "I did things I'm not proud of, but I...was effective. I obtained information that a Netherworld demon called Aeshma is planning on leading an invasion of this world on October 31st. He'll be commanding an army that will come through one or more of the gateways. He's also the one holding my husband."

Yi-kin fell back in his chair. His cup rattled against the saucer balanced on his lap, and he sat both aside on the table. "We cannot close all gateways by that time...."

"No," Diana agreed, "and they know that. That's why we have to try something else...or, rather, I do. I won't force you to do anything. In fact, I'd almost prefer you said no—"

"What will you do?"

"I can't close all the gateways, but maybe I can stop this Aeshma before he comes through."

"But Aeshma is in Netherworld...."

"Yes," Diana said, and she finally looked right at him as she added, "that's why I have to go through a gateway into the Netherworld."

Yi-kin nearly jumped from his seat in excitement. "Is it possible?!"

Diana shrugged. "Truthfully, I don't know. I'll need to do some research, but...well, we don't have much time...."

"Then we should go soon. Go *now*," Yi-kin said.

"You understand, Yi-kin, that this will be the most dangerous thing we've yet done. Our chances for survival will be quite slim."

Yi-kin thought briefly, then answered, "Chances for two are better than one."

"Are you sure?" she asked.

Yi-kin nodded vigorously. "I am sure. If you go, I go."

Although Diana knew she may have just guaranteed the young man's untimely death, she was secretly very relieved, and felt a rush of pride for Yi-kin. "Then we both go."

Mina looked up blearily, uttered a bemused meow, and leapt into Yi-kin's lap; once there, she turned to look intently at Diana, who laughed lightly.

"Of course, Mina," she said, correcting herself, "we *all* go."

Diana's real purpose in coming to London had been to visit Isadora, but first there was something else she wanted to do.

And so, on the afternoon of Saturday, September 4th, she arrived at the offices of the Hinton Trading Company with Yi-kin, only to be told that Sir Edward was spending the day at his private club.

Diana knew the name and location of the place—he'd spoken fondly of it on numerous occasions—and she arrived there twenty minutes after leaving his offices. The bellman, of course, tried to assure her this was a private *men's* club, but when he found his arm twisted most uncomfortably by Yi-kin, he reached over with the other and opened the door for her.

Yi-kin released him and followed as Diana strode angrily through the luxurious parlors, causing cries of male outrage.

"Is that a *woman*? With a *Chinaman*?"

One young man who was dressed in an expensive suit but smelled of liquor stood and leered at Diana while pulling at his lengthy mustache. "Madame, I'm afraid the house you seek is in the East End."

"I've no doubt you're well acquainted with it, sir," she said, leaving the man huffing as she and Yi-kin strode past him.

A man dressed as a waiter approached and grabbed Diana's elbow firmly. Before he could utter a word, Yi-kin deftly disengaged his hold. "She is great lady," he hissed, leaving the attendant to stare in disbelief.

She finally found Edward in one of the large sitting rooms, smoking a cigar with several companions, and enjoying a hearty laugh—which died in his throat as he saw her striding toward him, with a young Chinese man a few paces behind.

"Now see, her, Madame, this is a private club," an obese, bushy-browed companion of Edward's said to her, rising to his feet indignantly as he added, with a look towards Yi-kin, "a private club for English men."

Without taking her eyes from the mortified Edward, Diana told the man, "My business is entirely with Sir Edward Hinton."

"You *sit*," Yi-kin added.

The man sat down abruptly, as if his knees had been kicked out from under him.

"Diana, now see here—" Edward started, but his tone was quiet, his voice tremulous.

"Don't *see here* me, Eddie. I know full well now what your fortune rests upon, and an ill-gotten one it is—"

One of the other listeners interrupted. "What's she talking about, Sir Edward?"

Diana said, nearly shouting, "Opium trade, that's what I'm talking about. The attempted enslavement of an entire people, only to satisfy your own greed." She threw a hand back to Yi-kin. "These people, the Chinese people. You lied to me, Eddie. You told me you traded English woolens for their tea—"

"That was no lie!" Edward responded. "We *do* trade woolens—"

"And what percentage of your trade is that? Ten percent? Five? Your real trade is in opium. And you're little more than a contraband dealer. William would have been ashamed of you, Eddie, deeply ashamed."

And with that she turned on her heel and stalked out again, counting on Yi-kin to follow.

She was met at the door by two bobbies, just entering, but she waved a hand to them and lightly brushed past. "No need, gentlemen—we're leaving this opium den, never fear."

The bobbies turned and shared a puzzled glance, and let her go.

Diana and Yi-kin climbed into their waiting cab, then she gave Isadora's address to the driver and fell back against her seat, still huffing. At one point she looked over and saw Yi-kin eyeing her intently.

"*Dui m jue,*" she offered, apologizing.

Yi-kin barely stifled a laugh.

Isadora was happy to see Diana again, but was positively thrilled by Yi-kin; Orientalism had been much in vogue throughout Europe recently, and she thought Yi-kin far more interesting than a mere *chinosserie* or vase. She asked him a great many questions about China and her people, and Yi-kin did his best to answer.

Finally Diana had to step in, and she told Isadora that it was very important that she hear any news the medium might have received regarding the Netherworld.

Isadora confirmed that the Netherworld had been the source of a great deal of activity lately, and that she had received further whisperings of William. Diana asked if she would enter a trance now, and she agreed.

They waited quietly as Isadora closed her eyes and breathed deeply. She held Diana's hand, hoping that would assist in obtaining messages specifically relating to Diana's questions.

After a few moments, she began to moan softly. That was something new; she seemed to be in pain, which Diana had never seen her experience before. Her head rolled slightly, once to the left, then to the right, and she began to mutter.

"*Aeshma....*"

Diana and Yi-kin exchanged a look at that; Diana had been careful not to mention that name in Isadora's presence.

"No, not Aeshma...that's an older name...no, the name is...*Asmodeus.*"

Diana gasped.

"What?" whispered Yi-kin.

"Asmodeus is a famous Biblical demon...." she answered, but trailed off as she anxiously awaited Isadora's next words.

"You have one chance to save William, and stop the invasion: You must enter the Netherworld through the gateway at Cruachan before midnight on Samhain. If you do this, Asmodeus will stop the invasion, but only if you enter through Cruachan on the hallowed eve...."

Cruachan...the name sent a chill through Diana. Cruachan was one of the most famous gateways described in *The Book of Gateways, Conjurations and Banishments*, sometimes known as the Hell-Gate of

Ireland. For hundreds of years it had been the center of legends, of stories of murder, magic and madness. The ancient Celts had believed it opened each Samhain (or Hallowe'en), and poured forth a murderous horde of evil fairies and spirits. Even the modern Irish thought it held the "Cave of Cats," a mysterious underground passage which led to the realm of fairies. Diana hadn't sealed this gateway up 'til now because she thought it might need to be done— as the Hertfordshire one had been—on Hallowe'en.

And because she'd been afraid of it.

Suddenly Isadora's eyes rolled up in her head, exposing whites that gleamed almost as if lit from within. The air around her abruptly dropped at least twenty degrees, and was permeated with a horrible odor. Yi-kin and Diana both shot up out of their chairs Diana yanked her hand from a grip suddenly gone icy cold.

They stumbled back in shock as Isadora's chair—with her still in it—began to rise upward. Six inches above the floor...a foot...two feet...meanwhile, the poor woman writhed in the chair wildly, throwing herself from side to side, uttering something that could only be described as a lunatic howl of fury.

"What is this?"

"I don't know," she told him, "I've never seen its like."

Suddenly Isadora's eyes spun down in their sockets and fixed on Diana with piercing malice; when she spoke, the voice was plainly not hers, but higher, and with a terrible mocking tone:

"We're all waiting to welcome you over here, Diana. We have some very special things planned for you; I, in particular, look forward to finishing what we started, that night in the farmhouse."

Diana's heart was in her throat, then she swallowed it down and gritted her teeth. The last time she'd heard that voice, it'd been shrieking in agony as she dismembered its owner. "And I look forward to repeating what we did in the barn," she answered.

The reply infuriated the thing in Isadora, and it opened her mouth and poured forth a deafening roar. They both clamped hands over their ears from the pain.

Isadora fell from the chair and her limbs jerked. Diana and Yi-kin crouched, cowering. The medium's hands shot out, spasming, and the two observers jumped back. Isadora reached down to her desk, and twitching fingers fell upon a long, metallic letter opener.

They tensed for a fight until Isadora reversed her hold on the letter opener, turning the point in.

"No!" Diana cried out—

—too late to stop the demon from driving the letter opener into Isadora's abdomen.

The malevolence vanished from Isadora's eyes, replaced instantly by the shock of pain. Her mouth gaped in a silent cry, and she clutched at the horrible blade buried deep within her.

"No—Isadora—!" Diana cried out, trying to staunch the blood from her friend's wound with her own hand.

It was hopeless. Isadora's breath was slowing, coming out in tiny, convulsive gasps, and her own hands dropped away from the weapon, too weak to be held up any longer. Her head rolled towards Diana, and for a moment their eyes met.

"Dear God...." was all Isadora said.

And then she died.

Diana tried in vain to rally her, but finally Yi-kin gently pulled her away. "She is dead," he told Diana.

She stood up, not caring that her hands were covered with blood, or that she'd have to deal with the police. At that moment her only thought was:

Revenge.

The police arrived thirty minutes later and listened to their explanation: neither mentioning the demonic possession, explaining only that Isadora had seemed distraught and had stabbed herself before they could react. Although the police were somewhat wary of the young Chinese, Lady Furnaval's standing was accepted as above suspicion, and besides, they knew the medium bore the reputation of unmarried older woman who supposedly spoke to spirits. It took them only a short conversation with one another to accept the explanation of suicide, and allow Diana and Yi-kin to go on their way.

Although Diana knew exactly what they had just witnessed, she could answer few of Yi-kin's other questions: She had no idea if the voice they'd heard had actually—somehow—been that of the incubus she believed she'd killed, or some other entity impersonating it; she couldn't explain why Isadora had never been possessed before (although she began to realize, with an acute discomfort of guilt, that

Isadora had never before held her hand during any contact with the Netherworld). More importantly, she could not tell Yi-kin he was being ridiculous when he warned her that the Cruachan gateway obviously led to a trap.

What she did admit to him was that she had one of the world's finest libraries on the occult back at her estate in Derby, and she needed to begin searching that library immediately.

Although if Stephen Chappell was right, no amount of information would be enough to save them when they stepped through the gateway at Cruachan.

Chapter XXV

September 5-8, 1880
Derby, England

They arrived back at her estate the following day.

Diana was so moved that, upon stepping from the carriage, she nearly fell to her knees and kissed the earth beneath her feet.

Howe greeted her warmly, remarking on her tanned skin ("no more of that now," he chided her gently); he offered a heartfelt thanks and welcome to Yi-kin, whom Diana's letters had already described; and he even picked up Mina for a cuddle.

Diana immediately offered Yi-kin his choice of a suite of rooms in the manor, or his own small guesthouse on the grounds, and he chose the former. Diana suspected it was at least partly because he'd grown very attached to Mina.

After settling in, Diana took Howe aside for several hours and told of all their adventures. He asked to see both her buckshot wounds (which had healed nicely), and the scars on her left arm (which now totaled twelve). He agreed with Diana that it was suicide to enter the Netherworld through the Cruachan gateway, but offered to accompany her if she went. She thanked him, but told him that she needed him on this side, in case she failed—he would still have knowledge of the nature of the invaders, and could perhaps lead the counter-offensive, if need be.

She also asked him to contact her London solicitors to arrange services for Isadora, and learn if she had any relations that needed taking care of. Isadora had never spoken of any family, but Diana was determined to do whatever she could to honor her friend's memory.

The next day Diana fell into the research. She started with Asmodeus: Originally known by the ancient Persians as Aeshma, he was the spirit of lust and anger, and king of the demons. He once fell in love with a human woman named Sarah, and killed each of her seven husbands, thus earning the description of a destroyer of matrimonial tranquility.

Diana thought he'd certainly done his best to destroy her own.

Asmodeus was ancient and powerful, and Diana had no idea if her demon protections or talismans would work against him. Banishing him was especially questionable, since demons were normally exiled *back* to the Netherworld. Asmodeus would require banishing to Hell, something Diana had no experience with it. Stories of humans who had traveled through gateways were horrifying. There were literally hundreds of tales of unwary souls who had stumbled across *sidhe*, or fairy mounds, on Hallowe'en night; most had never been heard from again, although some had been seen again as tortured spirits. There were a few common threads in all of the stories: Those who partook of food or drink in the fairy realm would be trapped there forever, never aging; simple charms like a needle worn in a collar or sleeve were effective protections; and time passed quite differently in the Netherworld than it did in the mortal world.

Bolstered by this new information, Diana was growing in confidence, She presented her findings to Yi-kin and Howe, and told them she believed they should make a test.

"A test...?" Yi-kin asked.

"It's only the seventh of September today, meaning we have plenty of time until Hallowe'en. I want to step through a gateway right away. This week, in fact."

Yi-kin and Howe both gaped at her in disbelief.

"You can't be serious, m'Lady."

"I am, Howe. We need to know if it's even possible, for one thing. We need to know if we'll need special equipment or clothing—"

Howe muttered, "Might I suggest suits of armor?"

Diana ignored him and continued: "There's a gateway in Cornwall still open. I propose to go there promptly, and step through for exactly one minute. I will carry a watch and time myself."

Yi-kin immediately said, "I go through, not you."

"I appreciate the gesture, Yi-kin, but surely you understand that I can't let you do that—"

Howe cut her off, with the most anger she'd ever seen him display. "And you, m'Lady, are far too valuable to risk in such an experiment.

We're all in agreement with the need for some test, but you won't be much use to us if you return as a spirit. Yi-kin or myself are expendable. You're not."

"None of us are expendable," she argued.

"But you are the general," Yi-kin said. "General never fights with soldiers."

"He's right," Howe agreed.

Diana turned her back and paced to the fireplace. She considered all this for a moment, then finally turned back to them. "Very well. We'll talk about this further tomorrow, and decide then who it should be."

Howe breathed an audible sigh of relief, and Yi-kin smiled.

"Me," he boasted.

Yi-kin was awakened early the next morning by a knocking on his door. He leapt from bed, instantly alert, and ran to the door in his undergarments, opening it to reveal Howe. The butler looked very distressed, and was extending a sheet of paper towards Yi-kin.

"The daft woman's gone to do it anyway," he complained. "She left this in the kitchen."

Yi-kin took the note and struggled through Diana's flowing handwriting:

My Dears Howe and Yi-kin:

I'm sorry, but surely you realize I'd never be able to forgive myself if I let either of you go through the gateway and something happened. I already have William and Isadora on my conscience; I'm not sure I can bear more deaths.

I've taken Mina and a watch and gone to the Cornwall gateway. I will time myself very precisely, and step through for exactly one minute. Please remember that time may run very differently in the Netherworld than it does here, so don't panic if I haven't returned by the end of the day.

However, should I not return at all, please do not attempt to rescue me. It may be that human beings simply can't survive in the Netherworld; should that prove the case, this world will need you to lead the forces that will stand against Asmodeus and his armies come midnight of October 31st.

Affectionately,
Diana

Yi-kin looked up from the note to Howe, and saw that the man was on the verge of tears. "She took the fastest horse," Howe added.

Without hesitation, Yi-kin turned away from the door and began to get dressed. "I go after her," he said.

Then he looked back to Howe and asked, "Where is Cornwall?"

Chapter XXVI

September 11, 1880
Cornwall, England

It was late in the afternoon when Diana arrived at the gateway; both she and her steed were exhausted by three days of travel with little sleep.

Fortunately it had been easy to find: This one was located in the ruins of a very old abbey, near a main road. It was a bitter day, with the promise of rain heavy in the air, and the grey sky seemed well suited to the look of the place. *The Book of Gateways, Conjurations and Banishments* said the abbey, which dated back to the tenth century, was said to be haunted, and Diana could see why: It consisted of little more than a few stone archways and broken walls, their surfaces slick with dew and noxious-looking mosses. The land around the abbey was marshy and treeless, and the wind was blowing through the remains of one wall, causing an eerie whistle.

Diana's horse wasn't keen to approach the place, throwing its head about, rolling its eyes, and so Diana tied it to an old post near the road. She removed her satchel from the saddle, sat it on the ground and opened it, freeing Mina. The feline poked her little head out, sniffed the air, and then stepped out of the bag gingerly. Even she was intimidated by the desolation of the place.

Stepping carefully, Mina picked her way past banks of fungi and toppled walls, through a crumbling doorway and over a decayed casement. Finally she stopped, looking up and sniffing the air. And then she hissed.

Diana followed after her, glad for the heavy riding boots she'd chosen (along with tailored woolen slacks and jacket). She carried her familiar satchel, and set it down just behind the cat.

As usual, there was no visual hint of the gateway, but there was an iciness to the air and a particularly pungent stench of something rotten that she was sure didn't belong to this world.

Diana stopped, considering what she was about to do…and for just a few seconds her resolve left her. In all the time she'd been dealing with gateways, all the monstrosities she'd encountered around them, the twelve she'd sealed—she'd never so much as thrust a toe into one herself. She had only folklore to tell her that she wouldn't simply be obliterated when she stepped through; folklore, and the notion that William was alive over there, somewhere.

This was truly insane.

But this must be done. She couldn't wait until Hallowe'en to find out if this was possible; she needed to know now if special arrangements would need to be made, if she'd require equipment that might take her the weeks remaining to gather.

She needed to know if it was possible to return.

She reached into the satchel, and withdrew first a chain of garlic bulbs, which went around her neck. A small scabbard attached to her belt accepted the knife; on the other hip went a holstered pistol. She tucked a crucifix into one pocket, as well as a handful of herbs— rosemary, red rowan berries, and sprigs of willow. She stuck a needle into each sleeve, and lit a lantern. Lastly, she removed two stopwatches; one would go with her, the other would stay on this side.

Her heart was hammering. She took a few deep breaths to calm herself, and finally thought she was ready.

"All right, Mina," she said more to herself than to the snarling, arched cat, "I'll see you in a moment."

Then she started both stopwatches, placed one on the ground next to Mina, picked up her lantern—and stepped through.

Her first sensation came through her feet—she'd left the spongy marsh ground behind, and was now standing on solid stone. She was glad for that, at least—

—and then the visuals assaulted her; for a moment she feared she'd gone mad.

Before her was an impossible landscape: Blizzard-strength winds whipped her hair and clothing madly, and yet a thick, yellow fog roiled around slowly, unmoved by the fierce gales. The fog seemed to glow slightly from within, and billowed to a height of about ten feet;

overhead, the sky was a featureless black, without stars or moon. The ground was punctuated by large, bubbling obsidian pools. There was no life, either flora or fauna, to be seen, and yet Diana thought she could hear screams upon the foul wind.

Something touched her from behind.

Diana spun, raising the pistol she already held in one hand—

—and she nearly shot Yi-kin. He was holding Mina in his arms, and they both peered around, squinting against the blasts.

"Yi-kin," she shouted over the shrieking air, "how did you get here so quickly?!"

"It take me three days to reach Cornwall, and one more day to find you," he called back.

"But that's impossible...I've only just stepped through!" she told him.

He raised his eyebrows, unable to articulate an answer.

Then Diana saw what was behind Yi-kin, and she froze in astonishment:

The gateway—on this side, at least, here in the Netherworld—was surrounded by a great carved stone arch. Although Diana couldn't read the runic writing that covered the stone in bas-relief, its meaning was nonetheless clear: It very plainly told the inhabitants of the Netherworld that this was a gateway.

They're marked on this side, was all Diana could think for a few seconds.

And then she saw Yi-kin stiffen at something he spied over her shoulder, and she spun back around, her own adrenaline coursing:

There was something in the fog.

Or perhaps the fog *was* the something: The sulphurous vapors were forming the suggestion of a great face, with at least six eyes and a huge, circular maw lined with fangs. It seemed to roll in on itself, and then form again. Its form wavered, and then it was there again—but closer.

Diana could only faintly hear Mina's high-pitched howls of terror behind her, and she looked down at the stopwatch:

Only thirty seconds had passed.

She was determined to last the full minute; after all, if she couldn't survive her first sixty seconds in the Netherworld, how could she hope to find William and stop an entire demonic army?

She planted her feet against the gale and turned to face whatever was there. The fog billowed around her, and the face shifted throughout, taking shape on her left, then appearing on her right. She thought she saw other things in the fog now, too—a limb of some kind, reaching out.

Still holding the stopwatch in her left hand, she holstered the gun and reached into her pocket, removing a handful of the herbs and flinging them into the mists.

The leaves and twigs disappeared from view, but there was no other effect.

She withdrew the iron-bladed knife now, and held it before her. And she thought she saw the face quiver once in dismay.

Good.

Forty-five seconds.

Suddenly the ground vibrated beneath their feet. It was followed by another tremor, and another, as if something huge was pounding the earth near them.

Or approaching on gigantic feet.

Sixty seconds.

Diana spun to face Yi-kin. "Now!" she called.

They all started to step beneath the stone arch—

—when something wrapped itself around Diana's ankle.

She twisted around, and saw that the fog had extended out one of its limbs—tentacles? Pseudopods?—and wound itself around her leg. Although it still had the appearance of insubstantial vapor, its grip on her was all too real.

She tugged in vain, but the pull of the limb was stronger, and suddenly her feet went out from under her. She went down on the stone, and was dragged not just into the fog, but towards one of the churning, ebony pools. She grabbed desperately for any handhold, any purchase, but her fingernails shredded against hard rock. She had only seconds unless she did something—

—and then Yi-kin's hands were around her wrists, holding her. Mina launched herself over Diana's body and tore into the smoke-like limb that was wrapped around Diana's leg.

The appendage released Diana's ankle and surrounded Mina. It wrapped itself around the struggling cat, and began drawing her towards the swamp.

Diana acted instinctively, withdrawing the iron-bladed knife and slicing at the vaporous tentacle clutching Mina.

It vanished. It didn't release Mina, or draw back—it simply wasn't there.

Diana didn't wait to see if it would return. She re-sheathed the knife and let Yi-kin help her back up to her feet, then she gathered Mina and together they all sprang at the gateway.

They came out on the other side, and Diana was grateful for the soft swampy ground that cushioned her landing.

Yi-kin was already on his feet, in a defensive pose, and Mina backed away from the gateway, snarling.

Diana's first thought was of the thing on the other side—the thing that might be coming through any second....

She didn't even take the time to roll up her sleeve; she opened her left palm with the knife, and sealed the gateway. Then Mina quieted, but only somewhat, and Diana let herself fall back against a tumble of stones, exhausted.

Yi-kin leaned nearer to her and whispered, "We are not alone."

Diana pulled herself up, just now realizing it was full night, not the day she'd left only a moment earlier. She clawed at the stopwatch, forgotten in a jacket pocket, and witnessed that they'd barely passed two minutes.

Night already?

Then she saw the small fire that Yi-kin had noticed, burning nearby.

They all made their way cautiously towards the fire, and saw a complete small camp, with their horses tethered at one side.

A small camp? That wasn't here when I stepped through.

There was a man sleeping near the fire. As they approached, he heard them and jerked awake with a cry, then scrambled to his feet, plucking nervously at his clothing.

"Ahhh, beggin' yer pardon, ma'am," he exclaimed in a thick, working-class accent, "but you snuck up on me, you did...."

"Who are you?" Diana asked.

The man—who Diana guessed was perhaps thirty, and had the face and rough hands of a laborer—offered her a polite bow. "Name's Jenkins. Your man Howe hired me to keep watch—you'd be Lady Furnaval, now, wouldn't you, mum?"

"I would indeed," Diana replied, amazed, then added, "how long have you been here?"

"Oh, it's been a right long time now, mum. Never found anyone but them horses—I was beginnin' to think somebody'd pulled a joke on poor ol' Jenkins—"

"*How long?*" Diana demanded, stepping up to him.

Jenkins actually flinched and backed away. "Near on six weeks now, mum. Where did you come from anyhow?"

"Six *weeks?*" She turned away, ignoring the man's question, trying to calculate. Six weeks had passed since Howe had sent this man out—

and how long had passed before then? She turned back to him, trying to avoid shouting. "My god—what's the date *today*?!"

Jenkins hesitated, then answered, "October 25th, mum."

October twenty-fifth?! That gave them only six days to return to Derby, prepare, and get to Ireland.

"Yi-kin, we have to go," she said, already gathering up her things and running for her horse. "Mr. Jenkins, you earned yourself the reward of a hundred pounds."

Jenkins watched them go and called out, "So do I get paid now?"

Chapter XXVII

October 25-October 31
Derby England—Cruachan, Ireland

They left Cornwall immediately, and rode for three days, reaching the Derby estate sometime in the wee morning hours of the 29th. Howe was, of course, flabbergasted and delighted to see his mistress, but she told him there was no time to waste and immediately began preparations for the trip to Ireland.

Diana spent the rest of the time until dawn preparing everything Howe would need to run the estate for some years, since they now understood that time was indeed very much different in the Netherworld. He had initially begged to accompany them, of course, but had relented when Diana told him it was crucial that he remain behind, especially should they fail.

They slept on the train ride to Liverpool, and then again on the ship over to Dublin. There they bought food and two horses, and set out for County Roscommon before dawn on October 31st.

They rode west across the cool, green Irish countryside for six brutal hours, pausing only long enough to allow their exhausted mounts water. They arrived in County Roscommon shortly after noon, and by two p.m. they had rented two rooms in a small inn in the village of Tulsk, for a few hours of rest.

At six p.m. they rose, shared a small dinner with the innkeeper and his family (it was a traditional Samhain feast of *colcannon*, a dish made of potatoes, onions and cabbage, and a fruit cake called *barm brack*—the latter had a ring baked within, and the innkeeper's teenage daughter was delighted to find the trinket in her slice of cake, since it portended marriage).

Diana tried not to think of this as a last meal.

After turning down the innkeeper's invitation to stay and enjoy the annual Hallowe'en party, Diana and Yi-kin remounted the horses and forced the poor beasts the last few miles along the Rathcroghan-Lissalway Road. Although evening had already fallen, the night was lit by numerous bonfires, about which many of the locals danced with drunken abandon; but Diana also noticed farmhouses with branches of ash or rowan mounted over doorways and windows, and was reminded of what William had described seeing on Walpurgisnacht in the Transylvanian village. Apparently not all of the residents hereabouts thought of this as a night for parties and capering.

They rode past limestone outcroppings and great mounds of earth, and Diana recalled the research she'd done on the area while back at Derby: Connaught had supposedly been the kingdom of the ancient Celts, and had a rich tradition in local mythology. The mounds, she knew, all marked ancient burial places, and many of the rocky outcroppings were actually the stones from ruined structures. The cave they sought, called *Oweynagat* (which translated to the Cave of Cats) was also known as the "Cave of Cruachan"; it was the most famed entrance to the fairy world, and the setting for a number of unnerving Celtic legends. In the best known, a hero named Nera saw Cruachan in flames one Samhain Eve, and followed an army of fairies into Oweynagat. Nera crossed over into the fairy world and took a fairy wife, who told him the attack was nothing but illusion...but a *real* attack would take place next Samhain. Nera returned to his king, Ailell, and the legendary Queen Maeve, and warned them about the fairies' plan. The following Samhain the incursion was thwarted, but Nera ended up returning to the fairy world forever.

Diana could only hope that meant the Netherworld was more tolerable here than what she'd encountered in Cornwall.

It took them some time to locate the entrance in the dark, and it was nearly nine p.m. by the time they picked it out by the light of their lanterns. It was set into the side of a hill and was low and narrow, distinguished only by a large mound above its mouth, and an ancient Celtic *Ogham* stone, or marker inscribed with Celtic writing. They had no place to tie the horses, so they dismounted and trusted to their steeds to stay close. The horses wandered off a few feet, contentedly nuzzling at the low growth. Diana thought it unlikely that the scene would remain this peaceful much longer, not outside Ireland's Hell-gate on Samhain Eve.

Yi-kin was already kneeling and peering into the cavern, which they would need to crawl into one at a time. "It is bigger inside, I think," he observed.

Diana nodded, but was preoccupied with their final preparations. She had changed into her functional men's suit before they'd left the inn, with knee-high riding boots over her trousers; she added now the holstered knife and gun, (which she hadn't thought it prudent to openly display.) She kept the iron knife, but handed Yi-kin a silver dagger, which might prove useful against certain denizens of the netherworld that were unaffected by iron. She also released Mina, and was alarmed when the little feline ran at top speed for the cave opening and disappeared within.

"Mina!" Yi-kin called after her, as he started wedging himself through the low, narrow cave mouth.

"No, Yi-kin...wait," Diana cautioned. He turned to face her, and saw that she was hurriedly going through the satchel, stuffing her pockets with leaves and twigs, with both a crucifix and a Taoist talisman she'd saved from their experience with the hopping vampires. She checked something in her copy of *The Book of Gateways, Conjurations and Banishments*, which she placed back into the satchel, then she passed Yi-kin a pack which held food, water, candles and lanterns..

Diana took a last look into the ebony sky, studded with stars that seemed suddenly melancholy, and she didn't want to leave them. The smell of the countryside, the chill air, the blissful silence...she savored it all for a few seconds. Then Yi-kin called softly to her from where he knelt by the cave mouth. "We go?"

"We go."

Yi-kin wriggled through the cave opening first, and she followed. They crawled beneath the stone overhanging the entrance, and found themselves in an underground chamber about four feet in height. Stone lintels shored up the walls on either side, and Diana recognized another of the Ogham stones overhead. Although she couldn't decipher the runes inscribed there, she had read that it described the resting-place of a son of Ailell and Maeve.

"This place is made by man," said Yi-kin.

"Yes, this first part of the cave system was built by the ancient Celts. We should find the natural cave just at the end of this passage."

They hunkered forward, crabwalking, and Diana was distressed to see no trace of Mina. After perhaps eight feet the passage ended at an intersection: To the right was little more than a cul-de-sac, while to the left the passage slanted slightly downwards into darkness. They headed in that direction, and after perhaps another twenty feet they found they could now stand upright.

The passage had become a narrow limestone fissure, damp and cool. It began to descend more sharply, with jagged rocks underfoot, and they had to pick their way slowly.

"Why is this cave of cats?" Yi-kin asked, his voice echoing around the stone walls and down the length of the passage. "We cannot even find *our* cat."

"Well," Diana said, trying not to think about the last cave they'd been in, "she could only have gone this way."

The temperature dropped noticeably, and a somehow-familiar, musky odor tainted the air. This part of the cave showed no evidence of human workmanship, and Diana thought that probably very few had ever dared venture this far.

Especially on Samhain.

The odor became stronger, and now Diana could almost place it. There was something to its acrid scent, something of....

"Mina," Yi-kin commented, his nose twitching. "Cave smells like cat *siu bin*."

"Territorial marking," muttered Diana.

The cave flooring evened out beneath their feet, and the passage opened out before them to a wide cavern, perhaps twenty feet wide and at least forty or fifty long. Then they saw the source of the smell:

Cats. There were hundreds of them, in all manner of size, color and breed. They lounged on the hard floor of the cavern, strode lazily about, groomed each other, and batted playfully at tails and ears. Diana's eyes immediately sought out Mina, but there were dozens of gray tabbies, along with fluffy Persians, midnight black toms, sleek little tortoise-shells, regal Siamese, and battle-scarred old grays.

And beyond all the cats was the gateway. This one was clearly visible, shimmering in the lanternlight.

Diana heard Yi-kin gasp with surprise, and knew he'd seen it, too. It took up most of the far wall of the chamber, a rippling circular mass about ten feet in diameter. The rocky cave was dimly visible behind it, but its shimmering depths gave hints of other landscapes as well: Diana thought she glimpsed dead trees, headstones, a full moon....

"Why can we see this gateway?" Yi-kin asked.

Diana shook her head and answered, "I don't know, Yi-kin. Unless...it's simply because this one is somehow more powerful than the others, especially on this night."

Diana took another step onto the floor of the cavern—

—and hundreds of green and yellow eyes turned towards her, reflecting back the glow of their lanterns like lighthouse beacons, warning unwary ships to turn away.

Diana froze, and for a moment there was no movement in the chamber. Yi-kin tensed behind her, his lantern held high, and the sea of cats stared.

Then one of them hissed. And one started towards her.

She felt Yi-kin's hand on her shoulder, pulling her back. "*Siu saam*...." he cautioned.

Diana acquiesced and stepped backwards, moving cautiously. More of the cats were starting towards them now, but as Diana retreated backward into the passage, so the cats lost interest in them and strolled back towards the gateway. One trio stayed behind, eyeing the intruders with mild interest.

"Good—they stop," breathed Yi-kin.

"Well, at least we know why it's called the cave of cats, don't we?" Diana added. "They guard the damnable thing."

"How do we get to gateway?" Yi-kin asked.

Diana took the lantern from him and swung it about, searching out the dimensions of the cavern. There seemed no way around the mass of cats, and Diana was far more reluctant to injure a horde of what might have been family pets than she'd been to do likewise to loathesome lizard people. And she still couldn't find Mina; she could only assume her own beloved companion was out there somewhere amid that feline sea, meaning it was inconceivable that she would consider an offensive attack.

Given the length of the cavern, Diana calculated that she could dive the final quarter of the distance to the gateway. "We have to run for it," she told Yi-kin.

"But we step on cats—" he protested.

And then he stopped short when he noticed the cats regrouping, moving towards them now with more sinister purpose. They blocked themselves firmly between Diana and Yi-kin and the gateway, as if they were rows of tiny soldiers preparing for battle.

"Cats understand us!" Yi-kin whispered.

Diana answered softly, "That's ridiculous, cats can't understand human language—"

One of the cats stood up then, not on four legs, but on two. It reared up on its rear two legs, extending its lean body upright and balancing perfectly, as if born to bipedal motion.

"Of course," Diana admitted, "*normal* cats can't do that, either."

More of the creatures were standing now. Some stood taller than Diana's waist, and she saw with dismay that the claws on their upper paws (hands?) had been unsheathed, and glistened cruelly in the lantern's glow.

They began walking towards Diana and Yi-kin.

The two beleaguered humans began backing up the way they'd just come, desperately trying to keep one eye on the advancing felines and one on the jagged path behind them. The animals advanced on them with a matching, deliberate speed, and although Diana considering drawing her gun she feared exciting the cats to the point of attack.

And then the first cat launched itself at them.

Diana didn't see where it had come from, but before she could react a feline form was flying through the air at her, dagger-like claws extended, fangs bared. She instinctively reached up and caught it in mid-air, and it struggled madly in her grip, keening a nearly-human shriek as it slashed blindly. Diana felt pain in one cheek before she managed to hurl the beast away. She reached up and felt blood trickling down her face.

"Are you hurt?" Yi-kin cried out.

She ignored his question, instead gesturing behind her. "Yi-kin, I want you to go. Run back as fast as you can. These aren't cats!"

Predictably, he refused. "No! I will not leave you—"

"Then we'll both die here, Yi-kin. Now *go*—!"

"Diana saw more cats squatting back onto their haunches, preparing to spring, and she was drawing her gun—

—when Mina appeared at her feet.

She had come up from the sea of her murderous kind and positioned herself before the two humans, turning back to face the feline army. Her own teeth were bared, her hair bristling in a ridge along her spine, her hisses directed at her opponents.

Yi-kin called, "Mina!"

The advancing cats looked at her—and stopped.

Mina continued to snarl and spit at them, and Diana thought surely she would be attacked en masse by the horde of demon cats, but instead the guardians began to pull back, dropping down to all fours again, even turning their backs to walk away. Within seconds they had not only halted their threatening approach, they'd even opened a path in their ranks leading directly to the gateway.

Diana knew Mina had saved them. She reached down and stroked her animal's head, and Mina stopped her angry hissing long enough to look up at Diana and offer a self-satisfied meow.

"Mina, I adore you," Diana said, offering a few more caresses to the cat before rising.

Then Diana stepped into the cavern again, still walking slowly.

The cats were completely placid now; they seemed utterly disinterested as Diana, Yi-kin and Mina moved between them towards the gateway. Diana still kept a cautious eye on them, but the cats had returned to their usual innocent activities.

The human pair were perhaps ten feet from the gateway when one of the cats, an especially large black-and-white tom, roused itself and stepped into their path. They stopped, and then watched in astonishment as the animal began to change: It reared up not on furred hind paws, but on human legs, complete with feet enclosed in whimsical, curled boots. The metamorphosis continued on up the rest of the body, the shape melting and twisting, colors shifting and running, fur becoming skin and cloth, until a small man-like being stood before them.

He stood about four feet tall, with a slender build, a colorful tunic that shimmered in different colors as Diana looked at it, a wide belt seemingly made of leaves, and long golden hair that fell to his shoulders.

He also possessed lacey, translucent wings and gracefully-pointed ears.

His narrow face was as rosy-cheeked and unlined and hairless as a child's, yet there were ancient lines creasing his vivid blue eyes. He smiled at them, and executed an elaborate bow before speaking:

"Welcome, Lady Furnaval. My lord Asmodeus has sent me to welcome you to the netherworld."

Diana said, "I see. And you are...?"

He answered, "You may call me Robin."

Ahhh, of course.

"Robin Goodfellow, I presume?" she inquired.

He gave her a nod of acknowledgement. "Quite right, Lady. I salute you."

Yi-kin stepped close to her and whispered, "You know this...man?"

"*M hai yan*, Yi-kin. Mr. Goodfellow is a fairy—*siu gwai*."

Siu gwai...Diana didn't know the Cantonese word for fairy—if there was one—and little ghost was as close as she could come.

"*Ming baak*," Yi-kin answered. Apparently her rough translation had worked.

Diana turned back to the fairy. "Yes, Mr. Goodfellow's quite famous in Britain. He has a most impressive reputation for mischief."

Goodfellow feigned embarrassment. "M'lady is too kind."

"Oh no, Robin, you're really very well known, and I'm perfectly acquainted with some of your adventures. You see, Yi-kin," Diana directed back over her shoulder, never taking her eyes off Goodfellow, "our friend here is a shapeshifter. In the form of a will-o'-the-wisp, he's led travellers over cliff edges to their doom; I believe he's even taken the form of a horse, tempting a weary journeyer to mount him only to throw the unfortunate man into a river."

Robin laughed and then said, "Oh, but *that* chap only broke an arm!"

She offered Robin a tight smile, then told him, "You'll pardon us, I'm sure, if we proceed with caution around you."

Diana passed the lantern to Yi-kin, then shrugged out of her coat and handed that back to him as well. "Here, hold this, please."

Yi-kin took the coat while eyeing her with amazement. "Miss Diana, why do you…?"

But, she was working on the buttons of her vest. "You see, Yi-kin, according to legend, Robin Goodfellow can be gotten rid of by handing him a waistcoat. I thought we'd just test that folktale right now."

She was rewarded with a flash of fear across the little imp's face, followed by a nervous smile. "Now, Lady, you don't want to do that until you've heard why I'm here, do you?"

Her smile broadened as she finished unbuttoning her vest. She pulled her watch and fob from the pockets, placed them in one trouser pocket, and then pulled the vest off. She dangled it from her fingers, appearing to consider what next to do.

Robin backed anxiously towards the gateway. "Lady Furnaval, if you dismiss me now you'll never see William or Asmodeus."

She handed the waistcoat back to Yi-kin. "I'll have you hold this until we hear what our friend has to say."

Diana took her coat back and put it on again, while the fairy noticeably relaxed. "Wise choice. You see, I have very specific instructions for you. Were you to cross over on your own, you wouldn't stand a chance."

Diana asked, "And what are those instructions?"

Robin gestured to the gateway. "You'll receive them on the other side. Now, if you'll just follow me…."

Without a pause, he stepped through the gateway. Its surface trembled, resembling an impossibly vertical surface of clear water into which a stone had just been cast; then Robin disappeared, and Diana knew he awaited them in the Netherworld.

She did not move.

Behind her, Yi-kin nearly danced in agitation. "We cannot go! He will trick us...."

"Yes, I'm sure he'll *try*," Diana answered.

"Then...what...."

Diana answered, "The fairies of folklore liked nothing more than games, Yi-kin. I suspect Robin will offer us some sort of challenge on the other side. If we win, we'll probably be allowed to see Asmodeus. And...William."

Yi-kin said, "Maybe game already start. Maybe when we go to Netherworld *siu gwai* kill us."

Diana thought on that. "If that was all he wanted, he could have tried already."

She accepted a lantern from Yi-kin and took a step towards the portal.

"Lady Diana, *m ho*—!" Yi-kin cried out.

She stopped at the opening and turned back to him. "I'm sorry, Yi-kin, but I have no choice. And I'd tell you that you don't either, but it would be pointless, wouldn't it?"

Yi-kin paused long enough to parse her sentence, then nodded. "Yes. Pointless. I go first."

With that he raised his lantern and stepped through the gateway into the Netherworld.

Diana was about to follow when a voice caused her to draw up short.

"Diana...."

She spun about, both thrilled and incredulous. The voice belonged to Stephen Chappell.

He was there, impossibly, standing in the middle of the cavern; cats slept peacefully nearby, unconcerned by his presence.

In fact, the cats at Stephen's feet were purring.

He was looking at her seriously, with a hint of anger, or disappointment. "You were warned not to do this," he said.

She swallowed in a suddenly dry throat, and realized she had no idea how to answer.

He walked to her, and she noticed that his feet seemed to find their own way miraculously through the now-placid feline guardians, and then she wondered if his feet were actually passing *through* the cats. Still, his presence in front of her, now only inches away, felt real enough. If anything, it felt *too* real; she was acutely aware of him, of his very essence.

"I...." she started, then had nothing else to say.

"It may not be too late to save your friend. Step through only long enough to bring him back, then get out of this place. Samhain will be done by the time you come back, and you'll be able to leave safely. Leave...and don't return."

"Who...or *what* are you?" she asked.

"I told you before, Diana: Just as there are forces for evil in these worlds, so there are universal forces for good. I am simply a representative of those forces. And they are very concerned for you."

She demanded, "Then why don't they ever help me?"

"They have helped you," he affirmed.

"When?" she asked.

"On several occasions. I've provided information, and other times you've been given protection. For example, when you escaped the lizard men's realm in Los Angeles, we saw to it that you and your companions survived."

"There was a young man who was with me there, Manuel, who died. Why did your friends let that happen?"

Stephen thought briefly, then answered, "As I recall, that young man was killed not by any supernatural creature, but by a shotgun blast."

She nodded. "So I'm on my own when it comes to guns, is that what you're saying?"

Stephen looked away, seemingly chastened. "Believe me, Diana, if we could have saved that young man, we would have."

"My friend Isadora, then. Or will you simply dismiss that as an accident with a letter opener?"

"The answer should be obvious: Your medium's spirit had entered the Netherworld, as she searched for answers to your questions."

She wanted to tell him that wasn't possible, that Isadora hadn't died in part because of what she'd asked...but she felt the crushing truth of it, and the guilt threatened to overwhelm her.

Stephen sensed how distraught she was, and softened his tone. "You didn't kill her, Diana...but something in the Netherworld did. Step through that gateway, and you completely relinquish any protection from us whatsoever."

"Why?"

"We have no foothold in the Netherworld; it belongs to the dark ones. If you enter into their kingdom, you place yourself utterly under their control. We won't be able to aid you at all. You'll be quite alone."

Mina chose that moment to curl around Diana's feet, meowing softly. Diana smiled down at her, then looked back up at Stephen. "Apparently not quite alone."

He also offered Mina a fond look, but then returned to Diana. "You can't save William."

"Why not?"

Stephen looked away, silent, and Diana's ire rose. "I'm sorry, Stephen, but you're not much of a guardian angel. You offer only vague hints and try to tell me that your side has been protecting and helping me all along, but strangely enough it feels to me as if my friends and I have done everything on our own. Now unless you can offer me tangible reasons for not attempting to find William, or tell me exactly what to expect in the Netherworld, our conversation is ended, I think."

He suddenly reached out and took one of her hands in his. "Here's a tangible reason, then: *I* want you to stay."

"With you, you mean?" she asked.

"Yes."

She felt the warmth of his hand on hers, his almost magnetic pull, his lovely dark eyes; it would have been easy, so easy, to say yes, to take him into her arms, into her bed....

"I'm sorry, Stephen," she said, after a long moment, pulling her hand from his. "Were it not for William, we could perhaps have enjoyed many a pleasurable evening together."

He chuckled softly, then ran a hand along her jaw. "I adore your frankness."

"And sadly, that's all you can adore." She pulled away from him, stepping toward the gateway.

Stephen's jaw clenched for an instant, then he called after her, "You know you won't survive. And neither will the boy."

"Goodbye, Stephen." She turned toward the gateway, and Mina ran through ahead of her, disappearing into the Netherworld. Diana was lifting her foot for the final step that would carry her across when he called one last time:

"Wait, Diana...."

She turned back to see him holding a small object out to her.

"Since I've failed in scaring you out of this plan...this might save you."

She took the offering and saw that it was a bullet, but of some strangely-colored and shimmering material she couldn't identify. "What am I to do with this?"

Stephen's eyes betrayed his nervousness; he looked away, oddly uncomfortable. "I...must ask something of you, Diana, something I wouldn't ask were it not necessary."

"And what is that?"

He forced himself to look at her again. "I can't simply tell you how to use this bullet. Its employment requires more than simple knowledge; it also needs a—well, a quality that only those who made the bullet have."

Diana waited, but when he didn't go on, she asked, "And how will you impart that quality to me?"

"I must possess you, spiritually. For a moment."

Diana gaped, then couldn't hold back a laugh. "You can't be serious."

"I am."

When she didn't respond, he pressed her: "I assure you, it won't be dangerous, certainly not like what doomed your friend Isadora. It should only take seconds. Diana...I don't believe you can survive without this."

She studied him briefly, then thought of Yi-kin and Mina, waiting on the other side. How long had it been now for them—hours? Days?

"What's involved in this possession?"

"It's quite simple," Stephen said, "you close your eyes and try to think of nothing."

"That's it?" Diana said.

Stephen nodded. "Yes."

"Then do it."

She saw his smile, then closed her eyes.

Almost immediately Diana felt a strange sensation, like a strong wind buffeting her, but without physical force, and she stiffened.

She heard a small chuckle from Stephen. He said, "I knew you'd be strong, but...you can't fight me, Diana. It won't work if you do."

She uttered a slightly irritated sigh, and tried again to think of nothing.

"Better...focus on the purring of the cats."

She did as instructed, trying to push thoughts of peril and loss to the back of her mind, trying not to contemplate the horrors that awaited her, listening only to the gentle voiceless vibrato, the lulling rhythmic thrum....

And suddenly she was assaulted with a rush of feelings and sights not her own. From a maelstrom of thoughts she picked out images of herself, of London, of San Francisco, of places she'd never been, of places she knew didn't exist in her world.

Stephen had taken her.

She tried to move her right arm, and had a brief second of panic when she realized she had no idea whether she'd succeeded or not. Then she felt his thoughts, soothing her, reassuring, and her anxiety died away.

His presence within her was a warm companionship, more intimate than anything she'd ever experienced. She felt his desire for her, and it coursed through her until it met with her own equally strong attraction to him. Like mirrors set up facing one another that reflected infinity, their passions merged and were returned uncountable times, each return amplifying the intensity. Somewhere buried under that endless flood of feeling, she knew Stephen was working within her, changing something at her very core, altering her immutably. And Diana, in return, knew she was transforming him in some other way, taking in the essence of goodness at Stephen's center and returning it as something closer to human. His grace, her strength, entwined and replaced each other until Diana thought she would surely burst into white-hot flame.

And then he was abruptly gone, and she was staggering.

He caught her, and held onto her until her stamina returned, and she was able to stand on her own. She pushed away from him slightly, and knew she was flushed. "Was it...did it...?"

Stephen could only nod. He'd obviously been as affected by the possession as she.

Diana searched herself, examining both her thoughts and her body; she felt only a warmth just below her stomach, fading even as she explored the sensation. "I don't feel different."

Stephen took a deep breath before answering: "You are. You won't feel it until necessary."

"And when will that be?"

"When you face Asmodeus. *If* you face Asmodeus."

Diana frowned. "I don't understand—if?"

Stephen was suddenly very serious again, as he'd been when they'd first met. "What I've given you can't protect you from everything in the Netherworld. When you first cross over, Goodfellow will offer you a challenge. Should you survive it, you'll be permitted to see Asmodeus. At that point you'll have your chance to destroy him; it will require the bullet, and what I've left within you."

Diana had forgotten she was still holding the odd bullet. She brought it up to her eyes again, examining it. "Only one bullet?"

He nodded. "It was...very costly to us to manufacture even that one. You'll only have one chance, Diana."

She eyed the unearthly ammo a last time, then unholstered her revolver, removed one of her bullets, and replaced it with this new one. She snapped the chamber closed, holstered the pistol, and offered Stephen a last smile.

"Then one chance will have to be enough," she told him.

They looked into one another's eyes for a long moment, and Diana knew she would now be forever connected to Stephen, bonded to something not even human but immeasurably good.

She saw a tide of sadness wash across his features, and he took her hands in his own. "I'm sorry I cannot accompany you myself, Diana. I truly am."

She nodded, stroked his fingers once, then pulled away.

Just before she stepped through, she turned back. "Stephen, will you see to it that Mina is cared for?"

"Of course."

Then she left all goodness behind, and entered the Netherworld.

Chapter XXVIII

October 31
The Netherworld

The first thing they saw was the moon.

Or at least, the Netherworld's moon, since its size was impossible for any moon they could know; it took up a full quarter of the sky, floating what seemed to be a foot above the land, perfectly full and round and bright.

Its shadows also bore an amazing resemblance to a skull.

Diana tore her eyes away from the huge, gibbous thing, and turned to make sure Yi-kin was with her. He stood nearby, gazing into the distance.

"I'm sorry I took extra time arriving, but it was…necessary…."

Her voice trailed off as she saw what he was looking at:

The graveyard.

Because now that Diana's eyes, which had been dazzled by the moon, adjusted to the gloom beneath, she saw they stood in a true necropolis, a cemetery that stretched endlessly in all directions, a true city of the dead. There were granite headstones intermingled with marble monuments, crypts with wrought iron doors and carved angels of death, all shining dully under the light of that night orb. Behind them was the gateway, set into its own oversized monument, surmounted by a stone grim reaper complete with scythe.

"Impressive, isn't it?"

She turned, expecting to find Robin Goodfellow—and couldn't stifle a gasp when she saw not the charming fairy with elfin face and whimsical dress, but a towering, black-skinned demon. The thing stood at least seven feet tall, and was possessed of white horns, yellow eyes, and great leathery wings, which folded inward and outward as Diana watched. The lower part of its body was shaggy, and other than the long dark fur it wore no clothing.

It grinned down at her, its snake-yellow eyes creasing in malevolent mirth—and Diana suddenly realized, with a second small gasp, that it *was* Robin Goodfellow, in truer form.

That understanding gave her new strength, and she addressed the demon fairy: "So, Robin, a fairy in one world, but a demon in this other, eh?"

He laughed, a deep, guttural sound. "Very perceptive of you. Here you may call me Hob. "

Yi-kin stepped closer to Diana. *"Ngoh m ming baak...."*

She wished she could have explained it to him in Cantonese, but her grasp of that difficult tongue was not up to the task yet. "Usually fairies are nothing more than mischievous creatures, Yi-kin; but there are some tales which suggest that fairies may actually be demons in the *sidh* world...or...*here*. Robin Goodfellow was sometimes called 'hobgoblin.' Apparently those stories were correct."

Diana turned back to Hob, and swept the graveyard with a gesture. "I have to say, this isn't how I imagined the fairy world."

Hob responded, "It doesn't all look like this."

"Of course. And I would imagine there's some particular reason your master wanted us to see this particular part of it?"

Hob offered her a small nod of approval, "Very good. He wishes to offer you a challenge."

"I thought he might."

Hob walked forward a few feet, and waved a clawed hand at the ground. Diana looked down, and saw a narrow gravel pathway materialize at their feet—or rather, it was something *like* gravel, but it had its own ethereal glow, a slight greenish cast. About four feet wide, it led out into the graveyard from where they stood, and was lost to their view only a few dozen yards on as it curved around a large tomb.

"This path," Hob instructed her, running one talon a foot above its surface, "is your lifeline. If you follow it, it will eventually lead you through the necropolis, and to the castle of my lord Asmodeus...and your husband."

She looked into the far distance, but could make out no trace of a castle. She turned back to look at Robin, who seemed to be waiting for her question: "And what exactly is the challenge?"

"Simple: You must stay on this path. Confine your steps completely to it, and you will reach the far side safely. However, set one foot off the path, and...."

"And what?" Diana asked, not really expecting an answer, but curious to see what the demon would say.

"Well, there are things in the cemetery that will no longer consider you off-limits."

Diana looked around again, chilled at the thought of what things might be lurking out among the gravestones. In the distance, she heard a soft voice, moaning or chanting, although it could have been the wind....

Yi-kin looked at her curiously. "We only must stay on this path? Why is this *challenge?*"

Diana answered, "I doubt that it will be anything easy, Yi-kin—"

At that instant Hob suddenly roared—an immense, lion-like sound—and dove at them, his great wings spreading under the moonlight, his mouth open and eyes ablaze, and Yi-kin involuntarily stumbled backward. Diana reached out and steadied him just as he was about to step off the phosphorescent gravel. She turned with defiance back to Hob, who now stood only inches from them, laughing uproariously.

"Oh, you'll do just fine!" the demon howled.

Irritated, Diana snatched her waistcoat from Yi-kin and thrust the garment into Robin's hands before he could react. His laughter died abruptly and he stared from the vest to Diana with wide, shocked eyes.

"You know, Robin, I'm just glad the challenge wasn't a riddle, because I'm really not very good at riddles. Now goodbye."

The demon uttered a cry of frustration, then spread his wings and launched himself into the air. He flew away from the moon, and was lost from sight in seconds.

Yi-kin pulled his arm free from Diana's grip, returning angrily to the center of the path. "Just now I would not leave path—!"

Diana said, trying not to smile, "Of course you wouldn't. I'm sorry I over-reacted."

Yi-kin was mollified, then bent halfway down to stare at the ground just beyond the gravel stones. "What if we do? There is nothing."

Diana took a deep breath, then said, "I'm sure there will be plenty of somethings ahead, Yi-kin. Now let's go."

She set off, leading the way down the path, Yi-kin following slightly behind. She kept her eyes firmly on the ground in front of her, trying not to look too closely into the crypts and open plots that occasionally crowded their way. At one point, she realized her lantern was actually unnecessary, and was even making it slightly harder to follow the sickly green glow of the stones.

"Hold on," she stopped him, "let's put the lanterns away."

He shrugged out of his backpack, then unstrapped it and held it open while she snuffed out the lanterns, waited for them to cool, and secured them inside. Diana checked her pocket watch while Yi-kin shouldered the pack again.

The watch seemed to be functioning normally, and showed that only a few minutes had passed.

"Miss Diana—" Yi-kin suddenly whispered, and Diana looked up from the watch to see him staring fearfully at something.

She followed his gaze, and found he was looking at a life-size marble statue of a grieving woman, set near the front of a crypt. The sculpture was finely detailed and vividly portrayed a veiled woman with hunched shoulders, carrying a bundle of lilies. She guessed the statue was meant to suggest a mother's sorrow over the loss of a child.

Then the statue opened its eyes and looked at Diana.

Her heart quickened and she tensed, prepared to flee along the path, but the statue made no other move; it simply stared out at Diana with eyes that were somehow accusatory.

"Stone thing watch us," Yi-kin breathed.

"Well, yes, Yi-kin, remember—we're in the Netherworld now. I expect we'll see much worse than that."

He nodded, but his eyes kept darting back to the statue.

"Just try to keep your eyes on the path, don't look to the sides. Hob said we'd be safe as long as we didn't leave the path."

"What if he *gong daai*?" Yi-kin asked.

Gong daai... speak big...lie.

Diana decided to answer honestly. "If they really wanted to kill us, they would've tried already. Besides...."

She was unsure how much to say; were they being spied on even now? Did she dare tell Yi-kin of her meeting with Stephen, of how he'd secretly armed her for her encounter with Asmodeus? She was mulling over her answer when Yi-kin shushed her. "Something come on path."

Listening, Diana heard it as well: The sound of feet crunching gravel. It didn't sound large, but it was definitely on the path—where they were supposedly safe.

"See? Demon lie."

Diana glimpsed a low shape outlined against the glowing way, coming toward them. "No, wait—it's—"

"Mina!" Yi-kin cried out happily as the cat joined them. She seated herself at Diana's feet and meowed.

Diana groaned and picked up her companion. "You were supposed to stay behind. But you were having none of that, were you?"

Yi-kin joined in with the petting, and when they started off again, he held the cat firmly in his arms.

Mina meowed for Diana to follow.

With a small smile to herself, she followed.

Yi-kin kept his eyes fixed firmly to their path, walking rapidly. She did her best to follow his example, but she couldn't resist the occasional glance to right or left...although those glances nearly cost her the contest once or twice.

The necropolis was haunted.

The manifestations were small at first—a candle floating by itself over the grave of a child. The sound of sighs emanating from a sealed crypt. A headstone that trembled, as if whatever lay beneath it were recklessly trying to rise. Once Diana was reminded of a fake séance she had witnessed several years before, in which the so-called medium had supposedly levitated musical instruments and produced trailing strings of "ectoplasm." Diana had laughed at the obvious theatricality of it all. She wasn't laughing now. She knew there were no hidden strings holding up the candle, no unseen assistant pushing against the tombstone. This was all real. It was dead and deadly.

At one point the path zigzagged around a large tomb, and within the tomb Diana plainly saw a spectre.

It began as a faint glimmering deep within the tomb, the interior of which was visible beyond its iron-barred door. The bluish glow swirled and rippled, then coalesced into the indistinct figure of a robed and veiled woman. Although the ghost—for there was no question that was what Diana saw—lacked solid form or distinct features, Diana thought it had turned and was looking straight at her, its eyes nothing but black wells surrounded by glimmering ectoplasm.

"Miss Diana—" Yi-kin was calling, and then Diana realized she'd stopped to stare at the apparition.

Yi-kin had walked past the crypt without seeing it, and Diana thought it just as well that he not, so she pulled herself away from the sight and walked to him quickly, urging him along the path.

"Sorry, Yi-kin. Just...nothing."

"What...?" he started to ask.

"Just walk," Diana commanded.

A few paces later, it became impossible to keep him from seeing the ghosts, because they were everywhere now.

They appeared near graves, in mausoleums, came walking through solid crypt walls. Most were little more than rough human shapes, their forms indistinct as if they were so old that corporeality bore little meaning for them. Some seemed to be unaware of the pair; a few floated towards the path, causing Yi-kin to slow, then stop.

"*Hui laa!*" Diana blurted, hoping she'd used the right Cantonese inflection for issuing commands.

It must have been correct, because Yi-kin tore his eyes from their ethereal companions and continued on. Diana heard him muttering a mantra to himself, perhaps in hopes of drowning out the rising wails surrounding them: "*M hoh yi tai…m hoh yi tai….*"

Can't see.

When some of the apparitions took on more distinct outlines, she began to think that good advice, because not all of them were exactly human. The spirit of a soldier still bore not only his old uniform, but his gruesome battle wounds as well, including a large chunk of missing skull. One wraith seemed to have brought the decay of the grave with her, as her hair was largely missing, her eyes and nose sunken, and her teeth protruding from gumless jaws. One thing actually flew towards the path and stopped mere inches from Diana, fixing her with glittering eyes surmounting a death's head rictus grin, and Diana staggered back from that one, catching herself just before she stumbled off the path.

Still, she reminded herself, they couldn't really do anything to them while they kept to the path. At least that's what Hob had claimed.

And then one of the ghosts stepped onto the path directly before them.

Yi-kin, head down and eyes averted, didn't see the thing until Diana clapped a hand to his shoulder and stopped his forward movement. Then his head involuntarily jerked up, and his eyes went wide when he saw the six-foot tall spectre that stood in their way.

It was female, and dressed as a bride, in tattered white gown and veil. Although it was difficult to make out a face under the tulle, Diana thought she saw eyes gleaming with malevolence, set far back in deep sockets. The ghost hadn't moved since it had appeared on the path (although the shreds of its dress and train blew in the opposite direction from the breeze), and Diana began to have the uncannily strong notion that the spirit was somehow related to her.

Or that perhaps...it *was* her, the part of her that was still a young bride devastated by the loss of her husband; the part of her that died with William.

Yi-kin and even Mina seemed to sense some connection as well; He looked from the spectre to Diana and back again, while Mina—who thus far had hidden herself away in his arms—raised her head and spat furiously at the ghost.

Diana stepped forward, intending to to soothe Mina—and instead stared in shock as the spectral bride hurtled towards her. She forced herself to freeze, thinking that surely the thing only intended to frighten her off the path—

—and it passed directly through her.

Every molecule in Diana's body suddenly ached as if it had been paradoxically scalded by great cold. She was shaking so badly that she fell to her knees, and she might very well have tumbled over the edge of the path had Yi-kin not been there to catch her. He dropped Mina as he knelt behind Diana, and she crumpled into his arms.

"Miss Diana!" he called in alarm, holding her awkwardly. Mina stalked back and forth along the near edge of the path, apparently intuiting the dangers of stepping over its edges without needing to be told.

Instantly Diana knew that it was possible to feel a color, and the color she felt was black, the black of the infinite, cold void between stars, the black that comes at the cessation of life. Then, slowly, she began to feel warmth creep back into her, banishing the blackness and returning strength. After a few minutes she pulled away from Yi-kin, and began testing her legs.

"I'm all right now," she said, as she wobbled with only a hint of unsteadiness.

"That ghost—it go through you!" Yi-kin exclaimed.

Diana nodded, then turned to look behind them. The bride had disappeared, and Diana hoped they'd not see it again.

"You are fine?" Yi-kin asked, eyeing her warily.

Diana didn't take the question lightly. She searched within herself, but found that she really was fine; apparently the invasive spirit had left no taint, no piece of itself behind to poison her. She felt strong and warmly human again, and tried to smile for him. *"Jan ge ho.* Really, I'm fine. Let's go."

He eyed her doubtfully for a second more, then reluctantly scooped up Mina. "Good...but I will go first again."

Diana's experience turned out to have an unexpected benefit: Yi-kin no longer seemed quite so disturbed by the ghosts around them. Now that one had possibly injured his employer by passing through her, he deemed them all enemies, and was energized to fight...even though there was nothing to hit.

As, for example, there was nothing to strike out against at the first spirit who passed through *him*.

They had reached a point where the path wound through a stand of withered trees. Their branches were largely denuded of leaves, their wood cracking and gray, and yet they must have possessed some latent life, for thick clumps of parasitical growth prevented the moonlight from reaching the ground beneath the trees, and even the green aura of the path was obscured by fallen leaves. Yi-kin stopped fifty feet from the entrance to the grove and peered into it warily.

"I think we will need lanterns," he said, and was just setting Mina down to remove his backpack when Diana saw the spirit that floated towards him from the side of the path. It was half-formed, little more than a suggestion of human form, without distinct features.

"Yi-kin—!" she cried out, but was too late.

The amorphous thing passed through him, and he stiffened and abruptly toppled over. And the thing that had passed through him briefly gained strength, and some shape. It turned on legs clad in translucent shreds, and Diana saw that it now had a cadaverous face, with lips drawn back from gumless teeth. It was grinning at her.

Then it passed beyond the path and through a tomb wall, and was lost from sight.

Diana rushed to Yi-kin, who lay unmoving, his eyes frozen wide. At first she feared him dead, then she saw a tiny spasm pass through him. "Yi-kin," she called, taking his hands in her own. His were freezing cold, and she rubbed them briskly, trying to restore warmth and life.

She remembered a flask of brandy she'd stowed in the pack; she found it, then tilted it to his lips. Some dribbled over his chin, but enough found its way past his gritted teeth. The liquor seemed to work; he suddenly spluttered, convulsed, and grabbed her hand for another swallow from the flask. Finally he managed to sit up, still trembling, his gaze haunted.

"Cold thing go through me," he muttered.

"Yes," Diana said, "I'm sorry, Yi-kin. It was my fault. I saw it, but didn't warn you in time."

"I cannot do it again; my *chi* is not good. I will die."

Diana knew it was true; they had each lived through such passage once, and perhaps could twice, but Diana knew she didn't have enough warmth to survive a third such occurrence.

"We need to watch out for each other," she told him, helping him to his feet. "It should be possible to avoid them."

Yi-kin staggered, and Diana reached out a hand to steady him. His eyes darted around anxiously, and for a second Diana thought, *Stephen was right; we won't survive this.*

But for the moment she could see no more spirits, and although the path ahead was dark beneath the trees, Diana thought that might be good, since the ghosts had a faint blue light about them.

She reached into the pack, got the lantern, and kindled it. Nearby, Mina eyed the trees warily, but seemed calm enough.

Yi-kin re-shouldered the pack, then bent to pick up the cat. Hoisting the lantern, Diana led the way. "Let's go. We'll move slowly and cautiously."

Yi-kin nodded and followed behind her, still very tense.

They entered the grove, and Diana felt a new unease. The rotting limbs overhung the path, in places forcing them to duck as they walked beneath them; the dead leaves crackled underfoot, but even so Diana thought she could hear slithering among the woods on either side of the path. Once she heard a skittering overhead, and looked up to see several pairs of golden eyes glaring down at her. As she watched, they blinked and then vanished. She thought she heard a hiss, but whether it was the sound of a dry tongue lapping air or wings taking night flight, she couldn't tell. Behind her, Mina growled softly in Yi-kin's arms.

She brushed past several twigs (trying not to think of how they'd seemed to brush back), and then saw the thinning edge of the stand of trees a dozen feet farther on.

And beyond the trees were ghosts. Hundreds of them, hovering beside the path, over the path, and on the path.

Yi-kin joined her, saw the otherworldly road-block before them, and halted.

"Well," she could only say, "this isn't good."

The apparitions mulled around the pathway, having neither destinations nor legs to take them there; because they were transparent, Diana realized that she could see ghosts *through* ghosts, many layers deep. They were of all sizes, ages, professions and genders; some were so solid that Diana could have recognized them in daily life had she seen them again, while others (which she supposed were of great age) seemed little more than a few wisps, distinguishable from smoke or fog only by their movement, which bespoke some vague intelligence.

"If we try to pass through there, we die," Yi-kin said, stating the obvious.

Diana nodded, even while considering that death in the necropolis of the Netherworld would only be the beginning; they would doubtless be consigned to join these creatures, to aimlessly roam among the tombs for all eternity, feeling more and more of themselves simply drift away until they were little more than a few shreds, perhaps leaving only the awareness of great pain and loneliness at the end. Had these lost souls round her and Yi-kin once been travellers to the Netherworld? Had they each failed this same challenge, and now sought retribution against any who were likewise foolish enough to try? Or had they ever even been human?

Diana forced herself away from pointlessly philosophical musings, and back to the task at hand. Yes, it would certainly be suicidal to attempt to blunder their way through that deathless horde; however, even returning the way they'd come was no guarantee of safety. Both Stephen Chappell and Hob had suggested that this challenge could be won, so there had to be some way to overcome this obstacle.

She doubted that any of the herbs or talismans she'd brought would be effective against ghosts; she wracked her brain, trying to think of anything she'd ever read that might have mentioned a useful defense against otherworldly spirits, but nothing came to mind. After all, ghosts in her world—while frightening—were typically harmless.

She'd never heard of someone in the Great Britain of 1880 being frozen by spirits.

Frozen....

"Wait...of course...." Suddenly she was looking at the branches around them. She reached up and pulled one down, although it resisted being snapped completely off.

"Yi-kin, can you break this?"

He reached up and snapped the branch, then eyed the six-foot length of wood curiously. "Why?" he asked.

"Crack that in two," she commanded, already digging through the backpack without even bothering to ask him to remove it.

Yi-kin broke the branch into two yard-long sections, and waited while Diana rooted around in the pack. She pulled out two strips of paraffin-soaked cloth, which she'd brought expressly for torch-making, and wrapped them quickly around the wooden clubs as he held them, all the while his eyes darted nervously from her to the wandering spectres.

"You think *gwai* afraid of light, like lizard people?"

"Not light—heat. Something that cold would have to react to heat, yes?"

"But Miss Diana—" he started.

Diana cut him off, as she finished tying the cloth around the branches, then lit a twig from the light of the lantern. "If we have to, Yi-kin, we'll set fire to these trees."

Yi-kin looked around them, feeling distinctly uneasy at the idea of burning the malevolent trees. "*Due m jue*, but I do not think that is good idea." Somehow he thought the bole of the nearest trunk was actually soundlessly snarling at him, its bark whorled in a way that suggested an elongated, nightmarish face.

Diana finished lighting one of the torches. She put out the lantern and stowed it in the pack, took the lit torch from Yi-kin, and touched it to his. Then she stepped around him, wielding the torch like a sword. "Well, then—I thought of this, so I'll go first."

She took four wary steps toward the ghosts, reaching the edge of the woods. With only a few feet separating her from the spirits, she began to wave the torch in the direction of the nearest spectre.

And then her heart leapt into her throat as she saw all the entities turn en masse towards the source of the heat, and begin to converge on it.

She stumbled back, lowering the torch uncertainly. "Oh dear," she began.

"I am afraid this happen," said Yi-kin, also backing away. "In China we light fire at *Yue Laan* because ghost *like* fire."

"You might have mentioned that earlier," Diana chided him.

"I try," Yi-kin responded somewhat sheepishly.

And then a new idea occurred to her, and she stopped backpedaling.

"Wait, this still might work."

She stepped as close to the spirits as she dared, then pulled back her arm—and hurled her torch as far as she could into the graveyard to the left of the path.

All of the spectres turned as one to follow its arc through the air, and they drifted off the path in search of the torch and its heat.

Not quite all of them had been lured away; a few were still tempted by Yi-kin's brand. "Throw it the other way!" she barked at him.

He did, sending his torch sailing through the air to the right. And the last of the ghosts turned to float after it.

"That's it—let's go!"

Yi-kin paused only long enough to scoop up Mina, then followed Diana, who was moving along the pathway at a trot.

They had successfully cleared the ghosts.

Diana knew they were taking a considerable risk—after all, should they round the corner of some tomb and find themselves again confronting a wall of the undead, she doubted she'd have time to make and light more torches—but the path ran straight before them as far as they could see, again offering its green effluence beneath the moon's light, and there were no more phantoms to be seen.

They trotted until Diana's lungs could no longer keep pace with her anxiety, and she allowed herself to slow to a walk, then finally a pause. She was vaguely annoyed that Yi-kin, despite being burdened with both cat and pack, appeared not at all winded.

Ah youth. Or gender. Or race.

Yi-kin apparently caught her look. "What?" he asked.

"Nothing," Diana answered. *"Mo ah."*

Half-an-hour later they stumbled over the first body part.

Literally. Diana, who had been peering out into the unnervingly quiet gravescape, felt her foot snag on something and just caught herself before stepping off the path. Surprised, she turned back, and saw Yi-kin and Mina both peering down at the object that had caused her consternation.

It was a severed hand.

"Sau," mumbled Yi-kin.

Diana knelt to examine it more closely. It was old and mummified, shriveled flesh clinging to bone, ivory poking through in places. It included a few inches of narrow wrist, and the bone hadn't been snapped and cut cleanly, but looked splintered. Diana hoped its owner had been well deceased when the hand had been taken.

"Now how do you suppose that got here," she muttered, then rose to her feet and turned away from it. "Forget it. Let's go."

But the hand became harder to forget when they stumbled across a skull a few yards on. Then a rib cage. Then a foot that was the worst of all, because it looked alarmingly new. It lay sideways on the path, a small pool of blood that hadn't yet soaked into the ground surrounding its mutilated ankle.

"That one is fresh," Yi-kin noted, as Mina uttered a low growl.

Diana peered around the necropolis with renewed intensity, but saw nothing. No spirits, no malevolent fairies, nothing to indicate where the remains were coming from. Or why some of them gave evidence of having only recently been separated from living bodies.

Soon the gruesome fragments were in profusion, strewn across the path, dangling from the roofs of mausoleums, splattered up against headstones. Diana and Yi-kin were forced to slow their pace, having to pick their way carefully amongst the carnage. Their senses were assaulted by both the sight and stench; at one point Diana was swallowing back her gorge when Yi-kin prodded her, and she turned to find him offering her something that looked like a small wood chip.

"What is that?" she asked.

"Bark from tree used in many cures. Chew."

Diana took the bark, surprised. "How long have you had this?"

"I have bring it from China," he answered, then, added with a smirk, "I did not take it from Netherworld tree."

She put the inch-square tab in her mouth and began to chew. It was tough, but had a surprisingly pleasant, sugary flavor that preoccupied her taste and olfactory senses, effectively blocking much of the reek. "*Ho ho!*" she said, and Yi-kin smiled.

As they walked, her mind working better now that her sense of smell was dulled, Diana's thoughts circled in on one puzzle that had nagged her for quite some time: They had established that time moved differently in the Netherworld, and that each hour spent here meant perhaps years in the mortal world. So....

What was it? Something not quite right there....

And then she had it. If time was moving more quickly on this side of the gateway, then that would mean that the four years that had passed since William had been brought here would have been mere minutes in this place. But how then could Asmodeus have sent messages and invitations to her? Did the demon possess incredible speed? Could it read the future, and had planned all this years in advance?

Or did time move differently in various parts of the Netherworld?

She had to hope it was the latter. She thought that Stephen would surely have warned her, had Asmodeus been able to move that quickly. And if he could read the future, then he would already know the outcome of inviting her to his realm.

He would only have done so had he foreseen his own victory and her death. Again, she thought Stephen would have given her at least some hint, had that been the case.

Unless he and his fellows didn't know exactly what their demon opponent was capable of.

Diana was mulling these thoughts over when she became aware of a noise nearby, a rattling sound that she couldn't quite place. She glanced around, and once or twice thought she saw something in the shadows of the headstones, scuttling along, pacing them.

"Something follow us," Yi-kin half-whispered to her.

He was looking off into the gloom with Mina in his arms, her ears were twitched forward, her eyes wide, searching.

The sound was closer now, and it caused Diana's own hackles to rise:

It was unquestionably bone clattering against bone, but coming nearer.

Halted in caution, they followed the sound with their ears, turning their heads, scanning the left side of the path. There—a shadow of something short, or low. And there—a glimpse of gleaming white, flashing past....

And then the thing stepped out from behind a concealing tomb, and Diana couldn't restrain a harsh, single cry, half-laughter and half-gasp.

It was a living skeleton, but was missing its lower half; it balanced on two arms and a rib cage, with the spinal column dragging behind it like an obscene tail. A few bits of sinew or moss clung to it here and there, and the skull still bore wild strands of hair and—impossibly—two eyeballs, rolling in their fleshless sockets.

The thing goggled at them, and Diana had the impression that not only was it dead, but also quite mad.

"What're yeh starin' at?" it demanded in a raspy, high voice, tinged with Cockney accent.

They were at a loss for an answer. Mina meowed questioningly.

The thing yattered its jaws at them, making a clacking sound. "Well, don't just stand there. Yeh haven't much farther t' go, y'know. C'mon...." It turned and began trotting along the path, moving surprisingly well on its two arms.

Diana and Yi-kin shared a quick glance, then Diana shrugged. *"Ngoh dei hui ma."*

They set off after the thing, which glanced back to make sure they were following, and then slowed down to walk alongside them. "Yeh don't need to worry 'bout me, none, I can't hurt yeh...less you step off the path." The thing suddenly screeched laughter, and the sound caused them both to wince.

"Chi-sin," muttered Yi-kin, and Diana nodded.

Crazy, indeed.

"Besides," their new companion went on in that grating voice, "there's much worse'n me waitin' fer yeh ahead. 'Fact, I daresay yeh'll be missin' ol' Howie afore this day's done."

"Howie?!" Diana said, with a single laugh, "your name is *Howie*?!"

"Well, what'd yeh expect? What's wrong with Howie, anyway?"

"Nothing," Diana conceded.

"Oh, I know," the half-monster went on, "yeh thought it'd be somethin' scary, like Asmodeus or somethin'...."

Trying not to sound too interested, Diana asked, "Oh, do you know Asmodeus?"

"'Course I know 'im! We're like this—" Howie tried to hold up a hand with two bony fingers joined together, but had to cut the gesture short when he nearly toppled over.

"So, what's he like?"

Howie said, "Oh, he's a fearsome lord, he is. The two'a yeh are gonna be nice lil' appetizers for 'im! He'll crunch yeh up a'tween his teeth like yeh was just a handful'a nuts—"

Yi-kin stepped forward angrily, but caught a glance from Diana and restrained himself. She turned back to Howie, still trying to maintain a nonchalance about the conversation. "Maybe...or maybe not. I wonder if he knows about the little surprise we have planned for him."

Howie stopped, balanced on his hands, and turned to eye her, his eyes whirling madly in the sockets. "'Little surprise'?"

"Oh yes, quite," Diana said, then looked to Yi-kin for confirmation.

He nodded at her, then turned to Howie. "We not come here to die. We come to kill Asmodeus."

"And just how will yeh do that?" asked Howie, his head thrust forward as if ears still existed to catch the sound.

"First," Diana said, taking her gamble, "we'll lure him to one of the other areas of the Netherworld, where time moves differently."

Howie actually gasped. "Yeh know 'bout that?!"

Diana smiled and turned to see Yi-kin, looking puzzled. "Good news for us, Yi-kin: It would seem my suspicion was right, and that in this area of the Netherworld time moves as it does in our world."

Yi-kin considered, then said, "So when we come back it is not twenty years later?"

"*Ngaam ngaam.*"

Howie began to bounce angrily on his fingers, causing his bones to bang together in an especially noisy way. "Yeh tricked me! Yeh didn't really know that, did yeh?"

"I guessed," Diana said, then started on her way again.

Howie clattered along beside her, furious now. "Mark my words, miss, yeh'll regret trickin' Howie, yeh will! I've got friends here, powerful friends, they'll see to it that yeh not leave this graveyard alive. Wait'll yeh meet Thaloc—he'll rip yer flesh apart and eat yer souls—"

Diana abruptly stopped, and Yi-kin was so distracted he nearly ran into her. "What—?" he began, then saw the reason she balked.

The path ahead of them forked.

The divergent paths appeared identical. One wound off to the left, through more gravestones and tombs; the other to the right, through another stand of tall, grasping trees.

"Which way?" Yi-kin asked.

Diana nodded. "Which way indeed?"

Howie danced back and forth now, gleeful. "Yeh can't figger it out, can yeh? Both ways could be right, or one could be a trap, it could lead to certain death! I know which is which but I'll not tell—!" He howled more riotous laughter.

Diana tried to block the noise out to concentrate. The fork itself was very plain, and the paths looked identical to her.

"We can try one way, and if it is not good we come back and try other way," Yi-kin suggested.

"Maybe," Diana muttered.

Howie interrupted her thoughts again. "Or you could pick the wrong way and and step off the path!"

"*M ho gong!*" Yi-kin shouted at the grotesque little creature, but Howie only screeched with delight.

Diana was still contemplating when Yi-kin started to step around her. "I try left path, you wait here—"

"No!" Diana grabbed his arm, and he stopped, then watched as she bent down and retrieved two rocks from the path beneath their feet. She tossed the first rock at the right-hand path, and it landed with a slight clatter as it bounced off the other pebbles on the path.

"Oh, we're down to throwin' rocks now, are we?" Howie taunted.

Ignoring him, Diana aimed carefully and tossed the remaining rock at the other path.

It landed not with a reassuring clatter, but a splash. Suddenly the greenish rocks of the false path vanished, and they saw instead a dark green swamp, of liquid that bubbled slightly and gave off a low-lying noxious gas.

"Nooo! Damnation!" Howie cried out, shaking with agitation. "Damn yeh, woman, yer good, I'll admit that. But yeh'll not get past Thaloc!"

Diana exchanged a quick look with Yi-kin, who was clearly shaken by the understanding that he'd come dangerously close to stepping into that lethal pool. Then she turned and started off down the right-hand path, following it into the stand of trees.

Howie, unable to cross either the path or the swamp, called after them, "Yer deaths'll be slow an' painful, just like yer William, he's still dyin'—"

Diana abruptly stopped where the dead branches hung just overhead. She reached up to break one off, and Yi-kin stepped up to help. Together they snapped off a sturdy six-foot length as thick as an arm.

"That's right, I've seen yer William, I have, he's suffered the tortures of the damned, and yeh'll be joinin' him soon, both of yeh, and that animal, too—"

Diana hefted the branch and walked back to Howie resolutely. "What did you say?" she demanded.

The mad little monster screamed back at her, "Yeh'll die, just like that bastard husband'a yers—"

That's when Diana swung the branch. It connected with Howie and shattered him, sending shards flying in every direction. His skull landed in the middle of the path a few feet away, facing Diana, but continued to rebuke her: "The lord Asmodeus has something really special in store fer yeh, m'lady, oh yessss—"

She brought the branch down on the skull. Twice. Three times. Until it was pulverized into a fine white powder. A *silent* powder.

Satisfied, she tossed the branch aside, and returned to Yi-kin, who was staring at her appreciatively. "*Ho yeh*," he commended.

"He should never have mentioned William."

Sometime later, with no end of the necropolis yet in sight, they decided to take a break. At least the horrifying sight and reek of the mangled bodies was behind them, and so they tried to strengthen themselves with a small repast of bread, salt beef and tea. Diana shared the beef with Mina, who nestled in her lap and ate but remained alert.

They were just finishing the meal when an unexpected voice called her name.

It was Stephen.

She leapt to her feet and spun around, finally spotting him emerging from the shadow of a mausoleum a dozen feet to the right of the path. "Stephen—!" She had to restrain herself from running to him.

He stepped into the moonlight, but came no closer. "I'm pleased that you've made it this far. But then, I knew you would."

"I don't understand—I thought you said you couldn't cross over."

Stephen extended one arm to her. "It was very difficult to arrange, but necessary. I've come to take you back."

Diana frowned. "Back? I don't understand...."

"We know what Asmodeus is planning, and you won't survive it. Now just take my hand, and I can return us to your world."

Diana found herself desperately wanting to step forward, to leave this madness behind, this place of chattering, lunatic skulls and blood-chilling spirits, to return to the peace and safety of her home. Her arm came up, reaching towards him, leading her forward....

And then Yi-kin was beside her, also staring at the beckoning figure. *"Mui mui?"* he asked.

Diana's thoughts seemed hazy somehow, and it took a few seconds for that phrase to work through her consciousness. *Mui mui*...but that meant...*older sister....*

"Yi-kin, that's not your sister," she told him, "it's Stephen."

"No, it's *mui mui*—she says she can bring us home."

He stepped forward, reaching out, believing.

Diana looked away from Yi-kin, and plainly saw Stephen, beckoning her with tender concern, calling her forward. "Asmodeus is coming for you even now, Diana. Hurry—take my hand so we can leave here now—"

She was about to step forward, she wanted so badly to go with him, be with him—

—and then a paralyzing shriek filled the air, and something hurtled past them both.

That something was Mina. The feline's leap carried her forward half the distance to Stephen/*mui mui*, and one more leap brought her into clawing, screeching contact. As Diana stood dazed, about to step onto the ground beyond the path, she saw Stephen's image melt away, and instead Mina fought a winged, cat-headed demon that hissed and slashed at her with lion-sized paws. Mina dodged the blows and leapt away from the creature, running off into the necropolis.

"Mina!"

"M ho!" warned Yi-kin as he grabbed Diana, pulling her back from the path's edge.

The cat-headed demon whirled and quickly took flight, its wings propelling it up and away over the graves, looking for its tiny assailant, who had vanished.

Diana struggled in Yi-kin's grip. "We have to get her!"

"Miss Diana, we cannot. Mina is gone!"

Diana struggled briefly, weakening, then fell back, drained, fighting back tears.

Yi-kin held her arm, without restraint, only shared grief. "Mina save us," he said softly.

Diana exclaimed with realization. "Thaloc!"

Yi-kin thought briefly, then agreed, "That is name *gwai yeh* say."

Nodding, Diana chided herself. "Damn it, I should have remembered earlier. Thaloc was an ancient Egyptian shapeshifter. I saw Stephen, but you saw your older sister. It almost lured us off the path. It would have, if Mina hadn't...."

She trailed off, unable to continue.

Yi-kin waited.

Slowly, Diana stood, and Yi-kin released his grip on her, stepping back, slightly unnerved at the set of her jaw, her hooded eyes. He'd never seen this level of fury in her before.

"It's time for us to meet Asmodeus," was all she said, before striding off down the path, and it didn't escape Yi-kin's notice that her hands were now clenched into fists.

And so they finally came to the end of the necropolis.

Chapter XXIX

?

The Netherworld

The boundary of the necropolis was a high stone wall (although the moon's bilious light made it hard to guess its real height, Diana estimated one hundred feet) which blocked any view of whatever might lay beyond it. At first there didn't seem to be any way past, but finally the path rounded a last tomb and they saw a small, man-sized gateway set into the base of the wall, marking the terminus of their path.

As they approached the exit, Diana noticed it was barred by a gate made of impossibly long bones. She was just wondering if getting past the gate would be the final puzzle when a clawed hand gripped it from the other side and pulled it open. She and Yi-kin paused twenty feet away, waiting for some new vision of horror, when a familiar voice called out, "What, not ready to leave the graveyard yet?"

Diana led the way and offered Hob a wan smile as she saw the demon holding the gate to let them through.

Diana looked past him and saw that the area on this side of the wall was completely enshrouded in a thick, billowing fog, one that so far obscured any other details. The vapor had a rank smell, of rotting filth and metal slag and chemicals, and Hob's two human charges found themselves covering their noses with handkerchiefs, trying to block out as much of the nauseating stench as possible.

"I should have known," she said.

"As I suppose I should have," Hob answered, rattling the gate closed behind Yi-kin. "I really didn't believe you'd make it."

"You do not know us," Yi-kin said.

Hob glanced at him, before turning back to eye Diana. "Apparently not. Yet...weren't you *three* strong earlier? Your loathesome little pet seems to have deserted you."

Anger rushed through Diana, hot and sharp, driving out all other emotions for a moment. She felt no fear of this demonic thing, only outrage at its taunting tone. She took a step towards it, her limbs stiff as if built around steel rods, and she gave Hob a baleful stare that caused even the powerful, winged monster to back away one step. "I've slain demons before, Hob. Would you like me to demonstrate how?"

Her fingers closed on the silver dagger strapped to her belt.

Hob saw the movement, and for an instant there was a gratifying flash of bright yellow fear in his eyes. Then he bared his great fangs and declined, "Normally I'd welcome the challenge, but at the moment I'm acting under the specific instructions of Asmodeus, and *his* wrath is not one I wish to incur."

Diana didn't realize she was breathing hard until she felt Yi-kin's gentle touch on her shoulder, bringing her back. "Miss Diana," he whispered, leaning in close so only she could hear, "this *gwai yeh* will take us to Asmodeus. Then we will kill both."

The thought brought a grim pleasure to her and she let herself relax. "Yes," was all she could say.

With the situation thus defused, Robin stepped back and gestured widely. "Very good, then. The Lord Asmodeus is waiting."

Sounds began to filter through the haze, and they weren't happy ones: There were deep rumblings and rhythmic poundings, and Diana could only guess at some vast machinery...although why the Netherworld would require machines was something she couldn't begin to guess at. And then the other sounds: Piteous whimpers and groans. Sobbings. Cries of pain.

All very young.

"Hob, what is this place?" Diana asked, still trying to see anything through the mustard-hued vapors.

"All part of the Lord's grounds," was all he would answer.

As the noise changed slightly around them, Diana realized they had entered either an enclosure or a narrow passageway of some sort. A brightening glow overhead resolved itself into a streetlamp, one strangely similar to those found on any large city street, but not powered by gas; it gave off a steady glow, without trace of flicker. Diana's left foot suddenly slipped in something, and she looked down, disgusted to see she'd trod in a large pile of decaying rubbish—unrecognizable food and printed cartons of some unknown material all leaked foul liquids onto the paved ground.

They were in a city.

And now the city's dwellers began to appear: They were human, but so drained and glassy-eyed they seemed more like the wraiths Diana had seen a year before in the Hertfordshire cemetery. Men and women plodded along the grimy, reeking street, their eyes hollow, their footsteps slow and heavy. Some were horribly thin, their threadbare clothing doing little to disguise their emaciated forms; others were grotesquely fat but just as lifeless, as if the quantities of food they'd consumed had done nothing to nourish them.

Yi-kin sidestepped a woman with the unlined face of early adulthood, but the stooped posture and limp, sparse hair of someone elderly. "They do not see us," he muttered.

Diana nodded. At least these adults made no sound; somewhere nearby, she could hear the sounds of children in torment.

Robin led them through a doorway, and the noxious fumes thinned slightly, parting enough so that they could see they were in a cavernous building of some sort. The booming and grinding sounds were heavier now—nearly deafening—but not loud enough to drown out the children.

And then Diana saw them:

They were workers. They stood on either side of some sort of mechanical moving belt, applying small pieces to large, intricate-looking items that could only be guns of some sort. But it wasn't the weapons that held Diana's attention—it was the horrifying young laborers.

Some looked to be as small as five or six years of age; the oldest couldn't have been past mid-teens. They stood apathetically, going through their motions by rote. Some couldn't restrain cries of pain as they worked. Most were covered with sores, bruises, festering wounds. A few were missing limbs. One dropped to the ground, dead or unconscious, as Diana watched.

Suddenly, she understood. And felt faint herself.

"Oh my god."

She closed her eyes to the sight of the pathetic children, and Yi-kin stepped beside her, perplexed. *"Mat yeh a?"*

Hob turned and grinned when he realized they stopped behind him. He seemed pleased by Diana's expression. "But Lady Furnaval, we thought you of all people would appreciate this example of industry at its finest."

She looked at the walls of great machines lining the rows of toiling children; the machines displayed small lights in colors she'd never seen outside of carnivals, and she knew nothing like them existed in her world. "This isn't industry—"

Hob cut her off: "Oh, but it will be. You see, because time runs differently here in the Netherworld—a fact which I think you might have ascertained," Robin added with a wink that turned Diana's stomach, "we've seen the future of industry, and this is it. This is the endpoint of your beloved progress."

"Ridiculous," Diana scoffed. "Progress is forward movement. This isn't progress, this is some Netherworld farce, and I'm afraid I'm not amused."

"You weren't meant to be," Hob added, and then turned away.

Yi-kin watched the demon stride off, and then murmured to her, "I do not know this word, 'progress.' What is progress?"

She shook her head, then followed after Hob. "Not this," she called back over her shoulder.

None of the children turned to watch them go; they were too preoccupied building weapons.

Hob led them out of the hellish factory and down several streets—passing more of the city's zombie-like inhabitants—until they came to a large guarded enclave of some kind, bordered walls of black marble that bespoke wealth and crushing power. The sentries appeared to be normal until Diana examined them closely, and found that they were each horribly deformed or transfigured: Their features were broad and fleshy, their eyes too small, their hair bristle-like.

They were boar-like abominations, dressed incongruously in well-tailored black uniforms with gleaming brass buttons.

The porcine creatures acknowledged Hob as he led the pair past them, showing the way into the interior of what Diana now knew must be the lord's palace. By contrast, the sentries eyed Diana and Yi-kin with hungry stares, and several even licked their flabby lips with over-long, wet tongues. They stank of rotted meat and dung.

Beyond the guards and the outer wall now, Hob led them across a small courtyard towards a flight of wide steps. At the top of the stairs was a landing and portico; huge columns stood on either side of a vast doorway, which Diana thought could have admitted an elephant. Above this doorways stood a sculpted frieze, which seemed to be obscured by smoke. They climbed the steps and as they neared the portico, Diana realized the vaporous, hazy movement she imagined was actually movement in the frieze. The entire stone bas-relief—which depicted horrific creatures descending on terrified humanity—was writhing.

marble minotaurs, harpies, devils and gods skewered, strangled, bludgeoned, drowned and beat their victims. At the center of the frieze only one figure remained unmoving, a great horned and winged ruler that could only be Asmodeus, the demon general savoring his victory, maliciously serene in his pose.

As they reached the landing, huge doors—which looked to be made of a dark wood, perhaps mahogany, perhaps something that flourished only in the Netherworld—swung inward of their own accord. Diana forced her gaze away from the horrifying tableau (noting as she did so that Yi-kin was as transfixed by it as she'd been), and looked inside, expecting...what, a Gothic dungeon? Another industrial nightmare?

Instead, Hob brought them into a foyer that would compliment any of London's exclusive clubs: Luxuriously panelled walls were punctuated by tasteful wall sconces (that glowed with a steady light, although no sort of filament or jet was visible) and paintings in gold frames; the floors were tiled, and their heels clicked loudly, echoing off the expensive wood adorning the walls.

Diana would have liked to examine the art, which she was sure would have provided invaluable clues to the history and culture of the Netherworld, but Hob's pace quickened down the broad hallway, and she had only time enough to glance at them: Here a portrait of a haughty-visaged demon prince; there a battle scene of winged figures (angels?) fighting towering horned men.

Still, if the subject of the art were gruesome, the surroundings were not, and Diana began to wonder if this had been constructed to lure visitors (or, specifically—her?) into a state of false comfort, making their eventual torture that much more humiliating. Arrogant on her part, perhaps...but she suspected that, even had the factory not been constructed specifically for her, Hob had nonetheless been directed to take her through it. It didn't seem likely that Lord Asmodeus' usual guests would first be led through a weapon manufacturing plant.

They came to an intersecting hallway, and Hob turned, leading them into a new corridor which was smaller than the first, though no less elegant. They'd passed several closed doors when he stopped and opened one, gesturing within, wordless.

Diana hesitated, looking inside. She saw a tastefully-appointed guest room, one that would not have been out of place in any English manor house; chairs, tables, a canopy bed and a blazing hearth were all provided.

She turned to eye the demon, curious—did they intend for her to stay here? Was she to be treated as an honored guest? Hob's flat expression gave no clue; he only gestured again, suggesting—no, she knew it was *ordering*—that she enter.

She did—and instantly the door shut behind her, sealing her off alone.

She whirled and tried the doorknob, not particularly surprised to find it locked. As she spun back to the room, her hand went to the knife at her side, her eyes darted about, looking for danger.

There was none.

After a few seconds she relaxed slightly, lowering the knife she'd unsheathed and stepping away from the door. The room was quite large, and it took her the better part of a minute to examine it thoroughly. She peered behind draperies, into wardrobes, beneath the bed, expecting at any instant an assault from some horrific, hidden abomination—but the room was empty, save for her.

After being satisfied that she was alone—and hoping that Yi-kin was similarly placed in a nearby room—she moved up by the fire, which crackled with the same expected warmth and orange light of any earthbound fire. She stood before it, grateful to feel its heat on her hands and face. Her feet were aching after the long ordeal through the necropolis, and so she tentatively lowered herself into an overstuffed armchair near the hearth, half expecting the chair to suddenly spring to life in a smothering grip. Instead, she found only the pleasure of familiar comfort after a long journey.

She'd been that way for some time—ten minutes? An hour?—when the door opened. She was instantly out of the chair, knife in hand, ready to spring—

—when she saw William enter.

The door closed behind him and it took a second for his eyes to find her. Then his expression changed, from confused and terrified to disbelief and even great joy. "Diana—!"

Diana wanted to throw herself at him, to cry in relief as she buried herself in his arms, but she'd been tempted too many times by the Netherworld with the image of a man she longed for; and so she held her ground, eyeing him suspiciously. It certainly looked like her husband, with his unruly dark hair, pale skin, gray eyes and fine build; and his pleasing baritone sounded like her beloved. She knew well that voice—often felt its timber vibrating within her as he rested his head upon her breast and spoke sweetly to her while they lay together in their bed at home....

He stepped forward, his expression growing more confused and desperate with each step. "Darling, it's me, it's William—!"

Diana hefted the knife.

He saw it and stopped. "Diana, what—"

"If you're really William, then prove it," she commanded.

William—if such he were– gaped for a moment, then: "Diana, of course I'm William, I—"

"*Prove it.*"

His eyes darted away, as he thought. After a moment, he turned to her, and began spilling out words so quickly they tumbled over themselves as they left his mouth. "Of course you don't believe it's me here…remember that trip we took to London when we went to Highcastle and saw the carnival, and you looked at the sword swallower and said, 'That's obviously a fake sword,' and he heard you and stabbed the tip of the sword through your hat and took it clean off your head…or the night we were wed, when I tried to carry you all the way up the stairs and I nearly broke both our necks as I stumbled on that last step, and you laughed so hard I had to set you down—"

Then she knew it was him, her William. The knife dropped from her fingers to the carpet before the hearth and she flung herself at him, letting the tears flow. "William…oh my god, William, I thought you were dead, I thought you.…"

His arms were around her, and all she could think for a moment was how good he felt, how strong and familiar, and how lovely his hair felt under his fingers, and he was real, this was no shapeshifting illusion, but a real flesh-and-blood man.…

He looked at her distress and couldn't help but laugh. "Diana, what—?"

"It's been so long, William, so many years—"

He pulled away from her, puzzled. "Years? But I swear they only just brought me here.…"

She started to question him, or tell him he was wrong…and then she burst into laughter.

Time was impossible to reckon in the Netherworld.

When she'd contained herself again, she said, "Never mind. It doesn't really matter."

He kissed her again, sweetly this time, then pulled away to look at her. "How did you get here? Were you also brought here, as I was?"

She shook her head. "I came on my own. You'll have to trust me when I tell you that I've…recently learned a great deal. Asmodeus is planning to lead an army into our world. We have to stop him."

"My God," William said, looking away thoughtfully. "Did you see the factories out there? That explains the weapons."

Of course, Diana thought. Then she said, "Well, at least we know they can't just make weapons magically appear."

William smiled, then was looking at her again. "Has it really been years for you?"

"Four, to be precise."

"I'm so sorry."

He kissed her again, but this time the kiss didn't stop. It was rich and deep, and Diana was instantly lost in it. His lips moved down her jaw line to her ear, her neck, as his hands came up and found her breasts beneath the man's shirt she wore, and the woman's stays.

She let out a gasp, and her fingers tangled in his hair, holding his head as his mouth slid further down her neck, and his fingers worked at her more insistently. Her back arched towards him, and her quickening pulse moved to the space between her legs.

And yet....

She inhaled deeply of his hair, and a small spark of alarm was lit somewhere in the back of her mind.

It wasn't William's scent.

She knew his smell so well, the combination of sage and soap and musk that she so loved, and yet now it wasn't to be found on him. In fact, he had absolutely no scent at all, and somehow she found that even more disturbing.

Her hands moved to his face, and for the first time she realized that his skin was cold, as if chilled from within. She began to struggle to pull back from him. "William...."

She couldn't push him away. He clung to her with ferocity suddenly, his lips on her neck—and something else....

Instinctively Diana reached into a pocket of her gentleman's riding jacket and found what she'd placed there: The crucifix. She was removing it when there was a pain at her neck, sudden and sharp, and she cried out as her hand came up, dashing the crucifix against his face.

He shrieked in agony, an inhuman cry of fury, and staggered back as his cold skin smoked, a large cross-shaped brand beneath his left eye. Long fangs jutted from under his top lip, fangs that had just begun to open the skin of her neck.

She instinctively clapped a hand to her neck, then pulled away, trying to gauge the extent of her wound. Good—the blood on her fingers was minimal. She'd managed to pull away before he'd accomplished the killing bite.

He snarled once more, then his fangs retracted, sheathing themselves in his upper jaw, and some of the crimson fire left his eyes. "Diana, don't—"

She thrust the crucifix forward once more, indicating that she had no intention of surrendering.

He turned away from it, unable to look at her, and pleaded, "Diana, it's still me, William, your husband—"

She saw the blood on her fingers again, and held the crucifix out with trembling fingers. "William would never try to kill me."

"You're right, I wouldn't," he said, and now he turned his back on her completely. "It's not real death. Diana, I want us to be together forever. We can be."

Somehow seeing his back turned to her, not being able to see his face, was even more unnerving. "Turn around so I can see you," she ordered.

He did so, looking fully human once more. "You have no idea how much I love you—"

She felt a rush of heartbreak, and swept away tears from her eyes, leaving a swath of blood across her face. "Don't say that to me. You're not William."

"It would be so easy, love," he said, and his voice was a low purr now, "one moment of pain, then an eternity of happiness together."

"Doing what?" she said, "Laying waste to our world alongside our demon lord?"

"We could stop him."

She blinked in surprise—she hadn't expected that answer.

"You won't be able to defeat him as a human, Diana. But together, with new strength, new gifts...."

She wanted to believe that. *It almost makes sense*, she thought, and it would have been so easy to lay down the crucifix and welcome his last kiss, to reawaken free of her weaknesses and doubts, to tell Stephen—

Stephen.

She understood his answers about William—neither dead nor alive. What would Stephen say if she surrendered now, because of the promise of a monster.

A vampire.

William recognized her indecision and leapt forward. Nearly caught by surprise, she stumbled back towards the hearth, raising the crucifix again. He saw the symbol of good and hissed, drawing back.

She had to slay him.

She wasn't sure she had strength—either emotionally or physically—but Yi-kin wasn't here, and this was her task and hers alone. If she didn't...eventually she'd tire, he'd be on her, and the Netherworld would win.

She could not let that happen.

She needed a stake, and then realized Yi-kin had their backpack of equipment with him. The other means of protection she had with her— the gun, the knife, the herbs—might slow William down briefly, but they wouldn't slay him. No, she needed a wooden stake. She glanced around frantically, and saw a small branch of kindling in the fire; about the thickness of her wrist and the length of her forearm, the end had been partly charred to a rough point. It would have to do.

She leapt forward with the crucifix, forcing William to turn away, and in that brief instant she dashed her hand into the fire and grabbed the end of the impromptu stake, ignoring the searing pain that coursed up her arm. Forcing herself to keep hold of the hot wood, smelling the sickening odor of her own flesh cooking, she saw William look at her with a combination of fear and amusement.

"You can't be serious, Diana," was all he said.

The fire at the end of the burning stake had died down now, and she switched it to her right hand, taking the crucifix gingerly in her left. "If you were still William, you wouldn't ask that."

The reddish flames returned to his eyes, and his lips curled up in a bestial manner as he began to edge away from her. "You can't do this. Not alone."

"I know I can."

She pressed forward again with the crucifix, and he roared, now terrified, stumbling backward. She stepped slightly to the side—she wanted to trap him in a corner of the room—and pushed the cross at him again.

He fell back into the corner. She knew that if she failed to time this correctly, he could easily reach out and snap her wrists, and then his teeth would be buried in her throat and Asmodeus would be leading his army through the gateways. She had a split second as he turned away from the Holy relic, before he realized what she meant to do—

—and then she rammed the stake into his chest, putting all of her power behind the blow.

She was immediately rewarded with another ear-splitting scream, and a fountain of cold blood splattered across her. She closed her eyes against the gore and tossed the crucifix onto his chest so she could place both hands on the stake, driving it further into him. She felt the stake hit the wall behind him, but she didn't let up, she kept pushing, and he writhed and convulsed, and the wall behind him gave way with a loud *crack*, and more blood splattered Diana but she held on, ignoring the agony in her burned hand as she clutched the end of the stake so tightly that her muscles were corded like iron bars.

Finally it was over. Without opening her eyes, she heard the screaming become hissing and at long last silence; the movements juddering up through the stake ceased. She waited a few extra seconds, then took one hand from the stake, wiped the blood from her brow, and opened her eyes.

The vampire was dead. She'd pinned to the wall, fouled with its own blood; its head hung to one side.

Diana pulled her other hand away from the stake and took one step back, still watching him for any signs of life. There were none.

When she was certain, she let herself fall back to the canopied bed, and sank down onto the edge. She removed her gore-soaked jacket, and used it to wipe her face. She was dimly aware that, sometime during the struggle, her hair had come loose from its usual proper mass atop her head, and had also been drenched in William's blood. She didn't care. She only wanted it off her face, out of her eyes and nose and mouth. She wanted the tears gone, too.

When she'd cleaned herself as best she could, she pulled the few things she thought she might still need from the jacket, and put them into her trouser pockets instead. She retrieved the crucifix from the floor, and then before she knew it she was pounding on the room's locked door and screaming:

"I'm going to kill you, Asmodeus! Are you such a coward that you can only let your underlings face me?! You're going to pay for what you've done to William, you monster—!"

She broke off at the sound of laughter and applause.

It was coming from behind her. She spun about, but saw only the walls of the room, decorated in tastefully-understated wallpaper and molding. She approached one of the walls, and there was no question that the sounds were coming from behind it. She reached a hand out to touch the wall—

—and her hand went through it.

Illusion, like the false path in the graveyard.

She stepped through, and found herself facing a large stone room. Twenty feet away was a dais, holding a single carved and bejewelled chair.

A throne. And seated upon it was Asmodeus.

He was the source of the mirth, although he was joined by Hob, who watched from his position just behind the throne. Past them Diana glimpsed an opening onto an outside terrace or balcony.

Asmodeus stood, mocking her with a bow, and she had to admit he was an impressive being: Fully eight feet tall, with a broad, ovine face, long ivory horns, gold armor, and black cloak; he also possessed a rumbling basso voice that she could feel in her solar plexus.

"Asmodeus, I presume?"

Hob frowned and stepped forward to correct her. *"Lord* Asmodeus—"

The demon prince held up a hand, and Hob stepped obediently back. Asmodeus watched her with completely black eyes—no trace of iris or white—and they never left Diana. "Really very impressive, my dear. That's two challenges now I didn't expect you to survive."

Diana stood her ground, locking her gaze to his. "I'm happy to thwart your expectations."

"No doubt. Unfortunately—as entertaining as I find this—the game is nearly at an end. You see, I have a world to conquer, and since I won't be able to turn you to my own ends as I'd hoped, I'm forced to dispense with you instead."

Kill him, Diana. Kill him now.

Diana stiffened, feeling Stephen's presence stir to life within her. His whispered command was as clear as if he knelt at her feet; at first she wondered if Asmodeus had heard it as well, but one look at the lord's perplexed expression assured her that he hadn't.

"Is something the matter, Lady Furnaval? Surely you knew I'd kill you eventually."

Diana forced herself to relax, not wanting to reveal the secret of her unguessed companion. "I was hoping you'd answer a few questions first."

No, Diana, don't. Kill him NOW. While you have this chance.

No, she argued back, *I want answers first.*

Asmodeus threw his head back, roaring laughter, before asking: "Why should I?"

"Because you won't be able to gloat after I'm dead."

That brought fresh guffaws from the demon lord, and then he sank back onto his throne. "I suppose it does add only a few more moments to your existence. Very well: You have three questions, then your life ends. Choose carefully."

She didn't have to consider long; two questions had nagged her for a very long time, and the third required a more immediate resolution: "What about Yi-kin?"

Asmodeus exchanged a brief glance with Hob, who nodded his head in the direction of the room Diana had just escaped. "Your friend is enduring his own challenge in another room right now. I understand he's still alive...presently."

Diana absorbed that information, and realized it meant she needed to move quickly. "Thank you. My second question: Why invade our world?"

"Ahh, there it is!" Asmodeus exclaimed happily. "This answer will no doubt shock you, my dear: Yes, I plan to utterly lay waste to your world, but beyond that—I simply do not care about it."

Diana gaped for a moment, then managed a shocked, "What...?"

Asmodeus smiled, enjoying her confusion, then continued: "Your world means nothing to me—it's merely a strategic foundation, a launching point from which the *final* battle will begin."

He hesitated, waiting to see if she'd come up with the answer on her own.

She did, and felt a chill course through her.

"You mean to assault Stephen Chappell's realm...."

"Of course. I will put an end to this ridiculous struggle between good and evil once and for all. Now, one more question and then I end your life."

Don't ask it, Diana. NOW....

She did move a hand to the holstered pistol...but rested it there, waiting. She would ask her last question.

"Why did it take you this long to begin the attack on the forces of good?"

Asmodeus and Hob both giggled.

Then, Asmodeus said, "Oh, I am glad that was your last question, because I think you'll very much enjoy the answer: For centuries the gateways were carefully guarded, and only a few of our ilk ever managed to cross over. The guardians were powerful and talented, and we spent many centuries trying to find ways to destroy them, all to no avail. Until, that is, your own representatives of the forces of good did it for us."

Diana thought furiously, but couldn't guess the meaning of his words. "I don't understand...."

"The guardians were women, an ancient order of nature worshippers."

The answer began to form in Diana's mind. "Witches...."

The demon nodded. "Witches. And your church—the purveyors of goodness and morality—created an inquisition that sought them out and destroyed them. Where we'd been unable to slay more than a handful of these sentries, the church burned, drowned and tortured them to death by the thousands, and opened the gateways for us. I've been assembling my forces ever since."

Asmodeus eyed her for a moment, evidently enjoying watching the realizations and emotions that raced across her features; then he stood and gestured to the opening behind him. "Come—there's something I'd like you to see. As your last sight."

She hesitated, but Hob backed away submissively and Asmodeus stepped through, motioning her forward again. "You have one more moment of life, I assure you."

She strode forward, onto the dais, around the throne, and then through the opening and out onto a balcony.

She saw immediately that the balcony was set perhaps fifty yards above a vast open plain, illuminated by the great moon—

—and that plain held Asmodeus's army.

It stretched into the distance in every direction as far as Diana could see. Hundreds of thousands, probably millions, of monstrosities waited down there. She saw the moonlight glint off armor and weapons, she heard roars and screeches and loud booms as the strange weapons were discharged in practice. Although they were perched too great a height to make out the features of individual soldiers, she knew that some were too tall or too broad or moved too strangely to be anything even remotely human.

She had no doubt that this army would easily overwhelm her own world. And possibly the heavenly realm, as well.

"Glorious, isn't it," the demon lord and general murmured at her shoulder. "At my command, they will begin to cross over, through whatever gateways you've left us. At least no more will be closed now."

Now I'll kill him, she thought.

She backed away, off the balcony, giving herself enough room to draw her pistol. Asmodeus saw it, and merriment burst from him again. "I anticipated you would try to fight me before I ripped you limb from limb, although I admit I'm somewhat—*underwhelmed.*"

Diana backed all the way off the dais, keeping one eye on Asmodeus and the other on Hob—and her passage was abruptly stopped by the illusory wall, now become quite real.

Asmodeus, slowly edging towards her, savoring, saw the action and offered her an expression of mocking sadness. "Oh, I'm afraid there's no running, either."

Diana pulled the trigger.

The bullet slammed into Asmodeus's neck.

He smiled, plucked it from his skin and dropped it.

It's a revolver, we only loaded one chamber with the proper bullet, she heard, and she wasn't sure if it was her own voice or Stephen's now.

She pulled the trigger again. It hit the demon's head. After a second, he spat the bullet out. "Oh, please do try again."

She did. This bullet ricocheted from his chest plate.

Asmodeus was three feet away.

She jerked the trigger again. Another ricochet.

Asmodeus was reaching for her.

She forced it again. The bullet passed completely through his outstretched hand. Then he took the barrel of the gun, holding it almost tenderly, looking down at her with paternal disappointment.

She squeezed the trigger, knowing it was the last bullet.

The gun exploded, and Asmodeus suddenly fell back, roaring, clutching at an impossibly huge hole that had appeared in his torso, his golden armor blasted into pieces. A stream of liquid darkness, an anti-light, gushed from the hole as Asmodeus clutched in vain at his fatal wound.

Time suddenly seemed to cease: In the instant that Diana saw Asmodeus topple in ruin, Hob rushing in panic to his lord's side, she was suddenly flooded with a sensation of ancient energy unlike anything she'd ever known, and she realized this was Stephen's secret gift:

She had the means to create her own gateway, to escape the Netherworld.

In that timeless moment, she turned her attention inward, furiously seeking the presence of Stephen Chappell. She found it when his silent voice came: *What are you waiting for, Diana? GO!*

Why didn't you tell me? Why keep this secret?

Because you would have attempted to use the skill before you met Asmodeus, if not for yourself, then for your companions.

Diana's anger intensified. *And what if I had? Yi-kin might be dead by now, and I could have kept Mina alive—*

Like the bullet, Diana, we could only grant you a single use.

She bit her tongue, realizing its truth. Had she known, she would have sent Yi-kin and Mina back. And maybe even herself.

Then the moment unfroze, and Diana spotted a door on one end of the stone room, and she charged for it.

Diana, no—!

I won't leave Yi-kin.

Hob was kneeling beside his fallen lord, and in his disbelief he ignored her as she fled the chamber through the side door. Diana found herself in a long, plain hallway, with closed doors set into the stone walls at intervals. She ran to an intersection, and realized she had absolutely no idea of where to go. This palace might go on for miles; there could be countless rooms, Yi-kin could be in any, or all of them....

And then she heard it: A distant, plaintive mewling.

At first she couldn't be sure whether it was mortal or demon, but she ran to it anyway; she had nothing else to guide her. She turned another corner, and the sound was clearer now; she realized it was neither human nor demon, but animal.

Feline, in fact.

"Mina—!" she panted with anxiety.

She kept running, and although she heard the small voice more clearly with each step, there were other sounds now as well: Shouts, shrieks, commands, curses, orders, lumbering feet and hooves.

Asmodeus's assassination had been discovered, and the unholy soldiers mobilized.

She came to another intersection and hesitated, waiting for Mina's call again. She heard the other sounds coming from the left, and then she saw a mass of armored and armed guards turn the corner, spot her, and rush towards her. They were more of the boarmen she'd seen outside; they gnashed their tusks now and waved weapons as they rushed her.

The one in front shot at her.

She barely ducked back in time—and then heard Mina again, coming from the other direction. She took a deep breath and ran, hearing more shots behind her, shots which ricocheted around the narrow corridor.

A few paces brought her to another corner—and there was Mina, sitting a dozen yards away, before a bolted door, plainly looking at the door and uttering that desperate cry.

And Diana knew Yi-kin was behind it.

The boarmen couldn't be more than thirty yards behind her as she reached the door. In one swift action she scooped up Mina, unbolted the door, and leapt through, heaving the door shut behind her.

She might have just stepped into a long-forgotten Buddhist temple somewhere in China. The wooden floors and walls were covered with dust and cobwebs; a splintered dais held a decapitated statue of the Buddha. The decrepit room was lit only by moonlight entering through cracks in the ceiling.

And Yi-kin was launching a potentially lethal blow at her head.

She saw it just before it connected, and managed to duck. "It's me, Yi-kin!" she cried, as she dodged to one side.

He hesitated, maintaining his fighting stance, eyeing her suspiciously, and Diana realized that he saw a mad-looking creature covered in drying blood. "And Mina," she said, thrusting the cat forward.

Yi-kin took the cat. "Diana...?"

"*Hai ngoh*," she answered, and something in her pronunciation brought a welcome relief to his face.

Outside she heard her pursuers hammering the door, and she let Stephen's presence wash through her being. Later, she wouldn't be able to recall what she'd said or done, the motions made or the words uttered, but in seconds a gateway shimmered in the air before her.

"What—?" Yi-kin started to ask, but just then the door burst inward and the boarmen pushed in.

"*Hui ma!*" Diana shouted, pushing Yi-kin (with Mina) bodily through, before following.

Diana had an instant only to register that they were in a cellar or basement—before the first boarman followed them through. Yi-kin tossed Mina to Diana, and whirled into action, raining a devastating series of kicks and blows that propelled the invader backward to crash into the others attempting to come through. The force of Yi-kin's attack pushed the boarmen back in a cascade that toppled half-a-dozen of them, but others were heedlessly tromping over their fallen brethren in an effort to overwhelm the gateway.

"*Siu jeh—!*" Yi-kin shouted.

Diana dropped Mina and drew the knife from her belt. Yi-kin was already aiming a flying kick at the latest invader as Diana tore the sleeve up from her left wrist, made a quick slice, and cried out, "*By my will and by my blood is this gateway sealed FOREVER!*"

She flung her bloodied arm outward, and cast away the bloodied knife as well, just as Yi-kin knocked the latest boarman back through the gateway—and then they were looking at nothing but an earthen cellar wall.

The gateway was closed, and they had escaped the Netherworld.

Chapter XXX

November 11, 1880
Derby

They had staggered briefly about the large cellar (which, from the amount of wine racks and kegs, seemed to belong to a pub) until they found stairs leading upward. they found themselves in a kitchen, which was fortunately empty as they stepped out. Dull light entered through some grimy windows, and they realized it must be early afternoon...wherever they were.

There was a sink and water in the kitchen, and Diana paused long enough to scrub the worst of the blood (*William's blood*, some part of her whispered, but she wouldn't listen to that part yet) from her face and arms. Then they walked out into the pub, and found a single barmaid wiping down the bar. She gaped at them for a second, before exclaiming in a thick working-class accent, "'Ere now, where d'ye think you're goin'? The kitchen's off limits—"

"Sorry," Diana answered, "we got lost. We're new to this city—"

The barmaid laughed in disbelief. "'Ow can ye be new to London?"

We're in London. That's good to know, Diana thought, before asking the question she most dreaded.

"Can you tell me the date?"

The barmaid had had enough. "I think it's time for ye to leave. Go on, now, don' make me ave t' call the bobby...."

"We're going. Thank you."

They left the pub, and exited onto a filthy London street, one occupied by ragged, homeless urchins, staggering drunks and unhealthy looking prostitutes...and Diana could still have fallen to her knees in gratitude.

Mina cried, and Yi-kin set her down; she was evidently as happy as Diana to be back on home soil, and she ran off in pursuit of a juicy rat. "It does not look different," Yi-kin observed.

If this is the future, then perhaps progress really did die, Diana thought, but pushed that to the back of her mind, to be dealt with later. Right now she had to know *when* they were.

She spotted a boy selling papers, and tossed him a coin. He handed over a newspaper, and Diana grabbed it hungrily, her eyes seeking the date. When she'd found it, she looked up at Yi-kin, grinning.

"What?" he asked anxiously.

She turned the paper around to show him as she read aloud the date. "November first, eighteen-eighty."

Yi-kin took the paper, confused. "But...time...."

She wasn't sure whether she should thank Stephen or accept that time ran at various speeds throughout the Netherworld. Either way, all that mattered was that they were in their own world, and their own time.

Later that same day, safely ensconced in her London apartments, she'd taken a second hot bath (the first had turned the water crimson), and had finally let herself weep.

And afterwards she knew she could accept the truth that William was really gone.

The next day she asked Yi-kin what had happened to him in the room that had looked like a deserted temple.

He said he would never tell anyone. And she didn't ask again.

On November 5, nearly recovered (although her badly burned left hand was still swathed in bandages) and distracted by the antics of young Guy Fawkes Day beggars, they were making plans to return to the Derby estate when Yi-kin told Diana he wouldn't be going with her. He wanted to return to China.

He assured her he'd be back, that he only wanted to see his sister; but Diana knew his visit had something to do with what he'd endured in that Netherworld cell, and she feared she might never see him again.

Nonetheless, she bought his passage home and gave him a very large amount of money, which he tried to refuse. She did convince him to accept it by telling him to give it to his sister.

His boat left London on November 8. Diana brought Mina along, and when Yi-kin broke into tears as he stepped aboard the ship, Diana secretly wondered if it was for her or the cat.

She didn't really care. She hugged him long and hard, and told him they still had many gateways to close together.

He told her again he'd be back, and then he sailed away.

As she walked away from the busy port, Diana didn't immediately return Mina to her case; instead, she found herself clinging to the cat as if to her last friend.

Thusly preoccupied, she managed to collide head-on with a burly, bearded man who was similarly distracted with his own burden, a sheaf of pages. As they met, pages and squealing feline all flew into the air.

"Oh, I'm terribly sorry—!" they each exclaimed, as they bent to gather up animal and paper.

Mina was squirming madly as Diana stowed her safely in the satchel, and the man couldn't help but smile as he stood, assembling the disarray of his papers.

"What a charming little puss," he said.

Diana smiled down at Mina and rubbed her head. "Mina, you've captured another admirer," she said, then offered the man an amused look.

"A delightful name, as well," he noted.

Suddenly a shout sounded from the dock behind them. "Mr. Stoker, sir, you'll miss the Edinburgh boat!"

The man nodded frantically, still grappling with his pages. "Oh, dear." He turned back a last time to Diana and extended a hand to Mina, who rubbed against it happily. "Lovely to meet you, Miss Mina. I'm sorry we haven't time to further our acquaintance."

As he was racing off, Diana wondered briefly about the papers; there'd been several hundred of them, and she suspected they comprised some novel or other. *Well, Mina,* she thought, scratching the cat's chin, *perhaps we've given him a new story to tell.*

Later that day, Diana returned to Derby.

Although Howe was overjoyed to see her (and she him), her homecoming was not altogether joyous. Diana felt strange, roaming the estate knowing that William was now truly gone. Even though he'd been officially dead for four years and she'd inherited the Furnaval legacy some time ago, she realized that she hadn't really believed William to be dead before. Now the great manor house and grounds seemed somehow emptier than they were before. She was thankful for the companionship of Mina.

She also thought a great deal about the factory she'd seen, and Hob's ominous statements regarding the end results of progress. At first she tried to dismiss the glum future as nothing but a petty Netherworld torment, but the more she thought about London's factory smokestacks and hollow-eyed child workers, the more she realized the unrealistic idea of progress was *hers*.

What was the answer, then? Throw away her beliefs in man's ability to improve? Give up her basic optimism?

What would she be left with, then?

Her options, as she saw it, were: Dismiss her belief in humanity's forward motion, and become a jaded cynic; live in denial of what she'd seen in the Netherworld; or work to keep that future from happening.

She chose the latter.

On November 10th she arranged to meet with her solicitor, and so the following day she found herself in her sitting room at Derby, telling the astonished man that she intended to set aside a large portion of the Furnaval fortune for both charities aimed at improving the lot of impoverished workers and grants to scientists who created better, cleaner, safer methods of industry. Her solicitor asked her a great deal of questions, but she simply affirmed over and over that this was her decision, and she was quite set upon it.

Evening had come on while they'd debated over the arrangements, and Diana had been about to ask the solicitor (who was a pleasant if somewhat dull middle-aged man) if he wished to join her for dinner, when Howe entered, excusing himself.

A gentleman had arrived, asking to see her, Howe explained. He offered Diana a visiting card from a silver tray. Diana took the card and read the name engraved thereon:

Stephen Chappell.

All thoughts of inviting the solicitor to dine with her immediately vanished. Instead she told him that something most urgent had come up, and she'd have to bid him farewell. As Howe whisked the slightly-perplexed solicitor out, Diana poured herself a brandy and tried to decide what she'd say first to Stephen...whether she were furious, grateful, horrified, joyful, grief-stricken, or simply lonely.

Then the door opened behind her, and she finished the brandy, set the glass down, turned, and saw him.

It was a shock to see him in the flesh again, after having engaged in the most intimate psychic coupling imaginable. He looked as handsome and elegant as ever, and was smiling...although she also detected a wariness in that smile. Perhaps he was as unsure of her reaction to him as she was herself.

"Hello, Diana," he began, simply.

"Stephen," she nodded, but didn't approach him. "I trust your—what, employers? Elders?—are happy with the outcome of recent events...?"

"We are. You did very well, Diana."

"I had some very good help," she said, and hoped he knew that she meant Yi-kin and Mina, not the unknown forces surrounding him. "I expected to see you sooner."

"Did you? How kind."

"Not really. I wanted to tell you that I'm still extremely angry over not being trusted with the knowledge you kept concealed from me."

"Oh," Stephen answered, looking away. "I see."

"Do you? Just how human are you really? Can you understand why I'd be hurt by that?"

He took three short steps towards her, then stopped. "I'm more human than you might think, Diana. And you're right, we—they—were absolutely wrong to have underestimated you. I won't let it happen again."

That surprised her. Her anger (she had, in fact, more than once imagined hurling breakable objects at him) melted away almost instantly, and was replaced by a great swell of affection.

"So, any word from the Netherworld?" she asked.

"With Asmodeus defeated," Stephen replied, "the armies fell into disarray. They'll undoubtedly find a new leader eventually...but by then, you may very well have sealed every gateway."

"Perhaps," she agreed, then after a beat she asked, "I don't understand, Stephen: Why do these gateways even exist? And why is it up to me to seal them?"

Two more steps towards her, and now they stood only a yard apart. "As to why they exist, I can't tell you. I suppose they exist for the same reason that galaxies or mountains exist—they're simply some part of the vast scheme we call nature. And as for why you are the one to close them...well, my dear, perhaps you *don't* have to be alone in this anymore. If you'd like that, I mean."

Diana searched beneath his words, trying to find his real meaning. "Stephen, what are you suggesting? Can you just once come out and tell me, without hiding behind some metaphysical excuse?"

His jaw dropped open an inch, then snapped closed, "All right. I'd like to help you. And I'd...like to stay with you."

"Well, I applaud your newfound honesty, I suppose," she said, mocking him only slightly.

Suddenly she'd made a decision, and she took his hand and led him from the sitting room. "Diana, what—?" he laughed, delighted.

"Just come with me."

She led him out to the main flight of stairs that climbed to the second floor. "Where are we going?" he asked, as she pulled him up the steps.

"To my bedroom," she answered. "If that's acceptable to you, that is, dear Stephen."

And he found it was very acceptable indeed.

THE END

CPSIA information can be obtained at www.ICGtesting.com
Printed in the USA
BVOW05s0706020614

355041BV00001B/58/P